THE DEAD SOUL

A THRILLER FROM NEW YORK TIMES BESTSELLING AUTHOR

M. WILLIAM PHELPS

WildBluePress.com

THE DEAD SOUL published by:
WILDBLUE PRESS
P.O. Box 102440
Denver, Colorado 80250

ISBN 978-1-960332-40-0 Trade Paperback
ISBN 978-1-960332-39-4 eBook
ISBN 978-1-960332-41-7 Hardback

Cover design © 2023 WildBlue Press. All rights reserved.
Interior Formatting and Cover Design by Elijah Toten
www.totencreative.com

THE

DEAD

SOUL

*For those who appreciate how the mind
of a serial murderer works.*

Surgeons must be very careful
When they take the knife!
Underneath their fine incisions
Stirs the culprit—Life!
—*Emily Dickinson*

Note to reader

DO NOT *skip the prologue to this book (we know most of you have a habit of doing this!), for you will miss many important clues to the mystery.*

Now, turn the lights out, strap yourself in, and begin this ride ...

Prologue

MONDAY, MAY 3 – 12:10 P.M.

He did not plan on killing her. As he entered Sam Adams Plaza, a Cessna purred overhead, trailing behind it a banner advertising a one-day sale at *Shamrock's, Boston's #1 Automart*. The mobile billboard fluttered in front of a myriad of puffy white clouds. He carried a bag in one hand, a camera in the other. Over his left shoulder, the noon bells on the Customs House clock tower chimed. Street performers entertained throngs of people in the square.

Where is she?

A lanky college kid dressed in bulky parachute pants and a black-and-white-striped jailhouse T-shirt spun his unicycle in circles. He juggled three different-colored balls. Bongo music played, accompanied by tambourines and finger cymbals. The crowd clapped along to an a capella version of "Gimme Shelter."

The most dramatic of the street performers was a team of gargoyles spread out around the square, skulking and crawling. Some were hidden in places no one expected. Others sat statue-like on park benches, never breaking character. They were not friendly-looking creatures. Concrete-gray from head to toe, they appeared to have walked off the stony plinth of a medieval cathedral somewhere. Their fingernails were pointed. Tapered. Thornlike. The wings of Satan's angels strapped to their backs.

A hundred feet north of the Faneuil Hall entrance, he sat on the base of a water fountain, waiting for her. Impatiently, he checked his watch. It was hot in his uniform. He scanned the large crowd, using the telescopic lens on his Nikon as binoculars.

He stood up, frustrated. Walked toward Paul Revere Creamery. He had made sure to check his notebook before leaving the house. He was certain. She had purchased a plain vanilla cone every Monday for the past four weeks.

It was just after noon on a Monday. *Where in the hell is she?*

As he walked, a gargoyle followed him.

The man with the camera was determined to introduce himself to this woman who did not even know he existed. He wanted to show her the photos he had taken over the past several months; hundreds of black and white images of her.

A Northeastern student, Alyssa usually parked her orange VW Bug along a deserted alleyway between State and Milk streets. After volunteering at the soup kitchen nearby for a few hours, she liked to stroll about Quincy Market and shop.

He finally spotted her. Alyssa walked out from underneath a vendor's tent. Amid the mass of people puttering about, she passed right by him, brushing his right shoulder.

He stopped. Took her in. A long, slow inhale. Her fragrance went through his senses in layers—lavender flowers, nutty baby powder, mango body wash—as he closed his eyes.

Yum.

She walked toward Chatham Street into the dense crowd, weaved in and out of pedestrians. He lost sight of her, and a feeling of panic came over him in a rush of sweat. He gripped his camera tighter. The blue vein running along his right temple exposed itself like an earthworm.

"Alyssa," he yelled. "Alyssa?"

She turned. Scanned the crowd in puzzlement. Continued to walk.

Someone set off a pack of firecrackers nearby that startled everyone. It reminded him of watching Mardi Gras on the Travel Channel.

He moved faster. More focused. Then, from knee level, a gargoyle bounced up in front of him and stuck out his barbed fingers.

Boo.

"Sonofabitch!" he shouted. The crowd nearby took delight in how well the gargoyle frightened him. "You scared the shit out of me."

The gargoyle waved his cigar fingers as if he were performing some sort of ritualistic dance, casting a spell.

"Get the hell out of my way." He watched Alyssa walk out of the square, onto Chatham Street. "Move," he yelled. "Come on."

He shoved the gargoyle to his left. Ran after her.

"May the Father of Lies keep us from the wiles and temptations of your Lord," the gargoyle said in his best stage voice. He stood. Brushed himself off. "Jerk."

The crowd cheered. What a performance.

He slipped out of the square. Turned the corner. Directly in front of him, fifty yards away, he watched the object of his desire as she walked down a side street. Alone.

He tore off after her.

His heart thrummed. A single bead of sweat met his eyebrow. He watched her shapely calves, flexing and bouncing. Mounted his camera. Zoomed in.

The shutter went wild. Clicking over and over.

Do it now, he told himself. "All these photos." He slapped the side of his duffel bag.

"Hi," he said, coming up on Alyssa, out of breath, catching her off-guard.

Stunned, she turned to look at the stranger. Then quickly headed for her VW parked up ahead.

"I wanted to give you these." The stranger dug in his bag. Alyssa looked around, unsure of what to make of him. "I took them for you and, well"—this was a lot harder than he thought—"maybe we could, you know, do something together."

"Do I know you?" She rummaged through her handbag quickly.

Keys.

"No, you don't understand. These are pictures I took of *you*." He fanned out the photos as if they were playing cards, magicianlike. He pointed to one in particular. "I took them to show you, Alyssa."

"I need to get going." She stopped looking. "Thanks … but I need to get back to the dorm."

Alyssa was frozen by the driver's-side door of her car. He held a collection of photos in her face. He knew she would recognize the small tattoo of an angel on her left ankle in one close-up shot.

The look on her face told him she realized most of the photos had been taken from a distance. "Please, I don't want any trouble … I need to get going."

He rubbed his face as if he just woke up. "You don't understand."

Alyssa pushed the photos away. Knocked them out of his hand. They fell on the ground in front of him.

A burst of wind kicked up.

"Please, don't do that. Don't you *do* that to me. I took these for you."

He realized he was not stuttering anymore. It was wonderful and cathartic.

Shaking, Alyssa found her key, slipped it into the lock, and turned it to the right.

Several of the photos took flight with a burst of wind, carried down the alley, flying up and away.

He grabbed Alyssa by the arm. "No, listen. Let me start over."

Alyssa tried to shake off his arm. His grip was too tight.

"Let me go." She screamed, "I beg you. Please. Let me go."

"Don't yell. *Please* don't yell." He put a hand over her mouth.

"I'll do whatever you want." She had trouble getting the words out.

He didn't like her this way.

She broke free. But he grabbed her pocketbook and pulled. Then wrapped her in a bear hug. They were face to face. With her fists, she pounded his chest.

What am I doing, grabbing this woman?

As they struggled, he felt a comforting sense of power rise in him. The harder he worked at controlling her, the deeper the feeling of content. This soothed him.

He grasped Alyssa by the wrists. She gave him a knee in his side and he let go.

Then she slipped inside the car. He yanked her back out by her hips. They fell to the ground.

"Help …" she yelled. "Somebody help me …"

He cupped her mouth.

Shh …

Without realizing it, he put her in a headlock. Her right breast was cupped in one hand. It felt warm. Firm. Her head was tucked beneath his chin. He could smell her—lavender, dry baby powder. The aroma set him off. Reminded him of his mother when she got out of the shower. Not thinking about it, he twisted Alyssa's neck. It was not a conscious decision, but more of a reaction.

Her lower lip twitched. Her head stood mannequin-still as the lower half of her body squirmed. Then she went limp and collapsed to the ground.

"Hey?" he said in a loud whisper, his eyes darting from side to side. He turned. Nobody had seen what happened. Down the alley, a kid in a greasy apron tossed boxes in a

Dumpster. Not paying attention, he bobbed his head to the beat of his iPod.

"Hey?" He slapped Alyssa on the face lightly.

Nothing.

He pushed her into the car, over the shifter, and she plopped onto the passenger seat. He hopped into the driver's seat and started the car. Put the shifter in DRIVE. Hit the gas.

Alyssa came to. Groggy, but awake. "What's going on?" Realizing where she was and what had happened, she banged on the dashboard. Kicked. Grabbed the door handle.

He pulled up alongside a building wall, blocking her in.

They struggled again. She was weaker, the fight in her just about gone.

Still, she managed to scratch one of his eyes.

It burned. He felt a trickle of warm blood run down his cheek.

Please help me. No, I don't like the furnace.

With that thought a towering rage grew inside him. He grabbed the nylon shoulder strap of his duffel bag, wrapped it around Alyssa's neck, then pulled both ends as hard as he could, as if tying a knot.

She pawed at his forearms, gasped for air. The inside of the windows fogged.

He put his thumbs together. His hands around her neck. Then crushed her windpipe. The sound reminded him of breaking a Saltine. He had called on a strength he did not know existed inside him. White foam and saliva sputtered from her mouth like hot popping grease.

He stared into Alyssa's blue eyes. Her retinal veins burst before him.

He squeezed tighter, with more force, and felt an erection throb. The entire ordeal was intoxicating. He'd had no idea how gratifying this was. How much it calmed him.

Alyssa went quiet, flaccid. He watched her essence drift into eternal sleep. What a sense of authority. Life and death, all in his hands.

"You're so beautiful," he whispered. He kissed Alyssa on the lips.

In the struggle, her skirt had raised above her knees, exposing her smooth legs. The sight of them overtook him. And just then, staring at her bare skin, an idea hit him.

FOUR MONTHS LATER

1

WEDNESDAY, SEPTEMBER 3 – 6:28 P.M.

The smell of rotting flesh should have alerted someone. She had been lying on the ground in front of the Public Garden rose patch adjacent to Beacon Street for God knows how long. Her emerald-green eyes were wide open and cloudy, like a fish in supermarket snow. Her face had been beaten and bloodied; but, astonishingly, her features were easily distinguishable. Beyond killing her, someone had savagely pummeled the young woman over certain sections of her body. Shadows covered part of her body. Yet there was no mistaking the fact that her legs had been—some would later use the term "surgically"—removed. Just below the hip.

Stubs.

On late summer nights, the glow of Boston's Park Street Station around the Common took on a monotonous sense of surrealism. It felt lonely. Deserted. Gone was the steely taste of car exhaust from rush hour and the concrete dust from all the new construction going on near Charles and Boylston streets. In the magical twilight of dusk, steam floated out of the manhole covers in ghostly ribbons. Leaves, bursting with fall's early shades of plum purple and school bus orange, floated in graceful eddies onto a line of parked cars. And there was this young female, on her back, staring at the stars. Not hidden, or buried, but out in the open, amid this amiable, quaint cityscape. Waiting, essentially, to reveal the secrets of her murder.

2

WEDNESDAY, SEPTEMBER 3 – 6:44 P.M.

His heart pounding, Jake Cooper paced. The static-filled call came in over the Motorola as he was getting ready to leave. A jogger had stumbled over the girl. Jake was inside his office on the tenth floor of the Patriot Building, a stone and glass structure poking fifty-six stories into Boston's skyline, several blocks west of the Prudential Center. The Charles River and Mass Pike were at Jake's back. On his walnut desk, in a brass frame next to the telephone, a $19.95 Wal-Mart family photo package of Jake, his wife, and son stared up at him.

Stunned by the gruesome description of the girl, the detective froze.

"Cooper?" the lieutenant shouted over the radio. "Come on, answer me."

This was it, Jake knew. His last chance. They'd call it *Sundance's swan song* behind his back. The next major homicide case, the lieutenant had announced weeks ago, was Jake's. Only Jake wasn't sure he wanted it. All that locker room gossip and water cooler talk by his colleagues. The constant mocking and guilt trips ladled on by his former rabbi, Detective Mo Blackhall. Yes, Jake had fumbled that last homicide case, allowing the bastard to walk. Hell, he could still see the expression on the face of the little girl's mother. The color draining from her cheeks as the jury foreman stood … *"not guilty."* How she doubled over.

Stared daggers of hatred at Jake, screaming, "*It's your fault, Detective Cooper! You let my little girl die* TWICE."

It had been two years. Now Jake was gazing down the barrel of that second chance they say everyone deserves, those around him holding a collective finger on the trigger. He felt his stomach tighten. Those butterflies reminded the seasoned cop that there was nothing worse than a man unsure of himself.

"Answer me, Cooper!" the lieutenant screamed.

Jake sat. Put the heels of his hands over his eyes, elbows on his desk, his long fingers curling over his forehead.

This is your game, he told himself. *Get up … go!*

"Cooper … I know you can hear me. Get your ass over to the Garden—now. I'm on my way there."

It was a setup. Jake was certain the lieutenant wanted him on the case only to watch him fail. Then they could all laugh at him. Kick dirt from that little girl's grave in his face while shouting a chorus of *I-told-you-so's*.

6:49 P.M.

A damp chill hung in the air, thick and heavy, like the humidity following a soaking thunderstorm. When Lieutenant Ramunas "Ray" Matikas—the Loudmouth Lithuanian—arrived at the scene shortly after calling Jake, he stood stock still, shaking his head, caught in the aura of death on the young woman's face. In all his years, Matikas could not recall ever seeing anything like this.

As the lieutenant focused on the vic's purple lips and Goth-white torso, his thought was interrupted.

"I can't get ovah how much she resembles the Northeastern student who's been missing since spring, Lieutenant," a uniform blue said. The young cop handed Matikas a missing-persons flyer someone had brought out to the scene. "If you look at Alyssa Bettencourt's photo here, sized up against her vitals," the blue added, tapping the paper, "you'll see wicked similarities. Height, weight, hair. All the same."

Alyssa's boyfriend had reported that she'd gone to Quincy Market one afternoon in May and never returned to the dorm. No one had seen her since.

"Why isn't Cooper answering his radio? This is *his* problem."

"Dunno, sir."

Matikas wanted a positive ID before anyone called Alyssa's family for dentals or DNA. "The press is going to run with this. Her father is supposed to be some sort of shit-ass 'politician,'" Matikas said. "I don't need brass up my ass if we're wrong. Sure, it looks a lot like her." The lieutenant stood over the vic holding the flyer, going back and forth with his eyes. "Damn, if it is, you'd think she would have shown up months ago."

"Right, Lieutenant. Kidnapped and held hostage maybe?"

"No one move her until I say so," Matikas shouted. "Is Cooper on his way?"

"We're working on that, boss."

Blues and crime scene techs walked the knoll in back of the vic in parallel lines, conducting a grid search for trace. The area was taped off. Surrounded by park security and day-shift blues eating up overtime. Matikas eyed the vic again. Over her head was a sign, gold lettering set on a bronze plaque—FREEDOM TRAIL STARTS HERE.

There was a perfectly straight slice down the middle of the young woman's torso. North to South. It extended from the center of her breasts to just above her crotch area, where her pubic hairline would have begun if she hadn't recently gotten a Telly Savalas, complete bikini wax. There was a small tattoo of a cross on her belly, split in two by the incision.

"This doesn't bother you?" Matikas asked a young detective standing next to him who had just joined the squad. They called him Rookie. He wore those gaudy, out-of-style tortoise-shell glasses, circa 1970s Elton John. Patrol officers liked to tease him. *"B-B-B-Bennie and the Jets."* Rookie walked with a slight limp. He had gotten himself kicked off the force in Danvers, upstate, near Gloucester. Matikas got a call, decided to give the kid another chance.

Matikas elbowed Rookie, nodded toward the vic. "See that?"

"What, sir?" Rookie bent over. Pushed his glasses up the bridge of his nose.

Clearing his throat, Matikas went into one of his exasperating forensic lectures his men hated. "The absence of clotting indicates our perp cut this leg off while this young lady here, well, while she was still alive."

Rookie winced. He did not want to look at the woman. He was agitated and uncomfortable being around her.

Matikas enjoyed this part of the job. Made him feel in control of things. "There's no central clotting. She bled out. You see it?"

Rookie leaned in to make it look good. Nodded his head as if he understood.

"Yet there's no blood on the ground anywhere. Interesting, huh? Now, Rookie, look at the incision there on the chest." Matikas pointed to it with a pen. "You see that?"

"Yep." Rookie had no idea what his new boss was talking about.

"That's clotting. She died between that leg"—he made a circular gesture with the pen—"and *this* incision in her chest."

It was obvious the girl had not been killed at this location. The Common was a dumpsite.

Matikas wrote something in his notebook. Straightened himself. Stared at the vic. Then: "Has anyone found her legs?"

"Not yet, Lieutenant," Rookie said. He was pale, and looked as though he was about to upchuck dinner.

The blues standing around all shrugged.

The lieutenant walked over, put his arm around Rookie. "Welcome to Bawstin," he said, overdoing Bean Town's signature dialect on purpose. Then patted the newbie on the back. "You're in the Big City now, kid. Home of murderers, rapists, and the Sawx."

3

WEDNESDAY, SEPTEMBER 3 - 6:52 P.M.

The man in the light blue-and-white-pinstriped uniform leaned against the sink in his kitchen. Arms folded, he eyed the package on the table. Next to it was the *Boston Globe*, rolled up and stuffed inside a long clear plastic bag tied at the end like a loaf of bread. He had just picked it up from the front steps. The bag was covered in morning dew.

The inside of his small Cape was dated. In need of a Home Depot makeover. The walls were maple paneling. The rug, once a white-toned shag, now had travel paths of grunge where it looked as if he had scrubbed and washed to no avail. Tag-sale knickknacks crowded the tops of tables and shelves. An RCA Victor console color TV on four legs with rabbit ears sat in the corner. A relic.

To retrieve the parcel, he had made a special trip to the marina after getting out of work. He was tired now. He needed a bath and some sleep. Still, he couldn't leave the package as it was. Especially if he was going to use it.

He took each one out of the bag and placed it on the table. As he removed the second one, a single blood droplet oozed from the knee joint, hit the linoleum floor, and spattered in a starfish pattern near his right foot.

Damn it.

He hated a mess.

After folding the bubble wrap carefully over each leg, he taped the corners. Then slipped the packaged limbs into a brown paper shopping bag, all with a smile of satisfaction.

The freezer was right behind him. He placed the bag of legs next to a box of frozen pizza, in between a stack of frost-burned aqua blue ice cube trays he never used.

He walked to the closet in the living room—making sure not to step on the floor molding between the kitchen and the carpet—to get his cleaning kit. He needed to remove the blood from the linoleum. Tossing and turning, it would bother him all night if he didn't.

Hanging on the closet door were the priestly vestments he had just gotten back from the cleaners—black cassock, white collar. He locked onto them as a memory flashed before him.

The basement had cobwebs all the way down the stairs. I see them. No. Please. I will do what you say.

To block out the recollection, he whistled as loud as he could, a kid on his way to a fishing hole. He straightened the Catholic vestments. Ran his forefinger over the collar. Closed his eyes. Took a deep breath.

The cleaning supplies.

Get that blood off the floor.

He slammed the closet door shut.

I must cry out ... violence and outrage is my message.

He knelt on the kitchen floor and scrubbed the small spot of blood over and over. He used a brush. Sprayed the stain with a bleach and water mixture, wiped it in a circular pattern with a paper towel until any sign of blood was gone.

It was almost seven. Standing, he saw the newspapers on the table. Those articles in the *Globe* he wanted to clip and hang on the wall next to the others. They'd have to wait 'til later. After all, he'd be making headlines for the next several weeks.

4

WEDNESDAY, SEPTEMBER 3 – 6:56 P.M.

A slight drizzle fell. More of a cold mist, actually, rather November than early September, and clung to everything in its path. A lone crow, black and shiny as velvet, cawing loudly, landed on the iron gate leading down into the Garden. Squad cars lined Arlington, their red and blue lights reflecting off the glazed street, giving the scene a clear boundary, announcing to the neighborhood that something very bad had happened here.

About one hundred yards east of where the legless blonde had been discovered, Jake Cooper drove over the Beacon Street curb by the iron fence. As if his city-issued Crown Vic had won a marathon, the yellow plastic crime scene tape blocking off the entrance nearly snapped against the front bumper.

As he changed from his suit coat into a windbreaker, BOSTON POLICE in bright gold letters scribed across the back, Jake took mental note of his surroundings. News crews in vans with satellite dishes pointed toward the darkened skies stood around, waiting. Nosy neighbors from the nearby townhouses and three-deckers jostled for position. Blues held them back against the yellow sawhorses set up as though a parade was coming.

Jake spotted a photographer he knew. If this was his case, he needed to take charge immediately. "Get several shots of the crowd, would you, Paul?" Jake pointed. "Faces. Maybe our guy's still hangin' around."

"Sure thing, Detective. You alright?"

Jake stopped. Turned. Squinted a nasty look. "Yeah! Why?"

"Just asking. Gees, man. Don't be such a wicked pissa. Relax."

Jake Cooper ignored the remark, pulled out his iPhone and tapped the desktop App marked *CS*. He was calling up the GPS tracking device he had downloaded a few nights back from the BPD's encrypted tech support website. It was something new. Jake was told the program, if given enough information, could spit out a person-of-interest profile. Jake zeroed in on the location the body had been found as two intersecting lines on the small screen crisscrossed—a radar missile target locking. He saved the info to a chime. Then typed several notes to go along with the new file.

"Sundance Cooper," someone yelled.

Paying no attention, Jake walked down the asphalt path toward his vic.

A blue caught up to him and walked hurriedly by Jake's side to keep up. "Cooper? Hey, man, the lieutenant's looking for you. He's down by the Lagoon. Sounds pissed."

Jake smiled off to the side of his mouth.

At one time, Jake Cooper was the best detective Ray Matikas had on the squad. But Jake's relationship with Mo Blackhall and the fiasco that last homicide turned into destroyed all those fuzzy feelings, and almost got Jake booted off the force. Didn't matter how smart or tough a cop Jake Sundance Cooper had proven himself to be. Mo was poison. Jake had fumbled the last homicide. Matikas hated him for it. He wanted to see Jake out on his ass. Same as Mo. The sooner the better.

"What's the hurry, Lieutenant?" Jake asked. "Dead people won't walk away." He came up behind Matikas, who was explaining something to Rookie.

Matikas turned. "Ah, that's just great, Cooper. I've got the biggest homicide case of the year, and you're out and about, yanking y'chain."

"I'm here now, Ramunas. What do we have?"

"Funny guy." Matikas hated being called by his namesake. "What the hell. Where were you?" Matikas stepped closer to Jake, stopped what he was doing. Then called everyone to huddle up. "Oh, wait. Hey fellas, gather 'round. Detective Cooper is going to now tell us he knew where Whitey Bulger was hiding out all those years."

The blues laughed. Rookie looked down at his shoes.

Embarrassed, his blood pressure rising, Jake dropped his head. Clenched a fist. Felt the urge for a cigarette creep up the back of his throat.

Walking toward the body, Jake locked onto a single maple leaf that had fallen from a tree above and landed on the vic's stomach. He stopped, blocked everyone from his mind, taking in the grotesque nature of this scene. Then, in a low voice, not turning away from the girl: "Any info on who she is?"

Matikas lit a cigarette with a silver Zippo that let off a faint aroma of kerosene. He clinked the cover back in place, blew the first drag into Jake's face, then started toward his car. "You had better get me a positive ID by morning, Cooper. Listen, we think it might be that Bettencourt kid who's been missing from Northeastern. The vic's vitals match this flyer"—he gave it to Rookie to hand to Jake— "but her face is busted up and it's hard to tell. Still, I don't want her parents informed until we're sure. You got me?"

"You know what a Lithuanian is, Lieutenant?

Matikas didn't answer.

"I didn't think so—a poor Polack."

Matikas stroked his chin, then pointed at Jake: "You're a frickin' asshole, Cooper, you know that."

As Matikas walked up the path, mumbling obscenities in Lithuanian, Jake told the blues standing by to clear out. "Go watch the crowds, fellas, okay."

At the park's entryway, standing by his vehicle, Matikas yelled down to Jake. "Oh, yeah. One more thing. You screw this up, you'll be doing guard duty at Celtic games—that is, if IA doesn't find something to bring you and that asshole mentor of yours up on charges before that."

Matikas stubbed out his cigarette, and walked away.

Jake knelt beside the girl, one hand over his knee, the other smoothing his stubble. The detective studied the vic's position and posture. The empty look on the young woman's face and how her killer had staged the scene. He thought about the girl's last few moments. What a hell that must have been. Focusing, he heard the brittle leaves behind him crunch, a groan, then an "Oh, shit."

It had to be Dickie. No one else walked with such drama.

"Long time no see," Jake said without looking. "Almost lost your footing there."

Dickie Shaughnessy was an Irishman down to his dark orange hair and pockmarked pink face. He had an obsessive penchant for beer as dark as Coca-Cola, centuries-old overpriced whiskey, and colcannon. Dickie and Jake had known each other for five years. They had worked homicides together, but spent most of their time chasing dope dealers, rapists, and child abusers. Dickie supported Jake. He was unconvinced Jake was going down with Mo. Felt bad about the heat Jake had taken over that last case.

"Where the hell is she?"

"Over here, Dickie." It wasn't dark out yet, but with the oak trees casting umbrella-like shadows and the gloomy skies, it was hard to see anything until your eyes adjusted.

"Jesus," Dickie said, shining a flashlight on what was left of her legs, panning up toward her face. "What a frickin' mess … Christ Almighty."

Jake made the sign of the cross and looked up into the sky. "Hey, I told you about saying that shit around me."

"Oops, sorry there, Mr. Catholic. Thought you'd given up on all that faith stuff."

Jake stood, rapped Dickie on the back. "Thanks for coming out."

Dickie looked back toward his car. "Tired, Jake. We had a search and seizure in Medford. Up and down stairs all day long. You forget I'm fatter and older."

Jake leveled his watch. "It's not even eight o'clock yet."

"My Discovery Channel shows are on—what am I doin' here?"

They paused and shared a brief moment of camaraderie. Then Jake got serious. "Get a look at her face." Bending down again, the lead detective took a hankie from his pocket and picked up a plastic bristle attached to her shoulder. "Check this out." He held it up for Dickie to evaluate. "Piece of a broom?"

"Could be." Dickie moaned as he bent over and his gut rubbed against his belt buckle. He slipped on his Benjamin Franklin half-moon glasses. Studied the corpse they were now referring to as the "Unknown DB." Dickie focused on her eyes, noting how dull and glassy they were. The blood vessels mapping through the whites were clear, however. Not a spot in either one.

"You see that?"

"Clear conjunctiva," Jake pointed out. "I did." Dickie wrote it down in his pocket notebook. "She definitely wasn't strangled before the sonofabitch cut her open."

Jake snapped on a pair of latex gloves he took out of his pocket. Bending over the vic's head, he slid his cigar flashlight into his mouth, pointed it down—a coal miner's view—at her lips. Then pried open her mouth. He had learned from Mo years ago that with every homicide you checked the inside the vic's mouth. Light or dark, you could tell, within a respectable window, how long a person had been dead. The darker the skin tone, the longer. The lighter, the shorter.

"Months," Jake said out of the corner of his mouth.

Despite being stained with spots of blood, her teeth gleamed white. "A bleacher." Her tongue was purple as if she'd had a grape Blow Pop before meeting her maker. Her cheeks were pallid, dry, flaky, dark, and cold to the touch.

Jake spat the flashlight out onto the ground beside him. "Get a look at this." He leaned back so Dickie could go in for a closer view. "Odd, huh? Come here," Jake yelled to the crime scene photographer snapping photos around them. "Get me a shot of this." He pointed inside her mouth. "There's some scarring on her right cheek."

A series of quick flashes lit up the night. The photographer, Jake noticed, seemed to be taking more photos of the vic than necessary.

"Hey, enough already, huh. Head over to that pond. Snap the shoreline for me." Jake watched the photographer walk away.

"They seem to think she might be that Bettencourt kid," Dickie said without much confidence.

"She looks pretty damn good to me for a four-month-old corpse."

"Kidnapped? Held hostage? Killed later?"

Jake stood. "No way. There's no bruising on her wrists. No yellowing of the skin besides her face." They stared at her again. It was obvious she had never been tied up. "She could have been frozen. There, on her thigh, looks like freezer burn. The inside of her mouth indicates the same thing."

"Just when you think you've seen everything. Frickin' incredible."

The crime scene tape fencing off the area around the body fluttered against a blustery gust of Northeast wind. Jake and Dickie stood and looked down at Miss Unknown DB. Lights flashed against the corrugated bark of the trees around them, illuminating their faces in red and blue pulses. Several cops stood by. Sipped coffee. Talked Boston sports. They were waiting for the go-ahead to leave and get back to their cozy patrol cars. These were the smart cops, Jake thought. Do twenty in a uniform. Keep your trap shut. Collect a pension. That never worked for Jake. He needed the riddle a crime presented. Mr. Problem Solver, Jake Cooper. Finding the answers made him feel like it all actually mattered. That people gave a shit.

Jake popped a piece of nicotine gum out of a plastic foil sleeve. He had quit smoking six months ago. It had been a rough road. He'd been tar-free for thirty days and counting.

"There's something missing, Dickie."

"You mean, besides her legs?"

Jake ignored the wisecrack. "It's her face. Look closely. Since when are we using missing-persons fliers to ID DBs, anyway? The bruising on her face is fresh." Jake panned the beam of his flashlight over her chin and cheeks. Then down the length of her torso. "Look at the rest of her body. Doesn't add up."

"You think our guy froze her, thawed her out, *then* beat her?"

Jake looked down. "Maybe. But I know one thing."

"Yeah?"

"Nobody leaves a scene like this, or commits murder on this level, for the first time."

5

Dawn Cooper stopped at the District-15 squad room on her way to work. Jake's office inside D-15 was located along the west wall of the Patriot Building. It pained Dawn that the empty room lacked any serious decorating. The white-washed walls were naked, save for a few photographs Jake couldn't bring himself to remove until he was actually walking out the door for good. There was a framed motivational photo—TEAMWORK—of two rowing squads moving in unison up an unnamed river at sunrise. The smaller photo next to it was of Jake and his big (late) brother, Casey. But that was it. You walk into this cop's office and think, *Here's a guy in between two lives.*

Jake sat behind his desk in a swivel chair facing the large window looking out onto the city of Boston. He had his feet up on the dusty sill, lost in the charming grace of the jagged skyline in front of him. Inside, a well of concern brewed.

"What time will you be home tonight, honey?"

The question startled Jake, who turned quickly, stood, and kissed Dawn. "Sit. What is it? What's wrong?" His frayed nerves were implicit in every question. Any unscheduled visit or unexpected telephone call was automatically bad news to Jake Cooper. His insides were in a constant twist of worry. The sky was always falling.

"Relax, you. I'm running early for work. Just wanted to stop in and say hi on my way. Calm down." It was a lie.

"This is big, Dawn. My shot." Jake made a fist. Clenched his teeth. Stared at an empty space on his desk.

"What do you mean? Ray *gave* you the Garden case?" Dawn had heard the reports on the radio and figured it was the reason why her husband hadn't come home the night before. Not that he'd call and let her know.

"It's mine, yeah. Here's the thing. I think that body in the Garden is the first of several. Or the last of a collection we haven't found."

Silence beat a tense pulse between them as they considered this.

Dawn noted the I'm-back-in-the-game tone to her husband's voice. She didn't want to show it, but Dawn Cooper was worried sick. It was the reason for the visit. She knew a second chance for Jake was imminent. But had hoped for more time. She didn't want it to be *this* case. Here it was, Jake's first homicide since being back and he had been up all night already, a no-show at home. Dawn was there by Jake's side, helping him through that last fiasco. The girl was eight years old. She was brutally raped for two days after being abducted from her bedroom in the middle of the night. If that wasn't enough, the sonofabitch buried her alive underneath a neighbor's porch. Jake had found the girl, but destroyed a crucial piece of evidence in the process. The subsequent outcome of the trial—along with orders from brass—sent Jake to the psych ward of Faulkner Hospital to get his head straight. He'd been back on the job six months. It was too much, too soon.

"Oh my goodness," Dawn said. "And Ray's okay with this?"

"Of course. He insisted."

Jake hadn't spoken for days after the trial. The perp was freed because of that illegal search Jake had conducted. So Jake started stalking him until he finally left town. Why was Ray allowing Jake to jump back in now? And such a horrific case, with so much at stake. What if Jake's old nemesis had returned and graduated from rape to murder?

"Great, honey. I mean, that's what you wanted, right—another shot?"

Jake took a minute. "Yeah. Finally." He paced by the window, looking out, uncertain of his answer.

Dawn forced herself to say it. "We'll celebrate when you're done. I'll pick Brendan up tonight, then, at aftercare. We'll grab a pizza. See you at home later on?"

Jake shrugged without turning around. "Depends …"

Dawn looked over at the rumpled blanket and pillow on the couch in Jake's office. Walked out the door.

12:24 P.M.

Fighting back tears on the way to work, in her office a half hour later, Dawn Cooper turned her attention toward the kid sitting on the floor underneath the chair.

Denny Garcia. Such a cute twelve-year-old. Kinky light brown hair. A tiny sun spot on his right cheek blending perfectly with his olive skin. The bluest eyes.

"Come on out, Denny," Dawn said.

Denny's palms were white as chalk. Not from birth, but from a father who punished the kid by holding his hands over a lava red stove burner on high whenever he came home drunk and wanted to take out his frustrations for the personal failures of such a crappy life. Now Denny was with a foster family. And that was supposed to be better? It was Dawn's job to try and clean up the mess left behind.

Denny reluctantly sat in the chair. "Tell me about your week," Dawn said.

"Not good," Denny answered. "Bad. Bad. Bad." Earlier that day Denny took off all his clothes in class, complaining how hot he was.

"You know it's wrong to undress in public, right, Denny?"

The boy stared at a Monet-ish painting Dawn hung in the office of a woman sitting alone on a park bench, looking out at an enormous field of blurry flowers.

"I like that picture, Mrs. Cooper."

Denny told Dawn this at every session.

"It's beautiful, Denny, I know."

Dawn had a long road ahead of her.

3:14 P.M.

The transition from stay-at-home mom to working mother had been rough on Dawn. Before Brendan started first grade, spooning Jake in bed at night, Dawn looked forward to the daily jogs around the neighborhood every morning, pushing Brendan in a blue, three-wheeled canvas stroller. She missed the social gatherings at the park on warm days. The mid-afternoon Lia Sophia and Pampered Chef parties. Naps. *The Price Is Right* and *Guiding Light*. Bonding with her son. Now Dawn was a career-minded woman. Out of the PTA, busybody-neighbor loop.

Leaving work, she drove to the Pocahontas After School Daycare—everything had to be Disney-fied these days, didn't it, Dawn had told her too many times—to pick up seven-year-old Brendan, her and Jake's only child. The daycare was two miles from their home in Brookline. An argument with Jake the day before still bothered Dawn. She didn't want to bring it up at his office earlier, but she was upset by some of things Jake had said in anger. All she told him was that it might have been a mistake to take on coaching that soccer team on top of going back to work now that Brendan was in school full-time. Didn't mean she second-guessed herself. "I'm just venting, babe," Dawn had said. Her job as a school psychologist—her profession pre-Brendan—in Chelsea, was difficult. The school was in total disarray. Students fought. Threw feces at each other. Screamed obscenities at teachers. The stress on the family now that Dawn worked full-time and coached was getting to them both. She knew Jake hadn't mentioned it earlier because he was preoccupied with his new case. But in time the resentment and I-knew-its would resurface. Probably when he was at an impasse in the investigation and fed up with not making any progress. Dawn would bear the brunt.

"Can we get a Wii, Mommy?" Brendan asked. He sat in the backseat, his short legs not yet touching the floorboard.

Dawn looked in the rearview mirror at her son. "Who has one, Brendan?" She took a right onto Woodycrest, headed toward home.

"Nobody."

"Come on, fess up, kiddo?"

Brendan smiled. "Tara."

"Is her last name Jones?" Dawn laughed at her own stupid joke. "We'll have to discuss this, honey, okay."

"Car, Mommy," Brendan said. He pointed to their driveway. Brendan had a perpetual look of just having woken up. His hair always tossed about, clothes wrinkled, fingers in his mouth. He liked to wear shorts all the time, winter or summer. He had a hard time separating himself from his favorite Red Sox T-shirt. There was a picture Brendan had colored in daycare on the seat next to him—a sunset, house, stick-figure mom holding the hand of a sad child, the dad standing off to the side.

"I see, honey." Dawn didn't recognize the vehicle at first.

As she drove by a heaping pile of dry copper-colored maple leaves in the gutter of the road, they blew away like confetti from the whoosh of the car. The neighbor, Mr. Groeshel, was clipping hedges. He waved as Dawn went by.

"When is Daddy going to be home?" Brendan asked. He took one of his planes and pretend-flew it in front of him, making a buzzing sound, spittle spraying on the back of the headrest of the front seat.

"Soon, I hope." Dawn was puzzled by the presence of her guest after realizing who it was. Father John O'Brien stood, leaning on the trunk of his battered Ford Escort, reading the newspaper.

When Dawn emerged from her green Accord, Father John walked over and hugged her. Brendan grabbed his book bag, said hello with an embarrassed smirk. Being around clergy made the boy nervous.

"Hi, Father. What brings you around?"

"I need to speak with Jake, Dawn. Our last conversation ended on a bad note. Will he be home soon?" Father John's cloud-white hair blew in the slight wind. "It's chilly for this time of the year, eh?" He wore a knee-length black wool coat with a bat-wing collar, Russian spy-like. "I didn't want to call and warn him, you know what I mean."

She did. "Smart, Father. You want some tea? Come inside."

"You ready for First Communion?" Father asked Brendan, rustling the top of the boy's head. "Only a few years away, my son." Father John was in his early seventies. One of those old-school Boston Irish Catholic priests with rosy-red, chubby cheeks, bulging belly, and gentle manner. "I should have called first."

"No, Father. It's quite all right."

As Dawn and Father John chatted, Brendan ran off with a ncighborhood friend into the backyard. Dawn watched him and the other boy race around the corner, wishing life was as simple as a childhood game.

"Last one there's a rotten egg," Brendan screamed.

6

THURSDAY, SEPTEMBER 4 – 3:23 P.M.

Jake Cooper grabbed his keys and Motorola. Before heading out of his office, the big man stopped. One hand on the door, hesitation saddled him. It was time to man up, Jake supposed. Prove to all those bastards how wrong they were.

Just as he was about to leave, Jake turned and caught a glimpse of himself in the mirror on the opposite side of the room. He looked pale, pasty, and worn out. Six foot three, 210 pounds, all chest and arms, Jake hadn't changed much physically since becoming a cop fifteen years ago. He once read that variety was for the weak-minded. The undecided. So he went out and bought five of the same dark blue Hager suits, FBI-certified. Five white Ralph Lauren dress shirts. A collection of pastel-colored ties. Today he wore fire-engine red against that familiar G-man uniform. Mixing it up, Jake clipped on one of those American flag pins politicians started attaching to their lapels post-9/11, with the exception that Jake wore his for far different reasons.

Mo Blackhall was down the hall, getting ready to leave. He heard Jake's door click shut, then footsteps. Back in the day, Mo was *that* cop. The one you smacked on the shoulder every morning after roll call so the other cops saw you do it. The guy you blew off your wife for on Saturday nights to sit next to at the poker table. Had beers with at Red Sox games while screaming obscenities at slumping players. If you needed something, even from brass, Mo got it done.

As Jake made his way down the hallway, Mo came around the corner, and stepped in front of him.

Jake cut him off with raised hands. "Not now, Mo. I'm working a tip. Gotta run and meet Dickie."

"Yeah, I heard," Mo said. He sported a face full of salt-and-pepper stubble. Mo looked tired, raccoon bags under his eyes. Shaking his head, a cocky grin and smart-ass laugh Jake hated, he said: "This is your big chance, huh, kid?"

That hurt. *Kid*. What a slap. But Jake had no time to get into this now. Anyway, Mo had his own demons to contend with. He was on his way out. Sure, Mo had carried Jake Cooper up through the force, showing him the ropes. In many ways, Mo rescued Jake from the streets of Southie. But he'd been the subject of rumors the past year. No one seemed to know what was going on. The only thing certain was that Mo was too damn drunk to care or notice.

Standing, getting a good whiff of him, Jake could tell Mo had just hit his flask—and the drinking was, Jake knew, the least of Mo Blackhall's problems. Definitely not the reason why the lieutenant wasn't allowing him out of the office to investigate cases anymore.

"Mo, listen. I don't have time for this!" Jake pushed himself past his former mentor and made a beeline for the elevators.

Mo followed, fidgeting with an unlit cigar stub in his mouth. "We need to talk, Jake. You're part of this." He paused. "Don't forget where you're from. You got debts, too, kiddo."

Those contemptuous threats rustled Jake, making the anxiety flow hot, like nicotine, through his veins. The guy had some nerve.

"Jake, you on your way?" Dickie said over the radio. Jake was in the elevator, pushing the *G* button with the asterisk next to it.

Mo stood in front of the elevator doors as they closed. "You can only break so many times without shattering, Jake." He used his hands to mime an explosion.

"Give me ten minutes," Jake said to his partner, dropping his head as the elevator doors closed, and Mo disappeared from view.

In the lobby downstairs, Jake kicked the door into the parking lot open, those words shaking him up.

… You're part of this. …

There was that damn residue of ancient days, emerging like rust. Jake's legs were heavy as stone. What else could Mo be referring to?

"The past will always be there, Jake." The conversation took place two weeks ago. Jake was walking away from Father John O'Brien, throwing up his hands, saying he was finished with the Church. He had no faith left. He had gone to the priest for guidance. Support. Jake still couldn't reconcile with a God who could allow an innocent little girl to die the way she did? *"We carry all our sins with us,"* Father John continued as Jake stopped before heading out the rectory door. *"You either face them or allow them to destroy you."* Jake hadn't seen Father John since.

Before taking off in his Crown Vic, Jake took a deep breath.

One death at a time.

7

THURSDAY, SEPTEMBER 4 – 3:46 P.M.

Jake sat with Dickie inside his Crown Vic, talking. D-15's lead detective was preoccupied. Mo had got him thinking. Then the anxiety problem he had battled all his life took over from there. They were parked on Crest Hill Road in Somerville, the edge of the Mystic River, a putrid, skunky stank of oil and sewage infiltrating the car. Dickie was on stakeout. Couple of meth heads, a CI reported, lived in a nearby row house and cooked the drug in a mobile home parked in the back. Jake was there because a lead had come in from a couple of kids walking in the Garden the night before Miss Unknown DB had been discovered. The guards claimed to have seen a guy with a bag slung over his shoulder, walking toward the pond. Jake checked with park security who happened to note that one of its officers—he hated when security guards called themselves "officers"— had just been fired. The disgruntled employee warned his boss on the way out that payback was definitely going to be a bitch. "The guy had those serial killer eyes," the guard had told Rookie. "Weird dude. Lives alone. Keeps to himself." Another guard added, "Yeah, and, well, he liked his porn. I caught him checking out those Asian websites. Young girls in blond wigs."

Jake had heard his share of security guard theories throughout his career and knew it was probably nothing, but it needed to be checked out nonetheless.

"I'll take a ride over there this afternoon."

"You know, this case could be as easy as a whacko security guard," Dickie said. "I'll be tied up here"—he checked his watch—"until about three."

Jake made a point to tell Dickie he wanted D-15's top tech on the Garden job, adding, "Make sure Anastasia is ready for me. We need to go through anything she found at the crime scene." Anastasia Rossi was the *Sports Illustrated* swimsuit-hot Italian CSI in Jake's Crimes Against Persons unit. She had swept the Public Garden scene after Miss Unknown DB was taken to the morgue. Snapped photos. Collected trace. Poured molds of footprints.

Jake had not seen her report yet. "I need to get that info into my iPhone as soon as possible."

Dickie closed his eyes, gave a slow head-shake.

They were making some ground. Jake was eager to head out and begin digging into the case himself, hands-on. But then Dawn called. Father John was at the house. *"He said it was important."*

Now Jake was on his way home.

He drove by a woman pushing a stroller, her husband walking by her side. Watching them, it reminded Jake of the life he'd once had with Dawn. No matter how he felt about it, he knew the YMCA coaching gig Dawn had taken on this past spring was good for her. All those clichéd feelings that go along with giving back. It was an all-girls soccer team, composed of kids on welfare, abused, in all sorts of social situations many middle-class Bostonians never had to deal with. Jake had encouraged Dawn to do it. *"Get out, make a difference."*

Jake pulled into the driveway. Father John stood with Dawn on the porch.

Before getting out of the car, Jake hit the app on his iPhone and zeroed in on the location where Rookie had said he interviewed those security guards. He tapped out a brief note—*check Rookie's log*—and hit save.

The chime rang. He looked up. Sighed.

Father.

Jake walked up the path toward the house, noticing the spider-web cracks in the cement. Father John and Dawn sat on the porch swing. Brendan came around from the backyard after hearing his father's car, jumped into Jake's arms.

"Hey, how you doing, buddy?"

"Can we go to Buster's for ice cream tonight, Daddy?"

"We'll see, Bren. Let me talk to Father and Mommy first."

Jake made the stairs and leaned against the porch railing, folding his arms in front of himself. He looked above the bench seat at the tin star he had put on the house when they moved in. It was as big as one of those along the Hollywood Walk Of Fame. Jake wondered why he bought it. He had picked the thing up one day while trolling the aisles of the Christmas Tree Shops with Dawn.

"Always good to see you, Jake."

"You, too, Father. What's up? I have something going on right now." The tension of their last conversation buzzed between them like a family secret.

Dawn smiled, got up, and patted Father on the knee. "I'll leave you two be. Brendan, Daddy needs to talk to Father. Go play in the back, okay, honey?"

Brendan took off without argument.

"What can I do for you?" Jake asked.

Dawn walked into the house. "Stop by anytime, Father," she said through the screen door.

"Thanks." To Jake: "I'm having some trouble at the parish again. I need you to stop by when you can." He was referring to St. Paul's in Southie, a church Jake had attended since his baptism, walked away from after confirmation, went back to in adulthood, but had totally given up on since the little-girl case. Then there was that last conversation he and Father John had, Jake's faith once again in question, and he was sure he wasn't going back.

"Threats?"

"Yeah, but maybe it's more than that this time."

"What do you mean? I kinda got my hands full right now."

"That's your case," Father John commented, "the one in the papers?"

"It is."

"Well, I don't want to bother you, then." Father John stood, took a good look at Jake, slapped him gingerly on the right shoulder. "I have a couple to meet in fifteen minutes, anyway." The priest looked toward his car. "Young and eager to get married. You know the type. They live in the next neighborhood over. I'll let you be."

"Father, you okay? You come all the way over here to just leave?" Jake sensed something. He noticed how the priest had looked away when he mentioned meeting the young couple. Jake was no kinesics expert, but had been to several conferences on the interpretation of body language and facial expressions. The priest was anxious. Jake had known Father John all his life—and he had never mentioned reading about one of Jake's cases in the newspaper. Did he have information?

"Fine, Jake. Fine. Just stop by the parish when you get a minute, promise me." Father reached into his pocket, pulled out a pack of Marlboros. He offered one to Jake (who refused), took it for himself, struck a match, and then took a long, powerful pull, exhaling slowly away from Jake.

"Of course. But I'm here now. What's going on?"

The case of the Unknown DB was about to take its first major turn, as Jake Cooper knew it would.

Father John said, "It's Deacon Patrick O'Keefe, Jake. He's—"

"Hold on a minute, Father." Jake's attention was diverted by Dickie racing up in front of the house, chirping to stop. "What was that about the deacon, Father?"

"Nothing, Jake. It can wait. Come by and see me when you have time." Father took another drag, watched Dickie get out of his car, stubbed the cigarette out on the bottom of his shoe, put the unfinished butt back into the pack for later.

Dickie must have something good. Jake had made it clear earlier not to call him unless it was important. Plus, that stakeout. Why was Dickie here?

"I need to speak with my partner, Padre, sorry." Jake stepped off the porch. He and Dickie shared eye contact.

"I understand," Father said.

"What is it, Dick?"

Dickie waited until the priest was out of earshot.

"Well, Mr. Cooper, we were right."

Jake was impatient. Dickie liked to have fun when he had information. Jake hated it. "Let's have it, Dickie? Spit it out. I'm busy here."

"Jake, our DB wasn't the Northwestern girl, Alyssa ..."

"What?" Jake said as Dickie flipped through pages in his notebook.

"Alyssa … ah, here it is. Alyssa Bettencourt."

"That's what you get when you use a damn missing-persons flyer to identify a corpse." Jake waved to Father John as the priest got into his car and backed out of the driveway. Father made a gesture with his hand—thumb and pinky out, other fingers folded to make a pretend phone, and put it to his ear—to call him.

Jake and Dickie had somewhat expected this development.

"Tell me something I don't know here, Dick? What's the punch line?"

"That corpse was frozen. And you were right. She was thawed and then her face beaten post-mortem."

Jake found himself staring at the weeds overtaking the cement walkway leading up to his porch, thinking, hands in his pockets.

"The body is that of a young female," Dickie continued. "She's eighteen. She *was*, rather. Blond. Blue eyes. And get this, there was DNA—blood—found on her face that does *not* belong to her."

Silence from Jake. Then: "Male or female?"

"Female."

"So we now have a positive ID on our Unknown, then? That what you're telling me?"

Dickie shuffled about. "Yes, yes. Hold it. … Her name is … Lisa Marie Taylor. Graduated from North Cambridge Catholic High in June. Spent part of the summer with relatives in Dover, New Hampshire. We're on it, but that's all we got right now, Kid."

"How'd you ID her?"

"She was reported missing five days ago."

"The doc say anything else?" Jake keyed a note to himself on his iPhone—*Dover? A link?* "Any connection yet, Dickie, between Bettencourt and Lisa Marie?"

There *was* something else. Possibly the first major lead. But Dickie wasn't giving it up. Not yet. He was still waiting to hear from the lab. Nothing worse than getting Jake's hopes up only to let him down.

"Doc Kelsey wants us there first thing in the morning, Jake. She's still working things out."

"Alyssa's body is nearby. We need to find her."

"I put Rookie and a blue on it."

"Find out where Rookie grew up—isn't he from New Hampshire?"

"Not sure."

"You know what this means, Dick," Jake said. He looked to the left of Dickie. Stared off into the empty space between his house and the nearby woods. "Means we got ourselves a serial who favors young blondes."

8

FRIDAY, SEPTEMBER 5 - 8:02 A.M.

Mo Blackhall was in the squad room early, waiting for Jake to show up.

At one time Mo was a church-going family man who treated his wife, Colleen, as if no other woman existed. They took cruises every year to Alaska or the Caribbean. Mo bought her expensive jewelry for birthdays, Christmas, and anniversaries. He never missed a day of work. Out on the brick, there was not a smoother cop than Mo Blackhall. The guy knew Southie as well as the Irish ganstas running it. But his attitude had changed at some point. Mo got quiet. Then Colleen drifted as he started coming home late, disappearing on weekends. Three years ago, Colleen got fed up. Met an FBI agent. Took off. Thing about it was, Mo didn't give a shit.

Jake stopped before opening his office door. Tore off the note Mo had left. Crumpled it.

I need this shit now.

Mo was one of those old-fashioned cops. Bred from the traditional school of ill-tempered Irish law enforcement still hanging on from the sixties. Of Scottish descent, a touch of the accent still there, Mo had heard his share of Austin Powers-Fat Bastard jokes. The truth was, Mo had packed on a few pounds. With his crooked and caved-in nose, he could not escape his youth as a welterweight boxer. Mo became friends with former world champ Marvin Hagler, who grew up and lived in Brockton, after working a death threat case against the former champ. Mo didn't talk about his boxing days and no one ever asked. But Jake knew Mo had thrown a few fights in his day when money was short.

Jake's former rabbi sat behind a mahogany desk. The dust was so thick you could write your name. Papers were scattered all over the place. Mo chewed on an unlit cigar. Stared at Jake as he pushed open the door angrily, and walked in.

It was time, Jake knew, that he and Mo got a few things out in the open. Jake had been stewing over their last conversation. He needed to be certain Mo was not about to destroy what was the last chance Jake had to prove himself.

"What's this?" Jake asked, throwing the note at Mo.

Mo watched the balled-up paper fall to the floor. Righted his six-foot-two, 230-pound frame, hitched up his trousers. Jake's former mentor had developed a beer gut over the years. The flab protruded from his midsection, fell over his belt, tightened his shirt—a pillowcase full of sand.

"Sit down, Jake. Good to see you." Smugness. Jake had a short fuse for it.

"What's up with you, Mo?" A pang of the unknown smacked Jake's comfort zone. He paced in front of Mo's desk, feeling that angst well up. Here was his chance to show brass and all those naysayers he wasn't some burned-out cop, and Mo was messing with it. As a young patrol officer, during the heyday of the Big Dig construction project downtown (a three-and-a-half-mile re-routing of Interstate 93, changing it into a $15 billion tunnel under the city), it wasn't as if Jake knew what he was doing all those times Mo had asked him to deliver a package here, an envelope there. *Favors.* Every cop had debts. Was Jake a bit naïve about it? Sure. But back then he wanted what Mo had. And ignorance was a trait every great cop needed to master. The code of the successful: *Never question.* No one figured the Big Dig would go over budget by tens of millions and be the focus of a media frenzy and an internal investigation.

"Close the damn door before you speak, Jake, okay." Mo turned serious. "Have I not taught you *anything*."

Jake slammed it shut with his foot. "Hot case here, Mo. I don't need you fucking with it. Keep your damn nose out of this. Do your time. Leave with your pension. Be grateful for that, man. Whatever's up between you and brass and Matikas, it's not my thing. You and I, we're even."

"That Public Garden vic was mine, Jake. I'm the senior in this unit! Don't *ever* forget that." Mo had thought Matikas was going to use him. At the last minute, Matikas decided on Jake, telling Mo he was done for good out in the field. He would never investigate a case again.

"Come on. Give me a break. Ray was never going to allow you back out, Mo. You blew it. Accept that and be happy you still have a chance to get out of the department without being indicted."

Mo's computer stared at both of them, the screen saver set on 3D Pipes. As he sat down on the couch in Mo's office, Jake focused on the Etch-A-Sketch-like image of the pipes crawling around the screen.

Mo took a breath, sat. "How ya been, Jake? How's Dawn and Bren?"

"Don't go there. You lost the right to ask about them." Jake noticed Mo's hands shaking. "Haven't hit it yet today, I see."

"I can help you with this case, Jake—"

"No fucking way." Jake stood. Stabbed a forefinger into the top of Mo's desk, accenting each word. "No, Mo. Not in a million years. Don't *do* this to me. Shit, man. Come on."

"That's all I want. This one last dance. Forget all that bullshit about you showing brass you still got what it takes. You won't be able to do this without me, Jake. I taught you what you know."

"Even if I wanted you in, Ray would never allow it."

"Well, my former student, I'm confident you'll find a way to get around that little problem, won't you?" Mo sat back in his chair. Smirked. Twirled his cigar. Squinted.

Jake felt the juxtaposition of the past and present converging in front of him as if two blurry images had become one and the same. *What am I doing? I'm in over my head.* How long had it been? What, twelve years? No, fifteen, actually. He remembered meeting Mo that first time on Dorchester Street in Southie. Mo was working the Caddy's Liquor Store beat. He was like a fun uncle. The one you waited all year to see at Thanksgiving. He took Jake under his wing. Jake was just a punk kid then. Running "errands" for Bulger soldiers as part of his initiation, trying to find his place in Southie. Almost ten years later, Jake stood at roll call next to Mo, who viewed him then as the kid who'd made it out of Southie and fought like hell to make something of his life. It was a time when Mo respected the good in people. Throughout the years, as Jake grew into his role as a cop and stirred up the waters, Mo kept brass off his back. Jake looked up to Mo then. Mo taught him that solving cases was about how those on the street viewed you. No one, including the crooks who paid them, gave a shit about dirty cops. *"You don't mess with things, most of all,"* Mo once explained to Jake, *"that are none of your business. Keep your nose out of where it doesn't belong, no matter what you think."*

"I'm in deep here, Jake," Mo said. There was a beggar's distress to his gravelly voice. His demeanor had changed. "You're going to either make me part of this case, or I need a favor from you. Your choice." He paused. Then: "But you're doing one or the other."

Jake wanted to walk away. Slam the door in Mo's face. But something kept him there, listening, thinking. He walked closer to Mo. Those 3D pipes. How they kept going and going. Some things were forever.

You got debts.

"Mo, don't take me down with you. Please."

"Sit, Jake. Let me explain."

"I'll stand, Mo. Thanks. I really need to get going. One body's turned into two."

A sparkle came into Mo's eyes. He beamed. "Serial killer. Ah. You see, *that's* what I'm talking about. You were born for this shit. I saw it in you back in the day. That fire is still there. After all these years. Listen to you." Getting up, Mo walked over and grabbed his ex-apprentice by the back of the neck. They were almost nose to nose. Jake wasn't moving for some reason. He stared at the floor. "You need to solve this case or you won't sleep. Am I right?" Mo picked Jake's head up. Looked him in the eyes. Slapped him gently on his right cheek. Grabbed his chin as if he were a boy. "It's not about catching a killer. It's about reinventing Jake Cooper. Showing them who you are. Proving you're not like me."

Jake didn't respond. The exchange reminded him of the last time he had spoken to his father—that tension between them, an uncomfortable uncertainty. Like Jake was talking to someone he didn't know.

"You need them to like you," Mo said quietly. "You always needed people to like you, Jake."

Jake broke away. "I'm leaving, Mo. You're not part of this case. Forget it."

Mo walked back behind his desk. Jake could hear him laughing under his breath.

The idea that Mo needed his help made Jake's insides burn. His temples throb. The teacher had become the student. How could a guy change so much? Fall so far from grace. What happened to Mo must have been the part of the movie Jake had slept through. Why was the guy drinking like this? Talking crazy? What had Jake missed?

"I need to catch this sick bastard who cut the legs off this girl. And get him off the street, Mo. Don't come in between that. This is about nailing a killer, not me owing you anything. Think of these girls."

Jake walked into the hallway.

Mo relit his cigar, took a puff, then blew on the head to get it red hot. Ashes fluttered in the air around him like dust particles floating in a beam of sunshine. He looked at Jake. "You just keep an eye on that partner of yours, Detective Shaughnessy." Mo was as serious as Jake had ever heard him. Dickie and Mo had a history, Jake understood. Neither would say much about it. They were partners once. Had a falling-out. That was the public side of it. Jake knew there was more—much more. "Make sure he keeps his Irish nose out of what's none of his damn business," Mo said. "You tell him that. He'll know what I'm talking about. Don't give me that bullshit you don't know either, Jake."

Jake turned. It was too much. Mo's life was in stage-four turmoil.

"And that favor, Detective Cooper," Mo yelled from behind his desk, getting up. "I need you to do that for me and we'll consider ourselves even."

Jake looked in both directions, and walked inside Mo's doorway. "What favor, Mo? Make it quick."

"Take a peek for me in a file downtown. Mancini Construction. See if I'm tied to that investigation."

Jake rubbed his temples, paused. "Are you *kidding* me?"

"Come on, Jake. It's not so bad."

"Not doing it, Mo. Forget it."

"Okay." Mo took a breath, walked toward the door. "But hey, you might want to check if *your* name is part of it, too, son."

Mo slammed the door in Jake's face.

9

FRIDAY, SEPTEMBER 5 - 9:11 A.M.

As it normally did in Massachusetts during early September, the weather turned. This morning the sun was brutal, bright, and glaring. Fry-an-egg-on-the-sidewalk hot. The humidity was no help, heading off the charts at an unbreathable intensity. The kids near the Mission Hill Playground skipping school danced around an open fire hydrant.

Taking a right on Albany Street in Roxbury, Jake tried clearing his mind of Mo.

… that partner of yours, Detective Shaughnessy. ….

The stressed cop wore a pair of *Fear and Loathing* mirror sunglasses. Jake drove the candy apple red Chevelle he and Casey had restored together as kids. The car still had an 8-track deck, Fleetwood Mac's *Rumours* sticking out of it like a pop tart. The Crown Vic was in the garage getting tuned-up. It hurt to drive the old car. Jake could see Casey sitting next to him, smiling, laughing at some stupid joke of his. Always the big brother.

Jake pulled into the entrance, stopping at the guard shack. The wooden parking garage gate lever was down, a director's clapboard, prohibiting Jake from passing. To his left stood the towering Office of the Chief Medical Examiner Building. Not Jake's favorite place.

Howard Tiegs was one of those routine professionals Jake Cooper crossed paths with throughout his workday. Like many of the others, Tiegs saw Jake as a liability to himself. His own worst enemy. "You're one of those 'half-empty' guys, Cooper, huh?" Tiegs had said the last time Jake came to the CME building.

Jake wondered what cop wasn't.

"How are you, Howard?" Jake flashed his ID toward the kiosk. Sweat fell from his brow behind his sunglasses. "How's Tyler? Still hitting those boards like Reggie Lewis, I bet."

Tiegs laughed. Looked up from his clipboard. Shook his head. Signed Jake in. "Ain't no matter how long I seen you, Coop, you always remember my boy. Ty is great." A smile. "Thanks for asking."

Jake chirped the tires around the corner. A rumbling of the Chevelle's throaty four-barrel carburetor echoed throughout the two–tiered cement parking garage. He popped the door, walked a few steps, then hit the elevator arrow button DOWN.

There was, after all, no other place for the dead to go.

The sudden drop turned Jake's stomach to mud. He likened it to that feeling of ingesting too much cake frosting at once. Queasy, they called it. After his insides settled, Jake powered up his iPhone. Typed out a new file name: MANCINI. He'd heard of the company, a major contractor for the Big Dig who had hired on- and off-duty BPD cops as part of a deal with the local Teamsters. Jake needed to find out where Mo fit into that mix. Mo was up to something, or he would have never mentioned it.

The doors *ding*-ed open and made a Star Trek-like *swoosh* sliding apart. Jake stepped from the elevator onto the white-tiled floor. As he did, that smell wafted up and hit him square in the sinuses. The awful, unmistakable aroma of decomposing flesh. Heavy and thick, like a landfill.

"Wow," Jake said, choking, cupping both hands over his nose and mouth. The air conditioning made it worse. Fresher. More pungent.

"Hey, Cooper. How are you?" Dr. Leona Kelsey said. The pathologist had one of those proper, NPR, academic voices. Kelsey was often thrashed on the witness stand by defense attorneys, who chastised her for speaking to juries as if they were children.

Indeed, that was Kelsey. Miss Finger-Wagger.

Kelsey waited by the elevator door to greet Jake. Tiegs had called her to say Jake was on the way down. Kelsey had held off with her autopsy report on Jane Doe, now Lisa Marie Taylor. She wanted to get Jake down into her death suite first to explain a few things in person. From shoes to hairclip, Kelsey looked every bit of her fifty-six years. She was trained as a pathologist in New Hampshire at Green Mountain Institute. Her forensic training was in Albany. The BPD used Kelsey on just about every major homicide it put in front of a jury. She qualified in the state of Massachusetts as an expert by conducting thousands of autopsies.

Kelsey'd had a long day, Jake Cooper could tell, and it was only a little after nine in the morning. "This smell, it doesn't bother you?" It was worse than Jake could recall.

"We got an accident in yesterday afternoon. A real tar-burner. Some sweet little college intern forgot to put her in the cooler until this morning. Sorry, Cooper. About your gal, Jane Doe …" The doctor pulled a chart out and, having trouble flipping the top page because she was wearing yellow rubber gloves, asked Jake for help. "Lisa Marie Taylor."

"Right. Missing five days. We think dead for probably four."

They walked toward the autopsy suite. Orderlies in hospital greens passed. An African-American coroner Jake knew stopped. "Yo, been a while, Coop. What's up, son?" They bumped fists. "I'm feelin' the whole Russell Crowe thing you're rockin' these days. Suits you, man. Lookin' good."

"Not now, Nelsen. Call me, okay." Jake looked at Kelsey, continued walking. "You find out anything? Something I can use? This is no routine rape-murder here, Kelsey. Am I right?"

"No, definitely not routine. I can establish with ninety-nine percent certitude, however, that there was no rape, or sexual assault."

This surprised Jake. His man was strictly a killer, which meant the motive was buried deep inside him. Murder meant something to him personally. There was an emotional connection to killing. He wasn't murdering to cover up other crimes or part of a series of crimes.

"I've seen no other killer who cuts with such precision," Kelsey said, almost as if she envied his knife skills.

"What are we thinking, then? A doctor? Veterinarian? Some sort of medical professional? How 'bout military? Any of those ring a bell here?" The smell still affected Jake. He couldn't believe it didn't bother Kelsey. He pictured her apartment having the same odor, only mellower, like a convalescent home.

Pre-death.

"I won't take that leap just yet."

"Where's Dickie?"

"I'm told he's on his way. Have a look at the incision here," Kelsey explained as they approached Lisa Marie's body. The vic had been scrubbed and washed. Placed under the lights on a stainless-steel gurney with large-spoked wheels. There was a sink drain for fluids at one end. "It's important for me to tell you, Cooper, that Lisa Marie here, she was unquestionably dead when her chest was opened."

They both sighed. Some consolation that was.

"Tell me again how you ascertain these things?"

"Well," Kelsey pointed to where the incision in Lisa's chest started, "there's something very interesting here that I found." Kelsey circled an area of Lisa's stomach with her gloved finger.

"What's that?"

"My prelims tell me there were no poisons, toxins, et cetera, in her system. We found a minor trace of chloroform on her lips and in one lung."

"Knocked her out."

"Yep."

"Likewise for the legs?" Jake knew better but wanted to be sure. "I mean, she was dead when those legs were amputated, right?"

Kelsey closed her eyes. Turned slowly to Jake. "No."

"What?"

Kelsey took off her safety glasses and bit on the end of one of the earpieces. The doctor had been involved with the dead for thirty years. She liked to tell reporters she could separate her job from her emotions. But that was the public side of being in this game, Jake knew. Dr. Kelsey was beaten down by the disfigured bodies of children and countless other senseless means of death she saw every day. Kelsey's daughter was a few years older than Lisa Marie. How could she look into Lisa's listless eyes, photograph and study those stubs, and not see Christine?

"Any mysterious marks on her back?" Jake tried his best to keep the doc focused. Lisa was found face-up. If her body was frozen and then brought to the scene to thaw, Jake figured her killer might have preserved a piece of evidence without realizing it—her back was the largest section of her body left untouched.

The elevator sounded. *Dickie*. Jake wondered how in the hell the guy had ever made it through school or kept a job. He was late for everything.

Jake watched Dickie walk into the lobby, stopping first to pull up his trousers. Front first, then back. After that, both sides together before he tucked in the stray tongue of his dress shirt. Eying his partner all the way, Jake said to Kelsey, "I'm interested in one of the photos I saw this morning, taken at the crime scene. I thought I noticed an imprint of something on Lisa's back."

"Funny you should ask. Come over here and look at this." They stood over Lisa Marie. Stared down at her torso. Fluorescent lights shone on Lisa's teenage body. Poor thing. So young and delicate. Kelsey flipped Lisa's body on its side. She was stiff as a mannequin. Then pointed to a small indentation on the right portion of her back, down in the bottom corner, where the curve of her hip held that boomerang shape. It was postmortem, for sure. The indent would have been made after death. "It didn't bounce back into shape," Jake observed.

"Exactly. Rigor. Blood sinks. Pools. Coagulates into the lowest part of the body."

"Tissue hardens like mud in the sun."

"Right! Before it reverses the process, heats up like compost, and begins to decay. Whatever made the mark on Lisa's back was pushed into her skin and kept its shape."

Jake was interested. "Means she was placed on top of an object *after* death. Looks like some sort of light bulb, you think?"

"Not sure. That's not my thing. But I'd guess no. Just me. But it looks like, oh, this is just an educated assumption now, but it looks like some sort of handle."

"Get me several angles of that on film. I'll have someone run it down. Can you make an impression of it, too, with silicone?"

"Alexander?" the doctor yelled. A young Asian man stepped into the room. He carried a yellow legal pad and looked busy. "Do me a midsection tri-quarter-angle on this mark here. Get it done ASAP. Then have it sent over to Cooper this afternoon."

Jake was impressed by Kelsey's command. He took out his iPhone and scanned the image himself. Wouldn't hurt to get it into the database, see if he could come up with a hit. As he waited for the scan to finish, "You made it, I see."

Dickie had a funnel paper cup of water in his hand. "Bottoms up, Kid."

"Look at this," Kelsey said, reaching into Lisa's mouth, pulling her cheeks out as though she were a dentist, exposing Lisa's mouth. This took some effort, seeing how tight her muscles were from post. "Morning, Detective Shaughnessy."

Dickie winked. Jake bent down and turned his head to get a better view. Using a magnifying glass Kelsey gave him, he stared at the crude mark.

"We cannot figure it out." Kelsey held Lisa's mouth open with a pair of c-clamps and two hands as Jake studied what looked to be a scratch. "It's not a bite mark, like when you miss a chomp at a piece of food or gum and clip the side of your cheek. It's not a burn or a defect from birth."

"You mind?" Dickie asked.

"Go for it," Jake said, stepping back.

Dickie took a look. Then reached into his pocket, scribbled something in his notebook.

Kelsey reached above the gurney table and pulled down a square light. It was connected to the end of a metal arm she could maneuver around in an accordionlike fashion. The heat from the bulb as Kelsey pulled the light over his arms reminded Jake of reaching into a hot buffet. Kelsey exposed various areas of Lisa's torso as she explained things to Jake and Dickie they knew already—technical terms and medical explanations of no interest to the Dynamic Duo. Lisa's torso was wide open in front of them. Kelsey had used the same incision the killer originally made, but added two additional upward strokes, in a Y-pattern, toward Lisa's bony, pointed, supermodel shoulders. Then she peeled the two chest flaps back and clamped them down to the sides of the gurney. Lisa Marie had been filleted open.

Jake watched this with a jaded sense of envy, not paying much attention. He thought of the type of person who could do such a thing to another human being. It was not going to be easy to catch this psycho. Nonetheless, there was a clue here somewhere. A hair. Fiber. An imperative piece of the puzzle. All killers slipped up. Some left evidence on purpose.

The signature.

"Her face is in rather good shape, all considering," Dickie said.

"The inside of the mouth was purple yesterday," Jake observed.

"That color washed off. She was definitely beaten postmortem. Those bruises along her right cheek"—Kelsey pointed—"are superficial, they do not affect the muscle tissue. I cut a sample off her face so we could run a few additional tests."

"Where is it?" Jake asked.

"In the freezer. I placed it on a hockey goalie mask and froze it in the contour of her face to keep the texture and surface as natural as possible."

"Ah … *yeah* …" Jake said. He and Dickie looked at each other.

Yikes. What an image.

"Boston Bruin fan, I see?" Dickie said to the doctor.

She gave him a cold stare over the top of her glasses.

"We can check it out later." Jake put his hands in his pockets. "Please continue."

"We're ninety-nine percent alike," Kelsey explained, glancing down at the chart in front of her, then looking back up at them. "All of us. Our DNA is just about all the same. It's that one percent that makes each of us different. Just *one* percent. Two thousand proteins are created every second in our bodies. That adds to our make-up. But one percent separates us."

"Interesting lesson. Mr. Discovery Channel here," Jake looked over at Dickie, "loves this shit. But how's that got *anything* to do with my case?"

The doctor pointed with a pen to Lisa's chest cavity. "I'm getting to that."

Jake noticed that Lisa's rib cage on the right side was gone.

"What's that?" he asked, puzzled. "You take it out?"

"You don't know?" Kelsey said. "No one told you?" She looked at Dickie, who held up his hands as if someone held a gun to his back.

There was an empty space in Lisa's chest about the size of a man's fist. Her ribs were cut precisely with some sort of electric tool, exposing the tar-colored bone marrow inside like a dog bone.

"It's gone," Kelsey said.

"What's 'gone'?" Jake was missing something.

"Her heart."

Jake looked at Dickie.

"I'm no profiler," Kelsey said, "but someone who takes out the heart of his victim has sexual issues to compensate for. Impotence, maybe? Viagra complex. Loss of love."

"The father?" Dickie tossed out.

Jake walked over to the sink and turned on the water to wash his hands. "Wait a minute here. No. No. No. The heart has been extracted because he is telling us something. But the anomaly is somewhere else. Dickie, a father would never do that. Take out his daughter's heart to cover up a sex crime." Dickie had been hot on the father ever since they identified Lisa Marie.

"Never overlook the obvious, Jake. Who taught us that? Anyway, we can put," Dickie explained, scrolling through pages of notes, "Alyssa and Lisa Marie in the same library, same college café downtown, and *same* bar within the past few weeks." He tossed the little notebook on the table next to where Jake stood scrubbing his hands.

"Together?"

Kelsey walked over. "Um, we use that sink to wash organs, Detective Cooper. The hand-washing station is over there." She pointed to Jake's left.

"What? Damn it."

"We're working on that connection," Dickie said.

"Doesn't mean squat, Dickie. Or that they even knew each other." Jake dried his hands with a brown piece of paper towel.

"If they knew each other, boss, that certainly changes things."

10

FRIDAY, SEPTEMBER 5 - 1:33 P.M.

Dickie and Caroline Shaughnessy had lived on Plymouth Avenue in East Milton near Cunningham Park for the past twenty years. The neighborhood, dotted with three-deckers lined up so close to one another you could see what your neighbor was having for dinner, was an easy on-off jaunt from I-93, which made the trip downtown quick for Dickie.

Dickie stopped at home to grab lunch after leaving the morgue. Jake had radioed to say he'd be by to pick him up. Something about a tip Jake had gotten from a sheriff up north. The sun beat down on Jake as he walked up the short stone pathway, the flower beds edged in perfect lines of cut earth. Caroline was standing, drilling holes in the mulch with a strange tool she had impulsively purchased from an infomercial—this, so she could plant her tulip bulbs for next year. Dickie's wife had her bleached-blonde, shoulder-length hair tied back in a ponytail; her cell phone clipped to the side of her waist. She wore wool gloves so as not to damage a fresh manicure—purple polish with little white hearts and silver glitter at the tips—she had just gotten at the Somers Day Spa in Quincy, her weekly Friday afternoon treat. There was the perfect smear of dirt on Caroline's right cheek. All her adult life she had worked as an insurance consultant for Met-Life, just recently from home. She had dinner on the table at five every night. If Dickie wasn't there, Caroline ate in front of *Golden Girls* reruns on a TV tray by herself and told her man to fix his own damn plate when he came home.

"Does it really take 'the hard work out of yard work,' Caroline?" Jake asked about the gardening tool, referring to the pitch line in the commercial.

"You startled me." Caroline stopped working.

Jake kissed her on the cheek. Grabbed Caroline by the shoulders. Took a look at her. "You're a sucker for those TV gadgets, Caroline."

"How are Dawn and Brendan?"

Jake considered how independent today's woman was. He adored that about Dickie's wife. He wished Dawn was more like her. Free-spirited and tough. Caroline was one of those women who insisted on separate checkbooks and bank accounts from her husband.

"They're wonderful, Caroline."

"Right, Jake. Everything's just hunky-dory at home, uh-huh," she said, wiping a bead of sweat with the back of her wrist from her crinkled brow.

Jake walked away. Stepped up onto the wrap-around porch connected to the three-decker the Shaughnessys owned. "No one uses 'hunky-dory' anymore, Caroline. Let's you and I bring that one back, huh. Along with maybe 'a million miles an hour,' and 'highway robbery.' Now where is that husband of yours?"

"Downstairs in 'The Zone.'" Caroline looked up to the sky and shook her head. "Like a little kid sometimes—he is."

With his towering frame, Jake was forced to duck at the bottom of the stairs leading into Dickie's finished basement. He didn't want to hit his head on the ceiling above the final stair. Dickie had made some changes to the house since Jake's last visit. The basement was now decked out in Red Sox memorabilia.

"That thing tell you who our killer is yet?" Dickie asked as Jake came off the bottom stair keying something into his iPhone.

"Close, but not yet. Don't be such an obvious Luddite, Dick. Technology's our friend." Saying this, Jake realized he was speaking to a man who had a name for his basement. "You actually call this room in your house 'The Zone,' and you're making fun of my phone."

Dickie laughed. He gave Jake a quick tour, pointing out the new additions. "Got this from Yaz at a card show last year." He held up a baseball with the slugger's signature at twelve o'clock.

Jake shrugged off the memorabilia. "Come on, you know I could care less about this shit."

"You see, Jake, this is what makes us so different." Dickie threw the ball up in the air and caught it a few times. "I come down here to get away. Escape."

Jake thought of the drives he liked to take alone along Cape Cod Bay in his Chevelle. His muscle car was his Zone. But how rare were those trips? Dickie was right. The guy couldn't get away from the job. It consumed him.

"Any luck with that security guard lead?" Dickie asked. He shut off the lights.

"Naw. Nothing there." They both knew it was going to be a dead end. "Something's come up, though. That's why I'm here. Let's go. I'll explain on the way."

Outside on the front lawn, Dickie told Caroline he'd be back—"with any luck"— around six. She waved to Jake. "Give Dawn a kiss for me. If she ever wants to join me for yoga class, tell her to call."

Jake cranked the ignition. Put the car in reverse, got out onto the open road.

"You want to talk about Mo?" Dickie asked. "I did some checking, heard some 'things.' Word is there is some tension brewing between you two."

Jake gave his partner a look. "I'm dealing with that, Dick. Keep out of it." Then: "How's Maddox?" Maddox Shaughnessy was Dickie and Caroline's twenty-three-year-old boy, stationed in Baghdad, E-Co. 1/329th.The kid had been a Marine for almost five years. He was born, Dickie liked to say, with that camouflage green and black war paint under his eyes.

Rambo Jr.

"He's getting by. Should be home in about four months. But says his new tour starts two months later."

Military, Jake thought. *Huh*. He stared at Dickie. Listening to him talk about his son, Jake could picture some Muslim teenager wearing a backpack full of explosives and nails walking into a café, setting it down, blowing up the place with Dickie's boy inside. He wondered how Dickie lived with that fear day in, day out.

"What'a ya got, man?" Dickie wanted off the subject of the military.

Jake explained a call he had taken from a guy named John Branford. Branford worked out of the Danvers Police Department, an hour north of Boston, a small hamlet close to that fishing village made famous by Sebastian Junger's *Perfect Storm*. The cop claimed to have valid information about what he called "that serial murder case." Jake was skeptical, but knew cases got solved like this sometimes. One cop talking to another, both searching for the same answer. Old-school gumshoe police work.

As Jake explained it to Dickie, Captain Branford said he "saw an article in the *Globe* about the Boston Public Garden DB, and started asking around. Wanted to know if it's true that the Common case was connected to Quincy Market."

"Might be," Jake had told him. He pictured the cop twirling a toothpick in his mouth. Sitting back. Feet up on his desk. Enjoying the moment.

"I need to speak to you," Branford said.

"I'm listening."

"In person."

The guy is willing to travel an hour. Must have something.

Jake drove by the T near Fenway Park. Dickie was scrolling through his voicemail message numbers to see who had called.

"So we're heading over to meet him," Jake said, parking near a meter on Boylston Street in Kenmore Square.

They walked into the Back Bay Pub, a little dive tucked in between a Star Market and Riley's Laundromat. Branford was not what Jake had expected. A small man, five-foot-six, 120 pounds, skinny as a jockey. He wore a black blazer. Brown bolo tie. White dress shirt. Blue jeans. Cowboy boots. A ball cap with a large gold star on the front. He had a lazy eye that would not stop twitching.

Jake walked over and stuck out his hand. "This is my partner, Detective Shaughnessy."

Dickie waved.

"I recognize you both from the *Globe,*" the captain said as if he wanted Jake's job or an autograph.

Jake forced a smile. Dickie leaned against a wooden beam with names and obscenities carved into it. There were black cigarette burns in the red carpet below his feet.

"I think I have an idea of maybe someone you need to take a serious look at. It all made sense to me when I found out why he requested a transfer."

"So far you're speaking a foreign language, Captain. Sorry." Jake raised his eyebrows. "What do you have here?"

"He worked for me. Not a bad cop. Just wasn't any good." He laughed at his own turn of a phrase. "I did some checking. Found out he had a certain problem with young blondes. Also found out he got his self kicked off the Bangor force in Maine before coming to me, beggin' for a job. Apparently, he waited outside the local high school up there and drove some of the girls home in his squad car. Said some creepy things."

Jake wondered where this was going. A cop. Problem with blondes. It could fit. Then again, the guy sounded more like a loser rather than a killer.

Dickie watched a guy at the bar stirring his drink with a red plastic sizzle stick.

"We transferred him to your unit last May, a week or so before that Bettencourt kid went missing. Your lieutenant approved the transfer. Guess he knew the kid's uncle or something."

"Name?"

"He walks with a bum knee, kinda sliding it along. Name's Mark Stanhope."

Jake and Dickie looked at each other.

"Why did he 'request' a transfer?"

"He wanted to be," Branford said, "closer to the action downtown. Truth is, though, he knew we were about to find out he was peeping on some young chick—a blonde, of course—every morning where he stopped for coffee at this diner. He'd follow her into the bathroom. She never knew until one day she happened to look up and caught him peering over the wall, underneath the ceiling tile."

"Never liked Officer Stanhope," Jake said.

"I heard you guys got a nickname for him?" Branford said.

"B-B-B-Benny," Dickie said, laughing.

"We call him Rookie," Jake said. "Appreciate this info."

11

FRIDAY, SEPTEMBER 5 – 2:00 P.M.

Traffic was light for an early Friday afternoon downtown. Most everyone had their windows up, AC on. The digital temperature reading on the LCD clock over Copley Square read a balmy 97 degrees.

Driving into the city on the Mass Pike, eastbound, the Carmichaels were headed to Maine to spend the weekend with relatives. Jason Carmichael drove the family maroon Suburban. His wife sat shotgun. Their ten-year-old, Jeffrey, sat in back behind Dad. It was little Jeffrey's job to keep Sergeant Bilko, their four-year-old Lab, occupied. Jason listened to talk radio, WRKO, disagreeing with just about everything.

"See that, Jeffrey?" Jason leaned down, pointed to his right, looked out the passenger-side window. "That's the backside of the Green Monster, Fenway Park."

"Cool!" Jeffrey said. He moved over to get a better look. Stared out the window. Buckled himself into the backseat on his mom's side.

They drove under the Prudential Center and, as it got dark, the roar of a Harley echoed up along the left side, and the motorcyclist pulled in front of Jason.

"In about a half-mile," Jason announced, "we'll be coming up to the new Ted Williams Tunnel, part of the Big Dig project that cost the city billions. We'll actually be driving *under* Boston Harbor, Jeffrey."

Marjorie Carmichael said, "Billion, Jay. Not *billions*."

"Awesome," said Jeffrey.

It got a bit dark as they entered the tunnel. The fluorescent lights along the corner of the roof were bright, but only if you were stopped.

Jason noticed the Harley dude had one of those barbed-wire tattoos around his bicep. *How damn passé are those tats nowadays?* The woman on the back of the bike had an average ass, Jason considered. There was an angel tattoo above her plumber's crack. Jason checked her out. She was hot, he thought, in a skanky, Lucinda Williams sort of way.

Do-able, he'd tell the boys at work Monday morning.

The biker hit his brakes, illuminating the inside of the Carmichaels' Suburban.

Jason slowed down, a squeal from the vehicle's front rotors. "Traffic … damn-it."

"Relax now, honey. We're on vacation."

"Yeah, yeah, yeah."

"This is something, Dad," Jeffrey said from the backseat. "I can see my PSP like it's nighttime." Jeffrey played Super Mario Bros 3.

The line of cars, bikes, SUVs, and taxis inched forward.

Jason was fixated on the little license plate strapped to the back of the Harley in front of him. He killed time memorizing it.

CVD-431. Connecticut. The Constitution State.

Sitting, frustrated by the traffic, Jason was startled by the sound of a pebble hitting the windshield.

Huh? He watched it bounce to the ground just outside his door. It was white, like chalk.

Then another.

Weird?

Traffic moved up about ten feet at a time. Stop and go.

Several more pebbles fell on the windshield and bounced onto the ground.

"What the heck?" Jason said to himself. He looked out the window, up at the ceiling.

Marjorie fiddled with the dial, switching radio stations, trying to find anything other than the static coming in underneath the water.

"Screw it," she said. Then reached above, pulled down the sun visor, and looked through a library of CDs.

Jason zeroed in on a section of the tunnel's ceiling. It was loose and flapping, as if it wasn't attached in one corner. Several pebbles fell on the windshield.

What the hell … It wasn't registering.

A large piece of cement, about the size of a cigarette pack, fell and cracked the Carmichaels' windshield.

"What was that?" Marjorie asked in alarm, jumping back, CDs splaying all over her lap and floorboard.

Jason looked out the window, up at the ceiling again. "Oh my God."

The tunnel erupted with an enormous *boom*.

Dust spread everywhere, causing blind panic. People screamed. Car alarms sounded. Chirps of tires reverberated. It had happened so quickly no one knew what was going on.

The Carmichaels, the Harley dude with his biker babe, not to mention everyone else inside the tunnel, were not going to make it to the other side on this day. A twelve-ton section of the newly opened Ted Williams Tunnel had let go. One of the steel tiebacks holding a forty-foot segment of the ceiling over the eastbound portion of the interstate had caved in onto several cars waiting in traffic.

The fallen debris had just missed flattening the biker and his girlfriend. Unfortunately, as people got out of their vehicles and converged on the maroon Suburban behind the Harley, they were horrified to see that the heaviest section of the concrete had clipped the right-hand side of the SUV and crushed Jeffrey, Marjorie, and Sergeant Bilko.

Jason Carmichael sat inside his vehicle, unable to move, shell-shocked and speechless. To his right, on the now cracked inside wall of the tunnel, was a small sign indicating the company that had worked on this particular section.

Mancini Construction.

12

Jake got word that Dr. Kelsey had signed off on Lisa Marie's body. Two blues were heading out to Cambridge to tell Lisa Marie's parents their baby had been murdered. Jake called them off. He and Dickie were taking it.

Bringing an investigation out into a gated community near Cambridge Square gave Jake pause to despise the ultra-rich. The townhouses they passed on the way were straight out of *Architectural Digest* magazine and the cars in the driveways cost more than what most cops made in a year. A nun from India visiting Father John last year astutely observed, after Jake asked how she liked living in America, "You Americans, you like every-ting *veddy* large. Big home. Big car. Big stomach."

Jake looked over at his partner as they parked at the corner end of the Taylors' horseshoe driveway. Dickie's gut protruded tightly over the seat belt around him.

Who could argue with the woman?

"So how we playin' this?" Dickie wanted to know.

"You take the lead. I'll sit back and watch the old man. At least until we figure them out."

"Spoke to a friend from the FBI last night. Incestual relationships that have gone on for years often involve extremely *rare* and *extremely* violent crimes. 'Member that dude in California a few years back who fathered ten of his children's children, then killed each one of them, one by one, posed their bodies in the house … left them for weeks.

Several of them were dismembered. How 'bout that sicko in Austria? Locked his daughter in the basement for—"

Jake stopped him. "Yeah, okay. I get it, Dickie. We'll see." They walked up the pathway to the house. There was a line of strange-looking flowers planted in beds of mulch so clean and weed-free the landscaping looked fake. "Let's focus on what we need to do here. Nobody expects death to knock at the door." They approached the archway of the front porch. Jake took a glance around the yard. "They expect their lives—because they have money—to be carefree." He paused for a beat as Dickie rolled his eyes.

"Ring the bell, Jake. Your resentment is obvious. Let it go."

"You'd buy incest?" Jake shook his head in disagreement. "You get anyone on that Rookie lead yet?"

"Sure thing, Jake. Ring the damn bell already."

"That's some car, huh." Jake pointed toward the garage with his head.

"Gotta special-order those." Dickie stared at the red Ferrari. It was parked in front of the garage. They admired the car. But wondered why it wasn't *in* the garage. Expensive car like that just sitting out in the elements.

"Get a load of that, Dickie."

"What?"

"You see the way the worker cleans out those gutters?" The guy was about twenty yards away, standing on a ladder, spraying the gutters with a power-washer. He wore dark blue khakis, a white shirt, his name, Manuel, embroidered in cursive on the front pocket. When he noticed Jake staring, he stopped, winked, then went back to work.

Why was Jake so concerned with such trivial matters when they were here to tell Lisa Marie's parents their baby girl was not missing, as the Taylors had been led to believe, but dismembered? The Taylor family was on the opposite side of the door going about a normal day, thinking their daughter had simply run away again. In a few seconds their lives would never be the same.

"Hey, we leave out the details, got it?" Jake said. "A dead child is a dead child. The path to that end is meaningless right now." They were in search of information, Jake implied. The less the Taylors knew at this point, the better.

"And why is it," Dickie asked, "two hotshot detectives such as ourselves are out here telling these good people about their kid? Why not send a few blues last night?"

Telling Lisa Marie's affluent parents their daughter had been murdered was not something Jake had wanted to do himself. But reaction was everything. If the Taylors knew—or had dealings with someone who could have swiped the girl—it would show on their faces. Jake knew people hid things. Sometimes out of guilt. Other times because they didn't know better. Wealthy people had a lot to protect.

"The element of surprise, Dick. Back to basics here for the time being. It's all we have at the moment."

"No, Jake. You're wrong. We got teleforensics!" Dickie laughed, mocking Jake's iPhone crime-solving app.

"Funny. Hey, I mean that about Rookie—I want someone on his ass."

"Maybe tie him to Ray. I get it. Ray brought Rookie into the fold. Bring 'em both down. Ray's after your ass, anyway. Rookie is Ray's eyes."

Jake's mind raced.

Mr. Taylor opened the door. Looked at the two of them. Then noticed the gold badge hanging from around Jake's neck. "What's this?" he asked. "Who are …?"

Jake and Dickie looked down.

The Taylor father dropped his head in his hands, bawling as if he had been waiting for this knock on the door for the past two years. The mother shook her head, one tear falling down her right cheek, a sad frown, her shoulders slumped. "My baby," she said softly. "My baby girl is gone …"

After allowing the Taylors to catch their breath, Dickie asked the standard set of questions. He took notes as Jake wandered around the downstairs, looking at knickknacks, family photographs, admiring some of the window-size paintings in the foyer.

"We're going to need all of her computers, cell phones, friends' names."

"She had all that stuff with her," the mother said. "When we filed a missing persons report days ago, they told us not to worry."

"We're sorry, Mrs. Taylor." Dickie was terrible at delivering bad news.

Mr. Taylor did not speak.

"Can I take a look in Lisa's room, Mrs. Taylor? I hate to ask," Jake said, "but it would be very helpful." He kept his voice streamlined. Professional. Devoid of any emotion.

"No one's been in there, Detective, since she's been gone," the father said, speaking up.

"Even better." Jake headed up the stairs. He noticed a picture of Mr. and Mrs. Taylor, Lisa Marie, and their other two kids, taken at an amusement park. They were wearing western outfits. The photo was in that rustic, yellowish black and white. Every household had one of these. The kids were young. Everyone seemed happy.

"Hon," Mrs. Taylor said to her husband, "go with the detective."

Dickie stayed with the mother downstairs while Jake and Mr. Taylor walked up the long, three-foot-wide, arcing staircase. Lisa Marie Taylor's father was a Harvard professor who taught philosophy. He had been written about in many of the Christian journals because he believed religion needed to play a larger role in grammar through high school classrooms. He'd written books. But it wasn't Harvard money—or his literary endeavors—that had made the Taylor family wealthy. Mrs. Taylor's father, Artimus Raymore Samuels, took over a brewery in Boston opened at the turn of the century and turned it into one of the most successful ale companies in America.

"Those flowers out front, you know what they're called?" Jake asked as he and Mr. Taylor approached the top of the stairs. He had his hands in his pockets.

Mr. Taylor had a balled-up fist to his mouth. "Lisa … she," he had a hell of a time getting the words out, "… she planted them. Called them Night-blooming Cacti, or something like that. They open up at night after the sun goes down."

A faint smell struck Jake as he and Mr. Taylor walked down the hallway toward Lisa's bedroom. If you hadn't been around the dead before you wouldn't notice. It might instead smell like an expired mouse under a bureau. Or a family bathroom after a few days of the stomach flu.

They entered Lisa's room. The odor was far more pronounced inside. Rotten eggs and spoiled meat—that empty Dumpster odor in the summer. Maybe a funeral home.

All of them combined.

"Holy shit," Jake said under his breath, covering his nose and mouth.

Amid posters of Paris and Rome and a *Pulp Fiction* Uma Thurman, the smell made Jake's nose wrinkle. Acclimating himself to it, Jake noticed it was mixed with a fake air freshener perfume. Lavender and evergreen. Since he'd stopped smoking, Jake had his smell back. One of the perks.

"This air freshener, where's it coming from?" Jake asked. He looked up at the ceiling. Around the room.

"We have it pumped in," the father said, "through the air ducts."

Must be nice being *that* rich. *Geesh.* "You have perfumed air pumped in. Oh … K."

"You don't smell that?"

"Our maid is not the most efficient, Detective."

"No, not a laundry basket smell. Rotting flesh. Like meat that's gone bad. How have you and Mrs. Taylor managed to avoid it?"

"Now I do," Taylor tipped his head up in the air like a dog. Took in a few quick whiffs through his nose.

"What the hell? Hasn't anyone said anything about this?"

"We haven't been in here, *Detective*, since that first day Lisa went missing. My wife told you that. Ever since Lisa ran off, there was no need to come in here. The door has been closed. She's run off before. We never look through her things. She always comes back. When the house stinks, we turn the air freshener volume up and scold the maid."

The smell was stronger by the closet. Jake approached the door, but decided against opening it in front of Mr. Taylor.

"Why don't you wait out there?" Jake pointed to the hallway. Whatever was in the closet was something the father didn't need to see.

Once he was alone, Jake opened the door with caution, and walked in. It was a large room, the size of Jake's bedroom back in Southie. Dark, too. He found one of those bulb lights hanging from the ceiling, pulled the chain. Lisa Marie's shoes were on one side, clothes on the other.

Jake walked toward the back of the closet.

What?

The source of the smell came from what hung off two large hooks clipped to the clothes pole.

"Sonofabitch."

Mr. Taylor came up from behind. "What is it, Detective?"

"Get out of here," Jake yelled, pushing him out the door. "Go—"

A pair of legs, lopped off below the knees, hung there, bloated and dripping fluids—a piece of meat in a butcher's freezer. The toe nails were painted Barbie pink, same shade as Lisa's room.

Jake Cooper guessed he was staring at the remains of Lisa Marie Taylor's legs.

Dickie heard the commotion, ran up the stairs and into the room. He stood next to Jake, lost in surrealistic nature of such a horrific sight. After a moment, "Hey, kid," Dickie said, "your phone got an app for that?"

13

FRIDAY, SEPTEMBER 5 - 4:36 P.M.

Gregorian chants reverberated throughout the house. The booming voices of the choir made for an ominous, enchanting late afternoon. He loved the spiritual mood it put him in. Being a Friday, he got off work, then rushed home to see if that Web order from policesupplies.com had arrived. To his delightful surprise, he saw the brown package on the front steps after getting out of his Jeep.

He hummed with the music as he stood in front of a pan of photo developer mixed with 200 Solution. This, too, he had ordered online. The combination gave him the best bang for his Kodak buck. Developing photos at home, watching the images he snapped emerge from a solution that smelled of turpentine and chemistry class, was comforting and nauseating. The pictures in the solution were snapshots of dreams coming into focus. Amazing, he thought. A few simple ingredients—film, paper, and feigned darkness—unleashed a life frozen in time.

Lisa Marie's killer loved this.

He hung the photos from a clothesline in the room. When he finished, he inched his way backward, staring at each one.

I hate you. Leave me alone.

Memories attacked him like angry bees.

The first photo was of Lisa Marie's face, before he thrashed her. Lisa was completely thawed by that point. He tried to make her smile, but rigor had set in, her cheeks hard as a mound of clay left out overnight, not cooperating. Frustrated, he hit her one last time and gave up.

Next to the shot of Lisa's face were photos of pairs upon pairs of legs.

He looked down at his forearms. Those scars, the skinny bead welds. He relished in how good it felt to cut himself with a razor blade. How entirely in control of those moments in the basement he was when he cut his own skin open. The sluggishness of the blood oozing. The sense of power. There was no pain.

I alone adore you.

Out of those childhood memories, he was back focusing on the photographs of the legs—but whose were they?

One was of that young woman he had killed before Lisa. He'd recognize those legs anywhere. He had taken the photo before dismembering Alyssa, keeping her legs and heart, tossing the rest of her body to the sharks, easily fascinated by the swirling commotion of body parts and sea water before him.

An ocean of blood.

Same as he did after cutting himself, he tasted Alyssa's blood before scrubbing the deck of her remains and tossing everything overboard. He thought he'd had the boat entirely cleaned. Then turned, walked to the aft, and almost stepped on the girl's liver. Like a placenta, it slapped back and forth against the sides of the boat.

Alyssa …

She was now a woman, same as Lisa, without a worry in the world. In heaven, for certain. He knew this. The deacon—that bastard who had started this madness—assured him that all murder victims go to heaven.

The keepers of secrets.

He walked into the kitchen. Unfolded the morning's paper to see what they had written about him today. He had one wall in the living room dedicated to and covered with articles about his crimes. How Alyssa, "the college coed," went missing. How Lisa "vanished after leaving the library." How her body was found mutilated and dumped in the Garden. How Lisa's parents were offering some stupid reward in her name.

Pathetic. People with money think they can buy their daughter back.

He had made today's front page:

BODY IN GARDEN THAT OF MALE HEIR AND PROFESSOR'S DAUGHTER

Whistling, he took out the scissors, cut it out. Made sure the cuts were straight, taking his time. There could be no mistakes. He'd have to buy another paper and start all over.

Finished, he held it up.

"Now, look at that." He smiled. "Faking all of you bastards out. None of you can touch me."

He slipped back. Those bees again. He saw the menacing shadow coming at him.

"This is for your own good, Randy."

I don't hear you ...

He turned the page and fastened his attention on another article. The *Globe* had given him a name.

THE OPTIMIST: *Detective Says Killer Running Out of Options*

What did that mean?

Optimist?

Every serial killer needed a name. Was he supposed to be proud? Delighted? Where'd they get that from, anyway?

He taped the articles to the wall next to the others. Then walked back into the dark room. All those legs hanging before him. They were so vital now to his point. He started collecting them out of fascination, hoping to throw off the cops. But now he pictured his next victim begging for mercy on his boat. Struggling, crying, as he told her what he was going to do.

The CD skipped on a particular chant.

"*Fede … fede … fede … fede …*"

He didn't realize a chorus of monks were chanting faith, faith, faith as he walked out of his dark room and packed an overnight bag.

Camera.

Check.

Film, clothes, maps, toothbrush.

Check, check, check. Check.

Rope, flex cuffs, gauze, chloroform.

Check.

The Comfort Inn was just outside South Boston off I-93. "When you coming into town?" the desk clerk asked over the phone.

"Should be there before six, depending on traffic."

"Okay then. We'll see you at six, Mr. … didn't get your full name, sir."

He thought about it. What would it hurt? "Howard. Mr. Charles Nelsen Howard." He added Nelsen for effect.

"Like Charles Nelson Reilly from *Match Game*," the clerk said, brightening up. "Loved the show. Hated Gene Rayburn's corduroy suits and that long microphone."

"Not really. But yes. I believe you have what you need, then?"

He hung up.

The Optimist made sure the back door to his house was locked. He snapped the deadbolt four times, counting each one. Then did the same to the turnstile lock below it, again counting off.

Confident, he walked over and stopped at the mantel above the fireplace. He brushed the closed petals of the Queen of the Night flowers, taking a deep breath in through his nose, letting it out his mouth.

"Won't be here tonight to see you open," he whispered to the flowers, as if talking to a person, "but I will be back soon enough. A little boat ride is in order."

When he got to his jeep, he felt he should go back and check the locked doors once more. Just to be certain.

14

FRIDAY, SEPTEMBER 5 - 6:11 P.M.

Ever since discovering the legs in the Taylor kid's closet, a question nagged at Jake. How had this serial managed to transport Lisa's body down into the park, either the night before or that day, without being seen? Getting into the Taylor house to leave those legs made the guy a pro, for sure. But how had he staged such a scene in the Garden? Had he cut her up to lighten the load, or were the legs the guy's signature?

The answer was somewhere.

On his way home, Jake stopped by the Garden scene. He heard they were about to release it. He wanted one more crack.

The sun was still burning bright and hot, a fuzzy, unfocused ball of fire in an evening sky airbrushed with a perfect fusion of blue rouge and cranberry red.

Jake took off his jacket, left it in the car.

There was a safety-cone-orange outline spray-painted on the grass where Lisa had been found. White chalk lines were for Hollywood.

Lisa's death shape looked odd without her lower half.

When the sun fell out of view and behind the staggered skyline around Boston Common, a chill kicked up and Jake wished he'd taken his jacket with him. He pulled up his collar, bent down—a baseball catcher behind the plate— and stared at the empty sketch on the grass. Leaves had fallen all around, broken branches littered about the area.

Jake watched as people passed by the park going about their average lives. Talking. Laughing. Holding hands.

He looked through them, thinking.

Find his frame of mind.

He tapped on the side of his temple with a forefinger.

It wasn't hard to picture the madman at work. Follow him walking around the scene, planning to stage Lisa's corpse.

Where is she?

There were two types of killers, Jake knew. One enjoyed putting the rope around the woman's neck, relishing in watching her face turn a zombie-like hue of powder-blue. The other was more interested in the act itself. The technique. The methodical (and spiritual) nature of what went into taking a life. He was focused more on his own trauma while going about his business of torture, each moment a reflection of what he had gone through.

That's my guy.

Jake stood. As it got darker and the sounds of city life disappeared, it occurred to him how his mother used to demand he be in the house by early afternoon. He played by Columbia Point Project in Southie. At night, the place was a war zone of junkies and thugs. The thing was, Jake walked to and from school with his metal lunch box in hand, ready to strike at the kids looking to take it. Heading up Broadway once, the main shopping district in the all-white section of Southie, a gang of older kids surrounded him. Made him take off his pants and run home naked. All those Southie inbreeds drinking on their stoops, hanging out on the corners, screaming at one another up to the windows of row apartments, laughed at him.

There was an indentation in the mud by the pond. It was off the beaten path. Jake noticed it as he walked toward the scummy water. It was small, but noticeable, and looked as though someone had dropped a basketball and the claylike earth had recorded its imprint. He wondered how SIX-U had missed it. Jake reached inside his back pocket, took out his iPhone and double-clicked the scanning option app. "*Teleforensics, Cooper*," he heard the geek from tech say. "*It's the latest thing. Give it a shot.*" The guy showed him how to operate the scanner option. "*An app and two screens, you're done.*" Easy as taking a photograph. "*Only now, you can send the scanned image into a database and get results in minutes.*"

Jake moved the lens of the phone over the ground. He hit SCAN and slowly ran the phone's rays over the imprint as a fluorescent-green light glided over the outline of the shape.

He heard a chime. Hit the ENTER key. The image was now traveling through cyberspace, heading into the general database.

Jake copied Dickie and Anastasia on the send to keep them in the loop, with an added message to Anastasia, asking her how in the hell her team had missed this.

As Jake walked back up toward the body outline, the computer searched the system for a match, scrolling through thousands of images in seconds, much like it would for a fingerprint.

The hourglass turned as Jake stared at the screen.

Then came the e-report:

No data available.

Shit.

Then another chime. Jake looked at the screen again. No match, but there was a hit on the type of fabric. The scan had picked up on a crisscross pattern of material, fairly common. The main computer had compared its distinctive blueprint to thousands it had in storage.

Consistent with canvas. Military green in color.

Duffel bag.

Jake stood over the outline of Lisa. Checked his watch, pictured himself once again in the killer's shoes.

Duffel bag in hand—no ... bag on some sort of a cart—I stop here. He stared back toward the indentation. *Drop my bag. Unzip it. Take a look around. Make sure the coast is clear. Take her out and stage the scene.*

He tapped the glass on his watch, then looked up.

Forty-five seconds.

But where were his footprints? Anastasia would have found them.

He looked closely. Brush marks. The killer had used some sort of rake or tree branch to clear his footprints. How had the killer not seen the scallop?

Left it on purpose?

Jake keyed his radio ON. Called a blue standing guard at the entrance. "Don't allow this scene to be released."

"That you, Cooper? Shit, I didn't even frickin' see you go down there."

Jake shook his head. "Just do what I said."

"You got it."

Jake sat in his car on Boylston. "Rossi," he said into her voicemail. "I want the Garden scene reprocessed. We're looking for a professional—FedEx or UPS driver. A delivery person of some sort. Maintenance man. Maybe a cop. Or some ex-military nut." He paused. "Add a security guard in there somewhere."

Jake looked at the city of Boston before him. A taxi whizzed by, honking his horn. A woman jogger bounced along the sidewalk to the song in her earbuds. A guy behind her talked on his cell phone, using his hands to make points. A horse-and-buggy driver took a drag from a cigarette and read the *Globe* while waiting for a customer. Jake got lost in the swirling blue smoke hovering around the guy. He could taste the nicotine sting his throat, the tar burning his lungs as he inhaled. He popped a piece of nicotine gum. Chewed it once and then spit it out. A card Father John once gave him, congratulating Jake on his return to the church after getting out of the hospital, came in a wave as he drove away. The verse the card quoted was hard to forget.

"'*This is the verdict: Light has come into the world, but men loved darkness instead of light because their deeds were evil.*'"

Jake walked over to the horse-and-buggy guy. "You got an extra smoke?"

15

FRIDAY, SEPTEMBER 5 - 7:21 P.M.

CSI Anastasia Rossi sat behind her metal desk examining several photos spread out in front of her. It was late to be at work. But Anastasia had nowhere to go tonight. Cardio kickboxing class was on Mondays and Wednesdays. Her East Boston apartment, the one-bedroom overlooking Constitution Beach and Logan Airport, was not a place Anastasia wanted to be. Not tonight, with this case eating at her. What good was sitting home watching reruns of *Everybody Loves Raymond* and *Seinfeld*?

The break-up from her boyfriend, Todd Sacks, was still bothering Anastasia. Yet something kept telling her it was for the best. Long-distance relationships were doomed. Todd had left her, but had been there when her father died. Todd was one of those hard-bodied FDNY firemen, "Mr. July." When it came down to it, the guy was sincere, usually willing to drop everything and listen. Anastasia still called him once a week. Well, maybe a little more than that. Mostly on Sunday nights and Wednesday mornings before his shift. Last week they chatted for two hours. Talked about how Anastasia was faring in Boston. How she missed her father. Her goal was to make Grade One by the end of the year. Come to think of it, none of the conversation was about Todd.

Anastasia was promoted six months ago to Boston's A-list forensic team, Crime Scene Unit Six (or, as the team called itself in-house, SIX-U). They worked out of D-15.

By far, SIX-U was the unit with the most credibility. D-15's unprecedented conviction rate among the precincts made it the squad to work for. Anastasia had testified in four trials already. Each led to a conviction.

Not bad.

"You don't grow up in the Bronx," Anastasia had told Lieutenant Ray Matikas one day when he asked where her edge had come from, "and not learn a few things."

Anastasia stared at several close-ups of Lisa Marie's face, finding herself lost in the bizarre nature of this crime.

"You still here, Rossi?" Jake asked, walking by her desk.

She looked up, her big brown eyes lonely and curious, following Jake as he made his way toward his office. "Taking one for the team, Detective."

Jake halted before turning the corner. "I emailed you and Dickie something earlier, check it out. I need an explanation as to why you missed it. And, yeah, I need to speak with you, but not right now. Will you be around for a while?"

"Sure, Detective."

"Give me ten."

Snapping photos of dead bodies, tagging and bagging evidence, crawling around on all fours searching for fibers and hairs and chewed gum wasn't what Anastasia Rossi saw herself doing after moving from New York a year ago. She had transferred from the NYPD's hostage negotiation team. Coming to Boston, the twenty-nine-year-old had her heart set on wearing a gold shield like her dead father, Giuseppe Rossi. Crazy Joe was one of New York's most aggressive, if not infamous detectives.

Anastasia wrote something in a notebook she kept hidden in her desk under lock and key. She looked around before reaching into the drawer, then scribbled: *Jake Cooper, 7:32 PM, says he needs to "talk."*

Most everyone on the squad had gone home for the day. It was quiet. Anastasia heard the cleaning crew out in the lobby. Two guys were arguing about overtime, yelling at their foreman for being gypped a few hours in their last paycheck. Ignoring the commotion, Anastasia zeroed in on a few photos of the area surrounding Lisa Marie's body. Lisa was placed on the edge of the Public Garden Lagoon. There was a slight hill in front of her. How had Lisa's killer gotten her down that slope? Dead weight, Lisa weighed in at 115 pounds. No tire tracks were found anywhere on site. Did this mean the killer was a big man? A weightlifter type?

"Incredible case, huh, Rossi?" a blue from the front desk said as she walked by. She had her coat on, stopping to file a report in a nearby cabinet before leaving. "People can be so darn cruel. No legs. Incredible." She turned away from the color image Anastasia held in her hand.

"Hi-ya, Collins."

"Why don't you go home? It's late."

"I know," Anastasia said. "Cooper wants to speak to me, though. Can't leave."

Collins knew the real reason Anastasia worked so much overtime.

"Why don't you just put in for the promotion?" Collins sat on the desk in front of Anastasia's. "You'll get that job. There's a huge quota going on to fill a gender gap. Now's the time." Anastasia sat behind a small desk. This part of the office was set up like a school classroom. All the desks faced west, toward dispatch and the front counter. The offices were along the east wall, facing the city skyline. "You put too much pressure on yourself, Rossi. You'll never be noticed unless you speak up. You're a good cop. Good cops make Grade One. Take advantage of all the gender laws. They're written for people like you."

"That's sweet. Thanks. I appreciate it." Anastasia knew Collins was right, and meant well. All she ever thought about these days was finding that one piece of the puzzle in a big case that made her stand out.

Collins stood. "Think about it. I can make sure the paperwork gets into the right hands." She started to walk away. "Rossi?"

"Yeah?" Anastasia looked up.

"Unhappiness is a temporary condition, you know. It always passes."

"Good advice, Collins. Thanks."

Anastasia half-smiled. Inside, she wondered if her melancholy was that obvious. She thought she was over Mr. July. Her girlfriend back home had warned Anastasia about firefighters.

Her pager went off.

Dickie? At this hour? The guy was in bed by eight-thirty.

"What's up, Detective? Just getting ready to leave."

"Still hangin' around? I like your spunk, Rossi. So young and determined." Ever since Anastasia joined the team, Dickie had taken her under his wing.

"You know we got ourselves a hot case here. I want to do all I can to help."

"Listen, I was just talking to Jake"—*big surprise*—"and, well, first let me ask, are you busy this weekend?"

"No, why? What's up?" Anastasia bellied up to her desk, elbows on the large blotter with leather corners.

"Well, I spoke to a scientist at the Boston Science Museum. You know how they have that exotic, rare plant exhibit going on?" She didn't, but that was okay. "He suggested a botanist in New York we need to go see."

Anastasia was elated but confused. "Sorry, Detective, not following you. How is a botanist involved in our case?"

"His name is, oh, shoot, where is that piece of paper?" Anastasia heard Dickie shuffle papers around. He put the phone down. Cursed himself for losing everything. "I sometimes think I need to be tested for dementia, Rossi."

"You know what they say, Detective. If you forget where you put your keys, no biggie. It's when you forget what your keys are for—that's when you need to worry."

Dickie hadn't heard that one before. Cute.

"You there?" Dickie said. "Here it is …"

"Yeah, go ahead."

"We need to speak with the associate professor of plant genetics at Simmons University, in upstate New York by Erie … Doctor Albert K. Shelton."

"And again, Detective, this is for *what* purpose? If you don't mind me asking."

"I'll fill you in during the drive, but it involves that seedling you guys bagged from underneath the Taylor kid. It wasn't connected to any plant or vegetation in the Garden. In fact, one scientist claims, not anywhere in the state. It's definitely significant. Jake isn't sold on it yet, but I have one of those feelings. We might be able to locate the origin of the seedling. You know, where it's from. It's a start."

Jake walked around the corner. "Must have been Dickie, right?" He smiled. Anastasia stood. "No, please sit, Officer Rossi. This'll only take a minute. I'm on my way home." He looked down at his watch. "Late as it is."

Anastasia had become Jake Cooper's go-to. She was forever tagging along with Jake and Dickie during cases. It seemed just when they were about to throw up their hands on a case and send it to the cold case dustbin, she came up with a photo or piece of evidence everyone had missed. Never a smoking gun. But Anastasia seemed to always produce something that made a lead click. It was almost, Jake considered more than once, as if she held evidence back in order to make herself look good.

"You get that text on the scallop I found in the mud near the Common Lagoon?"

"Uh …"

"Check your email, Rossi. I won't even get into the fact that you missed that during your first sweep of the scene."

"I will, Detective. Sorry."

"Get back down there and process it again in the morning for me."

"Sure thing."

"I need you to do something else." Jake looked around to see if anyone was in earshot. "Needs to be kept quiet, though. You up for it?"

"Sure, Detective. Whatever I can do?" Anastasia knew what it was.

Simmons U.

"When you return from New York with Dickie," Jake whispered. This was strange to Anastasia. "I need you to go downtown and pull a case for me." File storage at HQ was off limits to just anyone.

Anastasia was absorbed. "Sure, but—"

"I don't care how you get in. The name's Carmichael. Marjorie and Jeffrey Carmichael were killed inside the Ted Williams Tunnel by falling debris. Probably a closed case already, written off as an accident, but I need your opinion on something. Also, check to see which law firm is representing Mr. Carmichael. I heard he's already lawyered up. And what construction company was hired for work on that quadrant of the tunnel."

"Is there anything I should know about it beforehand, Detective?"

"No. I don't want to taint your opinion. You heard of the case?"

"That would be affirmative, Detective. All over the news these past couple days. Poor woman and her son … that dog even." Anastasia looked over Jake's shoulder. She saw the elevator doors pop open and heard the floor number ding. A man walked out. He was dressed in sweatpants. A windbreaker. Boston Red Sox ball cap.

"Lieutenant Matikas, Coop."

Jake turned. *Shit.*

"What is he doing here at this hour?" Anastasia wondered out loud.

"You two, in my office," Matikas said, walking by them. "Now."

Jake dropped his shoulders. Followed. Waved Anastasia on.

Inside his office, Matikas folded his arms chest-high. Shook his head side to side. He could tell Jake wanted no part of this sudden meeting. Matikas's office was as messy as his car. Papers strewn all over the desk. Garbage can overflowing. Dust as thick as pollen on the tops of his cabinets. Cobwebs in the corners. Greasy fingerprint smudges on his computer screen.

"Why don't you leave your door unlocked, Ray," Jake said, "so the cleaning crew can get in here? Place is a shithole."

"Shut up for a minute, would you, Cooper. Oh, wait. I'm not keeping you from anything, am I?" Matikas tossed his keys on the desk. Medals, citations, and accommodations donned the walls behind his large burgundy leather chair, studded with gold buttons. The stuffed swordfish Matikas had bagged during a trip to the Grand Banks overlooked the three of them. Its marble eye followed Jake wherever he walked in the room.

"My dinner is getting cold, Ray."

"Why in the hell do you not answer your pager when it's important, Cooper? Can you tell me that, please?"

"I've been busy."

"You know, Rossi, this detective *really* thinks he's something. Some hotshot who doesn't have to live by the same rules the rest of us do. I've had it, Cooper, with your attitude and bullshit. I should *not* have given you this case—you're not ready for it." Sweat rolled off Matikas's forehead. He hadn't taken off his windbreaker, an old softball jacket from his days of playing in the FBI's summer league. He stunk like stale cigarettes and cabbage.

That remark smacked Jake. He was serious now. "Well, sir, I was here and I, well, you don't want to hear my problems, now do you?"

"The only reason I'm here now—believe me, I'd rather be home watching the *World Series of Poker*—is because Officer Collins had the decency to answer her damn telephone and let me know you were still here. It's the pathologist, Cooper. Kelsey has been trying to reach you for the past hour."

This sparked Jake's attention. "I'm all ears, Ray."

"Has to do with those legs you found in the Taylor closet. By the way, the father is pissed. Says you should have warned him there might have been something of a 'grotesque'—his word—nature in his daughter's room."

"What about those legs?"

Anastasia watched the exchange like a tennis match. She was curious, but did not want to get in between them.

"They're not Lisa Marie's legs, Cooper. Kelsey just confirmed that preliminary DNA does not match."

Jake had his iPhone out, dialing Dickie before Matikas even finished.

"I'm not done here. There's more. But you obviously have a few calls to make, so I'll wait." Matikas sat down.

Jake told Dickie to hold on. "What else, Ray? Come on."

"Kelsey found some sort of a mark, like lettering, on one of the legs. I don't know. Talk to her yourself. She'll tell you more. Just don't bother her tonight. She's at a wake. Her cousin. Or some uncle."

A thought passed through Jake: *Death truly* is *her life.* Then: "You hear that, Dickie?" Jake hung up.

"She wants you at the morgue first thing tomorrow morning. But said to call her office, she might have to meet you in Chelsea."

Two times in a week, Jake noted.

Jake turned to leave. Before walking out, he stopped at the door. "Rossi, you and Dickie leave tonight, not in the morning. I want you two up there banging on that Simmons professor's door while he's in the middle of a dream. Rustle his ass out of bed and get him working on that seedling."

"What about the crime scene?" Rossi asked.

"Let someone else go through it again."

"Cooper?" Matikas screamed. "What's this about Simmons University?"

Jake was on his way to the elevator.

16

SATURDAY, SEPTEMBER 6 – 7:45 A.M.

The soccer field was set against the backdrop of the old oil refinery tanks, rusted and unused, set along the Mystic River, west of the Tobin Bridge. Chelsea had changed since the days when the river was a means of industry. Now junkies and the unemployed loitered about, unafraid of corrupting Boston's historical character.

A frustrated Dawn Cooper blew the whistle hanging from her neck. It was loud and piercing, especially to kids who'd had no discipline in their short lives. Yet Dawn was not a coach who put up with any backtalk from a group of twelve-year-olds. They had better appreciate her giving up a Saturday morning to practice for the game next week. That is, if they wanted to beat the Revere Shamrocks.

"Julio Ortega," Dawn shouted, dropping her head, "you must pass the ball if you want to score. You are not Pelé, my little Latin soldier. Now pass-that-ball." She clapped her hands on the beat of each word. "Or you will sit out the game next week."

The boy looked at Dawn as if she were from another planet.

"Julio's a ball hog, Mrs. Cooper," Mantiqua Dawkins shouted from midfield.

"I'll handle this, Mantiqua, okay. Let's focus on what *you're* doing."

Brendan played with his Hot Wheels in a sandbox about twenty-five yards behind Dawn. He pushed the little cars through the sand, one by one, making *vrrrrrroom* sounds as he pretended he was part of the Daytona 500. At the basketball court nearby, a group of older kids traded Yu Gi Oh cards. Argued over who was a better superhero: Hell Boy or Batman. There was that autumn chill in the air, a cold, wet dampness generally reserved for late September.

Dawn glanced at Brendan every so often, smiled, and waved her little fingers. She took a look around the area where Brendan sat. Just to make sure all was copacetic.

"Pass the ball, Hugo," Dawn screamed. "We cannot win—how many times do I have to say this—if we do not pass … the … ball." She stopped play. Walked out onto the middle of the field. Her white Nike cleats kicked up wet grass behind her. She called everyone around in a circle. "You need to set your sights on the perimeter of the field and look for open teammates. Those who can drive the ball to your opponents' side and set up the best shot at goal."

"What's a perimeter, Mrs. Cooper?" Bertina Jackson really didn't know. She twirled a lock of her hair. Snapped a piece of bubble gum.

"The white lines, Tina. The outside white lines." Dawn pointed.

"Oh, sorry … *excuse* me." Bertina twisted her neck and head. "And I'm supposed to know that, right?"

The kids were loud and obnoxious. Soccer practice was a way to get off the street for the morning. Get a free breakfast out of Mrs. Cooper, some Gatorade, and not worry about being bullied for a few hours or waking up to hung-over parents.

"Now, let's try this again." Dawn had the soccer ball in her hands, whistle in her mouth. "Everybody understand what I'm saying?"

None of the kids responded.

Dawn backed off the field.

Thirty seconds passed. They were getting it, Dawn thought. That was all they needed, a little kick in the ass.

Some direction. "Yes, Hugo, that's it," she encouraged. "You got it, kiddo. Keep up the good work."

Dawn realized she had not checked on Brendan. Whenever she got actively involved in hands-on coaching, Dawn told Valerie Murray, nursing a broken leg on the bench, to keep an eye on Brendan. Dawn looked over and spied Valerie staring down at her cell phone screen, tapping out a text.

Bren?

Her stomach felt a kick as she turned.

The child was gone.

"No. Valerie, where is he?"

The girl looked up.

Dawn ran.

At the sandbox, Dawn saw his toys just sitting there. Large footprints—*a man's*—marked the sand next to where she was certain Brendan had been grabbed by some pedophile who now had him in his car, speeding down the road, salivating over all of the perverted things he was going to do to the boy.

"Brendan?" She surveyed the park in a circle.

Those kids trading cards looked at her. Went back to what they were doing.

"Brendan!" Play on the soccer field stopped. The kids realizing what was going on.

"Brendan, damn it, where are you?" Tears now. Dawn ran to the opposite end of the playground, which was blocked by several large maple trees and a large plastic playscape donated to the park by a man whose son died of cancer. "Adam's Land," that section of the park was called. The father was a doctor. A doctor who couldn't save his own son.

"Brendan?"

"Over here," a voice shouted, "Dawn. Over here, honey."

She stopped. Dropped to bended knees. Let out a deep breath. Thank God.

"He ran over to me," Jake said. He was sitting on the top of a picnic table under a tree. Brendan kneeled on the bench seat between his father's legs.

Dawn grabbed Brendan and tucked his head into her chest. Her chin rested on his head. She rocked back and forth. Stared at Jake.

How dare you.

"We'll talk about this later, Jake."

"What did *I* do? I was just driving by, thought I'd stop. He saw me. Came running."

"You could have said something earlier. You saw me panicking."

"I did not, Dawn." Jake shrugged. "Well, that might teach you to keep Brendan, like I've said, by your side when you're out and about." Under Mo, when he first came up, Jake worked a few years in the child abduction unit. He'd seen things he thought happened only in Third World countries. After Dawn had Brendan, Jake went on a stranger-danger kick. He became obsessed with the notion that someone was going to grab the kid. It was this same sort of behavior that had cost Jake a few relationships. The love of his life, Jenna Connors. They dated for four years, two in high school, two out. Jake's insecurity came in between them.

"I had Valerie watching him," Dawn explained, holding Brendan. "Or I thought she was. Maybe I need to keep him on a leash, Jake!"

Dawn wasn't a bad mother. She was more liberal when it came to Brendan. If it were up to Jake, Brendan would still be riding in the front seat of the shopping carriage and tied to Dawn's hip whenever they left the house. Dawn, on the other hand, wanted to teach the child that the world wasn't a bad place. You couldn't trust everyone. But you could certainly walk through life and not be afraid of every unfamiliar face you came in contact with. Jake was not a good judge of the real world. He lived inside that bubble of Boston's criminal element. It corrupted his thinking. All cops thought this way to some extent.

"He's not a prisoner, Jake. I'm so mad at you right now."

Just then the soccer team ran up.

"I have to go to see Dr. Kelsey, Dawn—" but she wouldn't let him finish.

"I'm sorry, Jake. I should not have trusted a thirteen-year-old. I know."

"Hey," Jake grabbed hold of his wife, "it's okay now."

Dawn shook. She went back and questioned every step of her morning. "I'm so sorry." More tears. This was the effect Jake had on people. He could turn things around with a few words. Lay on the guilt subtly. Make Dawn feel like it *was* her fault.

"Hey, listen, call your parents. I'll be done early today"— Jake looked at his watch—"probably 'roun' three. Let's go over there for dinner tonight, okay?" He knew that would make her feel better.

The team stood in the back of Dawn, a posse behind their leader. "Everything okay, Mrs. Cooper?" one of the kids asked.

Dawn got herself together. Stood. "Yeah. Yes. Of course."

The team ran together back to the field. Dawn said she'd join them soon.

"Brendan, you go with them."

"Okay, Mommy."

"Tyisha," Dawn told her oldest player, "keep an eye on him for me." She stared at the girl.

"Sure thing, Mrs. Cooper."

"This coaching thing," they walked toward Jake's car, "is too much. Work is draining you, Dawn. Me, too. What do you say we drop it all and move to New Hampshire."

"Watching *On Golden Pond* again?" She paused. More serious and calm now, "Listen, Jake, you can never do that again."

Jake kissed Dawn on the lips. Jumped into his car. Dawn stared at him. "I don't even know why I don't stay mad at you, Jake Cooper."

"Because I'm the Sundance Man," Jake said, mounting his sunglasses, "Boston's finest superhero." Dawn could see her reflection in those big blowfly mirror lenses. Alice Cooper-like, black mascara streaked down the channels of her eyes.

"Just don't forget about your dinner idea for tonight," Dawn reminded her husband. "Once I call mom, she'll hold us to it. We'll have to show up—or you'll have more in common with that priest of yours than you think."

Jake took off. The comment reminded him that he needed to get over to St. Paul's within the next few days and see Father John about that problem with the deacon. He owed the priest that much.

17

SATURDAY, SEPTEMBER 6 – 9:11 A.M.

The sun was blurry as if positioned behind stained glass. The sky a soft, varicose-vein blue. It had turned uncomfortably humid after a chilly start. Still, this was the type of morning in late summer you take without complaining. Jake parked on Franklin Street in Chelsea, next to a dangerously slanted telephone pole and white-brick retaining wall that looked to be falling over. Up ahead were ramshackle brick tenement buildings across the street from a dozen three-deckers. Blues had a name for the neighborhood—"Welfare Row."

Jake spied Dr. Kelsey as he walked around the corner of the U-Haul rental truck. It was situated at the base of a hill in front of the Miguel Village housing project. The pathologist stood on the tailgate. Handed out boxes and bags of food. Winter hats. Mittens and scarves. All donated by a local church.

Kelsey looked a lot better out in the real world. She was dressed in jeans, a tank top, white denim ball cap with a silver star made out of glitter on the front. She wore those white, nameless, nondescript tennis shoes made for housewives. Kelsey's nails were Goth black. She had make-up on, a Bahaman blue rouge above her eyes (borderline circus clown), cherry red cheeks, rock star black eyeliner. Large silver and gold bracelets clanked on her wrists. A gold skull pendant hung from her neck.

Nice touch, Jake thought, staring at the skeleton head.

Kelsey spotted the detective. "Get your butt up here, Cooper. Help us out."

"I need to talk to you," Jake yelled over the crowd, his hands cupped in a megaphone on the sides of his mouth. "Ray said you have something for me."

"Detective Cooper, this is Marilyn." Kelsey could throw her voice. "Marilyn, Sundance Cooper."

Jake walked over and shook the woman's strong, rough hand. She nodded without speaking.

"Marilyn's my sister."

"Nice to meet you."

Marilyn wore her gray hair in a military buzz cut. She did not smile.

"Don't mind my sister," Kelsey said, looking over at her. "Mad at the world—that woman."

Jake nodded as if to say he understood. "About those legs? Is it always this busy?"

The poor were huddled around the back of the truck as though Doctors Without Borders backed up to some Third World country village to hand out medical supplies and sacks of rice.

"This city is not into helping its people, Cooper. But that conversation is for another time." Kelsey said something to her sister Jake couldn't hear. Then jumped down off the tailgate, addressing Jake, "My car's over there."

They reached Kelsey's black Malibu. It was parked next to a red and yellow fire hydrant. They sat down inside. Kelsey took out her notes and read. Jake scoped out the inside of the vehicle. Clean. Tidy. He appreciated that.

"Right … yes, here we are," Kelsey said. She took off her librarian bifocals. Squinted one eye in thought. "I found what I believe to be the letter *m* underneath the ankle bone of the right leg."

"An *m*, you say?"

"Yes. Not a tattoo or anything like that. It's a crude marking of some sort as if it was burned into the skin—after death—on purpose."

A cipher?

Jake had a hard time with this notion. "Wait a minute, Doctor. Whose legs are we talking about here?"

"The new set. The set you found under the Taylor kid's bed?"

"You mean in her closet?"

"Right, sorry," she said, checking her notes again. "The Taylor closet."

"Yes, whose legs are those? Matikas said something about them not being the Taylor kid's. Are they Lisa Marie Taylor's legs or not?"

"Those legs are definitely *not* from your Lisa Marie. Who names their kid after a Presley, anyway?" The doctor shook her head.

"I'll ask the dad about the name next time I see him. Whose legs are they, then?"

"I need to run a few more tests, but I am ninety-nine percent certain, you can bet on this one, Cooper, that"—she winked—"those legs belong to the same DNA donor we pulled off the Taylor kid's face."

Alyssa Bettencourt. Jake saw all that blood on Lisa's face at the crime scene. It did not belong to her. Whoever beat her, slathered someone else's blood on her face and pummeled the girl after she was already dead.

"Go on."

"Beyond the prelim blood tests I ran, I know the legs had been previously frozen, likely in the same locale as the Taylor body. I found the same ice crystal residue. We determine this by analyzing the frozen air particles left behind. Sort of in the same fashion archeologists check layers of the Arctic for carbons. You know what I mean."

"I guess, yeah." Jake didn't care about science. He sat back. Considered the barbarity of these crimes. Took a breath. "Thanks, Doctor." He stepped out of the Malibu. Leveled his iPhone, hit speaker.

After one buzz: *"The Verizon customer you are trying to reach is out of a serviceable area."*

Simmons.

At the beep: "Dickie, call me when you have service back."

Kelsey tapped Jake on the back. "That's all for now. I'll have more soon. Gotta run. I need to get back to my sister and the civic duty she takes so much pride in. Not enough to be a lesbian, you know. She has to save the world, too."

"Yep, sure …" Jake hung up the line.

"Come see me on Monday. I should have more detail."

"One question, Doctor."

"What is it, Cooper? I really need to get back."

"Sure. But that marking inside Lisa's mouth, the one you thought wasn't a bite mark or a skin defect, what type of shape is that in?"

The doctor went back into the car and rummaged through the photographs, stopping on a close-up. "Look for yourself."

Jake took the color photo in hand, stared at it in puzzlement. "I don't see anything."

"You've got it upside down." It was hard to interpret if you didn't know what you were looking at. The skin, after a good washing, was a whitish pink, like chewed gum. The marking, all blown up like this in the photo, looked as if it could be anything.

Kelsey straightened the photo.

There it was in plain view.

"An *i*?"

"Yes. The letter *i*. Appears someone is sending you a message, Detective."

"Can I have this photo? You have one of the *m* on the ankle I can take, too?"

She handed it to him.

In his mind, Jake Cooper put the two letters together: "*i-m.*"

I-M.

I'm … what?

18

Lisa Marie's killer parked the 1972 American Motors Post Office Jeep he had bought at auction in a space nearest to the 1st Street entrance. How long had it been since he attended Mass inside this European-looking stone construction here in the old Southie neighborhood? Let's see … well, this was the first time since he left Bainbridge, where this same godforsaken establishment, St. Paul's Church, had shipped him off to. In Maine, the sisters had *made* him go to Mass. So the last time he actually sat in the pew and wanted to be there, praising Jesus and the Holy Spirit, kneeling and standing and believing in the gift of grace, it was here, in this church. In fact, the day before he had eavesdropped and overheard Deacon Patrick O'Keefe and Father John O'Brien decide his fate.

"Bainbridge is the right place for him, John," the deacon explained to the priest. "It's not a bad place. We've had successes come out of there. Kids we've sent. Southie is not a place where a kid can survive on his own. Look at the suicide rate. Anyway, this child will become a problem. Both his parents are not coming back. We know they're dead."

"I understand, Patrick. But this child is different. I don't think he can make it in that environment."

"Oh, come now, John. And living here is going to be better? This is not a decision for us to make. We cannot save everyone."

A flash of nostalgia passed through him as he walked through the large wooden double doors. He dipped in the holy water font. After pausing, thinking about it, he crossed himself. Time stood still. That statue of Mary, the blue and white shawl hanging off her young shoulders, was a bit worn, but still greeted him as he walked underneath. The gold cross above the door into the nave, polished once a week by the sisters, had not aged a day. Just like that, he was sucked back into this world he had come from. He watched the altar boys rushing around, getting ready for Mass. Years past, he stood in the same narthex dreaming of wearing that red and white cassock, preparing the incense for the priest.

Faith, the ultimate justifier.

Strange to be on the other side now, he thought, *representing the Evil One.*

He lived alone in that lice- and cockroach-infested Dorchester Heights apartment after his hooker mother left him to fend for himself. He accepted it, though, attending school and Mass and reading the Gospels at night. *Religiously.* He was stealing food from the local stores, getting by until he was old enough to get a job and take care of himself. It was God's plan, after all. His dad's miserable life was cut short by a "hot shot," a lethal dose of coke and heroin a dealer provides when he's sick of a customer not paying. That was followed by Mom's vanishing act. Why hadn't Father John and Deacon O'Keefe allowed him to live alone? What was so bad about it? He was better off. By sending him north, hadn't they intervened with God's work?

Sure they had.

"Good morning, sir," a guttural voice intoned. The mailman realized he had blacked out for a moment and lost track of where he was. He and Father John stood between the narthex and the nave. "Welcome to St. Paul's."

Startled, he turned. "Thank you … good morning, Father."

"Do I know you? You seem familiar."

"No, Father. I was passing through town. I'm from the north, Malden, Somerville area. Heading home to the wife and family after a business trip. I wanted to stop and take in the Mass. I've heard of your work here."

Lisa Marie's killer wanted to hit himself in the head with his palm. *Stupid, stupid, stupid.* Way too much information.

Father John O'Brien didn't pester the stranger. "Well, I do hope you enjoy Mass this morning, sir, and do join us again." The priest bowed. His hands palm-to-palm in front of himself. Eyes closed.

Kneeling, the music began. The mailman watched as a procession—Deacon Patrick O'Keefe, Father John, and the two altar servers—made that slow, devout walk down the center aisle of the nave. He had carried that same gold cross through that same aisle a thousand times. He dreamed back then of going to the seminary. He imagined himself dressed in friar's brown garb, shaved head, bowing and praying all day long, saying rosaries until his throat was like sandpaper.

Then the Teacher came into his life—the man who changed his outlook about growing up without parents in an orphanage. He was also, later on, the same man who took his soul and gutted it, before explaining to him that life was about choices. You had to follow your heart until you found your true calling. The seminary maybe wasn't for him. That was the day the doubt began. Spiritual desires are seen through a mature lens, said the Teacher. He pronounced the word *matt-turr*, like a Brit.

As he stood in the pew, the organist played. He watched God's chosen few walk toward the chancel. Father John kissed the altar. Sat down off to the right, in the south transept. The deacon sat beside him. As they did this, Lisa Marie's killer couldn't stop the thoughts and images this place evoked. He had no idea the horror of his past would be so magnified by just being in here. Yet it made him feel comfortable.

He saw the bandana go over his mouth. He couldn't scream.

Evil, he believed, was the main theme of Revelation.

Stop it … shut up …

He wanted to cut himself. Just a little slit along the thigh. Draw some blood. Oh, to do it here, in this church. How magisterial that would feel. How freeing. How satanic.

Cathartic bliss—a pressure valve let loose.

Don't make me do this.

Deacon Patrick O'Keefe stood at the pulpit in the north transept and read them from the Scriptures. When he finished, he cleared his throat and gave the homily. Off to the right Father John O'Brien sat in the chair with the big, pointed back, a relic given to St. Paul's by an outgoing bishop.

The gospel reading was Matthew 5:1-12. *The Sermon on the Mount.* The Beatitudes. Jesus' rules for living.

How appropriate.

Looking on, the mailman realized how long he had been away. Deacon O'Keefe looked old. Sagging skin. Gelled eyes, dripping a slimy clear fluid. The man walked with a slight curve in his back and had to *a-hem* several times before he found the right inflection to announce the Word.

The mailman thought of the article he pinned to his wall earlier that morning back at home. How the Boston archdiocese had uncovered an affair. O'Keefe confessed to Monsignor Belini, who confronted him with the matter. "I have a daughter, Your Excellency," Deacon said. But they allowed him to continue in his ministry.

Pathetic.

After reading the final beatitude, O'Keefe concluded with a simple bit of hypocritical advice: "To open your heart to the grace of our Lord, to partake in this reading and live these laws Jesus left to us," he stabbed his bony finger into the page, "is a peace you will not be able to find anywhere else."

The mailman smiled at the deacon, who looked at him several times.

A eureka moment hit Lisa Marie's and Alyssa Bettencourt's killer as the deacon concluded his homily. His next target was there before him. She had been within reach the entire time. "My fellow believers in Christ," the deacon shouted, "I need to say something on a personal note. Something that ushers into my heart such a grand sense of fulfillment and love." He smiled. "My daughter. Please stand, Mary." In the front pew, a young woman in a white sweater, her hair tied back in a matching bow, hesitated. Then stood and turned to face the congregation. "My lovely daughter, Mary, has decided to pursue a vocation in the Church. She is heading north, to Vermont, to study the Doctors of the Church at St. Faustina's College."

Mary took a bow as the parish erupted into applause.

The mailman stood and made single claps, slowly, out in front of himself—a trained seal. Mary cried and bowed, over and over. Embarrassed, she didn't know what to do.

Lisa Marie's killer imagined how Mary's neck was going feel in his hands. He relished in the sight of blood streaming from her legs after he cut them off with a hacksaw. He was going to tell her, as she screamed and pleaded with her god, that her father was nothing but a lying bastard sonofabitch who had cheated him out of a life.

An eye for an eye, Mary O'Keefe. *Study your Bible.*

19

A violent thunder and lightning storm rolled into the city, bringing with it torrential downpours that washed away the mini heat wave. As Jake walked out of his house, he could smell that after-rain aroma permeating the air, a mixture of sumac and pine, dead worms in the gutters, motor oil evaporating from the tar. The driveway steamed like a casserole, the red maple by the mailbox dripping perfect rainforest droplets of water.

It was a fifteen-minute ride from the Coopers' house in Brookline to Beacon Hill. A little less with Jake behind the wheel. The case nagged at Jake as he maneuvered his way around the rotary connecting Brookline Avenue and Boylston Street. The fact that a second victim's legs had been left in Lisa Marie's closet was a portent, a warning.

Additional victims would follow.

"Nervous, honey?" Dawn asked Jake. She glanced over the seat back at Brendan. "Excited to see grandma and grandpa, Bren?"

Jake had made a deal with himself that he wasn't going to talk about the case. Not tonight. He owed Dawn that much after scaring the shit out of her that morning at the park.

"I am, Mommy." Brendon wore his favorite Red Sox T-shirt. His hair was messy, as usual. He was looking forward to the five-dollar bill he knew his grandfather would slip to him. As Jake drove, Brendan colored in a book of dinosaurs. Going to see his grandparents was a good diversion for Brendan from not seeing his father all that much anymore. But the kid still hurt.

Jake mulled over those crude markings Kelsey had recovered on both bodies. Was it a message? Or was their serial throwing off the scent, playing games? So far, Jake's iPhone profiling program hadn't come back with anything—NOT ENOUGH DATA.

Worthless geeks and their 'technology'!

What would Anastasia and Dickie find at Simmons? They must be there by now. Why the hell hadn't Dickie called?

Anxiety flared. Jake realized his forearms hurt. He didn't know it, but he was squeezing the steering wheel, allowing his thoughts to run away from him.

"Not going to answer me?" Dawn asked.

"Sorry," Jake finally said. "Was thinking about things. Hey, unfoil me a piece of my nicotine gum, would you." His hands shook.

Jake took a left. Drove down the ramp onto Storrow Drive. Brendan liked this part of the trip. He loved watching the Boston University Terriers scull team. They sat in a line on those skinny canoes. Worked in unison. Pulled themselves against the Charles River current. True teamwork.

"Like pirates," Brendan said whenever they passed.

There were times—like this one—when Jake looked out at the water himself and could think of nothing but Martin Cooper, his father. They used to fish underneath the Boston University Bridge for pumpkinseed and smallmouth bass when Jake was in kindergarten. Martin would wear one of those white Fonzie T-shirts, the seams on the sleeves rolled up to expose his bicep muscles. Looking up at his dad, Jake felt an irreplaceable sense of safety. *The good years*. His most vivid memories now, however, were from years later, after Casey died. *The death years*. "Why would you ever want to be a cop?" Martin had asked after young Jake shared the news of being accepted into the state police academy. "Why not the service, like your brother? Like me! Military's not good enough for you, son, huh?"

This made Jake feel rejected. He tried to resist commenting back.

"You're probably not Army material, anyway," Martin Cooper said after Jake refused to give in and placate the man with an answer.

Ever since then, Jake had wondered if he had become a cop because it was in his blood and who he was, or simply to spite his father.

"Hey, anybody in there?" Dawn said, snapping her fingers in front of Jake's face as he drove.

"Sorry."

"They're excited to see you."

"Do you know what the average family income is in Beacon Hill?" Jake said, quickly changing the subject, more for his benefit.

"What, bored again at work, honey? Reading Wikipedia?" Jake heard Brendan laugh from the backseat. "You cannot count on that info. You should know that—you're a cop." Dawn put the sun visor down, flipped the mirror flap up. The little dome light shone on her face as she checked her makeup, flexing her face in different positions, puckering her lips, making sure her lipstick wasn't smudged. Dawn opened her mouth wide, then closed it, as though doing jaw exercises.

"Hear me out here for a minute. I'll have you know," Jake continued as he turned the corner onto Charles Street, looked down the block, and found his way onto Joy. Dawn's parents lived in a luxurious Beacon Hill red-brick town house next door to the Crumblers, whose great-granddaughter was the first Afro-American in the United States to receive a medical degree. "The combined income for a married couple in Beacon Hill is—drum roll, please, Brendan—five million dollars."

"Not Mom and Dad," Dawn said out of the corner of her mouth. "Please. Give me a break." The house had been an inheritance from Minnie's grandmother.

Every inch of space on Beacon Hill held historic value. Joy Street was indeed one of the wealthiest sections of the city. Besides the red-brick appearance and colonial feel, the town houses were known for their exaggerated brass door knockers. Residents insisted on keeping them polished to a glare. The brick sidewalks were spotless. Perpetually burning gas lanterns in place of streetlights. Pear trees. Hidden gardens situated around architecture from the Federal, Greek Revival, Colonial, and Victorian periods. Jake felt out of place.

"Indeed, you all here on Beacon Hill may have money, status, even fame," Jake held up a forefinger, "but we—and you're now one of us, Mrs. Cooper—in Brookline, we have JFK. No one can take him away from us."

"You're incredible," Dawn said. "Delusional." She paused. Smiled. "Thanks for suggesting this dinner, honey. It's a been a while since we've seen them."

Jake parked. As he got out, he stopped, looked down the block. At the end of Joy was the edge of Boston Common. Just a half-mile away from Cleveland and Minnie Benedict's town house was the Lisa Marie Taylor crime scene Jake Cooper could not let go of.

"Hi, Mother," Dawn said after ringing the bell. Jake stood behind his wife with his hands on Brendan's shoulders. As soon as Minnie opened the door, Brendan saw his grandfather and bolted into his open arms.

"Dawny, how are you? Jake, always good to see you."

The smell of braised lamb, rosemary, and fresh mint hit them as they walked into the foyer.

Dawn's father, Cleveland, wore a beige three-piece suit, white ruffled shirt, bow tie, Italian shoes. He had his trusty gold pocket watch tucked away, the chain hanging in a half circle, clipped to a belt loop. Jake Cooper couldn't deny the man looked sharp whenever he saw him, but had a weird Sherlock Holmes vibe Jake never understood.

"Sir," Jake stuck out his hand. "Always a pleasure."

"Detective." The old man enjoyed that greeting—calling Jake by what he did. "Any luck with the Garden case? Still cannot believe that happened *right* here." He shook his head. "Brandy, Jake?"

"Just a Mountain Dew, sir."

"Brendan, get your dad a soda pop." Cleveland walked over to a makeshift bar on a small table by the stairs, poured himself a snifter of brandy, cleared his throat. "What's the word on the case? Anything new?"

"Not much happening yet, sir. It's early in the game."

"I saw the Italian girl on New England News the other night. She said y'all think we've got a serial killer working in the city. How chilling to consider such a random, evil thing."

They walked toward a large room with oak floors, walnut shelves, shiny lacquered cherry wood walls. Jake admired how in shape Cleveland kept himself. His was no fake Jack LaLanne, juicer-body. Cleveland had real muscles, hard and ripped.

Walking, Jake noticed a bandage on Cleveland's right knuckle. "Cut yourself working in the garden again, Cleve?"

The old man lifted his hand, stared at the injury. "That, oh … well, you know, probably should have gotten stitches, but … What I did was, I smashed a glass accidentally while watching the Sox game the other night. Had serious money on it."

Jake had a strange look about him. "Bad luck, Cleve, huh."

"About the murders," Cleveland said. Jake felt his father-in-law wanted off the subject of the cut knuckle. "What can you tell me about them?"

"Officer Rossi, she said something like that, but I'm not going there, sir." The gruesome details of the case had not been released. Jake wasn't about to share anything, family or not. "You and Minnie are going to Europe, I hear, in a few days." Jake made a mental note to tell Anastasia to watch her tongue when speaking to the media.

"I'm getting too old for those trips. But you do what the wife wants long enough and she expects it. So I don't argue. I pack a bag and tell her I'm in, then complain of being sick a day before."

Dawn and Minnie sat by a window in two antique chairs near a large brick fireplace. A bookcase with volumes of leather-bound books no one read overlooked them. There was a rolltop desk, a family heirloom, nearby. Both chairs looked out into a courtyard flower garden.

Dawn and Minnie drank tall, skinny flutes of a 1995 Krug, Clos du Mesnil champagne from a bottle resting in an ice bucket between them.

"I don't know about your father, Dawn. He leaves at all hours of the night, never says where he's going."

"Probably to the club to play bridge, Mother."

"I don't know." Minnie was perplexed, seemed worried.

They chatted for a brief time. The oven timer went off. Dinner was done.

They sat at the dining table. "How are your mother and father, Jake?" Cleveland asked, snapping out his cloth napkin as if it were a tiny bedsheet, placing it on his lap. "We have not seen them in, oh, what has it been, Min, three, four years now?"

"They're good. Thanks. I'll tell 'em you asked. They'll like that. They adore Desert Winds, Arizona. It's hot. They stay indoors a lot and read. Once in a while they hit the early bird at the local Applebee's."

It was a lie. Jake's father was in the early stages of Alzheimer's. Most days the man didn't know his own name. Jake's mother took care of him. Jake and Dawn sent money at times and Dawn agreed her parents didn't need to know.

Jake took a pull from his Mountain Dew. As the green fizz burned his throat, he felt the buzz of his iPhone against his hip and looked down.

"I have to take this." He stood, pushed out his chair with the back of his knees, and walked into the study for privacy. Cleveland followed him with his eyes. "You're interrupting family time," Jake said roughly to the caller. "Better be good."

"We have something with that seedling, Jake. I spoke to this doctor at Simmons who thinks he can help us. We emailed him a digital photo before we left, so he could get started. But now that he's tested the actual seedling, he's certain it's from a rare flower that does not grow in the States. Means that the source of the flower could have ordered it."

"When are you coming back?"

"Tomorrow afternoon. We're meeting up with him again in the morning."

"Text me a brief report before you leave."

Dickie sighed. "I'll have Rossi do that."

9:57 P.M.

Brendan fell asleep as soon as Jake hit Storrow Drive. Leaning over the seat, putting a blanket over him, Dawn said, "Take the long way home."

"Yeah," Jake said. It was the last night with his Chevelle. The Crown Vic was going to be ready in the morning.

They passed a U.S Army billboard on Commonwealth. Holding an M-16, a fresh-faced young man sat on the edge of an Army helicopter. He looked serious.

Be all you can be.

"Still jolts you every time you see something like that," Dawn said. She moseyed over next to her husband as if they were teenagers at the drive-in.

"It's hard to forget. I often wonder what Casey'd be doing if he'd lived. He'd probably be a cop too." Jack scowled as he looked out the front windshield. "He would have been ten times the cop I am."

Casey Milton Cooper was a decorated marine pilot in Kuwait during the Gulf War. "I had wanted, and we joked about it as kids," Jake said, "so badly for my children to call him Uncle Milty."

Jake's older brother joined the military to get out of Southie. He was hanging with those scaly cap-wearing corner-dwellers of the Lower End in Old Colony Project. Got tired of running. Chasing a future in prison or a casket. Those Southie symbols—the shamrocks and claddaghs painted on the sides of buildings around the neighborhood— were said to represent "friendship, loyalty, and love." What a load of shit that was.

Jake was younger then. Looking at photos mailed to the house from Kuwait once a month made Jake proud to be Casey's brother. Envy eventually turned into respect. Jake realized he wanted to join the military, too. It was Father John O'Brien who talked Jake into the state police academy instead. Jake went to the priest one day to discuss how he felt about losing Casey. Explained that he wanted to pick up where his brother left off. He knew his father would want him to. Father John knew Jake wasn't built for military life. Plus, Casey wrote to the priest and made him promise to talk Jake out of it. It was almost, Father John admitted to Jake years later, as if Casey knew his time was limited. That he wasn't coming back. Mo Blackhall liked to take the credit for rescuing Jake out of Southie. But it was Father John. Mo was just the recruiter, so to speak. The priest changed Jake's heart. Turned his life around. Then one day it all fell apart.

There was a knock on the door. Jake had just come in from the Boys & Girls Club and a stop at the Donut Chef. It was snowing. He was smiling. No sooner had he closed the door did he turn around and have to answer it.

Two guys dressed in military greens asked for Mr. or Mrs. Cooper.

"Go to your room," Jake's mother said, walking up from behind, wiping her hands on her apron. "Go now, boy. Hurry."

Upstairs, his ear against the door, Jake listened to his mother wail as Martin Cooper put on his game face. Only thing the old man said was, "You know, there was a time not even an ambulance would not have come into this neighborhood without a police escort." He stuck out his hand. "Fifteen company. Korean War."

The captain handed Casey's dog tags to Martin.

Martin put them in his pocket.

Jake had always viewed his father as a shell of a man, hollow and unfeeling. Mr. Pokerface. Martin was kind of just, well, *there*. He had played the role of the father, as if he had read a how-to book, or taken some adult-ed class on parenting. But then Casey died and Martin found salvation in a pint of Popov he kept in the glove box of his car. Jake would see him staring at the white and red label before taking a swig. Martin started hanging out at McBride's and getting beaten up. As the years passed, Jake watched him sink deeper, never being able to pull himself out of it. Jake would walk out of the house or come up from behind the car unexpectedly and see his father tipping. He'd stop, watch, but never say anything to anyone.

Alcoholism, the middle-class white elephant.

As Mrs. Cooper cried, Martin put a hand on her shoulder. "Thank you, Captain. Lieutenant." Nodded to both men. "We appreciate you coming out."

Jake backed away from his door. Walked to the closet, where he had hid Casey's tattered and torn boot-camp training T-shirt. Jake planned on wearing it himself as soon as he could fill it out. Standing in his room that day, Jake held the shirt to his nose. He could still smell Casey.

10:15 P.M.

"I have to get over there and see Father John," Jake said as he took the left on Woodycrest, nearing home. Brendan was just waking up.

"You find out what he wants?" Dawn loved listening to Jake talk about Casey. She knew it helped him.

"No. But I suspect it has something to do with the deacon. He mentioned his name. Never trusted that guy, Dawn." Jake took a breath. "Hey, I want to drop Brendan off at school tomorrow morning, okay? Maybe once or twice a week from now on."

Dawn smiled. Jake would give up on it after two weeks. But it was a start.

"I'm thinking of clocking out for good after this case."

20

Dickie and Anastasia made contact with Dr. Albert K. Shelton. He was a rather academic-looking, owlish man who wore a bow tie. He had one of those Honest Abe mustache-less beards. Spoke in language that made two streetwise cops feel as though their community college degrees were worthless. They hooked up with the professor shortly after Dickie phoned Jake the previous night. Shelton decided it would be better to meet in the lab "as early as possible." He said he was scheduled to give a lecture that afternoon in Canada at a conference, and didn't have a lot of time to spare.

"The Queen of the Night," Shelton said aloud after introducing himself. He grasped the seedling found underneath Lisa Marie's body with a pair of tweezers. Placed it under a microscope. "I'm sure of it. This little seedling is the 'hot' plant of the moment. All the rage today, detectives."

"I'm a CSI, sir. Not a detective," Anastasia corrected. "A distinction not made quite clear on television these days."

The scholar ignored the comment. "What you officers need to do is conduct several more tests in order for the seedling to have any significance to your investigation." Anastasia took notes. Dickie stood, listening closely. "Just to be certain. You need random samples of bark and leaves. Other seeds taken from different trees, shrubs, flowers, and other foliage and plant species surrounding the home of the victim. Along with any strange plants you might come in contact with during your investigation. The science behind this tiny, naturally manufactured species is quite complicated. Same as, say, your DNA coding for blood."

"Okay, doctor … humor us, would you. How is the DNA similar?" Dickie couldn't help but think the professor sounded like one of the scientists he watched on Discovery Channel. Crass. Over-educated. Smarter than everyone else. The attitude the guy projected felt demeaning. It was hard to ignore.

Prick, Dickie thought to himself.

"Your toxicologists could probably answer this better, Detective. But I'll give it my best. When you come down to it, we are not so much different than plants. Our DNA, speaking scientifically, appears almost identical on paper."

Dickie picked his teeth with a toothpick he took from a bowl at the TGI Fridays the night before. As the professor spoke, he pictured two strands of the DNA ladder, the helixes, twisting next to each other.

"You see," Shelton continued. He held out the seedling. Pointed at different sections of it with the tip of his pen. He smelled of Old Spice and used bookstore dust. "In all of us, mitochondrial DNA is found in the energy-producing organelles of the cell called 'mitochondria.'" He peered up over the top of his glasses to make sure they were listening and paying close attention. "Most of our DNA is found in the nucleus of two types of what we call copies—nuclear DNA, which is routinely used for the typing you are likely familiar with. But also mitochondrial DNA, which is a shorter piece of DNA found in hundreds, I'd say, even thousands, of copies per cell."

Dickie and Anastasia shook their heads, as if to say, *Ah, now we get it.*

"If you come upon a scene, you should take samples of those plant species that might be out of character for that particular region. This way we can use this sort of mitochondrial DNA typing to wipe out other possibilities. It won't convince me. I'm already there. But you'll need this additional evidence when you prosecute."

"You get that, Rossi?" Dickie wondered how it was going to help them to find a murder suspect. Forget about courtrooms. He had made up his mind—this guy wasn't going to make it that far if they found him.

"I got it all, Shaughnessy."

The doctor looked at his watch. "I am stressed for time. Certainly, whoever allowed this 'clue' to escape onto the scene of this crime did not intend it to happen. That's one possibility. The other is, he *did* intend it to be left there. It's either a mishap or a deliberate attempt to confuse or say something."

Dickie and Anastasia took a breath. The professor paused.

"But then, of course," the doctor continued, "it could have been frozen. A test I ran indicated that it's dead. It would not grow, in other words, if we planted it. The flower it spawns is sometimes called the Dutchman's Pipe Cactus. Or the Night-blooming Cereus. The scientific term we use here is, *Epiphyllum oxypetalum*."

"Dutchman's Pipe sounds exotically erotic." Dickie raised his eyebrows.

"Great turn of phrase, Shaughnessy. Cinemax fan, I see." Anastasia laughed.

The doctor walked over to his computer and Googled "Queen of the Night." Dickie stood in back of the doctor's chair, waiting for the white screen to produce that list of water blue links.

"You see," Shelton said. He pointed to 7,230,000 hits the phrase returned. His glasses hung from a chain around his neck. He breathed laboriously, reminding Dickie of a chain smoker. "There are chat rooms and sites where you can buy these flowers. People today will start a chat room about anything—including the *Epiphyllum oxypetalum*."

Dickie was interested in this observation. "Make a note, Rossi. Maybe get inside a chat room, start talking like you're a young blonde hottie looking for these flowers. See what happens?"

Sounded totally *NCIS*, but what the heck.

"I need to run more tests. Call a few colleagues. Which will take some time. But I should be able to pinpoint where the seedling originated from and even track down its source within, say, a few dozen miles. Shouldn't be that hard with a little bit of patience, Internet searching, and study of the botanical patents filed for the species."

"Patents?"

"Correct. Each species has its own patent. Ever drive by a cornfield and see those signs along the side of the road with numbers on them?"

"Where are these flowers mainly from, Doctor?"

A strong wind blew outside, whistled underneath the cracks of the windows. They all looked out into the parking lot. The tops of the trees bent toward the east. A shiny, dark purple hawk with an orange beak and beady black eyes pecked at a squirrel carcass in between two yellow parking lines as a Lincoln Town Car with tinted windows drove up to the lab entrance and parked.

"Speaking specifically of the units traded on the Internet, most are from South America. They're imported into the states from buyers and sellers throughout the world. You see, Detective, people are attracted to the allure of her bloom. The *Epiphyllum oxypetalum* opens at night and closes before dawn. It's quite compelling. Brazil, I think, is the host country for the annual Queen of the Night Festival. You'll probably want to get your computer forensic people to amp up their end. There's probably an answer for you somewhere on this young girl's computer."

Dickie thought a minute. "What about eBay?" They had heard Lisa Marie traded on eBay, but the computer forensics lab hadn't found any sign of it on her computer.

"That is a possibility. Hold on." The professor Googled "Queen of the Night, eBay."

Hundreds of hits. There were literally dozens of eBay sites trading the Queen of the Night flower.

"Appears you two have your work cut out for you." Shelton scrolled down through all the eBay hits.

"In your opinion," Dickie paced in back of where the professor sat, "you think it's a dead end? I mean, like you said, this thing could have been on the ground for weeks— dropped there by some Boston College botany student."

"I did not say that, Detective. Please stick to the facts. Do not overstate my opinions." Anastasia didn't appreciate this guy's attitude. It was beginning to grate on her nerves. "What I *said*," he paused for a quick beat, "was that *perhaps* there's a chance the seedling could have been left at the scene a few days before your squad found that young woman. Seedlings are a lot like bodies, in a manner of decomposition. It takes time. In that environment, with moisture and a certain amount of protection from the elements, that time could be extended or sped up. Don't know. This is one of the tests I need to conduct in the lab." The doctor walked over to the coat rack near the exit, pulled his fedora off a hook, grabbed his trench coat and umbrella. He then took a peek at the clock on the wall. "I must be going if I am to make my flight north. As you can see, my car has arrived."

Dickie helped the old man put his jacket on.

"Thanks, Detective. These bones of mine sometimes do not want to cooperate."

Taking a look at Shelton decked out in his fedora, trench coat, white shirt and bow tie, an umbrella hanging from his arm, Dickie said, "Hey, doc, I gotta be honest with you. Besides the Amish beard, you've got this whole John Steed-Patrick Macnee-*Avengers* vibe happen'n." Anastasia looked on, puzzled. She was too young to get it. "I hope you're not holding out on us, like that secret agent, Steed. That would not be a smart thing to do."

"Don't insult me, Detective. Please. This is a two-hundred-and-fifty-dollar Vero fedora. Do I need to tell you what my clothes are worth?"

Dickie wanted to punch the guy in the face, but kept his cool. "So let me ask you then," Dickie said as they started for the door. "Hypothetically speaking. Let's say our vic was into these flowers and traded them on eBay. Would she have pollen or any sort of trace of these flowers on her possessions? Do they shed their DNA, I guess I'm asking?"

Neither Rossi nor Dickie could fathom a kid Lisa's age so engaged in the hobby of e-trading flowers. Her parents had said nothing about it.

"Of course. If she trafficked in the *Epiphyllum oxypetalu,* her bedroom, handbag, clothes, all of these would be covered with a fine layer of residue from the Queen that is quite easy to observe under the glass eye of a microscope."

Forensics probably overlooked this when they went through Lisa Marie's belongings. The scrub-down at the morgue would have taken care of any of it left on her body. "Anastasia, make a note to call forensics and tell them to FedEx any clothes taken from Lisa's bedroom up here to Mr. Shelton as soon as possible."

"That's 'Doctor.' Not sure I can get to that for you right away."

"Oh, I think you can, Professor," Dickie shot back.

Shelton looked at Dickie, who stared him down.

"Perhaps I'll make some time, Detective."

The big, beefy chauffeur dressed in black stood by the door of the Town Car.

"They treat you pretty good in Canada," Dickie said. "Shoot. Look at this."

"I'll be in touch, Detective." Shelton sat down inside the car. "A few more tests and I think I can break this thing open for you. I don't want to get into it just yet, but I have a theory. I may know who it is you're looking for. Driver, let's go."

Dickie and Anastasia stood, watched the limo drive out of the parking lot.

"So tell me, what stands out the most to you, Rossi?"

"If I had to pick something, I'd say that indentation on Lisa's back. This flower thing—it's probably meaningless."

"Did anything come back from trace yet? That mold Jake had cast?"

"Yep. No known source. They tested it against the FBI's database. Every type of vehicle they could. The idea was that she was put in a trunk and the backside of a bulb or some sort of instrument in the trunk made the indentation. But no one found a match."

The Town Car disappeared into the woods, out of view.

"Check into this douchebag professor's background for me, would you. I'm getting bad vibes from this guy."

"That's insulting, Shaughnessy." Anastasia tilted her head to one side. "But I'm on it."

Dickie didn't mean anything by it. He talked to Anastasia as though she were one of the guys.

"I suppose," Dickie said as they walked toward his Crown Vic. "You think you know what that indent is?" He opened the door and spoke to Anastasia over the roof as she held the passenger-side door handle across from him.

"I have my thoughts. Yes." Anastasia opened her door and got in.

"I knew it! What might that be, Rossi?" Dickie got in. Then, thinking about it, said, "I should probably take a leak before we go. This prostate of mine is not what it used to be, Rossi."

"TMI, Shaughnessy. And, yes, oh yeah, it's a handle all right. A briefcase handle. Or some sort of a handle on a box."

"That's pretty good, Rossi. Not only thinking outside the box, but inside of it, too."

She smiled, buckled herself in.

"Maybe Jake's iPhone will come up with something!" They had a good laugh between them. Dickie opened the door and stepped out. "Let me ask you, seriously now. What do you think of this seedling lead?"

"It's a ruse. Our guy left it to throw us off. Serials like to play tag, Shaughnessy."

"I might be with you on that." Dickie went to walk away, but stopped. "Let me take a piss and we can get back to the motel to pack up and go home. It's too quiet out here. Spooks me."

"I won't argue with you on that, Shaughnessy."

Dickie walked into the professor's lab. He had noticed a receptionist's office while they were inside. As soon as he got around the corner, out of Anastasia's sight, he found a landline telephone. He didn't want to use his cell phone. After taking one last look out the window, through the slit of the dusty blinds, making sure Anastasia hadn't decided to follow him, Dickie dialed.

21

MONDAY, SEPTEMBER 8, 10:00 A.M.

The man dressed as a mailman worked Saturdays, giving him Mondays off. This was the only reason why he had chosen the second day of the week to kidnap, torture, and kill Mary O'Keefe. It simply fit into his schedule.

Mary spent a few hours in adoration at a small chapel outside Brookline every Monday morning. How had the mailman found out? After Saturday's Mass, he walked out of St. Paul's and shook Deacon O'Keefe's hand. Congratulated him on such a "powerful and heartfelt" homily. "Your daughter," the mailman said, "what a wonderful young woman she is. So devout. The reverence in her eyes. My, my, are you a lucky father to have such a wonderful child of God."

The mailman disagreed with the Vatican's decision to allow deacons to marry and raise families. But who was he to question the magisterium's teaching?

Regardless, he now felt, in the scope of revenge, it had all worked out. Karma, he once heard—or, "the universe," what a joke—was like that, wasn't it?

O'Keefe smiled as though Mary had won a beauty contest. "Oh, thank you, my son. Are you ever so right." As they shook hands, the deacon placed his soft left hand over the top of the mailman's and tapped him gingerly in a comforting way. "She is blessed with such a grace and, I should add," he couldn't just leave it there, "going to adoration every Monday in Brookline, let me tell you," O'Keefe winked, "sure doesn't hurt."

File that one away. The mailman smiled.

He left St. Paul's, went to the library, did a quick Google search for adoration chapels in Brookline. And, wouldn't you know, there was only one on Mondays:

The Blessed Sacrament Chapel

Adoration of Our Lord Jesus Christ, 6:00 A.M. to Noon.

It was that easy.

10:15 A.M.

The mailman sat behind Mary O'Keefe inside the Blessed Sacrament Chapel and prayed to a Lord he did not believe in. As Mary recited the rosary in a whisper in front of the gold monstrance containing the consecrated, sacred host, the mailman could feel the palms of his hands sweat.

There were candles flickering on each side of the Body of Christ. The flame was soft and beige in color. He got lost in the gentle grace of the fire and black smoke billowing in swirls upward. The sight of this brought him back.

The furnace ... his nose pressed up against the grate. "No, Teacher. Please. Please do not do this. It burns. You're hurting me."

There were two additional devotees in the chapel. It was quiet, only the hum of a fan somewhere hidden in the drop ceiling buzzing to the soft breath of prayers.

At times, Mary folded her arms. She had gotten down on the carpet in front of the host earlier that morning, and prostrated her body on the floor like a novice taking her final vows. The mailman took careful note of this. He recalled once having to do the same for punishment at the Bainbridge orphanage. But not for bad behavior on his part.

As he lay there, face down, listening to the nun scold the child who had stolen food from the kitchen, he realized the punishment wasn't so bad. It had given him a chance to consider that no, there was no life for him in the Church. His calling was not to serve God. He had grown bitter by then toward a God who took everything from him. Southie, with its people lined up for block cheese handouts and gangs and drugs and welfare, wasn't Palm Beach, but it was home.

After an hour of adoration, he sat in a minivan outside the chapel in the parking lot, waiting for Mary O'Keefe to emerge. She lived a few blocks south. Whether she drove or walked made no difference to his plan.

He was impatient. It took intense concentration to ignore the pain. Thinking about it, he could cut himself now without thinking twice and treat one form of hurt with another. Emotional salvation, he liked to call it. Readdress existing objection. If Mary was there with him, inside the van, he could cut her open and get to the same place. Feel the same pleasure. There was rage inside him toward the Teacher. He could not express it alone. The man—the "powerful figure"—needed to be drowned out.

You will do what I tell you to ...

He dragged the sharp edge of the knife blade across his forearm slowly, closing his eyes.

Opening them, looking down, he watched as the warm fluid drizzled down the contour of his arm, clinging to its shape.

Ecstasy. He was swept away.

The blood of the innocent ...

"You will thank me," the Teacher had said, zipping up.

Instant relief.

He was drawn out of his trance memory by the sight of Mary opening the glass door. The blood still dripping down his arm, he tied a bandana around the small incision while watching Mary put a set of rosary beads into a little pouch, zip it closed. She held the door for the woman behind her.

Mary had a happy-go-lucky look about her. There was something fake about it, he felt.

He had put on his hoodie, a fake mustache he picked up at Party City, along with a standard, no-name security guard's uniform he bought online. That get-up, plus the sunglasses, made him look ridiculous and contrived, which was exactly the appearance he was after. Any bystander who saw him would soon say something like, "This security guard who looked like the Unabomber grabbed the girl and took off."

He pulled up alongside Mary, slid the door of the rental minivan open, then grabbed Mary by the hair. Pulling her down, he disabled her senses with a handful of gauze soaked in chloroform, then stuffed her in the back of the van, sliding the door shut. Driving over the curb, chirping the tires, the back end of the van bounced onto the street.

The young girl behind Mary screamed.

The minivan's license plate was covered with cardboard.

He drove out onto Route 9, into traffic, disrobing the disguise with one hand, the other on the wheel, placing everything inside a black plastic garbage bag. Doing this, he realized he probably looked like some villain from an episode of *Barnaby Jones* or *Hawaii Five-O*, and laughed at the image. Still, the important thing was that Mary O'Keefe was on her way to be sacrificed. He had just the right place in mind. For now, she needed that chemically induced sleep she was getting. The next twenty-four hours were going to be the worst of Mary O'Keefe's life. The path from this world into the next would involve every level of hell she had ever envisioned in her mind as she knelt and prayed day after day, night after night.

That and, of course, a power tool and a pair of pliers.

"Don't worry, Mary," the mailman said aloud, looking at her limp body in the rearview mirror as it rolled around in the back, "you'll make it to heaven."

22

Father John was in the confessional, waiting for a customer, the green light above the small room on. Jake made his way into the church through the double doors. Stopped, dipped in the font by the entrance to the nave, made the sign of the cross, and then questioned why, finally blaming it on habit. Father John heard him, came out, and patted the wooden pew in front of them.

"Sit down. Thanks for finding the time to come by, Jake. Can I offer you absolution today, I'm running a special?"

They laughed. "I'll pass, Father. Listen, about our conversation a few weeks ago—"

"Forget it. Faith is something we all need to keep working on."

"You know me. I question everything." Jake wanted off the subject. "Now, what can I do for you?"

"Well, as I said, it's Patrick O'Keefe. I'm worried about him."

They whispered as loud as they could. Being quiet in a Roman Catholic Church, Father John had instilled in Jake years ago, was a form of prayer in itself. The stained-glass window over Jake's back cast a starburst glow down the seat portion of the pew. Brightened up the tile floor. Jake appreciated the rainbow of colors. How they melded together. The room smelled of frankincense incense, bringing back too many memories for Jake to unravel.

"In what way, Father?"

"Threats. I'm getting these calls. You've been involved with this evil murder case."

"Yep."

The priest sensed despair on Jake's face, in his voice. Jake needed to catch this nut. It was beginning to fester inside him.

"Let's walk." Father John stood.

Jake dropped his head. It was hard to hide things from Father. Always had been.

"Unhappy, Jake? You have this aura about you, I don't know—an ambiguity."

"Who's happy, Father? Everyone is thinking about living another life, right."

"Indeed. Very few live in the moment."

"But that's not why I'm here."

"Right. I understand how much you have on your plate." Father John knew this was Jake's first murder case since that little girl. "How's your father?"

"Dad is fine, Father. Now, *what* am I doing here? Did my mother call you?"

"Jake, try not to allow the past to write your future. The little girl is in heaven. Forgive yourself. You'll drown in all that self-pity. It'll smother you."

There was more to this, Jake now understood. He had been conned into a talk with his parish priest. Jake's father, drunk from Alzheimer's, had wandered off from his Arizona home in the old people's community and disappeared the day before. Mrs. Cooper had called Father John and told him not to bother Jake with it. He was too busy. But Father knew better, so he let Dawn know.

Desert Winds Police eventually found Mr. Cooper strolling through the aisles of the local Safeway supermarket. He was standing near the shelves of soda, mumbling facts and figures about Sprite, Fanta Grape, and Orange Crush, which he had spent his life selling.

Jake was upset with his mother for not including him.

"She meant well, I know."

"She's human, Jake. Human beings will let you down. Your father lost a child. He didn't know how to face that. He found healing—in some strange way—in numbing that unbearable pain. I see it every day in this neighborhood. You know that."

"I need to catch this psycho, Father. For more reasons than you know. It's not about my father."

"Don't lose faith in yourself—dare I say it, Jake, the way you did in your father."

Jake shook his head. Could he argue with the priest?

"I had you come here for several reasons. I need to show you something." Father John knew it would cheer Jake up. "Been working on this for a while."

"How are things here? What about those threats, Father?"

"Okay. Always in need of more help and money, of course, but we're surviving. More than I can say for some of my fellow priests."

"And those calls? The deacon?"

"Ah, a few calls here and there. Idle threats all the parishes receive. I will say, though, this week I've gotten more than the usual. They seem to be centered on Deacon O'Keefe for some reason."

Jake followed the priest, who moved quite sluggishly. They walked down into the basement hall where the church held its post-mass socials and dances. There was a stage. Folding chairs and craft tables. A coat room. Men's and women's restrooms. The salt-and-pepper checkerboard tile on the floor was sixty years old and looked it. Along the wall were dozens of what appeared to be class photos. Some in color. Others black and white.

Jake didn't recall seeing them before. But then, it had been three years since he'd stepped foot in this part of the church.

"You ought to come for coffee after Mass more often, Jake."

They reached the north wall of the room.

When they stopped, Father John, one hand in the front pocket of his black pants, the other holding the right earpiece of his glasses in his mouth, pointed with a wink at the wall. "That's every class we've ever had here." There was sense of appreciation in his voice. It was as if the hundreds of kids were his own children. "Just finished gathering all of the photos. Took me forever."

Jake scanned the images. What memories. Here was an eclectic mix of Irish-Catholic kids from Southie. Many were dead. Suicides. Overdoses. Drive-bys. Stabbings. More were in prison. The boys wore the Roman-style cassocks with the white surplice. As the years passed, the Church introduced a white linen collar with a large black satin bow. The type Jake had worn.

"All of you added your own bit of grace to this parish over the years. You should feel good about that, Jake."

There were fourteen boys in Jake's class. The photo was of their final year as servers. They stood on a stage, lined up from shortest in front, tallest in back. Most smiled, their crooked teeth from being on Welfare clear. The two boys bookending the rest of the class held beautiful bouquets of vanilla-colored flowers with purple diamond-shaped petals.

"I don't even remember taking this." Jake had a tough time taking his eyes off the photo. He perused the names. "Haven't thought about most of these kids in years." He laughed under his breath, more to himself. "I've actually arrested a few of them."

Like Jake, many of these kids chose being an altar server over getting beat up every day in the projects they came from. It was a way to stay off the street. The Coopers were not poor by any means, but that just made life worse for Casey and Jake.

Father John said, "I think about how much I wanted Casey to be in one of these photos. But I searched and searched and could not find one."

They both went silent. Whenever someone mentioned his brother's name, Jake got those butterflies in his gut.

Jake was fixated on his class photo, probably running through a host of recollections. Some good, others not so good. There he was—the little Catholic soldier, standing tall, proud to be a part of God's army.

"Boy, Father, I was a nerdy kid."

Father John was in his own world. "Evil has insinuated itself into our lives *and* the Church," he finally said. "I think people forget that. The press certainly does. I don't need to tell you this. You see it every day."

Jake looked at the priest. *Here we go*, he told himself, *Father John stepping up on his soapbox*. Then focused on one boy who caught his attention. Black hair. Braces. Large, mousy buck teeth. Skinny and gaunt as a scarecrow. Something about the kid rubbed Jake the wrong way. *Who the hell is that?*

"We're involved in a cursed period of humanity, Jake"— Jake studied the boy, not really listening to Father—"and babies still come out of the womb sinless, their pink little bodies and cherub nature inherently established by God. Faultless, Jake. But give them a few years and they're assaulting His name. Why? Because we've taught 'em to."

"Society stirs up the flames, Father. We all make choices. You know the old argument—not every child that's abused abuses."

Who is that kid? Jake knew him.

"Sociology is supposed to solve all our problems, or so we're told. But in the end, we realize that's nothing but wretched ignorance on our part. The realism here is, we are sinners. We breed sinners. And all of us—including you and me, Jake—need to grow in moral goodness every day of our lives."

The overhead air duct fan kicked on. It made a loud intake sound, as if a fire had found an oxygen source in the form of an open door.

Whoosh!

Jake turned to Father John. "You've been reading. Sounds like a Harvard way of saying we have free will." As he said it, Jake thought of Mo—that little "favor" Mo had asked Jake to do. Mo wasn't going to let up. There was a conversation he had with Mo earlier that morning in the squad room. Every talk was now an argument. *"I pulled you out of the ghetto, Jake,"* Mo shouted. *"You seem to forget that so easily. I made you. You were a junkie. A numbers runner. Afraid of your own shadow. Always looking at the worst of things."* Most of it was untrue, Mo hoping the boys in the squad room would hear him. *"Why don't you go run to your priest friend. You're still a punk. You let some stupid case, one little dead girl, destroy you. And you thought you could run with those Southie boys? Shit. You're lucky I plucked you out of there—they would have eaten you. You're a cop because I allowed you to become a cop."*

That face. The kid. His dark eyes stared back at Jake.

"I've been praying, Jake. We don't trust a priest *because* he's a priest. We trust a priest because he's holy."

"Kids see a uniform—cop, fireman, security guard, soldier—and they trust what the uniform represents. A priest in vestments is about the most sacred uniform a human being can wear. Come over here, Father. I need you to look at something."

"I'm not making excuses here, Jake." Father walked toward the row of photographs. "Don't get me wrong. If we do everything naturally, we become barbarian perverts—all of us. Cruelty, lies, injustice. All that comes 'naturally' to many of us. Don't forget that."

"Like this animal I'm looking for, you mean? And those Satanic priests touching kids." Jake had left the Church during the sex abuse scandal. He couldn't investigate priests and then take Communion from their friends.

"Exactly. But he is a child of God, too. As are those fractured clergy."

Jake laughed. "Please. He is a child of Satan—same as those priests." Jake tapped on the face of the boy in the picture. "Who is that, Father?"

"To resist evil inclinations of nature takes discipline, Jake. You know that." Father John leaned in to get a closer look. "It takes fervent prayer. We need a Divine Presence in our lives. This man you're looking for didn't have that. I'm sure of it. I'll have to go to my list about the photo—I don't recognize the boy."

23

MONDAY, SEPTEMBER 8, 5:42 P.M.

A Grand Pause in a musical score is a break, strategically placed in the middle of an unfolding drama. It is there to fool the listener into believing that something bigger is imminent. Getting Mary O'Keefe onto his 32-foot fiberglass Trojan fishing boat, *The Grand Pause,* turned out to be trickier than expected. The dockside was bustling with people. Probably the weather. It was a pleasant, warm night. One of the last few of the boating season. The whole-belly clam shacks were open. The dockside tiki bars still allowed patrons to sit outside by the water. The harbor actually had a fresh smell to it. No dead fish or diesel fuel smog soiling the air.

The mailman had a stiletto switchblade with a pearl handle poked into Mary's back underneath her shirt. He whispered threats into her ear with his hot breath— something about gutting her father and returning with his liver for Mary to eat raw. It was enough to keep the deacon's daughter tamely walking by his side, groggy as she still was from being knocked out.

People looked. But the mailman and Mary appeared to be lovers, gently embraced, a little buzzed, heading off on a beautiful late-summer evening boat ride.

Beyond Boston Harbor, out in the open waves of the Atlantic Ocean, Mary O'Keefe drifted in and out of consciousness. The after-effects of the chloroform gave her a terrible migraine and she started vomiting.

"You're cleaning that up," he shouted into the wind, steering the boat. "Not me. That is friggin' gross."

On her knees, trying to keep her balance, Mary wiped her chin with her forearm. Every once in a while, she turned and looked up at her kidnapper.

"Pathetic, Mary. You're just a piece of flesh."

It took almost two hours to get to the destination he liked. No one was around for miles in any direction, just the open seas. Mary could scream until her vocal cords tore into raw nerve endings.

"I hate to have to sacrifice you, Mary O'Keefe." The mailman maneuvered the boat to face the east, stalled the engines. He had a tongue-in-cheek tone to his voice, patronizing Mary. "But your father did so many terrible things that I don't know where to even begin to illuminate you on the facts. You do deserve an explanation. I understand this part of it. But I am the one in control of this ship"—he laughed at his stupid joke—"and I do not feel the need to give you one."

6:12 P.M.

They were anchored in an area outside Boston Harbor where you could look in all directions and not see land. By now, Mary O'Keefe had accepted her fate. This madness was somehow God's plan, she figured. Her destiny. Her cross. Yet as insane as it seemed to die by the hand of this maniac, Mary had found her vocation. The truth was, as Mary sat in adoration earlier that morning, she hadn't told anyone, but she'd made a decision. Heading north, as her father announced to the parish without telling her, was not what Mary wanted to do with her life after all. It was her father's idea. *His* dream. Mary wanted to concentrate on acting school and travel with the theater. She believed Christ saved the world and repenting was one way to enter into the Kingdom. But she didn't want to devote her life to the cloth like her miserable father. He was a fraud. She did not want any part of being a liar. When she was bedridden sick for a few months one time, the deacon made Mary feel as if she was some sort of burden. An invalid taking up his time and wasting his money. The things he had said to her when she asked for something. Now she hated him for it; and yet, at the same time, had forgiven the man.

6:44 P.M.

As the mailman scanned the outer waters of Cape Cod Bay with binoculars to make sure no one was around, he spoke to an unresponsive Mary O'Keefe. She was lying on the deck of the boat in back of him, one arm over her forehead, the other on her stomach.

"You see, Mary, for the same reason that there is good and evil in this world and people question 'God's plan,' there is really no rhyme or reason as to why I chose to kill you. Some might say I am taking revenge on your father. And that may very well be true. But it is a subjective opinion." He wiped his brow as the wind kicked up and whitecaps crested on the swells. It got much colder as the sun set beyond the horizon. "To sum it up, Mary, you are, simply, the chosen one."

Still nursing her queasy stomach, Mary acted as though she was drifting in and out. While trying to gain her composure. The mailman walked over, grabbed Mary by the back of the head. Looked into her eyes. Studied her for a moment. There was no reason, he deduced, to tie up this pathetic woman. Her being seasick and still suffering from the effects of being knocked out was a sufficient enough prison for the time being.

Mary remained silent. A moan here, a deep breath and gag in her throat there.

The mailman's sonar told him the ocean floor was 350 feet below the boat. The swells calmed. If they were lucky, the mailman considered, standing on the deck, looking out at the rising moon, a humpback might surface and take a breath, put on a show.

"Incredible animals, Mary. The sheer grace. You can understand grace, can't you, Mary?"

He turned his back to his victim, walked over and took his murder kit out of a padlocked storage bin below the steering column. He set the thing on the seat and unfolded the knife set from a rolled-up pouch in which a barber might keep an inventory of scissors. One finger on his lips, he stared at the serrated knife.

Well, what do we have here ...

While lost in his own selfish satisfaction, a loud splash came from the stern of the boat.

Startled by the noise, he turned. It sounded as if someone tossed something overboard.

"Mary?"

She was gone.

24

Seeing that photograph in the church rec hall had set the wheels spinning for Jake. An idea sent him off and running. He called home, told Dawn to eat dinner without him. He needed to go see an old friend.

"Sure, babe. I'll make a plate and put it in the fridge. You want me to wait up?"

"No. Sorry, honey."

"I love you."

"Me, too."

Lots of couples used the phrase. But what did it mean— *me too?*

Dawn could sense that Jake was focused. Once he set his mind on something, that was it, there was no stopping the guy.

As Jake started for home from St. Paul's, it had hit him. He recognized the kid in the photo as Joe "Bags" Cane, a three-time Southie loser who Jake had arrested for all sorts of crimes. Robbery. Bookmaking. Crack dealing. You name it. Cane had even once started a pyramid scheme and ran it out of Old Colony Project. Jake had grown up with Cane. They hung around the church together as kids, trying to stay out of trouble. And yet it was a double homicide Cane got involved in that Jake thought about as he went in search of his old buddy.

The Ted Williams Tunnel into East Boston was closed because of the collapse, inspections, and repairs. So Jake took the Tobin Bridge over the Mystic River into Chelsea and Revere.

Cane hung out at a pool hall inside a bowling alley near Malone Park on Warren Avenue in Revere. Jake knew he'd find him there, probably trying to con some insurance exec stopping in for happy hour—tie loosened, top button undone, the dude half-drunk—out of his mortgage payment.

The rain started as Jake got off the Tobin. He drove into the end of town where the oil tankers docked and that smell of fresh gasoline enveloped the inside of his car.

Cane's past mattered little to Jake. The fact that he was tied to a Cambridge homicide just recently was where Jake got interested. One of the victim's legs had severe lacerations, as though someone had taken a knife to her. Cane was never a suspect in the sense that he killed the woman. But during his last bit, a three-year run for turning over a Korean grocery and beating the owner into a stupor, he claimed to know a guy who had some information about the case. No one ever followed up after D-12 failed to locate the snitch. But Cane convinced the DA to reduce his sentence for the info. Now was a good time for Bags Cane to pay for that free ride.

Jake unloosened his tie and unbuttoned the top button on his shirt, walked in, and spotted Cane by the video games in the back of the bar. He passed butcher-block Formica tables, chipped and carved up with patrons' initials, in between vinyl red booths with silver duct tape covering the rips. The bartender stared at Jake with a look that said he had five minutes.

Cane played an old-school, beat-up Pac-Man machine from the eighties pushed up against the back wall. Jake snuck up behind him while that annoying *wok-wok-wok-wok-wok* sound followed the Pac-Man around as it gobbled up blinking dots.

The jukebox was in the middle of Frampton's "Do You Feel Like I Do" and that strange guitar part where Frampton talks and plays his guitar at the same time.

"No kids around to swindle out of their paper route money tonight, Bags?" Jake put his arm around Cane's shoulder, gave him a strong squeeze, letting him know who was in charge. Cane wore a jean jacket, cut up and greasy. He had a blue bandana wound thick around his head like a gangbanger. A wallet chain hung from his back pocket. He got his nickname Bags from the Reilly brothers in junior high. Because Cane's dime bags of weed were more like nickels, the name stuck.

Cane didn't turn around. He looked at Jake in the reflection of the glass covering the screen. "Detective Cooper, hey, man. Long time, no see."

"You're rockin' that whole nineteen-eighty-three Bruce Springsteen, 'Born in the U.S.A.' look, huh. Doesn't suit you well, Bags." Jake turned to see who was watching. Some white dude with dreadlocks, wearing a visor cap, a pencil-thin mustache, was talking on his cell, staring down at the floor. The bartender was playing a game of liar's poker with two regulars sitting at the bar. It was clear to Jake no one gave two shits about Bags Cane.

Jake certainly had no respect for guys who dealt dope to kids. Cane had started with weed, graduated to crack, acquired his master's in heroin. Real scumbag, Jake knew firsthand. Cane was a guy who needed to be manhandled with that same street mentality he responded to.

"Let's go, Bags. Outside."

Hanging over the pool table behind them was one of those square Schlitz lights left over from the seventies. Two guys stood with pool sticks butted to the floor. They drank long-neck Buds. Laughed about something. Near them, some chick argued with her boyfriend on a pay phone.

"Come on, Jake. I ain't done nothing.'"

"Outside, Bags. We need to talk."

"I'm playing a game here …"

Wok-wok-wok-wok-wok. Frampton was guitar-talking those words from his song still.

"Looks like you got high score, too." Jake smiled. "That's too bad." He grabbed Cane by the ear and pulled him toward the door. "Do you feel like I do, Bags?"

No one paid attention.

"Jake, man, what are you doin'? You cannot embarrass me like this. Ouch, man. Stop it."

"Long time, Bags. How ya been?" When they got outside, Jake gave Cane a good push and he stumbled on the sidewalk. Almost fell. Jake looked both ways down the block. "Over there." He pointed. "Lean up against my car."

"What the hell do you want, anyway? I'm clean, man."

Jake patted Cane down, just to be sure. "Tell me about the tip you gave in turn for that get-out-of-jail-free card the DA handed you. The Cambridge case."

"Not sure I know what you mean." Cane leaned with his back up against Jake's car. A neon OPEN sign in the front window of the bar flashed red on his face. Part of its glare shone red along Jake's blue suit. It was dark. Cold. The streets had a shiny glaze from a misty drizzle. The music was still playing inside the bar, but it sounded muffled standing outside.

"I'm going to say this once more. Then I'm going to hurt you, simple as that. That tip you gave D-Twelve detectives to get time chewed off your last bit. The Cambridge murder, asshole. The one where the dude got all crazy with a knife. You have five seconds."

Jake walked over and, without warning, slugged Bags in the face.

"Shit, Coop … what was that for?" Cane said, spitting blood on the ground, holding his mouth.

Cooper cocked his fist back and held it.

"Oh, that one," Bags said. "Yeah, I think I recall now something about it." He kept rubbing his ear and chin. "You really hurt my earlobe, Jake, you know that. Now my chin, man … what the fuck."

Jake moved closer. "Come on. Don't fuck with me here, Bags. It's late and I'm in no mood."

"Look," Cane glanced right and left to make sure no one was watching them, "there's this guy out in Framingham, weird dude … likes to order the whores with limps and weird sorts of things wrong with them. Dead eye. Freakish scars. He's whacked, man. Screwed in the head. He, like, keeps knives and stuff on the walls next to posters of movies like *Hostel* and *Saw*. Collects serial killer memorabilia. Heard he wanted to pay ten K for any piece of clothing related to that JonBenét case. One of Charlie Tex's girls ran out of his house all freaked out was what I heard in the joint. She couldn't go back on the street for months. Said she'd never go back to the dude's house. I guess he wanted to pay her all sorts of money to cut on her legs as he was getting off. He showed her these snuff photos he said he bought on eBay. Called them four dead blondes. You know, like that band from the eighties—"

Jake interrupted. "Name?"

"Look, I don't know. All I—"

Jake moved nose to nose with Cane. "Name, Bags."

"I just know where he lives, man. Come on. Back off."

Bags pulled out a pack of cigarettes. Jake grabbed it, took one out of the sleeve, crumpled the pack, and tossed it.

After lighting the cigarette, Jake pulled out a pad from an inside pocket. "Draw me a map. If it's wrong, I'm coming back."

25

What the mailman didn't know about Mary O'Keefe was that she was a two-time all-American swimmer for Northrop High School before an illness saddled her. Not that she could swim to shore. But what if Mary had been able to finagle one of the small life rafts free from its ties? Several minutes had passed, he quickly realized, since he had taken his eyes off his victim. That was plenty of time for Mary to untie a raft and jump into the water.

"Bitch!" he screamed into the darkening skies above him, the stars now beginning to shine. "You are going to wish you …"

Mary was not afraid of the water. She could probably find her way somewhere. Maybe not back to the harbor. But damn it all, she might be able to find life again by morning. She had no chance aboard *The Grand Pause*. Mary was a survivor. She needed to do whatever she could. God's plan or not, she wanted to live. This was all rather clear to the mailman now that she was gone.

After the splash, he ran over and checked on the life rafts.

All were accounted for.

He panicked. Looked down into the water. Anxiety rose in him. From one side of the boat to the other, he walked the deck. Held his forehead. Scolded himself.

"Mary?"

Where was she?

"Mary? Mary?"

Nothing.

He paced. Rubbed his temples. Shouted. "Bitch. Bitch. Bitch. I am going to find you. Then I am going to *gut* you from belly button to throat and watch you *bleed*. You should have never done this!" Spittle projected from his mouth as he screamed over the side of the boat. "Do you realize what you've done? Oh, Mary, I was going to be nice. I was going cut your spinal cord first so you didn't feel anything—'a poor man's epidural,' the coroner would call it at the morgue. But now you will suffer. You bitch. How could you *do* this."

With his favorite knife in hand, the mailman walked back and forth, pacing. He needed to figure out what to do. He had lost control of the situation. It was the first time he had felt a sense of losing control since he started killing. And he didn't much like it.

The furnace. His hands tied behind his back. The Teacher.

"Don't hurt me, no …"

What the hell happened? He let Mary O'Keefe have a little bit of freedom and she took advantage of it. Damn, she had lied about being seasick. She had fooled him.

He thought of sitting down, cutting his thigh deep, teaching himself a good lesson. It would relieve the pain. But as he put the knife to his skin and began, an idea stopped him.

He stood. Found his search light. Scanned the water around the boat, lighthouse-like, paying careful attention to anything in the water that moved. A ripple. A splash. Any noise.

He realized rather quickly, however, that seeing a person out on this water at this time of the night, you had a better chance of reaching up and touching the stars.

He had let his guard down. *Damn-it-all*!

Dropping the light. "Mary!"

What would it hurt, he thought, not tying Mary O'Keefe up way out here? How far could she go? He had control of the radio. He padlocked the life rafts. No one was around for miles. All his weapons were locked up. She had vomited most of the way out here, for crying out loud.

There was nothing but water.

"Mary?"

Where there's a will ...

And now his next victim was gone. Poof! Swallowed up by the darkness. Mary O'Keefe was going to ruin everything.

26

MONDAY, SEPTEMBER 8, 8:09 P.M.

There was a pulse of discontent and anger surging through the mailman's veins as he wondered how he was going to fix this problem.

"Mary … oh, Mary … where are you?" It was a game now. He could not let the young woman know that he was in stage-four panic mode. So he mocked.

"Mary?" He talked slow and peaceful.

Rain came down heavily, large droplets drenching the deck of *The Grand Pause*, making loud popping noises on the fiberglass. Off in the distance the sky brightened in flashes as lightning zapped the water in near perfectly staggered Harry Potter bolts.

The mailman stopped. Another idea. This one better.

He stood with his hand on the ignition key.

No.

Yes. Turn on the engines and make a series of passes around the area. He thought about this while grinding his teeth. His temples, two small drum skins, pulsating like a frog's throat.

He was just about ready to crank the engines over, when …

8:15 P.M.

Mary O'Keefe was underneath *The Grand Pause*, floating

with the slow, up and down motion of the swells. Her toes were numb. Her blonde hair as soaked and salty as algae. Despite the grim outlook she faced, Mary relied on the same faith that had gotten her through all those lonely nights in her room by herself, rehabilitating from that bout of mono.

"'Seek good and not evil. Hate evil and love good.'"

She whispered passages from the Old Testament to herself she had memorized as part of a penance Father John had once given her.

The back of Mary's head was inches away from one of the engine's two window-fan-like propellers. She didn't know how close she was to having the back of her scalp peeled off by the blade—a sharp knife through the end of a watermelon. As much as Mary O'Keefe knew about swimming, she knew nothing about boats. She could not see two feet in front of herself out here in the darkness. She'd found a pocket of space inside the engine cavity. It was enough to keep her head above water while holding on to a steel bracket. Yet unbeknownst to her, the back of Mary's head was in the direct path of the propeller.

8:25 P.M.

The mailman started to crank the ignition key to the right. The engine turning over once would provide enough power to the engines to slice a good chunk of Mary's head clean off.

No … wait …

Another idea stopped him.

The mailman lowered the rescue boat, a small rubber raft, down into the water.

A splash.

He climbed onto it with a search light, then tied the small boat to the stern of the main vessel with two hundred feet of rope. He used an electric trolling motor to maneuver his way around *The Grand Pause*.

Mary stayed still as a bobber.

"Come on, Mary. It's over. I will find you." He sounded as if he and Mary were playing a friendly game of hide-and-go-seek. "I tell you what, Mary, if you give yourself up, I'll go easy on you."

He laughed.

There were quiet splashes of waves cresting and falling over. Gulls squawked overhead, but he couldn't see them. The rain had stopped. A white beam of light from the moon trembled reflectively across the water. The mailman focused on it. The menacing shadow clouds were gone. Tomorrow was going to be a beautiful day.

Mary was out here somewhere. He could almost smell her cheap perfume.

"Come on, Miss O'Keefe. You're a million miles from nowhere." He was twenty-five yards south of the main vessel. His searchlight passed over Mary's head twice already.

8:34 P.M.

Mary stayed composed. She thought about what to do. As she let go of the bracket to rub the salt from her eyes, a great swell came up and pushed Mary out to sea. She swam, pumping her legs with all her might. Her teeth chattered. All she thought about was dying out here, in the water, alone, without a hand from God. She'd heard drowning wasn't such a bad way to go. It was like being drugged, she'd read. You delight in the euphoric nature of a slow death after accepting your fate and allowing that first full breath of water to fill your lungs.

She heard him. "Mary?" That light again. A flash. It scanned over her head, just missing her. "Mary O'Keefe.

Now you come back home to me, darling, so we can finish what we started."

"'Let justice surge like water.'" Mary prayed. She tasted salt on her lips. Her eyes stung. A cut on her elbow burned as though rubbing alcohol had been poured on it.

She saw him motor around to the bow. With his back to her, in one quick move, Mary gave everything she had, swam out a few feet, hopped up on the back of the boat deck, then ran for the steering console.

Start the boat and take off.

It would work. She had thought it through.

Yet what Mary had failed to consider was that he had taken the keys with him.

The mailman was crazy—yes. Stupid—no.

Mary looked around in dread. Where was he? She couldn't see him. He had turned off the light.

Pray.

"'The man brought me back to the entrance to the temple, and I saw water coming out from under the threshold.'" Tears ran down Mary's face. Her whole body shook. She kept repeating the psalm.

8:45 P.M.

He stood quietly at the bow. Mary had her back to him, her head down, hands on the steering wheel. When she turned, Mary O'Keefe dropped to her knees.

He wiped a wrist across his forehead, aimed the crossbow at Mary's chest.

"I told you, Mary O'Keefe, you cannot hide from me out here."

That soldering iron in his hand. "If you say anything at all," the Teacher breathed in his ear, "I will finish what I started."

He squinted one eye, brought the bow to shoulder level, aimed it at Mary's heart, pulled the trigger.

Mary closed her eyes, her lips moving in one final prayer.

For safekeeping, he walked over, picked Mary's limp body up, exposing the right side of her neck, and slit her throat.

The blood gushed. A stream of it, like a burning wick, ran down a groove on the deck of the boat. White against red. Such a contrast.

"This is the cup of my blood," he shouted. He dipped two fingers into Mary's exposed larynx, then wiped the blood across his face, underneath both eyes. He stood still. Then took out his filleting knife and sharpening steel—that long, round tubular wand-like apparatus chefs use at carving stations—and ran the blade across the grooves.

Confident his knife was sharp enough, he looked down at Mary. Before making that first cut on her leg, he felt a strong sense of letting go. Such joy. A numbing high, as if he'd taken a tranquilizer.

The dawn of a new day. I win.

After the initial buzz of the kill wore off, every splash of blood on the boat irritated him. He knew it was going to take the rest of the night to get the deck clean. He'd be on his hands and knees, scrubbing and cursing Mary.

Then again, what did it matter?

As he rested the edge of the knife on Mary's shin, he knew what he had to do with Mary's body once he was finished. It would send a direct message to those investigators he had plastered all over the walls of his living room. Yes, he was going to speak to them now. It was time to say something. Mary had pushed him into it.

When he hit bone, he put the knife down and picked up the hacksaw.

They think they're *smart?* He sawed back and forth, back and forth. *I'll show them.*

27

TUESDAY, SEPTEMBER 9, 9:48 A.M.

The last place Angela Bizzetti wanted to be on a Tuesday morning during the second week of her sophomore year was aboard the Boston Tea Party Ship. "It's not even, like, real," Angela told a friend as they stepped on the school bus. "It's a replica."

The ship was an accurate model. The hull was tar black, with two yellow pinstripes running bow to stern, two masts centered perfectly on the vessel's deck. Beyond that, it was your typical tourist trap. People from Wichita who had never been to Bean Town were wowed by the vessel. And that was the idea.

"Smells like dead fish," Gina Belanger said as the children stepped off the bus and filed into a single line in front of the boat.

"Rat shit," Mark Tassel shouted, getting a roar from the group.

The boat swayed to the motion of the bay as the children, antsy and impatient, waited for their guide.

"He's not bad looking," Angela said, staring at the guy as he made his way to the front of the line, a clipboard in hand.

"I'm glad it's rather chilly this morning," the guide explained, "because on that cold night, December 16, 1773, when a group of patriots, disguised as native Americans, raided three tea ships like the one in back of me, dumping their cargoes of tea overboard and into the Boston Harbor to show their distrust of the King and disloyalty to taxes, all of your little iPod, text-messaging, boy- and girl-crazed lives changed forever."

As the guide explained the rules of the ship, Angela tapped out and sent a text to Bernadette Alden. Angela was pissed about what Bernadette and Marcus Hardy had done the previous night in the storage room of the Abercrombie and Fitch.

YOU SKANK. U 2 BETTA HOPE

I DONT FIND YOU. 4 2DAY YOU

SAFE. 2MORROW YOUR ASS MINE.

The tour guide wore jeans, a blue hoodie, SAVE THE WHALES written on the front, DON'T BUY CORPORATE COSMETICS on the back. He was able to project his voice like an opera singer. "The rebellion would have started about right here." He pointed to an area near the stern. The props—a chest, boxes of tea—looked like leftovers from the set of a Peter Pan play.

It was an awful thought: Sandy Duncan in green tights.

The ship was crowded. Boys and girls bunched together, talking, joking, making fun of how people lived back then. Their teacher stood with folded arms, captivated by the guide's tutorial.

"The rebel boycott reached a terrible climax when a band of irate colonists raided these British tea ships on Griffin's Wharf, right here, where we're all standing."

Angela got a text back.

LOL! WTF. BITCH. LET'S GO. ANYTIME.

"Look at this, Jackie." Angela turned the screen toward her friend.

"As they dumped the three-hundred-and-forty-two tea chests into the harbor, the rumor is that they all shouted what are now infamous words, 'Taxation without representation.'"

"You betta not, like, let that skank get away with that," Jackie said. "She stole yo man *and* dissed you?"

Angela tapped out another text. As she did, something fell on the screen. It startled her.

"What the …?"

The wind whipped a flag above them. It sounded like a sheet hanging from a clothesline on a blustery day.

The substance that dropped on Angela's cell phone screen was red and tacky, thick and creamy, the texture of Tabasco sauce.

"What in the heck?" Angela said. She couldn't figure it out.

Then she felt several taps on her shoulder.

Was it raining?

Angela and her two friends stood below the front mast of the ship. It was the only section of the boat you couldn't see getting on. Angela looked up instinctively, hoping to see the source of the red droplet on her screen. As she did, her mind didn't quite register at first what her eyes focused on.

Mary O'Keefe's legless, naked corpse was strapped about ten feet in the air, where a yardarm crossed the mast. She hung there as if some sort of a grotesquely dissected Christlike figure. Mary's chest cavity was filleted open. It was clear that her insides, at least partially, had been crudely removed. Her legs were lopped off directly below the knees.

Angela couldn't take her eyes off the dead woman as blood droplets peppered down onto her neck and into her mouth.

Then she screamed, a piercing howl startling everyone aboard the ship, grabbing their attention, beckoning them to gather around.

A gust of wind kicked up as mayhem ensued.

Two dozen teenagers ran for the exits at the same time. Two or three of them jumped into the water, swimming for the dock.

The tour guide stood on the deck staring up at Mary O'Keefe, calling someone on a walkie-talkie he pulled from his back pocket.

The devil had done his work aboard this ship, tainting this stop along the Freedom Trail forever. Generations of future schoolchildren would climb aboard the ship, then point—"Right there, on that mast. That was where the girl saw the dead woman with no legs, her insides hanging out of her like *The Walking Dead*."

28

TUESDAY, SEPTEMBER 9, 1:45 P.M.

Lieutenant Ray Matikas had an obsessive-compulsive nature about him when it came to locking the doors to his office, drawers in his desk, and the elephant-gray cabinets that contained files he needed to keep private. With the call of a legless body hanging aboard the Tea Party Ship, Matikas made the appropriate shout-outs from his office, rallying the troops over the radio to head out to Dorchester Avenue. Just so happened, Dickie was on the road. Jake too. No one had seen nor heard from Anastasia Rossi in hours.

"I want everyone there ASAP," Matikas shouted, tearing out of D-15's parking lot.

Jake called in immediately. "What'a we got, Lieutenant?"

Matikas passed through several red lights, siren blaring, pedestrians stopping to look as the tires on his Crown Vic squealed.

"Just get your ass over there, Cooper. Looks like it's connected to your case."

Jake's chest tightened.

1:47 P.M.

Back inside the D-15 squad room, one person lagged behind purposely, waiting for this moment when everyone was gone. The few blues hanging around, a Vice detective and two cops from Patrol, were in the locker rooms arguing over how the Red Sox had blown the third game of an important series against the Yankees.

Upstairs, the young cop at the front desk was calming a screaming wife. She said her husband had beat her up and took off with the family nest egg. All thirty dollars of it.

"I need you to relax, ma'am," the officer said, "and start at the beginning."

Getting by the front desk was not a problem for the intruder. Opening Matikas's office door, however, was not going to be as simple.

Even though the intruder was good with a lock pick, it took a few tries. Then, making sure the coast was clear down each end of the hallway, a twist and a slight push with a Visa card and *pop* … the door opened.

The intruder was in.

The file cabinets were a breeze, same as Matikas's desk. It was dark in the office with the blinds folded down.

Flipping through several manila folders, the intruder uncovered a file marked *Echo 1-Echo 2.*

"Ah, yes … the gold mine."

TUESDAY, SEPTEMBER 9, 2:28 P.M.

Looking east from Congress Street into Boston's Inner Harbor, standing on the bridge over Four Point Channel, the sky had turned menacing and mad. It had that dark gray color to it—same as you see on the Weather Channel in one of those tornado-hunter videos from Kansas or Missouri. A few cloud tails drifted downward, funneling, moving slowly in a vortex. Looked like ink being poured into a swirling glass of water. Yellow crime scene tape blocked off the dock leading to the Tea Party Ship. The Congress Street bridge was closed on both sides. The presence of the tape made the wharf look as though some sort of Revolutionary War movie was being filmed on location. The slight mist and increasingly darkening skies didn't help. The wind whipped. Having a ship like this as the scene of such a gruesome crime, reporters and television satellite truck crews jockeying for position on the other side of sawhorses, you worked under a microscope.

Matikas ordered squad cars parked on both sides of bridge, facing each other, lights flashing. The white sheet covering Mary's hanging corpse was staged in a circus tent-like fashion around her body so no one could see or take photos. Think of a cable lineman working on a telephone pole in winter under a canopy. You get the picture.

Jake and Matikas stood below Mary's body, looked up. Their gold badges against black leather pouches dangled from their necks on long chains. Both men shook their heads in disbelief and for several minutes, neither spoke a word.

Breaking the silence, Matikas said, "Holy shit, Cooper. This is unreal."

Waves crashed up against the sides of the ship. White caps crested over the swells in the channel. Keeping steady on the boat became a job in itself.

"Where's Shaughnessy, Cooper?"

"Don't know, Lieutenant."

"Fat bastard should be here."

"Does it always have to be personal, Ray? Damn. Look at yourself, for crying out loud. You could stand to eat a peach now and then."

Matikas didn't answer. He was paying careful attention to Mary's stubs. "Can you believe this? Look at her. Press gets hold of this, we're fucked."

Jake checked his watch. He, too, wondered where Dickie had run off to. And Anastasia, where in hell had she gone? Were they working together on a lead he didn't know about? Jake thought maybe it was time to pull in the reins on those two and get control of his team. It took a true leader to earn that respect back. They might say no one forgets. But cops remember everything.

Studying Mary, Jake realized he was now part of a case that had become much bigger than a homicide investigation. This was in a different league. He even caught himself looking away, wondering if he could now ever come out of this case with a sane head. It was a cliché to say that homicide cops latched on to vices—booze, drugs, sex, gambling—after a career of dead bodies. Yet Jake could see himself falling in, not being able to crawl out of that same hole.

"If we don't come up with something soon, Cooper, we're done. You got *anything* yet? How 'bout that super-duper, high tech CSiPhone piece of shit of yours?" Matikas lit a cigarette, titled his head back, blew the first drag up in the air. Then stared at Jake.

"I need a bit more time here. It's only been a week. Let's all just take a deep breath. Chill out. I'll turn up something soon."

Neither had to say it. Their killer had sent a message. The Optimist, as the *Globe* branded him, had turned a corner. He was now speaking to Jake and his team directly.

"A boat," Jake said. He twisted his neck, stretching it from side to side.

"What'd you say, Cooper?" Matikas kept his eyes on Dickie as he walked the dock. "Has Shaughnessy qualified lately at the range, Cooper?" He took one last drag from his cigarette, looked at the end of it, flicked the butt in the water.

"Not sure, Lieutenant, why don't you ask him?"

"What's this about a boat, Cooper?"

"Only way this guy could have gotten her up there like that was with a boat. That video surveillance along the docks would have picked him up otherwise."

Harbor Patrol motored up the channel by the Tea Party ship. Jake watched it go by. The driver waved. Jake nodded.

"Don't be so sure of that, Cooper."

Dickie walked up, gave the lieutenant a hand wave. He had a scorned child look about him. He knew what was coming.

"Where the fuck you been, Shaughnessy?"

"Takin' care of business, Lieutenant." Dickie stared at his boss.

Jake looked over from behind the lieutenant's shoulder, smiling at Dickie, wagging a finger at him.

Dickie looked up at the victim. "I had a feeling … shit."

Jake and Matikas turned.

"What do you mean?" Matikas asked.

"Well, I sensed a religious tone, maybe even motive. Now I know for certain."

Jake had thought the same thing as he studied the way the body was presented. How the killer had left her spoke to a man with issues against Christianity. The scene would be forever etched in Jake's mind, a blasphemous intent written all over it. Did their serial have a vendetta against the Church?

"Our guy could be a victim of the Church sex abuse scandal?" Matikas offered, thinking out loud. They walked to the stern after Jake suggested they view the crime scene from a different angle. The rain started without warning, as if someone had suddenly turned it on.

"Wasn't Anastasia with you, Dickie?" Jake asked.

"No. I thought she was at the station. You haven't seen her?"

"Nope."

"Cooper here seems to think a boat was involved."

"I'll go there, too, Lieutenant. There's no way one man could get a body up that high by himself."

"He docked off here, let's say." Jake explained, pointing, looking toward the side of the boat that faced the open ocean. "In the middle of the night, he hoists her up on that mast with a pulley system of some sort he has on his boat. All fishing boats are equipped with a hoist to load bait and remove the catch of the day."

"Like on *Deadliest Catch*, Lieutenant. Those crab cage hoists."

The lieutenant sighed. Massaged his temples.

"Vernon," Dickie shouted.

An officer in blue ran over. "Yeah, Dick, what's up?"

"Listen, I want a canvass of this entire marina along the Channel. All the fishing, private and party boats, et cetera. I want every boat accounted for last night."

Jake interrupted. Thought about the look that guy had given him. "Including Harbor Patrol," he added.

"Yeah," Dickie echoed. "Where they were? What time? Find out if anyone reported a boat in this area of the channel late last night. Haul their ass in if you run into a problem. Got me?"

Officer Banks flipped his police cap, covered with plastic, dripping wet from a harder rain that had picked up. The wind blew west, throwing the downpour in slanted sheets.

"Okay," Jake said, yelling over the sound of the rain, covering himself with his jacket, "so he docks off here. He hoists her up there. Tacks her arms. Ties off her elbows with that rope and duct tape. Then ties her knees, right above where he cut off her legs, to the mast with fishing line." He shook his head at the thought of the description. "He's grabbing whatever is available to him. He didn't plan this part well. Then he speeds away? Something's not right here. We're missing a step."

Jake walked over to the body, stared upward, covering his face by making a visor with his hand, as if blocking the sun's rays.

"That's *your* problem, Cooper," Matikas shouted. "I have a crapload of paperwork to get done. I'm not about to stand out here all afternoon, getting soaked. You need to start thinking about a specific type of killer. Call in that FBI profiler." He snapped his fingers. "SA Talbot. Get me something I can work with." Matikas watched Anastasia Rossi work her way through the officers guarding the docks and onto the ship. "I cannot bring your theory of a boat and pulleys and strange characters in the night to brass, Cooper. They're already up my ass. I need something tangible. Like a fucking killer!" Whenever Matikas became irritated, he spoke in English and Lithuanian. "You've got, what, three bodies now? Three!" He held up the appropriate amount of fingers, then said something in Lithuanian. "All blondes— all with their legs missing."

Dickie laughed.

"Funny, huh. This is hilarious, isn't it, Shaughnessy?" Anastasia walked over with her forensic tackle box in one hand, flashlight in the other. "Hey, glad to see our CSI could make the party. Rossi, how are you?" Matikas threw his hands up in frustration, walked toward the exit. "Follow me, all of you."

"Sorry I'm late, Lieutenant. Cooper. Shaughnessy." Anastasia gave head nods to both.

"I'm wondering, Lieutenant, do you think in that funny language of yours, or do you think in English?" Jake mocked.

"Up yours, Cooper. Laugh all you want. But damn it all, get me something today, before we're all in a heap of shit. If the press makes a connection to the Church, it's gonna get nasty." Matikas walked off the ship, stopped halfway across the little catwalk, put a hand on the rope railing for balance, turned around. "I don't need to tell you, Cooper, that the hourglass on your career is almost out of sand."

Jake, Dickie, and Anastasia turned, went back to the mast where Mary's body was strung up.

"I want this entire deck swept tonight, Rossi," Jake said. "Outside of the ship, too. Pay particular mind to rope burns and markings on the side of the ship facing the water. Things like that. Text me a brief on what you find by the end of the night."

"We know who she is yet?" Anastasia slapped on a pair of latex gloves. "Damn, it's pouring out, huh." She took a poncho out of her box, stretched it open, placed it over her head.

Dickie went off to get that info. Anastasia and Jake waited. "Hey," Jake asked in a semi-whisper, looking around, "you get a chance to check that thing out for me yet?"

Anastasia fiddled with her flashlight, turning it on and off. "Not sure I can do that, Cooper. I kinda feel dirty about going in there."

Dickie came back. The rain made a tinny sound, almost as if hail was falling on a metal roof, as it hit various sections of the canvas sails.

"Looks like, um, from what the blues are telling me, she was identified by one of the kids on the tour. Said he recognized her from church. It looks like we got us one Mary Margaret O'Keefe, thirty-one. She lives in …"

"… Brookline," Jake finished for Dickie, looking up at Mary, "with her father, who's a *freakin'* deacon at St. Paul's Church. I knew she looked familiar. Sonofa*bitch*." Jake unfoiled a piece of nicotine gum. Chewed it violently.

"You know her?"

"Yeah, Dickie. Of her, actually. I know her father, Deacon Patrick O'Keefe." Jake thought of Father John wanting to speak to him about the deacon. Was there a connection? Maybe more to what Father John knew but didn't want to say?

"Incredible. If our guy knew that, he's got some serious issues with the Church. Maybe an abuse victim?" Anastasia turned to get out of the windblown path of the rain, pulling her arms inside the poncho.

"We've been down this road already, Rossi," Dickie said.

"I better get over there and tell Father John and the deacon myself." As Jake spoke, they all turned. There was a commotion going on over by the catwalk entrance to the boat. Two blues were arguing with a man. With the rain pelting harder, it was hard to make out who was who.

Jake moved closer. *Mo. Shit.*

"I'll handle this," he said to Dickie and Anastasia, who looked at each other with an embarrassed turn-away of their heads.

"What do you want? Let him be, fellas. It's cool." The two blues went back to guarding the entrance. Jake walked up to Mo.

Mo brushed himself off, as if he had been manhandled. "You boys know who I am? … Jake, how are you, buddy?"

Jake could smell the booze, even through the steady rain. "Mo, I'm working here. This is not a place for you. Not now."

That hurt. The student dictating to the teacher what to do. Mo felt two feet tall. "Just wanted to stop by and see if … you know, if I … I could help out." Mo looked up, saw Mary. "Shit almighty. What the hell?"

Jake didn't want to deal with this problem anymore. "Mo, you have to get—"

From behind Jake, Dickie interrupted. "What happened to you, Blackhall? They called you the 'King of Southie' at one time. More collars than any cop on the force. You busted the Bulger crew when other cops were afraid." There was anger and hate in Dickie's voice, coming from somewhere deep. Jake had never heard him like this before. "I remember you were once talked up as the *reason* why Bulger's crew broke up. Some said you—by yourself— turned Bulger into an FBI snitch. I often wondered, what in the hell happened to Mo Blackhall to end up like a skid row bum? Look at you." Dickie turned his head to the side and spit.

Jake was concerned. Why was Dickie getting involved? Why such animosity between them? Jake could feel both his left and right carotid arteries throb to the beat of his heart against the damp tightness of his necktie. He stuck a finger inside his shirt and loosened the wet collar up some.

Mo smiled a drunkard's smirk, staring glassy-eyed at Dickie, wiping his rain-soaked face off. "Shaughnessy, you are something. The shit-ass nerve you got telling me"—he pointed his right forefinger into Dickie's chest—"what *I* was. I could quash you like a bug. Have you cut up into pieces by those same assholes I used to pinch—"

"Hey, now, none of that," Jake said. Mo and Dickie moved toward each other, face-to-face. Dickie pushed Mo. "That's enough!" Jake got in between, pulled Mo away, grabbing him by his shoulder. "It's pouring out here, Mo.

We got work to do. Murphy?" Jake caught the eye of a blue. "Get him home."

"Right, Cooper." The linebacker-size cop took Mo by the arm, led him away.

"Watch your back, Shaughnessy," Mo mumbled, tripping over his own feet.

Dickie and Jake walked back toward Anastasia. "What happened to that guy, Jake? I've been quiet and stayed out of this long enough. I cannot stand to watch him bring you down."

"Wish I knew, Dick. But I'll fight my own battles on this one, got me."

Dickie didn't answer.

Anastasia bent down near the base of the mast, kneeling directly underneath Mary's stubs. The rain had washed Mary clean of any trace, which had pooled into the rainwater and drainage where the mast came out of the deck. There were hairs and what appeared to bits of flesh and gray duct tape. "I'm betting," Anastasia said, picking something up off the ground with a pair of tweezers, staring at it, "this was mistakenly left here by our guy."

"What's that?" Jake walked closer. Dickie right behind.

"I don't see any red, white and blue paint on this boat— at least none with this metallic texture." She held up a small paint chip. It was the size of a fingernail clipping. Anastasia peered at it with a spyglass lens connected to one eye, like a jeweler. "Seems our guy got a little sloppy."

"You wanna bet he left that paint chip here for us to find?" Dickie offered.

"Just get it to the lab, Rossi. And get me that damn report." Jake rapped his partner on the shoulder, started walking away. "Dickie, let's go."

30

TUESDAY, SEPTEMBER 9, 6:19 P.M.

She had her blonde hair pulled back, set in a braided ponytail. She wore large, Clark Kent, black-framed glasses with thick lenses. "Coke bottles," the high school kids called them, giggling. From behind, standing like she was, she looked to be about thirty-five. Yet that was a guess, since all he could see was the contour of her heart-shaped ass filling out that ankle-length denim skirt. She was bent over. Her head buried in a file drawer.

The mailman stopped at the Revere Public Library on Beach Street on his way home from work. Walking into the red-brick building, spotting the woman, he took a look side to side and started toward the counter. A plastic holder with different colored free bookmarks—red and yellow and orange and turquoise—noted the library's address, website, and hours of operation. Odd, he thought, that she was the only librarian around. The Info Desk was generally a busy place this time of the evening. Students studying for tests. Mothers and daughters and sons looking for SpongeBob and Stephenie Meyer books. Where was everyone?

What luck—*Alone in a library with a blonde*?

He walked with a road-tested, smooth grace, not making a sound. He had practice at this, sneaking up to mailboxes while vicious dogs slept on the grass. She was focused on her Dewey Decimal system filing project. He had one shot at her.

Not three feet away, he stopped. Something told him no. But then he took another two steps. He was close enough to grab her by the throat and drag her down the stairs into the basement of the building. Nobody would see a thing.

"I called earlier today, ma'am," he said. He took off his hat, twirled it in his hands. "About an article in the paper. Well, several, actually."

His voice startled her. She turned quickly, put her hand over her chest, gasped. "Oh, my goodness! You scared me." Then she laughed at herself.

"Sorry 'bout that, ma'am. Didn't mean to."

She found the counter and sifted through a pile of Post-Its. "I remember the call, yes." Her breath almost back, "It's in here somewhere." She lifted the little yellow papers, having trouble unsticking them, reading each one. "I remember you … hold on one minute, please." Then, "Ah-hah, here we go."

Looking at her, face-to-face, he could see the beginnings of crow's feet at the corners of her eyes. She had another chin starting to form. "Take your time."

She's too old. He heard the Teacher speak to him. *Choose carefully.*

"I have it right here, yes." She picked up the yellow paper. "Cooper. You called and asked about a Detective Cooper. Am I right?"

"You got it." A smile. "That's him."

The mailman wanted to learn as much as he could about the man in charge of catching him. He had articles about Jake and D-15's supposed "super squad" taped to the north wall in his living room. But he knew little about how Jake solved cases or his past.

"You were interested in any articles published in the *Globe* or *Herald* about Detective Cooper." She blinked her eyes fast, thinking, titled her head to the right. "Something about putting together a scrapbook for him. He's a friend, I assume?"

"Indeed, you have a great memory." He looked down at the photocopier next to her desk. Taped to the top was a sign written in black Magic Marker on white copy paper: **.25¢ PER PAGE**. The tape was yellowed. The paper old and torn at the corners.

"We get this all the time. People want old newspaper clippings. Class or family reunion coming up, am I right?"

"Right again!" He looked around for more people. But couldn't find anyone.

The librarian signaled for the mailman to follow her toward the microfiche area of the library. Soon, they arrived near a series of large cherrywood tables with green and gold desktop lamps. The mailman was overwhelmed to see that the librarian had pulled out all of the old newspapers containing the key words "Cooper, Detective, Boston Police," and had them ready for him.

"You never gave me a first name for your friend. But I found a Jake Sundance Cooper." She smiled, palmed the top of the stack of papers. "I hope that's your friend's name. I mean, how many Jake Sundance Coopers could there be on the Boston Police force, you know what I'm saying."

"Good old Jakester," the mailman said with a Grinch grin. "The Sundance man. I thought for certain I told you his name. Huh. Sorry 'bout that. Jake and I, we go *way* back."

"If you need anything else, don't hesitate to ask." She looked down at a forefinger nail she'd chipped while tapping on the table.

"You're the best. Thanks so much."

"Just doin' my job."

Me, too, he thought, sitting down at the table, a stack of newspapers in front of him.

The first article was dated early last year. Jake had hit a parked Mercedes as he chased a gang-related drive-by suspect. No pictures. No mention of anything personal. Yet it was clear to the mailman that the press did not like Jake

Cooper. The headline accompanying the brief article giving that away.

ROGUE COP IN TROUBLE WITH
BRASS ONCE AGAIN

The mailman had considered Googling Jake and his squad. But he wanted to smell the ink on the page, stare at the photos in their original context. The computer was overrated, he had told coworkers who asked him why he wasn't interested. He didn't keep one at home. He used the library's whenever he absolutely needed to. A computer was a good way to get caught, he knew. One mistake online and the feds were banging on your door. Same with a cell phone. Technology was great. Sure. But when you didn't want to be found, you had better have alternative ways of getting your information.

The next article showed a photo of Jake standing in front of several pounds of hashish. He and four DEA agents had confiscated the drug from an informant Jake was using while investigating the murder of a Korean grocery clerk. Jake stood with his broad shoulders and firm chest filling out his white dress shirt. He looked younger, happier. His eyes were slits, his cockiness still not yet squeezed from him by the loss of the little girl. His dark hair was slicked back around his ears, curling just below his jawbone. He had that Crockett and Tubbs stubble.

BOSTON PD DETECTIVE BLOWS MURDER CASE
TO SOLVE LARGE-SCALE HASHISH RING.

This is fun.

The mailman looked through a series of articles that didn't offer much. Jake's name popped up because he either played on the BPD softball team when he was a patrol officer, or made some sort of real estate transaction for his parents. Then Lisa Marie's killer turned the page of a recent newspaper and saw Jake standing, the Public Garden over his shoulder. Jake had that *no comment* look, his hands up in front of his face. There were microphones all around him. There was an air of defeat about him. Lisa Marie's murder had shaken the color out of the guy.

BOSTON POLICE DETECTIVE WILL NOT COMMENT ON DISFIGURED BODY FOUND IN PUBLIC GARDEN.

Interesting …

The mailman recognized the article and was sure he'd even cut it out and put it up on his wall. But at the time Detective Cooper was not part of the case, he believed. Staring at the detective now, the mailman never thought he would find himself tied to this cop in such a personal way.

Six degrees.

The article said something about Jake being given a "second chance" to "redeem a career that is up in the air," outlining how it had been "hindered, some sources claimed 'destroyed,' by a stint in a mental hospital after solving the case of a Brighton girl who had been raped and buried underneath the porch of her neighbor's home." With a smile, he read how Jake had dug the girl's fresh body out of the ground with his hands after "torturing" the burial location out of her killer. But Jake had failed to get to her in time. More than that, Jake had beaten the guy so badly, most of the important evidence he had collected throughout the investigation was tossed out of the trial. The guy walked.

The mailman got gooseflesh while reading the story. He felt a sense of satisfaction in being the one to bring Jake back into the game. Getting inside Jake's head was going to be easy, the mailman now knew—especially with *that* history.

He turned the page of another newspaper and there was a photo of Jake, Dickie, and Anastasia. They were crouched down, examining something on the ground near the bike path in the Garden.

The seedling. He looked up, picturing himself placing it there, smiled.

Anastasia was looking toward the camera—the only cop credited with a quote. Jake's name wasn't mentioned.

"We have a feeling our victim and her killer knew each other. Beyond that, we're not prepared to say anything more. But if anyone has information about this case, please contact the BPD immediately. We've set up a hotline."

He wrote the hotline number down on the back of his hand.

While skimming through a newspaper four years old, the photo jumped off the middle of the page. She was stunning. Much more so than he would have imagined. So beautiful, in fact, the paper had printed her photo in color. Dirty-blonde hair, razor cut, stylishly on a serrated, biased pattern to the curve of her shoulders. She had those supermodel cheekbones, sharp and chiseled. Caribbean sea-green eyes. Above all that, her smile showed off her flawlessly aligned, white teeth. He thought she had the most gorgeous button nose a woman could ever hope to have without surgery.

DAWN COOPER, STANDING BESIDE HER HUSBAND, BPD DETECTIVE JAKE SUNDANCE COOPER, SMILES AS THE COP DEDICATES A MEMORIAL TO HIS FALLEN BROTHER.

Sundance and Dawn. Mr. and Mrs. Cooper. Lovely.
Reading the story, the mailman learned Jake had taken up a collection for three years. Then purchased a stone monument to celebrate the heroism his brother displayed in Desert Storm. The dedication was placed at the entrance to Thomas Telegraph Hill Park in Southie on Pacific.

The mailman tore the photo out of the newspaper. He could cut the jagged, ripped edges off when he got home. He stuffed it into his pocket, got up, started for the exit.

"Is there anything else I can do for you?" The librarian yelled from behind the counter. She was reading a James Patterson novel. Her glasses down to the tip of her nose. Raised eyebrows, she looked at the mailman over the top edge of the frames.

"Oh, no. I have exactly what I need. I do thank you. Jake is going to *love* what I have planned for him and his wife."

31

WEDNESDAY, SEPTEMBER 10, NOON

Jake sat on the bench seat outside D-15. He stared down at the screen of his iPhone. The sun was bright in a cloudless sky. He scrolled through the notes he'd made the past few days. Several thoughts came as he ran the new program D-15's tech support had raved about. "Operation Bull's Eye" was the name the techies gave it. All you had to do was answer computer-generated questions—*WHERE WAS THE BODY FOUND? HOW? CLOTHING? AGE? KNOWN SOURCE OF DEATH? WEATHER?*—and add your own thoughts and theories as you developed them into an empty space box. When it was ready, the program spat out a profile of your killer. Jake had spent many sleepless nights going over things again and again. Writing notes. Deleting thoughts. Adding details he hoped would help move the program along. With everyone else on the squad laughing at him, Jake felt it certainly couldn't hurt to give it a try.

He sat and watched the screen with anticipation.

NOT ENOUGH INFORMATION TO PROJECT PROFILE, the phone shot back.

"What's missing? Damn it."

Considering the Tea Party scene, an idea struck Jake that he needed to head out to Framingham. It was time to pay a visit to that sadomasochistic scumbag Bags Cane had told him about, and confront the dude head-on, poking a finger in his chest for information. Jake knew he wasn't their man.

But the guy could maybe point them in the direction of a cult, or some sort of underground society that got off on cutting up women.

Dawn pulled up in her Accord. Stepping out of the car, Dawn carried a plastic Stop & Shop bag. She had picked Jake up a salad and his favorite, mac and cheese, topped with breadcrumbs.

Comfort food.

"What's this?" Jake stood, kissed Dawn on the cheek.

"I can't go out." They had made plans to meet and sit by the Charles River and have a quiet lunch. It was a gorgeous end-of-the-summer day in Boston. The swans would be out in numbers. Those annoying, yet humorous, Duck Boat tours would motor by, tourists taking photos of the graceful fowl. It would have been fun. "I have an appointment with Denny Garcia. Something came up. He's acting out. I don't know why. I thought I was helping …" Dawn sounded stretched to her limit.

"Sit. I want to hear all about it."

"I wish I could. But I can't." Dawn looked down at her watch. "I have fifteen minutes to get back."

That freakin' job. Dawn needed to be home, working on her master's, writing, doing research, taking care of Brendan, conversing with the neighborhood busybodies. Jake hated the idea that she was tied to a time clock. Things had been so calm when Brendan was home, before kindergarten. Dawn enjoyed her life then. All she did now was run from one place to another. The working soccer mom.

Jake walked over, kissed his wife on the mouth. After that, he held Dawn by the shoulders, stared down into her eyes. "Relax, honey. You can do this. We'll figure it out."

"Reminds me. I need to tell you about Denny Garcia—"

"I know, I know. That professional insight." Jake stepped back, put his hands in his pockets, jiggled the loose change.

A flock of pigeons fluttered down from the ledge of the building after a guy on the bench tossed some seed.

"Unless you want to rely on a cell phone to tell you what the make-up of your killer is. Jake, serials grow into the role through trauma. You know that. I studied Bundy in college. I'm telling you. Denny can help you glimpse into that world."

"You've been OD-ing on DVR'd episodes of Dr. Phil again, haven't you, Dawn? Anyway, my guy is nothing like Bundy."

"Write me off, okay. I get it."

"So I'll keep me eye on Denny when he gets out of high school."

"I have to go. We'll talk about this later."

Jake knew Dawn only wanted to help. She yearned to dig into something and come out of it with an *ah-hah* moment. *Look, Jake. Look what I found!* It would make all of that time away from home worth something.

As they walked toward Dawn's car, Jake's phone buzzed. "Hold on," he said. "Don't leave. … Yo, Dick. What's up?" Jake didn't take his eyes off Dawn as he listened.

"We got ourselves a hot lead, Detective." Dickie sounded excited for the first time since the case began.

"The seedling?"

"Well, sort of still working that out. No, this is bigger. Come on. Hurry. We're heading out now. I'm in the back parking lot."

"What is it?"

"Couple of blues were questioning a friend of Lisa Marie's and scored."

Jake put his iPhone away. "Gotta run, Dawn. Don't worry about Denny. Do your best. That's all you can do, right?"

"I won't give up on this kid, Jake."

"Of course not."

Jake leaned in through the window and pecked his wife on the cheek. She watched him run toward his car around the corner. He turned before disappearing, "Eat that mac and cheese, okay."

12:25 P.M.

Across from D-15, on the opposite side of Harrington Street, he sat on a park bench near a fountain. The small stone-lined garden housed a granite statue of Lady Justice. On a plaque in front of the lady were the names of Boston's dead police officers.

The mailman had some time to spare for lunch. So he decided to sit outside the precinct and get a better look at the man in charge of investigating him. Not for a moment did he consider that he would run into Dawn, too.

Watching Dawn get out of her car and approach Jake, he held up the photo. It was then he realized the picture in the newspaper had not done the woman any justice.

Wow.

Dawn Cooper was a true hottie. An eleven!

While waiting for Dawn, Jake spied the mailman sitting there. But considered him to be just another city worker enjoying one of the last few warm days of the year. It had rained so much over the past few days, it seemed everyone was outdoors.

After Dawn drove away, the man the *Boston Globe* had dubbed the Optimist walked into D-15. He went up to an officer sitting at a chest-high desk inside a cage, asked if he could use the bathroom.

The officer pointed to the left. There was a sign—a funny cartoon picture of a keystone cop sitting on the toilet eating a donut—on a door marked THE LOO.

"It's really not for public use, but since you're a quasi-government employee, what the hell."

"Thanks for nothing."

Inside the bathroom stall, the Optimist unzipped his pants. In the process of relieving himself, he thought of how much he had accomplished thus far. Here he was, inside Detective Jake Cooper's world, having stalked Jake and his wife, and no one suspected a thing. It was such a simple pleasure. Such a wonderful way to enjoy the game. The next murder had to be personal, he knew. Jake needed to feel it.

His mood changed as he went to zip up. It happened this way sometimes. Going to the bathroom forced him to look down. Once in a while, those grotesque scars carved on his shins stood out and spoke. On each leg were the marks left behind from that moment in the basement with the Teacher when life went from bad to worse. Those two letters, so grossly stamped—skin welds—by that man, were a reminder of what he had been made to feel like all these years.

The human stain.

That's why he wore the handcuff key around his neck as a pendant—to remind himself that he could escape from anything. Any time. The Teacher could no longer hold him hostage.

He flushed the urinal. Buckling his pants, he couldn't stop his mind from spinning backwards in time. This was when hurting himself meant the most. When he cut, it stopped the pain. The memories stayed, but fogged over. Yet he couldn't chance it here. Not the restroom. He had to let the recollections flood him.

That knife. The fire in the furnace. The Teacher had him by the throat, forcing him down the stairs.

"It's time. You resist, you're dead."

But just like that he was back inside the bathroom. Looking at himself in the mirror. Washing his hands with that foamy soap, drying them under the hot air.

But the screaming in his head was too loud.

He stared at himself, through the reflection in the mirror.

"Leave me alone ... Stop touching me like that. I don't like it."

Total recall. The Teacher walked over to a table set up amid the cobwebs hanging from the dirty pipes in the basement of Bainbridge. In his mind it was a movie. He watched the Teacher pick up a soldering iron that looked an awful lot like the hair curling iron he remembered his mother once using on him. The Teacher bent down. Rolled up the boy's pant legs. Then he screamed as the Teacher carved the letters into his shins, branding him for good.

"No ... no ... please ..."

"I would cut your legs off," he heard the Teacher whisper in his ear, *"but I cannot keep you alive at the same time. I need to teach you to have control if you are to carry out my plans."*

The Optimist was back in real time. Walking out of the bathroom, he realized how gratifying this game he had begun months ago with Alyssa Bettencourt at Quincy Market now was. The past and present had juxtaposed so well. With each victim, a small part of that moment in the basement was erased. And soon, with this next victim he had planned, every tear would be wiped away.

32

Barton Colby was white as milk, his face frozen. Two blues stood at the doorway. Another pair were stationed at the end of the driveway. Dickie and Jake stood in the kitchen. Barton's father, Dr. Nathan Allen Colby, was handcuffed and told to sit on the living room floor. Mrs. Colby was in the foyer, hyperventilating, talking fast, gasping for air while trying to speak to the family lawyer on the telephone.

Instead of heading to Framingham, Jake followed Dickie to the Colby house. The blue colonial was about a mile from the Taylors'. Barton was good friends with Lisa Marie. Narcotics came up with a tip that Barton was stealing his father's prescription pads. Barton Colby was the local high school Oxycontin dealer.

"Operating a drug factory is a serious crime," Dickie said to the elder Colby. "You're a doctor, sir. Oxy is a prescription-only drug. Let's see how this looks. You're writing out scripts for your neighborhood friends. Trying to make a few extra bucks to pay off that breast job you just bought your wife."

Jake raised his eyebrows. "Sounds like ten years in the federal pen to me."

They had Barton Colby in a squeeze. Seeing his father bound like a criminal, Barton was going to open right up. Questioning teens was tough. They protected themselves, even if a best friend had been abducted and butchered. Jake had sent a team out to question Lisa's friends. Not one of them had mentioned Barton. It was clear the fear was in being found out themselves. Still, what if Lisa was one of Barton's customers? If so, the stakes had changed. Buying drugs would put Lisa in sections of the city Jake had not yet connected her to. The theory Jake was working under had Lisa being swiped off the street by her killer as she headed home from the library.

"Maybe he needs to go downtown, Jake. Maybe get tossed in with a few dudes that like middle-age, gray-haired doctors who get their nails done at the salon. What are they calling them now, heterosexuals?"

"*Metro*sexuals, Dickie." Jake looked up in the air.

Dickie called for two blues to come get Mr. Colby. A motorcycle roared by outside the house. A nosey crowd of neighbors gathered at the end of the driveway.

"Hold on. Hold it!" Seventeen-year-old Barton Colby stood from his seat at the dining table. He had been rubbing his temples. Thinking. His leg bouncing. "Just wait a damn minute." Barton wore a tattered T-shirt, black, a dragon on the front, red Chuck Taylor Converse sneakers, ripped jeans, and gauge earrings.

"Something you need to tell us, son?" Dickie walked toward the boy.

Barton's mind raced in ten different directions. He tried to figure out what to say. Or how to say it, actually. Whatever information he divulged was an admission of something illegal.

Barton stepped into the kitchen, brushing shoulders with Dickie in the doorway. The granite countertop sparkled from the overhead light. The stainless-steel fridge with French doors was restaurant big. The floor tile was Italian. Certainly, imported. "Listen, I can help you guys. Just take the cuffs off my dad."

Dr. Colby grimaced. He hadn't said a word. His wrists burned, the skin rubbing against the metal and bone.

"We're investigating a possible narcotics ring here, one that might involve murder. Your dad is a grown man." Dickie looked toward one of the blues. "Officer Martin, take that scumbag dope-dealing doctor out to your car. Get him to D-Twelve. Lock his ass up."

"Wait, man. Just wait a minute."

"Martin, take him away."

A blue on each side, Dr. Nathan Colby was hoisted off the floor, carried out of the house like an Occupy Wall Street protestor going to jail.

Jake stood next to Barton. Kicked out a stool along the marble breakfast bar. "Sit down, kid."

The other blue in the house knew enough to walk Mrs. Colby outside. That left just Dickie, Jake, and Barton Colby.

"You're screwed, kid." Dickie leaned over the boy's shoulder, spoke in his ear. "You're going to jail. We know you're writing your own scripts."

"Dickie, relax. Give'm a chance. Lisa Marie, Barton, let's start there."

A routine arrest led to the Colby house. A couple of high schoolers in a BMW had been stopped outside Fenway Park after running a light. The cop spotted a bag of dope the passenger tried hiding underneath her thigh. As soon as the blue mentioned the pot, the little rich boy started shaking, crying. "I can help, I can help … That girl who was murdered; she went to my school. I heard that this kid, Colby Something, was selling her Oxy. Word is that Colby gave her an overdose, covered up that crime by knifing her."

The tip was off. But here they were. In Barton Colby's house asking him about Lisa. All because an astute cop knew enough to bring the information to Narcotics, who took it to Jake.

Teamwork. Sometimes it actually worked.

Barton put his face on his palms. Elbows on his knees. Rocked back and forth. The hum of the refrigerator kept the pace in the background.

"Take a breath, kid. Relax a little. Begin with Lisa's buying habits."

"That's just it, man. She was not a user." Barton looked up. Stared at the kitchen appliances lined up along the countertop. "She just liked to hang with me over here to get away from her nagging parents. Freakin' father of hers is a weirdo. I think he liked to touch her."

"She ever tell you that?"

He shrugged. "No."

"When was the last time you spoke to Lisa?" Jake pulled up a chair. He put a foot on it. His knee was level with Barton's chest. Dickie opened the refrigerator, took out a Coke. Barton didn't turn to look. He could hear the sharp metallic crack of the lid followed by the fizz of tiny bubbles bursting inside the can.

"I'm not really sure. I was so wrapped up in that game, that stupid friggin' computer game. When she came over and talked, you know, like, I wasn't listening. She'd hang in my room. Sit down on my beanbag chair next to me. Say stuff that was bothering her. Watch me play. She'd tell me what she was doing. What was going on at home. But the game. I listened and nodded and didn't hear anything she said."

"I bet you wished you did now. All that, 'Why wasn't I there for my friend?' bullshit." Dickie took a slug of his Coke. Continued: "Hindsight, kid. It's the plague of the guilty."

"I didn't *do* anything."

"Any text messages from her we can look at? Emails? Letters? Notes?" Jake wanted to stay focused on getting a lead out of the kid.

Barton Colby dropped his shoulders, a telltale sign that he was ready to talk. Then he stood.

"Whoa there, cowboy." Jake put a hand on Barton's shoulder. "Sit your ass back down. You move when we say so."

"I'll take him, Jake. What, you want to go upstairs into your room?" Dickie put a hand over his stomach, burped. "'Scuse me there."

"Yeah."

Jake motioned that it was okay. As Dickie and Barton walked up the stairs, Jake wandered around the den. He looked at family photographs. Flipped through address books. Notes the family left one another on an antique rolltop desk. *Pick up bread. Drop dog off at vet's. Honey, we need to talk* ...

Pretty normal dysfunctional American family, from what Jake could tell. No love in the notes. All business. A family on the run.

Jake walked into a second living room. One of those with furniture nobody ever sat on. It was spotless. A photo above the fireplace featured Barton and Lisa Marie. They over-smiled. Wore graduation hats and gowns. Held diplomas in hand like relay race batons. A pair of best friends getting ready for high school. They were younger. Eighth grade, Jake figured.

Dickie came in carrying Barton's cell phone. "Holy shit."

"What did you find?"

Barton Colby stood in the kitchen. He had both hands in his jean pockets. Shoulders slumped. Eyes on his sneakers, withdrawn.

"Text message from Lisa right around the time she was killed." Dickie held the phone up as if he were in an ad for it.

"You're kiddin' me?"

There were several, actually. Most were meaningless in the scope of the investigation. Normal texts between kids. WHAT R U DOIN 2 NITE? PIZZA? MOVE-E?

But then ...

CANT DO DINNR ...

2 BY THAT THING

"Sit back down, Barton." Dickie pointed to the sofa. "There."

The boy fell on the soft leather couch, which swallowed him up.

Jake stared at the text. Then sat down on the coffee table in front of Barton. "Okay. You see it? Now tell me what it means."

Barton stared at his nails, picked one of them with the other. "That's the thing. I've been over it a thousand times, man. I don't remember what she said. She was here that day. In my room, early. I was playing that game. She talked about buying something. I don't know what. She left here and went to the library. I got that text an hour after she left."

"Look at me when you speak, Barton. You had better think harder, boy. A lot harder. You understand me."

Dickie stood in back of Jake, laughing under his breath. Rubbed Jake's shoulders like a boxing coach. "Kid, you won't like David Banner here when he gets mad."

"Come on. I didn't do anything. I don't know."

"You'll have to do better than that."

"She started getting into selling stuff on eBay. I don't know what. But she bought and sold all types of car parts and rare cactuses and other plants. It kept her busy. She didn't need the money. She liked the thrill, I guess. She liked meeting people. She'd set up eBay purchases, met customers at the library and the park across the street from it."

Computer forensics hadn't found anything on Lisa's computer to indicate such a thing.

"We never found one iota of evidence on her computer, Barton, to support your theory," Jake said. "Why are you lying to us?"

"She brought it over here once a week so I could wipe it clean."

"Why would she do that?"

"Because she was chatting with a former boyfriend her father hated. She was afraid her parents were snooping in her computer. We all do it. Wiping computers clean once a week for a kid is like cleaning your room. Some kids have parties just for that purpose."

"When she said 'that thing' in the text, what did she mean? Was it something from eBay she was hoping to sell or buy?"

"I swear, man, I *don't* know."

"What about the chatting? Why would she want to keep it hidden from pops?"

"She said her parents, if they ever thought she was talking to that kid again, would take the computer away and keep her confined to the house like a prisoner. And she really liked the dude."

The front door opened. A middle-aged man with hair plugs, wearing a double-breasted, shiny Armani suit—circa 1983—trounced into the living room. "Barton, don't you answer *another* question." He took out a business card and threw it at Jake. "Allen Jacoby."

"Hey," Dickie said, snapping his fingers, "I've seen you on TV, late at night, after Leno. Those commercials. It's you!" Dickie did his best impression, dropping his voice low. "'Never again will you be left alone by a system out to trample on your rights. Malpractice. Auto and work injuries. Unemployment. Sexual harassment. We got you covered.'"

"Barton here has no trouble answering our questions. Ask him for yourself."

"They read you your rights, Barton?"

The kid just sat there, dazed. Tears streamed slowly down his cheeks.

Jake got in the lawyer's face: "We're investigating a murder here. You need to leave."

"And you, Detective, need to arrest my client or let him be. My other client, out in your car, needs those handcuffs off before I cause you big trouble."

"And you're good at finding trouble, aren't you?" Dickie walked up beside Jake. "I didn't notice an ambulance out there in the driveway, counselor. How'd you find us?"

"I've been through it, over and over," Barton said, interrupting. They all turned toward him. Barton was referring to Lisa's last text message—"*Find m-m, find Lisa's killer*. I don't know anyone with those initials. Neither did Lisa. At least that I know of."

Allen Jacoby said, "Barton, no more. Stop right there."

Dickie motioned for a blue to escort Jacoby out of the house.

"It's killing me, eating me inside and out. If I had just listened, I could tell you what you need to know. I gotta live with this." More tears. "I have to go on knowing that I could have been there for my friend."

"Barton," Jake dropped his voice into a whisper. He sounded serious. Dickie put a hand on the lawyer's shoulder, holding him back. "Listen. You could not have saved Lisa. Trust us on that. But we need you to dig deep. Really, really deep, boy. Figure this out." Jake nodded to Dickie. It was time to leave. "You call us when you have something. We'll table the rest—the Oxy, you know—until then."

"Just don't wait too long," Dickie added before they walked out the door, "or Daddy will be out of work."

33

Anastasia sat behind her desk, seething. How could that bow tie-wearing prick do this to them?

Shelton.

She calmed herself. Then dialed the professor at his Simmons University office. He just happened to be coming off the heels of an interview with the *New York Times* regarding his role in finding a killer the national media was now calling the Boston Butcher.

"Professor, you are not to be running to the press about what you're doing for the Boston Police Department. It's an ongoing investigation, sir. We need your total commitment and silence where it pertains to what you uncover for us. I thought I made that perfectly clear in an email to you."

"CNN *and* Geraldo's people called my office today," Shelton squealed. There was flames in his voice. He sounded energized. "Nancy Grace live tonight. In fact, I'm in a hurry." This was his fifteen minutes. No one was taking it away from him.

"Well, I suspect more will be calling." Anastasia leaned back in her chair with a squeak. The office was loud this time of the day, first-shift cops coming in off the road, second-shifters getting ready to head out. Bosses barking orders. The phones. It was hard for Anastasia to block it all out. She liked the idea of a private office for herself some-day.

"Indeed, *Officer* Rossi. I think you might be correct. I was also contacted by a few publishers. I may get a book deal out of this." There was that crass, I'm-better-than-you-because-I-have-a-doctorate tone back in his voice again. "I get your title right that time?"

Anastasia ignored Shelton's tactless attitude. Gave him a few seconds to enjoy the gloating. Then: "I hope you understand that you won't be going on any of those shows, Professor. And a book? Please."

He was puzzled. "Excuse me?" Anastasia heard him laugh. "I am *not* an employee of the Boston Police, Miss Rossi." She could picture him fixing his bow tie. Twisting his neck. "I can—and *will*—do anything that helps further my academic career."

"Indeed. True. And I can also release the fact that your first wife accused you, let me see"—she rattled a piece of paper to make it sound real—"some thirty years ago now, was it, of visiting your son in his room late at night. Dose boys in the dean's office know you're an accused kid-toucher?"

"I was cleared of those charges." His voice turned hostile. "It was never proven and my son denied it ever happened."

"A bell was rung, Professor. I can re-ring that bell. Doesn't matter if you're innocent. You'd be over."

"You wouldn't."

"I would, sir."

Silence.

"Professor? You there, sweetie?"

"Your tactics, Miss Rossi, are vile."

"I'm from New York, what can I say? We get the job done."

A beat.

"Now, where were we? Oh, yeah, let's talk about my seedling?"

Shelton hesitated. The snappy tone gone. "I … I …"

"Get on with what you've found out about my seedling, doctor. I won't even bother getting into the fact that it's Wednesday and I had to call *you* about this."

Shelton had finished his work on the seedling. He confirmed it was from a Queen of the Night. The variety was of a South American origin. From his perspective, there was no doubt about it. Whoever left the seedling behind did it not long before or after Lisa's death. The seedling the professor tested in the lab showed no decomposition after a few days inside a similar environment. The seedling in opposing environments—warmer and colder—deteriorated quickly.

"You're looking for someone who knows this is a rare flower."

"Why do you say that?"

"Because they are not your ordinary roses or lilies. They take great care and a tender touch. A green thumb, if I must use such pedestrian language."

"Still doesn't answer my question." Anastasia watched a ruckus flare up at the front desk. There was a woman with bruises on her face. She was crying, holding both hands over her mouth.

"As I was saying, the Queen of the Night—"

"Lay off with the tone, okay?" Anastasia snapped. "Enough of the academic snobbish bullshit from you. You got me? Now, start again."

"You can find the Queen in waste areas, streambanks, near gardens, bush margins, gullies, alluvial flats, places like this—but not around here. Only in extremely warm climates. She prefers higher rainfall areas. She is extremely tolerant of frost."

Anastasia hated that he called the plant a she. It sounded dirty.

"You know what, I'm through with this call."

"Well, there's more."

"Email me what you have right now. Don't make me wait."

Anastasia hung up. Waiting for the professor's email, she Googled "Queen of the Night." Scrolled and read.

The seeds, in remote areas where you wouldn't normally find them, were dispersed by birds and water. Pieces of cut root, one Website said, can spread the flower by cultivation. It also reproduced from buds and creeping roots. Seeds remained dormant in the soil for many, many years.

She wondered how any of this could help them catch the Optimist. Then it hit her: "He sold Lisa plants?" Anastasia said out loud, staring at the monitor.

It made no sense. A teenager who bought rare flowers? Anastasia heard her inbox blow a flute sound.

----- Original Message -----

FROM: BotanistSheltonP101@aol.com

To: ARossi@BostonPD.D15.gov

Sent: September 11 - 3:57 PM

Subject: The Queen

Officer:

I don't appreciate being treated like a common criminal. I am helping you.

I sent some information to your home address via FedEx, as you suggested in your last email.

The Queen has enemies. This particular variety that was found at your crime scene is extremely toxic to farm animals. Your killer is not a farmer! Dense infestations exclude all vegetation. No other plants can grow near the Queen, hence one reason for her name.

Anastasia was bored with this guy and his useless information.

> What we found in retesting the seedling was a trace of sodium chloride and H2O—salt water. Interestingly enough, we also found saturated hydrocarbons, or paraffins and cycloparaffins, and aromatic hydrocarbons that include naphthalenes and alkylbenzenes.
>
> -Professor Shelton, Ph.D.

"In English, Professor," she said to herself. Then Googled those words: *aromatic hydrocarbons that include naphthalenes and alkylbenzenes.* She was certain the professor didn't explain their meaning just to get her back on the phone.

She scrolled through the top results and found a site of microbiology fluids that had profound effects on the environment. The professor was apparently referring to diesel fuel.

Diesel fuel?

"Yes, a boat could be a source, or a Mack truck," said a croaky voice from over Anastasia's shoulder. It was Mo Blackhall. He was on his way out the door. "Your killer has a boat, Rossi. Check that out. Looks like the Sundance Man was right after all."

Mo was enemy number one in the squad room. But at last, a lead.

"Thanks, Blackhall."

Mo stopped before heading out of the office space. Stared Anastasia in the eyes. "You tell that boss of yours, Cooper, that I stopped by your desk to say hello, okay. He'll know what I mean."

34

It was the closest Jake Cooper came to a good feeling these days. Stepping beyond the large oak doors into St. Paul's had always humbled him. With its cathedral ceiling, stained-glass windows, burning candles, and smell of roses, frankincense, and carnations, Jake was at home here. Protected from that world outside. The past and present. Both pulling at him. In here it was safe.

He found Father John in front of the altar. The priest knelt before the blessed sacrament. As Jake watched his old parish priest pray, he thought how strange it was never to have seen Father John shed a tear. He could not recall seeing Father cry. What hardened the emotion of this priest in such a way? With all the death he faced—funerals, sometimes three a week; bringing Communion to the sick and dying in the hospital; cancer wards; abused kids; the Southie junkies and prostitutes with AIDS—on a routine basis, you'd think he'd be more prone to melancholy. But not Father John. He seemed flat-lined, emotionally. A lot like a cop who'd seen too many dead bodies. Jake wanted that. He wondered if you could learn detachment. If you could train yourself to be immune to life's heartache. But then, weren't those the same people he chased?

Jake walked up to Father John. "Father?"

"Jake, how are you?" Father John whispered. "Twice in one week, how 'bout that?"

"This is a not a personal visit, Father. We need to talk."

"I suspected as much. Help an old friend off his knees, would you." The priest groaned as he stood.

They walked out of the church toward the rectory. In the hallway, Jake stopped. "I'm so sorry, Father. What happened to Mary is …"

"Nobody has the answer to why evil happens, Jake." They stood just outside Father John's office. "If you read your Bible, you'll see that even Christ questions it on the cross: '*Eli, eli, lema sabachthani.*'"

They said the English translation together, out loud: "Why hast thou forsaken me …?"

Father John said, "You remember your Aramaic! I'm impressed."

Inside Father John's office, Jake sat as the priest looked through several messages written on those pink WHILE-YOU-WERE-OUT slips of paper his secretary had left him. He sat down with a tremendous thud. "We just had cake and a celebration with Mary on Sunday night." He rubbed his forehead and eyes with one hand. "This is awful. I do not understand. This girl was as pure as summer rain. Please tell me she wasn't violated sexually."

Jake had not heard from Dr. Kelsey on that yet. He could say with certainty, however, that their killer was not prone to rape. "Father, no. She was not."

"Praise the Lord, Jake."

"How is the deacon, anyway?"

"As expected. He's being cared for at home by Carla and Ramsey, our devoted sisters. The doctor sedated him. Perhaps this is retaliation for the Church's sex scandal, but I don't know." The father put his fists up to his lips. Took a minute. Tried to find an answer in his thoughts.

"No, Father. One would have nothing to do with the other. People threaten, sure. They make prank phone calls. But this? Not a chance. There was hatred and deep-seated anger here. A psychology deeper than revenge. This was direct. Mary O'Keefe was chosen specifically."

Father John stood. Walked over to a table near the window. He reached down into the cabinet nearby and took out a bottle of Jack Daniels, lifted it to Jake, asking without speaking if he wanted one.

Jake nodded no.

Father poured himself three fingers worth and sat back down.

"I don't know, Jake," he said after taking a sip. He was responding to Jake's suggestion that the murder was for other reasons than the sex abuse scandal and possible retaliation. "I was at Logan a number of weeks back, just waiting to board my flight for a conference in Seattle." Father John took a breath, stared at Jake. "This young boy, maybe five or six, was playing in front of me, pushing one of those cute little John Deere tractor toys around on the carpet, making funny engine noises like kids do. I smiled at him and waved. His mother must have been watching. She ran over, grabbed the child, looked me in the eyes. The hate. You should have seen her. 'How dare you! You're disgusting,' she said. 'You should be locked up like the rest of them.' All I did was smile at the boy, Jake. There was hate in that woman's eyes. Considering what happened to Mary, I could see someone loathing us this much."

Jake shook his head, commiserating. Then took out his iPhone and opened up a new file to begin taking notes. "We're going on the record now, Father. I need to get into some uncomfortable areas."

"First, I need to ask how your father is doing, Jake?"

"Not bad, considering. It's my mother I worry about."

Father John felt Jake wasn't being completely honest. Yet knew him well enough to understand that when Jake Cooper was ready, he would talk about what was bothering him under the surface.

"You need not struggle to find an answer, Jake. Sometimes we just wait it out and that in itself becomes a solution—time."

Jake shook his head. "My integrity has been put to the test, Father. There's more to what I thought at first. You remember Mo Blackhall?"

"Years ago he had this beat, down here by the parish. Good cop, if memory serves me. Seemed to take a liking to you."

"Right. Well, some things are erupting between us … but hey, let me stay on point here."

"What can I help you with?"

Father John's office was dark, no matter how many lights he had on. The walls were paneled with a caramel-colored oak leftover from the seventies. The red curtains, heavy and thick as a comforter, allowed little light into the room. It smelled of dust and frankincense. Mildewy, like a basement.

"I am under the impression, Father, that this murder was directed at the O'Keefe family, not necessarily the Church. Have you seen anyone 'different' hanging around lately?"

"Jake," the priest took another sip of his whiskey, "we have new attendees at Mass every day. It's that type of parish. People stop in. We never see them again."

"But anyone stand out? Like, has anyone been asking questions?"

The father considered this. "Not that I know of."

"The deacon, Father. Any problems with his daughter?"

"Come on, Jake." Father John had a strange look about him. He knew something, but held back. Jake picked up on it.

"What is it?"

Father John closed his eyes.

"Father? If you know something—"

"Jake, I cannot divulge Church information without due reflection and speaking to the bishop. You know that."

"Father, his daughter was dismembered."

"It's about him, Jake."

Father John got a call on his desk phone.

"Excuse me. Yes, Eleanor?" There was a pause. "Okay. Send him in."

"What is it?"

"Your partner, Mr. Shaughnessy, is here."

"Here?" Jake's face straightened as he pointed down at the floor with his forefinger. "Here … now?"

Dickie knocked. Father John yelled for him to come in. The priest stood, grabbed Jake by the shoulder, squeezed. "Meet me in the rectory when you're done. I have a project started that I need to get back to. Keeps my mind," the old man had a hard time walking, "darn knees … weak as gum … off this horror."

Jake was on his feet. "I'll be over in a few minutes, Father."

Dickie nodded hello to the priest. Father John motioned the same back. As soon as Father John crossed the threshold of the door, Dickie closed it.

"What are you doing here, Dickie? What's so important you gotta come over here?"

"Just came from the morgue."

Jake didn't say anything.

"Kelsey seems to have found something underneath Mary O'Keefe's right titty."

Jake rolled his eyes. *Titty.* "You're in a church building, for crying out loud, Dickie."

"Sorry, Kid." He made the sign of the cross, missing the second station—the Son—near his belly button.

"Nice try. What is it? Or, rather, what does Kelsey think it is?"

"Another marking. She's pretty firm on this one. Letter *c*. Looks to have been carved with a knife. Or some sharp object, like maybe a screwdriver. 'Very clear,' was the quote. Kelsey said she's putting in her report. She made a point to tell me that."

Jake thought about it. *A cipher?*

"Makes no sense, though, Dickie—*i-m-c*? What could that mean?"

"Anastasia and I brainstormed it through. Switch them around."

"Switch what around?"

"You're basing your rationale on the point that vic number one was Boston Common Lisa Marie. Vic number one, don't forget, was Quincy Market Alyssa Bettencourt, who supposedly had the *m* on her. Now it becomes *m-i-c*."

Dickie picked up a chalice off Father John's desk. Looked at it. "Pure gold, I bet. This is heavy."

Jake wasn't sold on it. *M-i-c? Maybe.*

He walked out of the office. Across the parking lot. Up the stairs toward the rectory. Father John sat at the large dining table gluing little bells onto green felt Christmas trees he liked to drop off in the Southie housing projects around the church during Advent. The old man was lost in this simple act of giving.

Dickie followed. "A town, maybe?" he said to Jake as they made their way into the rectory.

"Not sure. I might be on board with a name—and that's a stretch." Jake held the door for Dickie to go in before him.

"He's not going to give us his name. That'd be too obvious."

Jake stopped. Turned to Dickie. "Right. Okay. Let me get this straight. If nothing else, he's subtle, Dickie." He dropped his voice to a whisper. "Remember, he tacked the body of a deacon's daughter to the mast of the Tea Party Ship. Cut her legs off. Dug her insides out. Don't you think he's a bit narcissistic?"

"Got your point. But—" Dickie hit a nerve.

"But nothing! Give me something substantial. Not three letters that might be letters, that might be a name, that might be a town. Come on."

"I didn't kill these girls, Jake. I know it hits home for you with Mary. Relax."

Father John looked up from what he was doing, startled by Jake's outburst.

"What do you have? Don't come over here," Jake raised his voice as Father John looked on curiously, "giving me some crap about a name that starts with *m-i-c*. I need more than that. I need leads, Dickie. Speculation is for TV detectives."

Father John watched Jake walk toward the library in the room adjacent to where the priest sat. There was a large opening between the two rooms. Father John hummed something, a hymn probably, to try and lighten the mood. The memories of being an altar boy came back for Jake as he looked at all the yearbooks lined up by year. He could smell the burning incense in the thurible during special Mass processions, the ball-shaped apparatus at the end of a chain the priests swung as they walked down the aisle, consecrating the altar and chapel. It gave the church an Old Testament aroma, made the room smoky and feel ancient. Jake delighted in preparing the incense.

"What I'm telling you, Jake—" Dickie started to say, but was cut off.

"Dickie, forget it." Jake was calmed by the smell of the old books. "Father? I have to go. But we need to finish our conversation ASAP. When can I come back?"

Father John got up from his seat, walked over and searched for a book on the shelf to Jake's left. It was a large leather-bound yearbook. Jake wondered what he was doing.

"The one good thing about getting old, Jake," Father John hobbled with pain in his limbs, the book unfolded in front of him, "is that I can see the end of the road. I can feel the warmth of the light. And I know in my heart I've spent my whole life preparing for it. Thank the Lord, though, that my memory is still intact."

"What are you talking about, Father?" Jake was out of patience. He needed to get out of the rectory and into his car. Alone.

"This book," Father held it up, "may help you."

It was a compilation of St. Paul lectors for the past fifty years.

Dickie walked over. Stared at it over the priest's shoulder. Jake didn't seem interested.

The photos were black-and-white. Nothing stood out to Dickie. Father John had a look about him, though. He was taking this somewhere good.

"Jake," Father John stared down at a name and photo, "I heard you yell a moment ago about someone named Mic."

"Father, what are you getting at here? I need to be other places."

Father John took off his glasses. "Stuart Micah, you recall him?"

The name was not familiar to Jake.

Father pointed to his picture. The name sounded so biblical. "Micah."

M-i-c, Jake thought.

"Tell me about him, Father?"

Stuart Micah was a small kid when he showed up at the church. Buzzed-cut hair. Buddy Holly-type horned-rimmed glasses. Lanky frame. In the photo, he looked as if he wanted no part of his photo being taken.

"Sad story, Jake. And, well, you just told me about Mary's murder being personal."

"Sad?"

"Stuart and his family were devout Mass attendees. His parents pushed him into becoming an altar server, then a lector. But it wasn't in Micah's heart. He was here because he had to be. Anyway, he grew into his role as a Catholic. Excelled, actually. He was around twenty, I think, when this photo was taken in 1967. I heard he went to Boston College, stayed in the area. Never married. Contemplated going to seminary but gave up on it after an incident he said he didn't want to discuss. Stuart became a teacher at a local grammar school. Not sure of the name, but I can look it up. Might be JFK in Malden."

"What does any of this have to do with my case, Father?"

"That's what I'm getting at. I need to sit."

Dickie grabbed a chair from the dining room. Father John sat. Jake stood in front of him. Arms folded.

"Stuart Micah got bored with teaching grammar school. He wanted to make a difference, or that's what he told us—and worked very hard to make us believe. We had an opening in one of our orphanages up north."

"Which one?"

"Bainbridge, the orphanage St. Paul's is affiliated with. Or was, I should say."

"And this Stuart Micah, he went up there to teach?"

"Well, he had nothing holding him here. His family was dead. No wife. He started a class up there for the kids who were smarter than the others. The gifted ones, I suppose they called them. Things went smoothly for years. The kids loved him."

Where's the but? Jake wondered. He could almost hear the drum roll in Father John's voice as he paused before delivering the sobering punch line.

"Then, well, one of his kids came forward and accused him of the worst thing imaginable—which opened the floodgates. There's much more to it. But the short end of the story is that he was tried, convicted, sent to prison."

"And he's there now?"

"I believe he's not in great health, but yes, Stuart Micah is still alive."

Jake's interest piqued. At least for the time being. What else did they have?

"He's been incarcerated for nearly twenty years, Jake. Everyone has his Calvary—the place of the skull. He cannot be your killer. That's not what I'm saying. But the *m-i-c* fits. It's a start."

"I'll be in touch, Father. Do me a favor. Dig out all you can on Mr. Micah and have it sent over to my office—immediately. And don't tell anyone what you've told me today. Especially Deacon O'Keefe."

Father John frowned. "You noticed that?"

"Come on, Father. Of course." Jake walked out of the rectory.

Dickie turned to the priest, shrugged his shoulders in a what-am-I-missing-here gesture.

The priest pointed to the photo. Dickie looked at it.

"That is Deacon O'Keefe standing next to Stuart Micah in their class photo," Father John explained. "The deacon trained that class of lectors. He and Mr. Micah were once very close, Mr. Shaughnessy."

35

WEDNESDAY, SEPTEMBER 10 – 4:32 P.M.

Lieutenant Ray Matikas stood outside the captain's office downtown. In the corner of the room, to his right, was a plastic fern plant, its spiked leaves covered with a coat of dust. Matikas sat on a cheap, stiff sofa. The room reminded him of going to the doctor. How we all get lost in the perpetual act of waiting. Always waiting. Hurry up and wait. The life of a white shirt cop. Your appointment was scheduled for four. Four-thirty rolls around and you find yourself still working the next hemorrhoid out.

Control. Everybody elbowed for it.

"Is he around, Candis?" Matikas was sick of sitting. The captain's secretary was playing solitaire on her computer. "Your *People* magazines are weeks old. I cannot sit anymore."

"Funny, Ray. He is, as a matter of fact. But like I said, he's on the phone. Very important call. Just give him a few more minutes." She never looked away from her game.

Matikas ran a hand across his face, freshening himself up. Then poured a paper cup of water from the big upside-down jug, pounded it in one loud gulp. Crumpled the cup. Tossed it in the basket ten feet away. He hated this. Being summoned to Captain Annadel Morely's office. It was never good news. Matikas knew when he screwed up. He didn't need to be told.

Candis was focused on finding a home for a nine of hearts when the lieutenant went for it, walking angrily, grabbing the doorknob, barging into the captain's office.

"Ray!" Candis shouted, getting up, running.

The captain was on his computer, serious look on his face, reading something. "It's okay, Candis," he said, not looking up or turning away from the monitor.

Matikas went straight at him. Palmed the desk. Stared at the monitor holding the captain's attention.

The captain was reading an article on WebMD.

"Important call, huh, Captain."

Morely smiled. "Sit down. Relax, Ray. Be with you in a minute."

Matikas did what he was told. Waiting, he scanned the captain's desk and considered how well-connected Morely was. The captain smiled in a framed photo with the late Ted Kennedy. They were at some black-tie function, looked to be Harvard. In another, he stood next to Red Sox wunderkind GM Theo Epstein. They held Cuban cigars, smiled like winning gamblers. There were commendations from the mayor and City Hall on the wall in back of Morely's desk. Photos of the captain golfing with the likes of the governor and Bill Clinton.

Morely donned gold bars on the side shoulder of his white shirt, three stars on his collar. Matikas believed deep down he should have gotten the promotion Morely took from him only, Matikas thought, because Morely was black.

"What's the problem, Captain?" Matikas finally said after giving the guy his minute. "I'm busy downtown. I need to get back to my people."

"Ray, let me tell you, this Google thing is amazing—but very dangerous." The captain still had not looked at Matikas. "I woke up this morning with a tiny bubble on the roof of my mouth. Thought nothing of it. But then it grew bigger as the morning progressed. So I did what everyone told me to. Hopped onto Google and diagnosed myself. Within ten minutes of comparing the bubble to some photos, I thought I had mouth cancer."

"Captain, what is it that you want?"

"Come to find out, it's just a skin rash. Very common." The captain spun around in his swivel chair and faced Matikas, a serious tone and look to him now. "I understand someone broke into your office."

"Yes, but I—"

"Uh, now, now, Ray. I don't want to hear your excuses." Morely had his eyes closed. Hands up in front of himself. "What I need from you is to know how far you've come with your inquiry into this Mo Blackhall, Jake Cooper thing. Mo is causing us some problems. He needs to go. I cannot have a cop hitting the bottle in the office. That's so nineteen-seventies, Ray. *Barney Miller* stuff. And this Ted Williams Tunnel thing. If my people are connected in any way, the Big Dig just went over budget again. Now, I don't want any of your bullshit, I just want answers, Ray."

The police scanner in the captain's office let out a static-filled cough. A cop said something about a *10-54d*, possible dead body, in Chinatown. When he came back on, he requested a *10-78* ("ambulance") ... *Looks like a heart attack.*

Matikas waited for the transmission to conclude before speaking. "Blackhall is definitely involved with Mancini Construction and that work on the Ted Williams, just don't know to what capacity. He moonlighted as security for Mancini when they dug the tunnel."

"And Cooper?"

"Not sure about Cooper yet. Still looking into it."

Candis rang up the captain on speakerphone. "Mrs. Morely is on line five, sir."

The captain pressed the button, held it down, "Tell her we're having dinner with the deputy chief at Gitano's in Quincy. I'll be picking her up at six." He looked at his watch.

Matikas stood. "Look, I'm still working on this, Captain." He used his hands to plead. *Come on, cut me some slack here. We've known each other how long?* "But I have a full boat with this serial case Cooper's working on."

"I was getting to that. Sit back down, Ray. The deputy chief is friends with the Bettencourt kid's father."

Matikas's stomach turned over. *Great.* The color drained from his face.

"Yeah, Ray. Tell me about it. He's up my ass on this." The captain could sense the distress via Matikas's body language. "I need answers, Ray. Not your typical ass-kissing. I'm tired of carrying you. This Mo thing. The idea that you put Cooper on this serial case when the guy cracked up a year ago. Gees. People around here think you're losing your touch. I tend to agree with them. We're not chasing Whitey Bulger around Southie anymore, Ray. Things are different today. The stakes are higher."

The captain got up. Walked over to a small table next to the large window looking out onto the Prudential Center Building to the north. Fenway Park was due south, the Citgo sign in back of the Green Monster spinning. Looking down, you could see cars that looked as small as kids' toys zipping underneath the building on the Mass Pike. The city was quiet, staring out at it through the thick glass of the thirty-fifth floor. Not a peep of social noise. The captain didn't say anything, arms behind his back, rocking, taking it all in like a president. A Swinging Wonder sat on the windowsill in front of him. The small square structure with five chrome steel balls hanging from strings was modeled after the original Newton's Cradle. The captain pulled back one of the balls, looked at Matikas through it, then released it. The apparatus clicked back and forth, metronome-like.

Matikas watched, understanding the message.

Time was running out.

"Keep an eye on Cooper. He likely knows more about this Big Dig problem of Mo's than you think. And if it becomes my problem, Ray, well, let's just say, losing your job will be the least of your worries." These guys were once friends. They hunted. Fished. Played cards every Saturday night.

"Understood, Captain."

Matikas sat in his car outside thinking about what the captain had said. He had known Morely twenty-five years. Still, there was a new code of blue in the BPD. One thing mattered when you sat in a position of power—your loyalty to higher-ups. Matikas didn't want to play ball anymore. He was tired. Stood to retire in two years.

Before driving away, he reached into the glove box, pulled out the phone number he swore he'd never need, better yet use. Then typed out a text:

LOOK, CAPT. IS PISSED.

WE NEED TO RESOLVE THIS ASAP.

I CANNOT WAIT ANY LONGER.

After he hit SEND, Matikas peeled out onto the street, keying the radio.

"Cooper?"

No answer.

Matikas dialed up the office. As he did, Jake responded. "Yeah, Ray? What is it?"

At a stoplight, Matikas looked left and right down Commonwealth. The T train, whining its tinny electric squeal as it passed, glided through the middle of the street. The Boston Museum of Art was on Matikas's right, several blocks away. A Star Market dead ahead.

"Cooper, I need to speak with you first thing tomorrow morning."

"What's up, Lieutenant?"

"Just come see me, Cooper. I'm warning you. Don't blow me off."

That night, Ray Matikas and Jake Cooper did not sleep.

36

Dickie walked into the squad room. He opened the plastic lid to his medium cup of Dunkin' Donuts coffee—light and sweet—just as the lieutenant came around the corner and started in.

"Are you two out of your minds?" Matikas screamed. "Holding the Colby kid hostage like that, the father out in the car, handcuffed? Where are we now, Shaughnessy, Guantanamo Bay, doin' friggin' terrorist interrogations? I didn't hear from anyone that the Colby kid was reading the Koran and building pipe bombs in his room."

For no reason, Dickie thought of the term waterboarding. How he had just seen something on TV the night before about the United States being accused of using the torture technique.

"I got a call at home last night from our attorney's office, Shaughnessy. Big problems with the Colbys."

Dickie had the morning's *Globe* tucked underneath his arm. He took a sip of his coffee, slurping it the way the lieutenant hated. Looking around, he wondered, *Where is Jake when I need him?*

"Did you hear what we got out of the kid, Lieutenant?"

"That's beside the point." Matikas looked at his watch. "Where is Cooper, anyway? Tell him to get his ass in here to come see me. You two do not go out on the road today without stopping in my office."

"Right-o, Lieutenant." Dickie saluted. He took out a Lactaid pill. Popped it. Swallowed. "Listen, love to sit and chat, but I gotta drop me a deuce. You know what this coffee does to my colon. I got a bubble rolling around in here." He massaged his stomach in a circular motion.

Several blues standing by the front counter looked at one another and laughed. One yelled, "TMI, Shaughnessy ..." The time clock nearby made a *pop* sound as it hit fifteen minutes before the hour.

"Screw you, Shaughnessy," Matikas said. "You're just like him. As a matter of fact, where in the hell are my reports for the Public Garden and Tea Party scenes? I won't even get into the Bettencourt case."

"I'm still working on those, Lieutenant. Give me a day or two."

"End of today, Shaughnessy."

"Okay, Lieutenant." Dickie took a sip of his coffee. *Not a chance.*

"It looks to me like we got a connection now to St. Paul's Church, with this O'Keefe girl's father. Isn't that Cooper's spiritual turf?"

"I'm a non-believer, sir ... sorry."

"If that's his church, Shaughnessy"—a blue walked over, asked Matikas to sign something—"Cooper needs to step back and maybe, if this ever goes to court—a big *if,* mind you—we might not run into legal trouble. Make sure you two clear this with the DA before Cooper runs over there badgering those clergymen. I don't need the Catholic Church up my ass."

"Sure thing."

Briefcase in hand, Matikas stomped into his office. Slammed the door behind him. Dickie went to the bathroom. Came back. Sat at his desk.

Callahan, the day desk sergeant, mentioned that Barton Colby was on the phone.

Dickie picked up the line.

The kid still didn't have any idea what "*mm*" stood for, he said, but recalled something about the guy Lisa met online. He was an older dude, Barton said, "Maybe like, thirty-five or even forty."

"Yeah, that's old all right. What was it that she bought?"

His name was Nick Miller. A stocky man who had helped Lisa Marie locate a nursery on the other side of Worcester that sold rare flowers. Miller called the police once he realized Lisa had been murdered. Mr. and Mrs. Taylor confirmed that Mr. Taylor drove Lisa to Worcester a week before her death to meet with Miller. He had flowers, all right, but not what Lisa wanted. Mr. Taylor never inquired what type of flowers his daughter was looking for, only that she get there and back safely—without making a stop by her old boyfriend's house.

"That's *n-m*, though," Barton said. "Nick Miller … *mm* doesn't fit."

Dickie looked down at his keyboard. The *n* was right next to the *m*. Typo, perhaps? "We checked Nick out, Barton. Nothing there. But thanks for the call. Keep thinking, kid. Hopefully, it'll come to you before we lose another girl."

Dickie hung up.

Anastasia Rossi sat on Dickie's desk and faced him.

"Fancy seeing you here, missy. Coffee?"

Anastasia nodded her head. Opened the lid. "Black. You know me well, Shaughnessy. Thanks." Jumped off Dickie's desk.

"Anything new?"

She put her bag down by her chair. Sat behind her desk, swiveled toward Dickie. He leaned back in his chair to listen, elbow on the armrest, palm holding up his chin.

"I heard from the lab on that paint chip."

"Stuck on that, huh, Rossi? It could have been left there by a tourist. Blew in with a gust of Bean Town wind."

"Right you are. Forget it, then." She turned. Acted as if she was working on something.

"Come on, Rossi. You gotta be able to take it. What'a ya got?"

She looked up. "It's from a state vehicle. Special brand of metallic paint used on cop cars, government vehicles, and those vans the towns and cities use for utility jobs."

"That could mean a thousand different things. Tell me something straight, Rossi. Something I can use right now."

She had anticipated that reaction. "How 'bout that I narrowed it down, using computer records I pulled from the Net last night, to about four hundred vehicles from the postal service. Worcester, actually. They service most of the vehicles used throughout the city. I spoke to a guy there late last night, second shifter, who told me that this type of paint, speaking generally, was used on the Jeeps and vans to make those red, white, and blue pinstripes. Thing is, they discontinued the paint about ten years ago and went back to pin-striping stickers."

"Let me guess—lead-based, right?"

"Bingo."

"Not bad, Rossi. Not bad at all. So we know our guy, if a tourist didn't leave it behind, is driving a ten-year-old (or more) vehicle. And that he could even work for the post office." That did narrow the search. "What about our professor? Anything new out of him?"

Anastasia tossed a file on Dickie's desk, about thirty pages thick. "There's a transcript in there of my last phone call with Shelton, a few email exchanges, along with some Google research. You'll enjoy it."

"Do you sleep?"

She smiled.

37

THURSDAY, SEPTEMBER 11 - 10:31 A.M.

Dickie took a radio call from Jake not long after speaking with Anastasia. "Meet me in Framingham. The Kohl's parking lot on Route Nine. Bring two shotguns from the cage."

"You got it."

Dickie grabbed the weapons, two uniforms, and took off.

Forty-five minutes later, Dickie hopped in Jake's Crown Vic as shoppers walked out of Kohl's in front of them. The blues followed in another vehicle.

No lights. No sirens.

Stealth.

The guy whose name Bags Cane gave to Jake lived in a gated, million-dollar contemporary laid out on about fifty acres. There was a brand-new cherry red Cadillac in the driveway, a pair of steer horns on the front hood, twenty-two-inch gold rims with tires so thin they looked like rubber bands.

Jake and the team parked down the road from the house. Jake explained the situation Bags Cane had related to him. This guy was a Class A scumbag. He wasn't their guy, but he might know something. Anyway, getting a piece of garbage like this off the street was all in a good day's work. Jake could sense another victim of the Optimist's coming. Any lead—no matter how remote—was worth checking out.

The clock was ticking.

"No search warrant?"

Jake looked at Dickie. *Mr. By-the-book.*

"Probable cause in the scope of a murder investigation."

"Matikas know?"

Jake didn't answer.

They hopped the four-foot chain-link fence. Dickie had a rough go of it and fell behind.

Flanking the gate on each side, they walked along the driveway. There was a line of black solar lights stuck in the ground—gigantic mushrooms—near a row of evergreens. A bread-crumb trail to the front door.

Jake explained how he wanted things to go down.

The two blues agreed.

Dickie came up, huffing and puffing.

Jake knocked on the door with the barrel end of his shotgun.

It opened. The guy stood in front of them wearing a bathrobe untied. Boxer shorts. Fuzzy slippers. He was smoking a cigarette. Looked as though he hadn't showered in days.

Jake and Dickie looked at each other: *Get a load of this.*

Vice gave Dickie his name after Jake provided an address. Tad "Cowboy" Peterson, a real piece of shit if there ever was one. Tad had moved into the area two years ago. He had run a whorehouse in Las Vegas. Got busted for providing bowls of cocaine to his johns during the Tony Montana-*Scarface* era. Did five years, was granted an early release. Made some money selling the ranch. Brought his sleaze show east.

"What do you want?" Tad Peterson said. He did not look alarmed. "I saw all of you on my security cam. Pretty funny shit, actually."

Jake said, "Just to talk, Tad. Nothing else."

"Put the weapons away."

"Come on, Tad. You know we can't do that. Just want to chat a little bit about a few girlfriends of yours."

There was a beat of tense silence. No one said anything.

The door popped open. Tad beckoned them inside, turning his back, walking away.

The living room just beyond the foyer looked like something out of a 70's porn film. Furry shag rugs. Stuffed animal heads hung from the walls. Pinball machine. Sunken floor with a projection big-screen television in one corner. Incense burning on plates. Multi-colored wax candles on every table.

"Where's the lava lamp?" Dickie said, laughing at his own joke.

"You ever leave here, Tad?" Jake didn't want cause a panic. He came across relaxed, calm. "We'd like to look around. That okay with you?"

"Wait a minute, man. You got a warrant?"

"No. Why, we going to need one? Warrants involve judges. Charges. We just thought we'd pop in and have a friendly conversation. But if you insist on a warrant, hell, we can get that done."

Peterson thought about it. He could read Jake. He'd been shaken down all his life by country cops, unlike Jake Cooper, he had no trouble paying off. After considering the alternative, "Yeah, go ahead," he said. "Have a look."

"Dickie, take a blue and search the bedroom upstairs."

"Wait a freakin' minute," Peterson said, moving closer toward Jake.

"So, *Tad*," Jake said, "you gonna set some boundaries now?" Jake cracked his shotgun in half, checked the chamber with one eye squinted, snapped it back in place with one arm.

"Ah, shit …" Peterson said, dropping his head.

Jake could smell that unmistakable aroma of crack cocaine. He had lived in Southie too many years. You walk into a housing project hallway. Around the playgrounds. You smell someone blowing crack smoke. Once it got on your skin, your clothes, in your hair, like a day-old corpse in a stuffy apartment sitting underneath your nose a day later, there was no getting rid of it.

A skinny redhead with orange lips and freckled pale skin came out of the kitchen. She was Nicole Kidman-tall. Half-naked, she wore a thong, wife-beater T-shirt. Her nipples popped through the cotton like raisins. She looked as if she'd been up all night. When she spied Jake standing there, Dickie and a cop on their way upstairs, she turned around and headed back into the kitchen.

"Why don't you join us?" the blue with Jake said.

Tad Peterson was on the phone with his lawyer. "Yup, okay. No, I will."

Jake looked around. "You know why we're here, Tad, right?"

Peterson lit another Marlboro with the butt end of the one he'd just finished. Blew the smoke off to his right side. Didn't say anything.

Jake moved closer. Peterson stepped up, took another drag, blew smoke in Jake's face.

"Simple stuff, Tad. Just answer some questions and we're out of here. That simple."

"Come on, man. Nothin' is ever that easy with cops."

Dickie came down the stairs with a glass bowl, spoon burned black on the bottom, and several small beer-bottle brown vials of what appeared to be crack. The blue behind him had a two-liter plastic Coke bottle, half full of water, a hole cut in the side, tin foil stuffed inside. A makeshift bong.

"That crack is so nineteen-nineties, Tad." Jake shook his head.

"Get a look at her," Dickie said of the redhead sitting on the couch, "higher than Hosanna, huh, Jake?"

"Very funny, Dick."

"An hour and I'll be out," Peterson said in his quick and breathy voice. He meant jail.

"Look, tell me about your fetish for cutting on women. Or should we ask your girlfriend here, instead?" Jake looked down at her shins. Scabs and scars. He knew them from the jimmy-jam leg itch junkies get, not from cutting, but went with it, anyway.

Tad Peterson laughed. "Different strokes for—"

Jake bumped Peterson in his pigeon chest, pushing him back against the wall. Got right in his face. Jake was at least a foot taller. "Tad, Bags Cane has been talking since he got out of the joint." Peterson and the redhead looked at each other quickly. "Come on, you read the papers lately?"

"Me? No way."

"We got ourselves a witness putting you in the Public Garden with that young girl. Now, we know you didn't kill her, Tad."

"Listen, I had nothing to do with that shit. You know that. What is this'?" Peterson pulled away. Jake let him go. "I'm calling my lawyer back." He went for the phone.

"Sit down, Tad," Jake said. His voice ratcheted up a notch. Then he took Tad's cordless phone and threw it at the sliding glass door as hard as he could, shattering the glass.

Dickie went into the kitchen. Returned with a knife he said he found underneath the sink. He held it out in front of Peterson by the tip with a hankie.

"The boys in forensics are going to love this." Dickie held it up. "Bag that up for me, fellas. Then call in and get us that signed search warrant we'll need."

"Get Tad into the car and get him downtown." Jake sat on the couch. Dropped his head. Another dead end. Tad Peterson and his girlfriend were escorted out of the house.

"What do you think, boss?" Dickie asked. He had his shotgun cradled over his shoulder like a hunter.

"Have the boys interrogate him all day, but he doesn't know a thing." Jake rubbed his right hand through his hair and blew a long-winded sigh.

38

THURSDAY, SEPTEMBER 11 - 11:53 A.M.

Inside D-15, Jake had his hand on the doorknob to his office, when Matikas emerged from around the corner.

"Now, Cooper. Let's go."

Jake had his back toward the lieutenant. He dropped his head. Under his breath, "Shit. Come on."

"I warned you last night on the phone not to blow me off, damn it all."

Jake looked at the whitewashed walls in Matikas's office. They were a blurry shade of gray from not being painted or cleaned. Two chairs faced Matikas's oak desk. Jake sat opposite the lieutenant and explained how his connection to St. Paul's was not going to make one bit of a difference when it came time to prosecute. Anyway, where was their suspect? They were far from having to worry about prosecuting a serial killer they had not yet captured.

"If you recall, Cooper, you messed up the last time I put you in charge of a high-profile murder case. You ever consider that? I stuck my ass out here—again!"

Cheap shot.

Jake looked down at his shoes. He saw the little girl's face. Dirt covering her eyes. He heard Dr. Kelsey a day later. *"We found dirt in her lungs, Cooper, sorry. That means she was alive when she was buried. She was breathing."*

"Don't go there, Ray."

"No? Why, Cooper? You going crazy on me again?" Matikas threw his hands up in an it's-not-even-worth-it gesture.

Jake stood to leave.

"Sit. Down."

Jake stopped. Turned. Stood, instead.

"I was doing my job," Jake explained. "Doesn't matter that I was a parish member of St. Paul's. The DA agrees with me, Ray. Non-issue. Now, what else do you want?"

Matikas bounced an index finger off his pursed lips. "Fine, but listen. There's been some talk downtown about Mo that is not, let's say, in his favor. What do you know about him being tied to Mancini and that security company? I can't have them coming after you—not now, during this investigation. If we make an arrest and then you're sucked into that Mo vacuum by Internal Affairs, I won't be able to save your ass. We're done. I'm thinking of taking you off this case anyway, until this thing with Mo is finished."

Jake became animated. "What? No, Ray. You cannot do that." He stopped talking. Was the lieutenant playing him? "You think I'm going to give you Mo, is that it? What the hell is wrong with you? Forget Mo. Allow me to do my job here." Jake went to walk out of the room for a second time.

Security company? He was floored by this revelation. It was the first he had heard of it. He hadn't thought about the situation much lately, but it made sense now. Mancini was the ruse. Mo—and maybe Jake, too—was in deeper than Jake had ever considered.

"Your nose better be clean with this Mo thing, Cooper. I'm hearing things about you I don't like."

Jake considered walking away without answering that little jab. But he stood by the door. *How could Ray know?* Was it a bluff to get information?

Matikas walked over to the tall picture window in back of his desk. He looked down at the parking lot below. He had a serious buzz to his voice. Concern. Jake hadn't left.

"You need to focus on getting this butcher off my streets," the lieutenant said. "Killing a deacon's daughter and a Harvard professor's little girl doesn't sit well with brass. The captain is up my ass. He wants answers, Jake. You got *anything*? Don't mess with me. I'm pleading with you here. My ass is on the line, too. What do we have?"

Jake could hear the anguish in the lieutenant's voice. He was being pressured. He needed to produce. It seemed the entire plight of D-15 was riding on this one case.

"I have a few leads, Ray. But I need to get the hell out of here and work them."

"You have two days to get me something I can use to quiet the captain down. After that, well…," Matikas walked away from the window, put both palms on his desk, propped himself up, "I cannot be responsible for where you end up. I'll hold off HQ and Mo's keepers as long as I can. But no promises." He pointed his index finger into the desk, accentuating each word. "One more thing. Don't be barging into anybody's home again without a freakin' search warrant."

"Peterson's scum." Jake paused. Then: "I'm clean on the Mo thing, Ray. I won't take that hit."

"Where is Mo now?"

"I have no idea."

"The guy is never around. Comes and goes from this office like he doesn't work here."

Jake went to grab the door and noticed a *Boston Herald* article framed on the wall. Matikas had rescued a few kids from a warehouse fire. There was a photo of him with the mayor below it. The guy was considered a hero at one time.

"I can look into that thing about Mo," Jake said in a near-whisper. He wasn't facing Matikas.

"Are we clear where we stand with Mo, Jake? I'm not going to mention this again. And I certainly am not going down for that sonofabitch."

"Clear, Ray."

"You better do something, hotshot. Or they won't be as friendly to you as they have been with your rabbi there. You'll be out on your ass, with charges to follow. Don't matter what you did or didn't do. They want you, Jake, you're history. You're from the old Southie boys club—don't ever forget that."

Jake pushed the door open. He wanted to turn and scream at Matikas. Tell him to go to hell. Then run to brass downtown and let them all know he was waiting for them anytime they wanted to come after him. And for a moment, Jake Cooper considered walking down the hall, packing up his things and leaving. Never coming back.

But he did none of that.

39

THURSDAY, SEPTEMBER 11 - NOON

Jake grabbed a Mountain Dew from the machine in the hallway by his office. Tapped on the spout before snapping it open. Walked in, shut the door behind him, sat down in his chair with a heavy thud. He needed to take a serious look into Stuart Micah's criminal record. Dickie was downstairs with Tad Peterson, digging, buying time, so the team searching Peterson's house could maybe find something to tie him to that Cambridge case.

There were only two photographs left on Jake's office wall. He had packed all the others and most of his personal belongings into a box, which sat on the small sofa by the window. One photo was of Jake standing next to Casey, who was dressed in his Marine greens. Casey stood straight as a rake. Chest out. Arms folded behind his back. Jake was a teenager, sporting that cocky I'm-a-bad-ass Southie look all the kids had.

Underneath that photo was one of Jake decked out in his full cop blues, white gloves, standing next to Casey's memorial. Jake stood and stared at it. He couldn't bring himself to pull it down off the wall. Not until he was walking out of the office for the last time.

On his desk was a family photo of Jake, Brendan, and Dawn. It was a farm scene. Fake fence. Some hay. They all smiled.

The good times.

Jake fired up his computer and connected his iPhone to an open port, hit the interface icon on the desktop to synchronize the two.

His gut told him not to tell Matikas about Micah yet. It would just cause more problems. The dilemma with the lead was, of course, tracking down Micah's victims. It was going to be difficult on a number of levels. As Jake figured, the victims' families had sued the state of Maine and the Boston Archdiocese of the Church, which made their cases extremely *un*-PC. Add the juvenile factor to it and the white shirts would not like Jake sniffing around. There was an unwritten rule between cops and City Hall—once government money exchanged hands, the vic was off limits.

Politics is for the weak.

It took a minute for Jake's computer to pull the latest data from his iPhone and send it into the main database. As Jake waited, he considered the idea that catching a serial murderer usurped any and all political meddling attached to the case. He would be glad to answer questions later. Hell, if he stuck around long enough to catch this lunatic, he would be glad to resign. The idea of leaving consumed Jake these days. Did he really need all this bullshit with Mo and Matikas? He was supposed to be a cop. Not some sort of babysitter and political scapegoat. Where had their integrity as police officers gone?

With a few keystrokes, Stuart Micah's mug shot appeared on Jake's monitor. He downloaded it, along with Micah's complete file, into his iPhone. The main system sent back a message that it needed more data before a projected profile could be completed.

Fine. Micah's mug shot and file would suffice for the time being. It was Micah's latest prison intake photo, taken last year. The guy had a steely gaze. Dark brown eyes. Crinkled brow. Acne scars. He'd make a great extra in a Nazi film, Jake was thinking, staring at him. His hair was gray and wiry, like pipe cleaners. He looked as if prison had aged him some. Still, it was clear that Stuart Micah was doing the time, the time was not doing Micah.

Big difference, Jake knew.

Jake read through several reports the prison compiled on Micah. The guy had accepted his punishment, knowing he was going to die in prison. Most cons could not admit guilt, or come to terms with the reality of prison life forever. But it was clear Micah was not bred from that same ilk. *He wants to be left alone*, said one psychological analysis. He suffered from *Borderline Personality Disorder characterized by the standard*, across the board, *pervasive instability of moods, along with an inability to maintain interpersonal relationships*. He possessed *a self-image of a man who hated himself*, but could not *do anything about it to change or make reparations to his victims*.

Jake was able to access an older file on Micah through the interoffice computer system (ICS-KPAC). It was a network cops used to swap suspect info from precinct to precinct without worrying about some zit-faced Geek Squad Lisbeth Salander-wannabe with a supercomputer having fun in his room hacking into the BPD. Reading Micah's criminal report further, Jake learned Micah was battling emphysema. The guy was on oxygen. Weighed 95 pounds. He used a wheelchair to get around inside the prison. And yet, beyond all that, "I'm comfortable," he told a psychologist a year after he was caught, "knowing that my victims deserved the abuse they suffered by my hand. They were chosen because they needed a teacher—their parents abandoned them. They were sent to me by God."

Jake called the DA's office. He ordered a complete copy of Micah's trial transcripts. The clerk said she would have it delivered by the end of the day—tomorrow. Jake figured he could spend the weekend reading through the testimony of Micah's victims. Maybe come up with some useful information.

Next, he called the prison, explained himself. Then asked how hard it would be to get in and see Micah later that afternoon.

"No problem," said the chief of security. "You come see me, Detective."

Jake could hear it in his voice. *A budding cop. Perfect.* So he went with the moment. "This is a big case in the city, Chief. Your help would be greatly appreciated. How is Mr. Micah?"

"Frail, but sharp as a tack. Detective Cooper, anything I can do to help, you just say the word."

"I'll be up there late this afternoon."

40

THURSDAY, SEPTEMBER 11 – 1:30 P.M.

Anastasia Rossi drove back to her apartment in Chelsea's Little Italy to retrieve a notebook she left behind that morning. It was no bother. Dickie had a department-mandated eye exam downtown. She dropped him off, said she'd be back in an hour.

"I'll be out front," Dickie said. "Don't be late."

She parked in an open space in front of the three-story, red-brick tenement building. There were those cast-iron ladders, sharp chips of green paint flaking off, leading up to the small verandas hanging over the street. Outside on the lamppost hung a red, white, and green Italian flag. People sat on the stoops, talking, eyeing anyone who looked out of place. Smoking. Talkin' shit.

Inside her apartment, Anastasia had the latest bestselling self-help books—*The Secret* was bedside—and diet magazines strewn about. The refrigerator was empty, save for a half-gallon of green tea, cream for coffee, a few out-of-date condiments she'd never use, and a six-pack of Diet 7-Up. White Chinese food cartons, stained with tacky red duck sauce, sat next to a half-empty green bottle of Pellegrino spring water on one of the refrigerator door shelves.

After checking her messages (nothing from Todd) and grabbing the notebook, Anastasia stopped by the door on her way out, stared at a photo she kept up on the wall over the thermostat near the door. It was Todd and her at a friend's party, his arm interlocked with hers. They held red keg party plastic cups up in front of themselves. Saluted the camera. Both looked glossy-eyed, but happy.

She touched the photo gingerly. Smiled slightly. Tilted her head to the right. It was hard, but she was going to get through this.

Fake it till you make it.

Outside, Anastasia walked down the ten steps and toward her car. Almost there, she bumped into, of all people, a man she presumed to be the neighborhood mailman. He was common-looking, she noticed. Wore sunglasses—those yellow-tinted types you buy on late-night TV and get two pair for $19.95 plus a free fanny pack carrying case. He had a pock-marked face. *Craters*, she thought. Dark brown— nearly black—eyes. He seemed to be about five foot eight inches, maybe 160 pounds.

Mr. Nobody.

No, Mr. Everybody.

Anastasia's mind was off somewhere. In fact, she wouldn't have looked twice at him if they had not bumped into each other.

"Oops," he said, dropping the load of mail from his hands. "Sorry."

"Oh, no. It's my fault." She bent down. Helped him pick up the mess. "Don't know where my head is these days."

"I know how *that* is. You have a good day now, Officer."

Anastasia got in her car. Called into base to let dispatch know where she was headed. It took several minutes. When she was finished, CSI Anastasia Rossi sped off with a chirp of the tires.

1:46 P.M.

He sat in his Jeep. Watched Anastasia Rossi speed away like some television cop off on an urgent call. He wondered if she had figured out that tiny little detail yet. Or was she so consumed with her own issues, she had failed to notice.

Officer.

If she was such a smart cop, as she had projected herself to be in the newspapers and on TV, she'd realize there was no way for a stranger to know she was a cop. Anastasia dressed in casual clothes. Not traditional blues.

She'll never figure it out.

The mailman took out a photo he swiped from the Chelsea Public Library.

It was her, definitely. "Officer Anastasia Rossi, Forensics."

Sitting in front of her apartment, staring down at Anastasia's photo, the mailman smiled, relishing in how easy finding CSI Rossi had been.

He had logged onto Yahoo! Search inside the library, keyed her name into that little magical box to the left of the Yahoo! Trademark symbol. With a few quick keystrokes, the man in the mailman's uniform came up with two *A. Rossi* names in the Boston area. One lived in a high-rise outside Beacon Hill, which anyone with a grammar school education knew a cop in Boston could not afford. The other lived in an apartment building outside Revere. He printed out the information along with MapQuest directions and headed out the door.

Officer Rossi. My hero.

41

THURSDAY, SEPTEMBER 11, 4:15 P.M.

The drive up to Shirley, Massachusetts, took Jake a little over an hour. He enjoyed the time out of the city. He could clear his head without the noise of the past intruding. Northern Massachusetts was a beautiful part of the state, with lots of evergreens and rock-strewn streams bubbling off to nowhere. It was hard not to feel a calming sense of letting go up here.

Jake came out of a wooded area, turned a corner, and there it was—a mountain of concrete and steel standing tall, as if it had been planted and grown from a seed. The prison itself was surrounded by a fifteen-foot-tall fence, topped with coils of wire and Chinese star-like razors. The prison seemed incongruous inside the dynamic of preserved forest country. So contextually and environmentally out of place.

The Souza-Baranowski Correctional Center was Massachusetts's most modern prison. It held the distinction of having the maximum degree of technical security out of any prison system in the United States. Jake had read up on the place before leaving, even downloaded some of the data into his iPhone. He was fascinated by the sheer mass of the structure now seeing it in person. The 500,000-square-foot maximum-security facility housed about 1,000 cells. It also had over 125 special management cells. And two dozen health service beds, which was one of the reasons why Micah had been transferred from Massachusetts

Correctional Institution at Norfolk, south of Boston—maximum health care within maximum security.

The security system at Souza-Baranowski was something out of *Battlestar Galactica*. The brain of the facility consisted of forty "graphic interfaced computer terminals," a geek's way of saying there was only one way into the keyless building. The computer controlled the prison's 1,700 doors, lights, receptacles, as well as the gates. With one of the largest matrix systems in the world at their disposal, guards used nearly 400 cameras to oversee and record the ebb and flow of the prison, twenty-four/seven.

Jake flashed his badge into the camera's eye, and was zapped into the main lot.

At the guard shack, Jake unloaded the one live round in his .40- caliber Glock into the fifty-five-gallon drum full of sand by the door. All armed law enforcement visiting the prison were mandated to stick their hand into a rubber hole on the top of the barrel and fire any live rounds of ammo into the mound of sand inside. It was to protect the inmates more than anything else.

Jake handed the guard five additional rounds. Showed him the gun was empty. Holstered it. Then followed his escort to an empty waiting room past four sliding steel doors banging shut—with that dramatic prison echo—behind him. The room was devoid of any color whatsoever. Reds, greens, and purples stimulated inmates. The gray kept them calm. Chairs and tables were welded to the floor. Remote- controlled camera eye lenses stared down at Jake from all four corners. The hum of fluorescent lights kept pace, while the shiniest—and cleanest—white tile Jake had ever seen glared up at him.

"We spoke on the mobile," the guard said with a British accent, sticking out his catcher's-mitt-size hand. "Name's Derek Minster." He was freakishly tall. Bald by choice. Fit as a weight trainer. "Anything you need, Detective, you get hold of me. I'm the shift supervisor here. They call me 'Chief.' Nothing gets done without my signature. Of course, I'm pulling a double tonight because we're short, but what can you do?"

Jake was impressed. Two guards with five o'clock-shadow-shaved-heads stood in back of him at attention. They stared at nothing in a creepy, Heil Hitler-like fashion.

"Thank you."

Jake read through his iPhone notes as Micah was wheeled in. There was an oxygen tank strapped to the back of Micah's wheelchair, a long, clear hose running from a ventilator up to his nostrils.

"Take all the time you need, Detective."

The door closed. The lock snapped into place, clicking loudly inside the room.

With labored breath, Micah asked, "What do you want?"

"Your help. I need information you have."

Jake and Dickie had theorized that Micah might be pulling the strings of some nut on the outside. Maybe coaching an old student to kill. Jake needed to be careful with his questions. He didn't want to allude to this. He needed Micah to believe that he had some sort of control over the investigation.

"Not interested."

"All I need is information, Mr. Micah. Just a few yeses and nos. Then I'm out of here."

"Why would I help you?" The heart rate machine hooked to Micah's pulse beeped at a methodic, medical pace. The room smelled of fresh paint and cleaning chemicals. Micah had a hospital aroma to him, Jake could tell by sitting so close. It reminded the detective of his mother putting Vicks VapoRub on his chest when he had a cold.

"Did you smoke, Micah? I've wondered. I'm conducting a little un-scientific survey of my own. Looking over your medical history, I've thought, 'How much did this guy smoke?' I'm sorry you're so sick. Must be doubly worse in a place like this."

Jake took a piece of nicotine gum, popped it into his mouth. He offered a piece to Micah.

"I did not smoke, Detective. Actually, the medical care in here is ten times what I would have gotten on the outside." Micah gave Jake a fake smile, then went straight-lipped. "I'll ask you again—what do you want? Look at me. I have a death sentence. I am in no mood to waste any of my time. I have a card game to get back to. I'm prepared to die in here. I could care less about your investigation."

"I'm interested in your students. Those you abused, that is."

"No."

"Tell me about the orphanage. Your classes."

"No again. Next?"

"What if I can get you out of this high-tech prison and into a lower security facility downstate? Same healthcare. Some hot nurses to take care of you. Good food. I can talk to the DA. She's a personal friend."

"You're not going to do anything for me, Detective." Micah chuckled for real this time. "Don't make transparent promises. It won't work here. One thing about a prison with such tight security—nothing is private. There's probably ten people watching and listening to us right now."

Jake looked around the room. Big Friggin' Brother.

"Listen, no bullshit," Jake leaned in to whisper. "I need you to step up to the plate here, or I'll make your life in this joint a hell you have never thought existed."

Micah smiled. "This has nothing to do with that serial murder case in the papers, Mr. Cooper. Now does it?" Micah had a sarcastic, one-up tone to his gravelly voice.

Jake was puzzled by this.

"You heard me, Mr. Cooper. This is more about a little girl you couldn't save, am I right?"

Blood rushed into Jake's face and hands. His pulse went off the charts. He stood. Walked away from the table.

"You need to redeem a career so you can walk away from the job feeling like it wasn't your fault that little girl died. I can smell it on you."

Jake bowed his head. Had one hand in his pocket. The other clenched into a fist, up to his mouth. He considered how he had lost that fire for the work he once had. He was running on the past, using it to fuel every move. Once a cop lost his nerve, Jake was certain, he was finished.

"What's a matter, Mr. Cooper, I hit a nerve? You're so quiet."

Jake got nose-to-nose with Micah. He thought of that little girl's final moments, what it must have been like to smother and not breathe. He grabbed the oxygen hose, pinched it. Put his mouth up to Micah's ear. "Don't fuck with me, you freakin' diddler—I'll have you castrated in here, you got me."

Micah couldn't breathe. He started coughing. Couldn't stop on his own. Guards rushed in. Ended the interview. Wheeled Micah out into the hallway.

Jake followed them. "I'll be back tomorrow morning."

"Don't bother," Micah said, trying to catch his breath, hacking and coughing.

Derek Minster stood nearby, listening.

"I won't leave you alone."

"Promises, promises, Mr. Cooper. Spare me the drama." The guard wheeled Micah a few feet down the hall after Minster motioned with a head nod to take him away. Halfway down the hall, Micah tugged at the guard's shirt to stop. "Turn me around. I want to see his face when I tell him."

Jake looked. "Tell me what?"

"I know who you're looking for, Detective." He laughed, and it started another coughing fit. Then he grabbed the guard's shirt again, as if he was some sort of villain in a Peter Sellers movie, gesturing to be taken away. "I even know his name."

The guard wheeled the child abuser away as he laughed and coughed.

6:05 P.M.

When Jake returned to his car in the prison parking lot, he checked his iPhone.

Dawn had sent him a text saying to call her as soon as he could.

"Hey." He started the car. "What's going on? Everything okay?"

"Fine, Jake. Listen. I got a call from an 'old friend,' didn't leave his name. Said something about Mo—"

"What's going on, Dawn?"

"This guy said Mo was upstate in some bar, drunk off his ass, saying things that weren't making much sense. Told me to get ahold of you right away with the info."

"Name of the bar?"

"Yeah, hold on, let me get the note."

Silence. Static.

"Dunstable, a place called Larry's. Mo was apparently heading up to Vermont to go fishing. Meet some old cop buddies."

"Who called?"

"Said he didn't want to get involved."

"Did you recognize the voice? Caller ID?"

"No. Private name, private number. Voice was muffled. Male, though, for sure."

"I'm about an hour from Dunstable. Maybe I should go. I'd like another crack at this clown Micah tomorrow morning. I'll get a hotel in Dunstable. Call you later."

Jake groaned after he hung up. Going to rescue a drunk from himself was not what he had in mind for the rest of the day. But maybe it was time to confront Mo and lay it all out.

What is he doing up here, anyway?

Guy never fished a day in his life.

Driving away, Jake was reminded of a time when he had pulled his father out of Touchie's Shamrock Pub on the corner of H and 8th streets in Southie, a few blocks from the Coopers' row house. It was one of those scorching July mornings. Several teenagers loitered outside the bar, standing on the corner bare-chested, T-shirts tucked into their back pockets. They held quart bottles of beer in brown paper bags. Unlit cigarettes tucked in their ears. Jake stared them down and walked into Touchie's just as two guys were getting ready to pummel the old man. Jake's dad was yelling, "Fookin' tinkers!" He and two local union guys were arguing about the Boston Bruins losing in the playoffs the night before. A friend of Casey's had called Jake to warn of the impending ass-kicking. It was the first and last time Jake bailed his father out.

42

Ribbons of smoke from the oil tankers docked in Mystic River near Alford Street rose in perfect corkscrews. For the first time all year it actually felt like September. There was a bite in the evening air. By nightfall a damp, cold mantle of Canadian air would settle on the city. It would be a comforter night.

The game was going well for the Jaguars. Dawn's team was ahead by four goals. Watching things wind down, Dawn realized she couldn't get Denny Garcia out of her mind. She needed to focus on helping the boy. As if things weren't bad enough for the kid already, his foster father had hit Denny the day before. He was okay. But the open-hand slap was so hard, Denny walked into school with a black-and-blue handprint on his face. The authorities got involved. Denny was moved to another home. Fifth one in four years.

Dawn wanted to cry.

The ref blew a whistle. Held up a forefinger. "One minute to go."

Dawn snapped out of it and turned to look at Brendan. As usual, he was in the sandbox just behind her, playing with his Hot Wheels. Such a gentle, agreeable kid. His one lot in life these days was to convince Mom and Dad that the playscape he wanted—$3,000 worth of pressure-treated bliss—was well worth the money because Aden, a fifth grader up the street, had one, but he was too old for Brendan to play with.

Dawn had a bead on her son this time. He was fine. What kind of world was it that a kid couldn't play in a sandbox by himself, his mother twenty-five yards away? Dawn wasn't interested in living in that place, regardless what Jake warned. Didn't matter how dangerous those Catch a Predator shows on television made life seem. There was so much to fear today. It was a wonder anyone sent their kids out to play at all. Dawn was not about to shield her only child from, well, his childhood.

As she turned to call Brendan over—he liked to help collect the balls and pick up the equipment after games— the ref blew his whistle. Two girls were involved in a shoving match in the middle of the field.

"Now?" Dawn said to herself. She ran out onto the field. Grabbed Tyisha Harris by the shirt. "Stop that, Ty. Stop it right now."

The other girl screamed obscenities.

The ref got carried away with his whistle.

Dawn yelled, "Stop it, Ty. Calm down now. Let her go."

Tyisha said something and released the girl. Everyone's hearts thumped out of their chests.

Dawn walked back to the sidelines, scolding Tyisha for allowing her anger to get the best of her. As she started to say, "You should know better than …" Dawn glanced over at Brendan and her heart raced. There was a man standing beside him. Brendan sat on the sand, looking up. It was hard to make out who it was because darkness had settled and the park lights weren't bright enough.

Dawn ran toward her son.

Arriving at the sandbox, Dawn realized the guy was nothing more than the neighborhood mail carrier. Coming up on the two of them, she let out a deep sigh. It was okay.

He's just a mailman.

Dawn was out of breath. With her hands on her knees, she asked, "Bren, everything cool here?"

The mailman didn't speak. He looked at Brendan.

"Yes, Mommy … this is a mailman, you know."

"I know, honey." To the mailman, "What do you want with my son? No, in fact, what are you doin' here?"

She wondered if she was overreacting.

"Oh, gees. Sorry to alarm you. I was passing through after finishing my route, heading toward my Jeep over there." He pointed. It was parked along the road in front of them. "Saw that your boy here was playing Hot Wheels." He reached down and picked up a Corvette, held it eye level, and stared in through its little window. "God, did I love these cars. Brought back so many memories. I had to stop."

"He's okay, Mommy. He just wanted to know what was my favorite car."

"The Hummer!"

Brendan said it with him, adding, "Jinx."

"Double jinx."

They laughed.

"Just brought back so many memories. Déjà vu … you know. I looked over and saw myself as a child, having grown up in this very same neighborhood, sitting, playing with my cars, not a care in the world. Didn't mean to alarm you. I apologize."

"It's fine. I'm sorry. I worry. My husband's a cop. Lots of crazy people in this world."

Dawn felt she was making a big deal out of nothing. Too many late night television shows. Too many "Stranger Danger" infomercials. Too many lectures by Jake.

The mailman walked away. "You have a good day now, Mrs. Cooper."

"You too, sir."

"Bye, Mr. Mailman."

Dawn bent down to help Brendan pick up his toys. "Come on, let's go home."

They walked back to the team bench. "How did he know your name, Mommy?"

Dawn turned to look.

The mailman was gone.

43

THURSDAY, SEPTEMBER 11, 7:05 P.M.

Larry's Café smelled of stale beer and urine. Cigarette butts floated in half-full glasses of brown and black liquids. Pickled eggs sat in a gallon jar on the bar. Beef jerky, Slim Jims, and pretzels were in dusty display boxes along a mirror. All of this, as Jake walked in and looked around, made it clear to him that men went to Larry's to get their drunk on.

Jake spied Mo leaning on the bar, hunched over, his arm slipping off the cushioned bar rail. There was a six-ounce glass of draft beer in front of him, full. A five-dollar bill and some spare change underneath a shot of Jack Daniel's he had not touched.

Mo didn't notice as Jake sat down and snapped his fingers for the bartender. Then ordered a Mountain Dew and Bacardi. "With a lime."

The bartender, a rugged man wearing a stained apron, chewing on the unlit end of a stubby cigar, brown dishrag in hand, laughed. "Yeah, right."

"Mo, yo?" Jake said. He hit him on the back. Mo couldn't lift his chin off his chest. "Come on, Mo. Wake up." Jake slapped him gingerly on both cheeks.

Mo drifted from side to side, mumbling things. He tried to push Jake's hands off him, unaware it was Jake Cooper trying to revive him. "Leave me … alone …"

"Mo? Hey, man … time to get going."

Mo said it again: "Leave … me … a … lone."

Leave me alone. It sounded so familiar. Martin Cooper's favorite saying near the end. The first time Jake heard it, he stood outside the door to his father's bedroom. Jake was eighteen. His life finally on track. He heard his father's muffled voice through the door: *go away.* Jake knew Dad was in the bedroom, sprawled out on the floor, drunk and powerless as a skid row bum, and had probably pissed all over himself.

"Jake?" Mo was seeing double. "That you, Jake?"

"Hey, man. Gotta get you outta here."

"Jake?" Mo rocked slowly, as if he was underwater, back and forth.

The bartender put Jake's drink down. "Five dollars for the rum and Coke."

"How long has he been here like this?" Jake gave him a twenty. The bartender looked at it. Turned the bill over and back again. Laughed.

Jake reached into Mo's front pocket and found a fifty-dollar bill, gave it to the guy.

The bartender said something about Mo sitting there since early afternoon. "He was with some other dude, a fat and really white guy who was definitely a cop."

"They seem to get along, or was it business?"

"Said he was looking out for a friend. Called himself 'Sunshine.'" The bartender folded the bill in three, put in his front shirt pocket.

Jake ran through his mental Rolodex.

No Sunshine.

Mo was nodding in and out again.

"This Sunshine, him and this clown argued at times. Toasted at others. He was here for, oh, I don't know, three hours. Your boy here, he gave 'Sunshine' an envelope. Then the fat dude left. All I can tell ya."

Jake took a sip from his rum and Coke. Took Mo by the arm, placed it around his shoulder. Then hoisted him up and off the stool. Mo was out cold.

"Why keep serving the guy if he's passing out like this?"

"You got money, you drink."

"Asshole."

As Jake and Mo walked toward the door, three guys, rough, backwoods, *Deliverance* types, came up to Jake, stepped in front of him.

"He ain't leavin' without paying," the tall one said. He was rugged. Unwashed. Unshaven. Poster child for grease monkeys everywhere.

According to these clowns, Mo had played pool and lost. Drinking wasn't enough, apparently. Guy had to gamble, also.

Jake looked the men over. Put Mo down on a chair beside the door. He slumped over. One arm flung off the chair, nearly touched the ground.

"Listen." Jake addressed the tall one, who seemed to be the leader. "No trouble here. How much?"

"Two hundred."

Jake gritted his teeth. Put a thumb and middle finger on his temples. Looked up. "This guy wouldn't bet two large on a guaranteed winner. He's a cheapshit. Screw you. Get the hell out of my way."

The three guys moved closer. There were four other patrons in the bar. One sat next to a neon Pabst Blue Ribbon sign buzzing on and off in the window. Another sat at the bar, watching a hunting show on ESPN, sipping from a longneck Miller. Two more were in a booth, a hooker and her john, laughing, touching each other playfully. The bartender put an elbow on the bar, cradled his chin in his palm, stared.

Jake was the entertainment for the night.

"Look, I am not going to be able to take the three of you." Jake put his hands on his waist. "But bet on this—I'll put one, maybe two of you, in the hospital before you get me down and kick my ass."

They looked at each other.

"Eat shit and die," the greasy dude said. He would have fit the part better if he had a chain in his hand. Or maybe a nightstick to swat against his palm while he spoke.

Jake thought about it. Growing up in Southie, you learned things. One was to never get involved in a fight you knew you couldn't win. So he opened his suit jacket as if modeling the inside pocket and exposed the shoulder holster fit snug up against his rib cage. The handle end of his Glock was easy to see. "If that doesn't work, well, I guess my forty-caliber friend here will do the trick. I'm a cop, you assholes. Now help me load this drunken sonofabitch into my car and we'll see how much money he has left on him."

44

THURSDAY, SEPTEMBER 11, 8:00 P.M.

The Sea Shore Motor Inn was the first motel Jake came upon. He pulled into the parking lot, Mo passed out on the backseat. Jake could send for Mo's car later on.

The name of the motel baffled him. There was not a shoreline for fifty miles. The "a" was missing from the sign, several other letters buzzing, not lit up. Grass had grown waist-high around the pool, which was filled in with dirt. The door to the office had one of those black and orange signs you get at the hardware store—HELP WANTED.

Jake rented a room hoping that Mo would sleep off his bender, wake up, and explain what the hell was going on, once and for all.

Inside the room, Jake plopped Mo on the bed. He didn't blink. But instead started to snore a day's worth of beers and whiskey away. Jake knew once his former mentor was out, trying to revive him was a waste of good energy.

After tossing his keys on the small desk, Jake locked the door. Took a deep breath. Freshened up inside the bathroom. At the local diner a half-hour later, he had a strong cup of coffee and a plate of homemade pot roast and gravy with a side of mash that bore a striking resemblance to cottage cheese. He spoke to Dawn. Explained that he was staying overnight as he had originally thought. Said he would be home in the morning. Dawn said she was probably taking tomorrow off. Something about being stressed out. "Can't wait to see you, babe."

Jake's pulse raised. "Something happen? Everything go okay at the game?"

Dawn hesitated. She wanted to tell him. But not now. "We won."

They said goodbye and goodnight.

Matikas called and asked Jake what the hell he was doing way up north. Jake said he'd fill him in first thing tomorrow afternoon. "The case is coming together, Ray," he lied.

"You better have something substantial here, Cooper."

Jake rolled his eyes. Didn't mention Mo. Or what else he was up to. He gave Matikas some excuse about following a lead Dickie had come up with.

When Jake returned to his hotel room, he went to put a hand on the doorknob, but immediately retracted after looking down and noticing that the door was propped open about two inches.

He drew his Glock without thinking. Checked behind him. Then shuffled to one side of the jamb, as low as he could get to the ground.

He couldn't hear anything inside.

With his Glock leveled in front of his chest, Jake did one of those kick-the-door-open-and-dart-inside moves every cop learned his first week at the academy. The rookie motion made Jake feel like Robert Urich's *Spencer: For Hire*. Stupid, flashy. Way too Hollywood. Still, the move was effective if you didn't want to get shot or blindsided.

Inside the room, Mo was still sound asleep. What looked to be a Hallmark card in a white envelope sat atop Mo's stomach, rising up and down with the drunken cop's labored breathing.

Jake cleared the room first. Made sure no one was in the shower, behind a door, or under the bed. He grabbed the envelope with a Kleenex, sat down on the sticky chair. With his iPhone set on fingerprint mode, he scanned the envelope. Saved the data.

Detective Jake Cooper, the front of the card read.

He opened it slowly, without getting his prints or the acid from his hands on it. Inside was a folded card. Jake pulled it out carefully, as if someone had sent him an envelope full of anthrax.

How stupid do I look? he thought after doing it.

Typed on the inside of the card in all caps was a simple message:

> *MR. MICAH HAD A VISITOR A WHILE*
> *BACK ... CHECK THE PRISON LOG.*

45

Dickie wanted to be home. His feet up on the recliner. Remote control in hand. Zapping his way through the one-hundred-and-eighty-seven channels of cable television he complained of overpaying for each month when he got the bill. But he and Anastasia were out, waiting for Lisa Marie Taylor's folks to get home. Dickie had stationed a blue at the Taylor residence that afternoon. The Taylor family, however, was nowhere to be found. So Dickie and Anastasia, after getting a call that Mr. and Mrs. Taylor had returned, were now standing on the Taylor doorstep, preparing themselves to question Lisa's father again. Dickie was banking on a hunch he had that the Taylors knew more than they had previously offered, hoping this horrible story would go away and not taint the family legacy.

"Good cop-bad cop?" Anastasia asked as Dickie knocked.

"Leave that *Law & Order* bullshit to the actors, Rossi. This is the real deal here. Just watch and learn. Follow my lead."

Anastasia didn't mind. She understood Jake and Dickie were giving her more responsibility. At least she wasn't cooped up in that office all day studying crime scene photos. Or lurking around the lab in a white coat, digging through pairs of panties with tweezers, collecting DNA from cigarette butts and other trace. She was an investigator. Out in the field. Tracking leads, questioning people. Where all the action was.

Andrew Taylor sat by a window in the library as Dickie and Anastasia entered the house under Bernadette Taylor's direction. The maid offered coffee. Both refused. Dickie said something about being up all night if he drank caffeine after four.

Anastasia walked around the Taylor library, taking in what Andrew liked to read. Lisa's father and Dickie got comfortable with each other. "Leave us be a few minutes," Andrew told his wife. From a sofa in the middle of the room, she got up, said nothing, then walked into the kitchen around the corner.

Dickie had already decided to take a chance. Solving difficult cases required risk. They had made some headway in the case, but not fast enough. Dickie had read the ME's report and decided to put a volatile subject out in the open. Enough time had elapsed. Mr. Taylor could take the hit.

"So, what was going on between you and Lisa?"

"You guys are quick," Andrew said, staggered by the question. "I'll give you that." He felt the loss now more permanently. It took several days to settle. This was what Dickie remembered most about being in uniform—how a parent's reaction to their kid's death came with that unfortunate, terribly compounded delay.

"Talk me through this, Andrew, as I give you the benefit of the doubt. We have a source says you liked to touch your daughter. That's enough to blow this fake-ass Ozzie and Harriet world you and the missus have to pieces. We also know Lisa had an abortion recently. Help me understand what's going on here."

Andrew took a long, slow breath, let it all out from his nostrils. "I guess, in light of your investigation, you need to scratch some things off your list, Detective. So I'll oblige. If I didn't care about my daughter, I'd throw your ass out of my house for making such an accusation. Then sue the blue out of the Boston Police Department. You'd be directing traffic in Jamaica Plain with the connections my wife and I have."

"Come on, Andrew, were you sneaking into your daughter's room in the middle of the night? We can find this out the hard way if you choose."

"Not a chance, Detective. The problem that Colby kid was referring to—it is Barton Colby making this erroneous claim?—involves my daughter sneaking around with some older man she met in the hospital. You see, Lisa spent some time in McLean Psychiatric Hospital in Belmont. We paid this guy off to forget her. The bastard actually shook us down. What, did you nail Colby on drug charges? We call that a deflection at the university. You forestall attention on yourself by pointing a finger at someone else."

"We'll need that name, Andrew. Did he get her pregnant? And this has been bothering me. Where was Lisa going that day she disappeared?"

"Look," Taylor stared out the window, lost in a haze of mourning, "you were going to find this out soon enough anyway, but please don't let the press know about it. Lisa got the help she needed. We had someone watching her almost twenty-four hours a day. But when she went to the library," he looked down at the carpet, swallowed a lump, "we allowed her that space—without intrusion. She was doing research on some 'project' she said we wouldn't be interested in. She was, most likely, checking her eBay accounts on the library computer. To be honest, she was right—we weren't that interested. We were too involved in our own damn lives to care about what mattered to Lisa. It's so true, Detective. You have no idea what you have until it's gone." He choked back tears. "It was Barton Colby's child—and we paid for the abortion. Gladly, I might add."

Hindsight. The ultimate reality check.

Dickie was disgusted with the guy. He saw that cross tattoo on Lisa's stomach and realized Lisa had put it there as a memorial to her aborted child. Andrew obviously loved his daughter. But hadn't treated her the way he now wished he had. Colby's insinuation was ridiculous. Dickie knew the art of body-language lie-detecting. He noticed that Andrew had a habit of dropping his right shoulder and running a hand across his chin whenever he spoke the truth. Dickie had asked several common questions he knew the answers to and Andrew made the same gestures when asked about an inappropriate relationship with his daughter.

"That name, Andrew?"

"Robert Tanglewood. You won't find him, though. Shot himself in the head after a bad acid trip. He was in that psych hospital for a reason, Detective."

"What's this about the eBay stuff?"

Taylor played with a tissue in his hand. "I'm not really sure because … because, well, we never really asked her about it. The eBay trading kept her busy and we thought that's what she needed. She believed she was hiding it from us. We allowed her that." He changed the subject. "Are you telling me this sonofabitch cut my baby's legs off? How was he able to get into our home to put the legs in her closet?"

"We're not sure yet." Dickie was glad no one had gone over the initial autopsy report with the family. The Taylors had never asked specifics regarding how Lisa was murdered, other than a cause of death. Most families didn't want particulars. Death was enough information. But the Taylors had assumed the legs found in Lisa's walk-in were hers. Jake didn't want any facts about the legs released.

"What else did this animal do to her?"

"We're working all of that out now, Andrew. Takes time. Let me ask you, the Colby kid said you and Mrs. Taylor, you didn't want Lisa trading on eBay. You knew about eBay. But why would you make Lisa think you didn't want her to do it?"

"MySpace and Facebook, we did not want her on those social sites. We come from money, Detective. Once people understand that, they think they deserve a share. Lisa told Barton eBay because she didn't want to admit we wouldn't allow her on the other sites. She said it was embarrassing."

The response sounded legit enough to Dickie.

"How did this animal get into my home? How did my daughter's killer get into my house? Do you know how much money I spend on security? This guy comes into my house and leaves behind a reminder of what he did to our little girl."

The tears turned on. Taylor had worked himself up into a frenzy.

Dickie was glad he didn't manage the Taylors' security company. "We've had a twenty-four-hour watch on your house since."

He put one arm up on the tic-tac-toe pane and leaned, staring outside into a maze of what-ifs. The gardener, an olive-skinned man of about thirty, pruned an apple tree. He stood on a stepladder. Whistled. Andrew Taylor looked through him.

Dickie appeared behind Taylor. "The eBay accounts, that 'research' she was doing at the library. Where did Lisa keep it?"

Taylor didn't answer.

"Andrew? That research—you know where it is? It could be important. If she left it somewhere in the house, we need to see it."

"Probably in her backpack in the closet."

"Take me there."

The closet was outside the doorway leading into the library. Andrew Taylor opened the door slowly. Lisa's smell wafted up and out. It was a gentle, flowery mixture of pomegranate body wash and Johnson's Baby Oil. This was where Lisa kept her coat and backpack. Scarves and hats. As the dad got a whiff of his daughter, he sighed and sobbed. His shoulders bounced up and down as tried holding in the tears. "You're going to … please, if you could … come back, Detective."

Dickie took the bag. "Sorry, Andrew. Of course." Taylor started up the spiral Colonial-style cherry wood staircase. "You mind if I take this with me?" Dickie held up the book bag. Anastasia stood by the front door, held it open. She stared down at the marble tile with an embarrassed crinkle. This part of the job sucked.

"Whatever you want," Andrew Taylor said, one hand on the gnarled railing. He did not turn to look.

"Was that laptop you gave us the other day Lisa's only computer?"

"Yep."

"If you come up with her cell phone, please call me."

"Tell my wife. She'll help." Andrew Taylor was at the top of the stairs, marching fast for his bedroom and a fresh bottle of Xanax the local Walgreens had just delivered.

Dickie and Anastasia walked out of the house. "Evidence, Shaughnessy?" she said, referring to the backpack. Shouldn't we be taking precautions with handling Lisa's belongings?

"It would have been if it was under a warrant or grabbed when we came over here last week. We never got a warrant to search the Taylor home. What for?"

"Got it."

The backpack could be a treasure trove. It was heavy. When they got to the car, the first thing Dickie pulled out after un-Velcroing the flap was an encyclopedia—*Rare Exotic Plants*. The others were a mix-and-match of rare coin and stamp catalogues. A few books of cheap jewelry. A rather thick copy of *High Performance Auto Parts for the Fast and Furious*.

"Big money in trading that car stuff," Anastasia said and pointed to the auto parts catalogue. "All the kids are doing it. Thank Vin Diesel for that."

"Vin who?"

"Nobody."

What did it all mean? So Lisa sold everything from rare plants to auto parts to jewelry on the Internet. She didn't need the money. What was her interest?

"Take this, Rossi, and see what you can find. There's more to this than that girl having a hobby."

"It's late, Shaughnessy. The lab is dark and lonely this time of night. Tomorrow?" She steepled her hands in front of Dickie as if praying. "Please?"

"How 'bout you take it home? It's nothing we can use in court, anyway. It's more for our own investigative purposes."

Anastasia held up a forefinger. Closed her eyes. "One question that's bothering me. Something you ignored in there with Taylor."

"Shoot."

"How *did* Lisa's killer get into the house to leave Alyssa's legs?"

Dickie shrugged. "I guess they have lousy security."

"Come on."

"I asked myself the same thing. Then it hit me. The Taylors are always having work done on that house. Carpets cleaned, catering, all that rich people stuff. So our guy disguised himself as one of these people. He watched the house for a few days and got in as a workman. It's either that, or our killer and the Taylors know each other."

"I'll take a second look at that security company."

"I want a list of the vehicles every employee drives, you got that?"

"A Jeep in there, perhaps …" she said.

"Maybe."

"Consider it done."

46

THURSDAY, SEPTEMBER 11, 8:50 P.M.

Anastasia returned to her apartment. What a day. Approaching the door, she looked down and found a white and blue-striped USPS envelope sitting on the doormat. She bent over and picked it up. Eyeballed the package out in front of herself with a quizzical look on her face.

The center was bulky, soft. It felt foamy, like a stuffed animal.

Anastasia tilted her head back, smiled, pressed the package against her heart.

Todd.

Her birthday was a few days away. Regardless of the break-up, the guy insisted on sending Anastasia "a little something" on special occasions. *"We can still be friends."*

She opened the door. Walked in. Placed Lisa Marie's backpack on the empty wooden wire spool she used as dining table.

After listening to her voicemail, Anastasia walked into her bedroom and got her forensic tool kit. Sitting at the small dining table, her back to the TV, she pointed the remote at the mirror in front of her on the wall and zapped the television on. The Boston News recap was coming up at ten, a bumper said. A rerun of *Sanford & Son* was almost over. When Anastasia heard that whiny voice of Aunt Esther, "You fish-eyed heathen," she stopped, turned around. Fred Sanford held his chest with one hand, the other waved toward the sky. "You hear that, Elizabeth? I'm coming to join you, honey."

Anastasia snickered along with the laugh track. Those random voices in the background of single life. The company of the lonely. To her, it was heaven.

Bored, she got up and grabbed a bottle of red wine, a $5.99 two-year-old merlot she bought at Star Market. She poured four fingers worth into an empty grape jelly jar. Taking a sip, she started to go through the papers and books and whatever else Lisa Marie had collected over the course of her research. Every once in a while, Anastasia looked at the package at the far end of the table, smiled.

Todd.

Maybe there was hope for the two of them, after all.

The package was going to have to wait. She wanted a little glow on first. Whatever it was—a tiny stuffed bear, music box, small red pillow with *Happy Birthday* embroidered on the front—warranted a phone call. She needed to be prepared to say things to Todd she was thinking about lately.

Raising the jar in a toast to the package, Anastasia took a good, hard swallow. Thank goodness for liquid courage.

It was clear to the CSI that Lisa liked to take copious notes for whatever eBay project she was working on. She had conducted research on the Queen of the Night flower after realizing how much money could be made selling them, studying every aspect of the plant. Going through it all, well into the end of the news (the sports was already on), Anastasia thought she just might end up with a Ph. D. in botany. At least where the Queen was concerned.

Meticulous didn't cover Lisa's need to know everything she could about the items she sold. Must have helped her get better prices, Anastasia figured.

Professor Shelton was spot-on with his assessment. The seedling found near Lisa's body in the Public Garden was from South America—Fortaleza, Brazil, to be exact. The most expensive breed available. Lisa understood the real money was in selling *direct descendants of a certain pedigree*, she wrote in her notes, *of Dutchman's Pipe over 100 years old.* She got her plants from a guy just outside Boston. She called him "Papa."

Strange. *Papa.*

Further along in her notebook, closer to the day of her abduction, Lisa wrote of a meeting she had set up with "MM" to purchase several Queen of the Nights. MM claimed they were from that same Brazilian pedigree. According to Lisa's notes, he said he was willing to knock off ten percent if she bought within a week's time.

"How gullible," Anastasia said out loud. "My God." She reached across the table, took another gulp of merlot.

The printed email was folded and placed inside Lisa's notes.

----- Original Message -----

From: s&snurse@gardennest.com

To: lmtaylorseller@comcast.net

Sent: August 31, 6:06 AM

Lisa … great to meet you. glad I could be of some help. You're right, eBay buyers are crazy for these … i'd sell them myself if I had the time. i do have a few south american dutchmans left over… seems you have another local green thumb pipe lover nearby, Mr. MM, you know him? Stop by anytime, I'm always here. addy below.

all best, allen

Smith & Sons Nursery

54 Industrial Park South

Braintree, MA 02185

Sent from my BlackBerry® wireless device

Anastasia wrote a note to herself. She needed to give the name to Dickie first thing in the morning. They could go see Papa and find out what he knew about MM.

Comparing the entry to notes Lisa had written in the days leading up to her abduction, Anastasia concluded that MM had a contact who was going to sell the flowers to Lisa, who was going to double her money by reselling them to an eBay buyer in Canada. *How gullible these freakin' people are,* Lisa wrote. Then told a story of how she had once bought fifteen broaches at the Dollar Tree for a buck each and turned around and sold them on eBay for $40 apiece. *Suckers will buy anything.*

On paper, it seemed like a drug deal, which was probably why Lisa took such an interest in it all. The thrill of buying and selling. eBay was floating out there in cyberspace creating armies of pushers.

Studying those days leading up to the abduction, Anastasia was startled by her ringing telephone. She glanced at the caller ID.

TODD, NEW YORK, NY …

It rang again.

Don't seem desperate. Three rings was the rule.

On the second ring, she picked up the empty bottle of merlot, held it up to the light, let out a quick laugh. Clearing her throat, "Hello there, Mr. Firefighter."

"Ana, how are you, honey?"

She loved that. *Ana.* No one in Boston called her Ana.

"Good, I'm fine … and how are you, sir?" She let out a shallow, drunken laugh.

"What's up with the I-know-something-you-don't-know tone, Ana? What's going on?"

"I got something today. I'm holding it in my hands." Anastasia cradled the phone in the crook of her shoulder. "You never call me on a Thursday night, Todd. I know what you're up to."

"*What* are you talking about?"

"Come on." She shook the package. "It's twelve by twelve, white, a little bulky in the center, soft, little cold. Chocolate, maybe?"

"You're crazy."

"A big chocolate heart from my favorite Fifth Avenue store, *J. Pierre's*?"

"Ana, please. I didn't send you anything." Todd was serious. Impatient.

"That's funny, lover boy. What, did you break up with your new bimbo? Feeling a little guilty, huh, cowboy?"

"You been drinking?"

Duh.

"I'm gonna have to open this now while I have you on the phone."

"Go right ahead. I know when your birthday is, Ana. I never send you anything early." He sounded like her brother. She hated him for it.

Then a thought. Todd was right. He was late with his gifts, yes. Early, never.

Anastasia sat down. Placed the package on her lap. Ripped open the tab. Reached inside.

The tips of her fingers stuck to something cold, the texture of Styrofoam.

Dry ice?

She put the phone down on the table in front of her. Turned on the speaker function. "Todd," Anastasia yelled louder than she needed to, "did you send me one of those LobsterGrams?"

She felt bubble wrap. The size of a fist. Soft. Semi-flat.

She slipped it out of the envelope.

"Todd, what did you send me …?"

Anastasia unhinged the tape. Unfolded the plastic wrap. The gel-like package popped open as if it had been rigged to spring apart. The contents oozed all over Anastasia legs, and then onto the floor.

Gasping for air, Anastasia got up. Walked slowly backward. "Oh, my God. Oh, my God." It was as if the wind had been kicked out of her.

Both her hands covered her mouth.

She stood with her back flush to the wall. Tears rolling off her cheeks. She had a hard time catching her breath.

Todd yelled, "Ana? Ana? What is it? What's going on?"

Her back to the wall, Anastasia slid down slowly and landed on her butt, sobbing uncontrollably.

47

FRIDAY, SEPTEMBER 12 - 7:00 A.M.

Jake had found a few hours of sleep. After dozing off on the tacky chair, about halfway through the night he grabbed a blanket from the trunk of his car, hit the bathtub.

When he walked out of the bathroom, rubbing sleep from his eyes, Jake saw that Mo was gone. At the window, he pushed the drapes aside.

"Coward." Jake said, shaking his head.

Standing there, staring at the empty parking space, Jake went into a drowsy daydream centered around Martin Cooper. How the man had run from situations that involved any sort of emotional responsibility. Jake's dad drank himself silly right through mourning Casey's death. Numb as a cavity. This, of course, while Jake and his mother withstood the brunt of it all—calls from family and friends, packing up Casey's clothes, dealing with the military. Now, with Alzheimer's stealing Martin's memory, the old man managed to escape guilt, too. Bastard. How the universe sometimes got it wrong.

Why would you ever want to be a cop?

It was too early for this. Jake wanted a cigarette. Instead, he popped a piece of nicotine gum.

Then another.

He could call and scream at Mo for taking off. Ask why he didn't face up to being a loser. Yet Jake had other things on his mind this morning. Anyway, he could take a drive over to Mo's when he got back to town and demand answers.

Then again, maybe the best response was to catch this sicko and quit.

Sitting on the edge of the bed, Jake wondered why a burglar needed to tell him to check that visitors log. Why hadn't he done it himself yesterday while he was at the prison? This was probably a good indication as to why he'd been passed over before now on these big cases.

You're probably not Army material, anyway.

There was Martin again.

8:05 A.M.

Jake rolled up on downtown Dunstable and found a Starbucks. A tall Pike's Peak all the way out here in the sticks. Go figure.

As he walked out, he heard his cell phone chime.

He looked at the home screen. A profile, although incomplete, was finally waiting for him.

Jake pushed the "load" key. Sat down inside his Crown Vic.

It took a moment. He sipped his coffee, waiting.

Then, with the magic those techies had promised, there it was.

----- Profile Incomplete/Need More Data -----

Developed: Friday, Sept. 13, 6:58 AM

Subject: RE: Public Garden Murder Suspect

FAMILY / HOME

Mother: Drug addict, abandoned child at young age, likely blonde, average looking, loner, prostitution possible, welfare case

Father: Not a daily presence in home, unavailable emotionally to mother and children, unfulfilled promises, may have abused children sexually, did not hold down steady job, likely discharged dishonorably from military

No siblings.

Urban dwellers, low-income housing, lived alone at a young age, likely lives no fewer than 50 to 100 miles outside of crime scene zone

CHILDHOOD

Seemed in total control of life, look for "good will" offerings to make up for loss of love at home, probably scorned by one or two adults early, felt let down, a driving force behind the anger he now feels, dismembered and/or mutilated animals

MOTIVATING FACTORS

Self-importance, easily feels upstaged, greedy, collects objects (beyond relics from murders) of fascination, hate for mother is projected toward victims, childhood sexual abuse initiated feelings of loss of control, will try to improve and increase "cat-and-mouse" with LE with each crime, will not stop until fully satisfied, may begin to take long breaks in between murders

PROFESSIONAL LIFE

Involved with the public, prefers to wear uniform to hide behind mask of sanity, works second or third shift, excellent attendance record and work performance evaluation, will be described by coworkers as "quiet," "keeps to himself," "excellent worker." No friends

DIAGNOSIS

Antisocial Personality Disorder, Anger-Retaliation Signature, likely 32 to 41 years old. Will have no trouble gaining the trust of his victims, who view him as nonthreatening

A college kid whizzed by Jake's car on a mountain bike. Jake watched. Thought about the *greed factor* the program mentioned. He knew that as it manifested inside his killer, the more he killed and got away with it, the larger the thirst for blood was going to be.

And that's when he'll get sloppy.

Jake found Dickie and Anastasia's email addresses. Tapped out a brief message—"Work this into whatever you have … I'll be in touch soon"—and forwarded the profile.

Jake drove back to Souza-Baranowski. Parked next to a 1999 black Z-28 with tinted windows. He crouched down in the passenger's side of his vehicle, looked at his watch. It was ten minutes past eight.

Five minutes went by. He heard footsteps. Then the Z-28 door open.

Jake popped up and startled the guy. "Whoa, there, hold up."

It was that British security guard, Derek Minster. The tall, bald one.

"You scared me, Detective." Derek had his trench coat folded over his arm. "Got a minute?"

"Sure. What's up?"

"Work a double last night?" Jake took out his iPhone, ran the green light scanning option over the driver's-side door handle of Derek's hotrod. Waited for the image to load. Then hit the *compare* App.

"Yeah. I'm beat. Looking forward to going home and sleeping it off. You going in to speak with Micah this morning? Good luck with that, Detective. What's that thing you have there in your hand?"

"I thought I saw you last night in the parking lot of Larry's. That you, Derek?" Jake kept looking down at the iPhone screen to see if it had finished the comparison task.

"Me? What. No. Must have been someone who looked like me."

"Derek. Come on. You're a bald, giant man. Very British-looking. I've been a cop a lot of years."

"I was here all night working. Couldn't have been me."

"Didn't really realize it was you until I saw the car here this morning—and then it fell together." Jake walked around the front-end of the vehicle, ran his index finger—the white glove touch—along the pin stripe. Derek stood still, following Jake with his sad eyes. "Why tail me? How'd you know where I was heading?"

The chime sound rattled Jake's attention. He looked down—CONFIRMED MATCH was all it said atop a split-screen of the two fingerprint images: one from Derek's hotrod and the other from the

doorknob back at the hotel Jake had scanned before he left.

"You must have me mistaken with someone else, Detective. Not sure what you're bloody insinuating."

Jake tilted his head. "Please, Derek. Don't insult me." He held up the phone, raised his eyebrows. "Let's stop dicking around here."

Derek Minster hesitated. Then opened his door. Tossed his coat onto the front seat. Straightening, he put his hands up like a suspect. "Okay. You caught me."

"What's happening here, guy? Why the interest in Micah? How in the hell did you know I was at Larry's?"

"I got people."

"You got people?" Jake laughed. "How long you been in America?"

"Can we sit over there?" Derek pointed to a bench behind his car under an elm tree.

"Sure. I have all morning."

Derek took a deep breath. Together they watched a bird peck at the grass. "I have cousins. Lots of cousins. Too many bloody cousins, actually. We were poor. A few of them went to Bainbridge when my mum, well, when she couldn't provide anymore. It was kinda like, okay, pick of the litter. She had six of her own. Her sisters' kids were derelicts. One of them, a mate I actually liked, became one of Micah's students."

"'Nuff said." Jake held up his hands. "But why the interest in this 'visitor' you mentioned in that note you left me? If anything, I could see you allowing your cousins into the prison some night when"—Jake looked around at Orwell *1984* security—"all this technology mysteriously loses power."

Derek considered this. "I figured you were looking to maybe get Micah charged with more crimes. My cousin's case was tossed out of court. That's why you're up here, right? You have more witnesses? There's no statute on what that bloody sonofagun did. Plus, if my cousin's case goes to criminal court, it will look better for his civil suit. They're still poor. They're suing St. Paul's Church for recommending Bainbridge."

"Gotcha," Jake said. "You would make a great cop, Derek. You've got me all figured out. And breaking into my hotel room. Great touch."

"I know the proprietor."

"Well, okay, anyway. We're hoping to maybe take a few more cases to the DA soon. You're absolutely right." Jake reached into his pocket. Took out a business card. Crossed off his name, numbers, and email. "You tell your cousin, if he's now willing to talk, to call this guy." He showed Derek Minster what he wrote: *Detective Lieutenant Matikas*, "Call this number." Jake wrote Matikas's home phone, underlined it. "You tell him to start at the beginning with the lieutenant. This is Matikas's case. I'm just up here doing him a favor. He would love nothing more than to hear about this."

"Hey, thanks for that. You really think I could be a bloody cop?"

"'Course. Ask Matikas about that, too. You got what it takes, kiddo. He'll help you out." Jake tapped him on the side of the arm.

"One thing, though, Detective. Micah, he won't talk. I sent a couple of my boys in last night." Derek looked around as though someone was listening. Then brought his voice down to a whisper, and winked. "Made sure the cameras were off. He wouldn't budge."

Jake looked toward the prison. "Yeah, I guess I should head back to Boston. Forget Micah for now."

"You might want to talk to that mailman who was up here to visit him, though. Come on, I'll take you in and get that log. He signed in. Checked his ID myself. Seemed to be a strange mate."

Jake flashed on that red, white, and blue paint chip Anastasia found on the Tea Party ship.

"Did you say, 'mailman' Derek?"

A line from that computer profile he'd just read came back.

Involved with the public, prefers to wear uniform to hide behind mask of sanity.

48

FRIDAY, SEPTEMBER 12 - 8:42 A.M.

With a quick test, Forensics determined that the bag of blood sent to Anastasia Rossi's apartment was a mixture of Lisa Marie Taylor, Alyssa Bettencourt, and an unknown donor. The plastic package, similar to an IV bag, was engineered to pop open when CSI Rossi pulled it out of the envelope. The lab had also found traces of cornstarch inside the package and on the bag—which meant their serial had worn latex gloves.

Anastasia had been up all night. She was shaken. She had washed her hands obsessively. Getting the smell of death off her body and out of the apartment was going to be tough. Blood can really start to have an odor when not chilled to the proper temperature. Anastasia was a trained crime scene technician. She'd scraped the remains of teenagers off the highway with a shovel—literally. She'd picked the charred remains of fire victims and found organs to identify them. Yet having the blood of two dismembered vics in a case she was actively involved in spread all over your hands, thighs, and carpet, the man she still loved on the telephone, had proven to be too much.

"At a crime scene you're, um, detached," she told Dickie. "You're working."

Dickie had rushed over. His wife Caroline with him. He took Anastasia in his arms. Consoled her. From this point on, all mail delivered to the squad room or to any of the detectives' homes, Dickie ordered in Jake's absence, was to be put through X-ray.

Anastasia sat at her desk the morning after the incident, but she was not there. Todd called to make sure everything was okay. He said he was heading out the door on a three-day tour, and wanted to "check in."

"I'll be fine, Todd," Anastasia said, trying to sound strong. "Don't worry."

"You call if you need me. I'll try to phone you tonight." She knew he meant it, even if he was just trying to be nice.

"Screw him," Dickie said after she hung up. "He had his chance."

The package had been dropped off. There was no way to trace its origin, logistically. No postmark. No fingerprints. Nothing.

Dickie called Jake to fill him in. "This is his game now," Jake said. He sounded sure of himself. "It's going to get worse. Expect additional morbidity. He's showing us what he's capable of doing. You read that profile I emailed you, right?"

Dickie had no use for computers telling him how to do his job. "Yeah, 'course, boss."

"Well, we got a serial who is in the business of upstaging himself with each crime. Egomaniac. I'll be back in the city by noon. I think I made a discovery up here that can help."

"You want to share?"

Jake was taking charge. "Nothing you need to know right now."

Dial tone.

9:05 A.M.

Matikas sat behind his desk, the phone in his ear. Someone from HQ had called to run up and down each side of the man because of Jake Cooper and his inability to catch a killer. As he listened, Matikas noticed that one of his file cabinets had been jimmied open.

He stood, cradled the phone between his shoulder and ear. Opened the drawer. Dug through several files, searching for what he knew the intruder was after.

Indeed, it was gone.

Sonofabitch.

"Gotta go, Henry. Let's meet this afternoon and discuss. I'm all over Cooper's shit."

Matikas stood in his office alone. Wiped his mouth in dread.

What the hell am I supposed to do now?

9:15 A.M.

"You up for a brainstorming session, Rossi?" Dickie leaned on her desk. "Scratch that. Why don't you just go home? Get some sleep. You're tired. Emotionally drained. Jesus, a bag of blood in your lap."

"How is your son, Dickie?"

Dickie was surprised by the question. He righted himself. Looked at Anastasia with a twisted face.

"Yeah," Anastasia stood. Kicked out her chair. "Your boy in Iraq. How is he?"

"He's okay, Rossi. Getting by. Tough kid. Knows his limits." Dickie thought about it. Then segued into, "Okay, Rossi, I get the picture here. I'm just saying, if you need some time off, it's understandable. You're human. Lot on your plate these past few months."

She held out a hand. Closed her eyes. "Nope. I'm good, Detective. Let's get to work and catch this psycho."

Inside the large conference room on the same floor, tablet armchairs were set up facing one direction, as if it were a classroom. Dickie picked up a cylinder of white chalk. Spent a minute laying the case out on an old-school blackboard. Cases were mapped out and analyzed here. Important meetings with the entire squad.

"Sit there, Rossi, in front of me." Dickie pulled up his pants. Drew a bull's-eye diagram on the board. "In the middle, the bull's-eye," he pointed to it, tapped on the board with the chalk, dust blooming, bits of chalk falling on the metal eraser holder below, "those are our victims. These rings around the victims are all of our leads and suspects— for which we have very few. We have options, Rossi, of where we can take this case. The question is, where does that bag of blood fit into this matrix?"

Anastasia was numb. She'd just wiped the blood from two of those *victims* off her hands. Here was a guy who had trouble keeping his pants up all day sounding as though he was a professor, teaching a master's course in Law Enforcement Investigation.

"Lisa's friend." Anastasia stopped, snapped her fingers with her eyes closed. "That girl … um, Martina Clarkson. Yes. She led us to the Internet source who sold Lisa the first batch of flowers on eBay. Turned out to be nothing. The guy was clueless."

"Right!" Dickie pointed at Anastasia with the chalk. Then turned and used his forefinger to smudge out that ring of the bull's-eye. "Keep going, Rossi." He made a circle motion with his free hand.

"What about Jake's profile—the one he texted us?"

"Screw that computer nonsense. We solve cases by gumshoe police work. Forget about that and focus, Rossi."

"We know that the paint chip—which may or may not be part of our Tea Party crime scene—is from a government vehicle, possibly a mail truck. But we're still waiting on additional tests to confirm the paint type."

"You're on a hot streak here, Rossi. Keep it up."

They stared at the board as though it was a calculator. If they could just put in the right combination of thoughts and theories. Screw Jake and his iPhone. This was how you caught a killer. Mind against mind. Good versus evil.

"We know there's only one location in the state that uses that specific type of paint to detail vehicles. And the paint is ten years old—at least. But we do not know the chemical makeup of the paint, which can lead us to a source."

"Not yet. And we have a list of what, about three hundred different vehicles we're looking at, right?"

"Which does us no good."

"Wrong. Keep thinking it through, Rossi."

"We know that Lisa was communicating with 'MM' about buying something, presumably rare flowers."

Dickie moved to an open area of the chalkboard. He drew two large *m*'s on the board. Put the chalk down. Clapped the dust from his hands.

Anastasia went to say something.

Dickie interrupted. "Just sit and think. Don't speak now."

With the solemn drone of the air duct above buzzing, Dickie bent down in front of the tablet armchair desk where Anastasia fit into it like a high schooler. As gentle as a father to his daughter, "I want you to sit here, Rossi," Dickie said, "and I want you to go through your databank. You're a smart investigator. You have the answer somewhere. I had a blue go over to your apartment and grab Lisa's bag. I'll have someone bring it down, along with some coffee. I want you to begin to cross off any 'MM' you can think of, however stupid or silly or extreme the name might sound to you."

Anastasia was quiet, sinking into the chair. This was her chance. Still, she didn't want it now. She wasn't ready. She started to speak again.

"Uh-uh," Dickie put a forefinger up to his lips. "Shh … You sit here and you study this case. Because once we find the meaning behind MM," he stood, tucked in his shirt, "we got our guy, Rossi. You hear me? We got this sick bastard."

49

FRIDAY, SEPTEMBER 12 - 10:40 A.M.

Dawn called in sick. That episode at the soccer field had rattled her. She was a mess. Dropping dishes. Putting laundry detergent in the dryer. A flashlight in the refrigerator. Yet after putting Brendan on the bus, she realized there was no way she could blow off her appointment with Denny Garcia. If nothing else, Denny needed to know there was one constant in his life—the time he had with Dawn twice a week.

The drive to the school took fifteen minutes. Dawn pulled into the parking lot, opened the car door to the smell of fresh-cut grass wafting up. That aroma reminded Dawn of walking through Boston Common as a child with her dad, eating a snow cone, the city crew cutting the lawn around them.

Denny was waiting by the door, one leg bouncing a mile a minute.

Dawn gave him a high-five. "Sit today, Denny, will you?" She looked down at the boy. Placed her pocketbook on her desk. Noticed the red voice-mail light on her phone blinking.

Denny smelled as if an adult had rubbed Brut cologne off on his clothes. He wore a faded Star Wars T-shirt—Luke Skywalker holding his light saber above his head in victory.

Dawn could tell Denny fought an urge to get underneath the chair. After contemplating it, the boy sat, knees to chest, head resting on the top of his legs. The bruise on his face—

now a tie-dyed collage of yellows and purples—was almost gone.

Denny gave Dawn a few of his most recent papers from English class. They talked about schoolwork when Denny didn't want to address life. Looking at one paper in particular, on which Denny's English teacher had left a note about, Dawn mentioned that they needed to discuss it.

She pointed to a story Denny had written about lions. On one entire page of the story, Denny failed to use periods, as though he had forgotten how.

"Denny, you know how to use periods, right?"

The boy shook his head yes.

"How come, Denny, you didn't use periods here?"

He rocked back and forth in the chair, shrugging.

"Why do we use periods, Denny?"

He looked up. Then: "So the words don't fall off the side of the page."

Dawn winced. Such an intense response from a strange kid. But that was Denny. He had the highest IQ in his class. Yet at times came across as borderline retarded.

"Daddy. Daddy. Daddy. Daddy."

"It's okay, Denny. Take a deep breath. This is your 'safe zone.' You remember me telling you about that?"

He stopped.

"Mrs. Cooper?"

"Yes, Denny."

"Good is good, right?"

Dawn wondered where this was going. "Yes …"

"And evil is evil, Mrs. Cooper, right?"

"Denny, where are you getting this from?"

"One cannot come from the other, right, Mrs. Cooper?"

"Denny, where did you hear this?"

"Is it true?"

"I guess it is, Denny."

"I read it in the library."

"There is an instinct in all of us to want to do bad, Denny. We need to be mindful of it at all times. Do you feel like being bad today, Denny?"

"Only when my daddy hurts me."

Dawn sensed a breakthrough.

"But he's gone now, Denny. He cannot hurt you anymore."

"Yes. But there will be other new ones."

Denny said he wanted to draw. Dawn kept him focused on his thoughts.

"Tell me more about this, Denny."

"Mad. Mad. Mad."

"That's good. Keep going."

Denny jumped up and wiggled his way underneath the chair.

Dawn pushed her chair aside and got on her stomach. She was nearly nose to nose with Denny. "Good, Denny, what else? Tell me what else you're feeling, honey."

Without warning Denny screamed. Then stopped.

As Dawn went to speak, Denny put his hands over his ears and let out a high-pitched shriek. When he didn't stop, Dawn buzzed security to calm him down enough so the nurse could give him a glass of water and a tranquilizer.

Dawn drove home in tears.

50

Jake was in the kitchen leaning against the sink, arms folded. It was a quick trip back from up north. Looking around, the wallpaper peeling back a little by the stove, Jake was thinking how long it had been since he'd actually broken his tools out and did some work around the house. Maybe it was time to throw it in and go back to living the life of a normal person.

Dawn walked in. Seeing her husband, she ran over and kissed him hard on the lips.

Jake grabbed her butt cheeks with both hands and lifted her off the floor.

Dawn slapped his hands. "That's what's on your mind as soon as you see me?"

"I just got home myself."

Dawn put her keys down, picked up the mail on the kitchen table, started sifting through it. "There's a package for you on the dining-room-table chair," she said. "Came yesterday morning. Weighs a ton."

Jake moved fast. Picked the package up. He didn't see any writing on it. So he put it down. Stood, staring at it, wondering if he should make Dawn leave the house.

"No one was here to scan this?" he yelled.

"Huh?" Dawn said something about not being home. She had no idea. It was on the front steps when she walked in from the grocery store earlier that morning.

Jake flipped the package over, quickly realizing it was the transcripts from Stuart Micah's trial. They had been sent over from the DA's office as he had asked. His heart settled.

Then his iPhone buzzed. It was on the countertop. Jake got to it before it vibrated onto the floor.

"I'm at a pay phone. Listen, I did that thing. Company is Lawler, Clein, and Keiser. Thirty-million-dollar lawsuit just filed."

Jake walked out onto the front porch, closing the door behind him. "Rossi, sorry 'bout that package. It's part of being a good cop, you know, taking hits like that. Crazy shit's gonna happen sometimes."

"I know. You'd think a girl from New York would be able to take a little blood, Cooper. I got my period when I was eleven."

Jake didn't know how to respond to that. "What else was in the file, Rossi?"

"There was something about Mo and his working traffic duty back during the heyday of the Big Dig. He was in a bad spot, gambling. Doing a lot of overtime on city pay for this one company. That was the only red flag I saw. Someone lobbied for him to be tossed, but he pulled a favor and got put behind a desk. I have one more place to look, though. I heard HQ has a sealed file in that SEG room downtown. But it's going take some time, and maybe a little cleavage, to get my hands on it."

"Good work, Rossi."

Anastasia looked down at her cell phone. Dickie was calling. He was probably wondering why she wasn't in the conference room. "Gotta go, Cooper. I'm supposed to be having lunch."

"Don't talk about this in the office or around anyone—including Dickie." Jake felt strange saying that. "Call me in a few days."

51

"We like to believe we can overcome anything," Anastasia's father once told her after she worked her first homicide. "Truth is, some things are just too despicably evil to get over."

Time—the healer of all wounds. Nothing but bullshit. Ask the Taylor and Bettencourt families. How do you ever get over burying pieces of your child?

The case was weighing Anastasia down. That bag of blood was maybe the final thread. Anastasia was going home to get some sleep. As she made her way toward the elevator after collecting her things, the desk sergeant yelled from behind the counter. "You have a phone call, Rossi."

Todd.

Her insides felt fuzzy, but conflicted.

"I'll take it downstairs in the lobby. I gotta get out of here."

"I understand. That I do, Rossi."

She pressed *G* for ground. The elevator smelled of leather and several cheap replica mens colognes. Anastasia pictured patrol cops buying from Indian vender kiosks at Weston Mall. In the reception area of the lobby, cops sometimes used the phone for personal business. It was set up like a break room, a Poland Spring water cooler, microwave oven, a table, and some chairs. Anastasia's call had been transferred to the phone on the wall. Cops were coming and going. In and out the room.

"I knew you'd call." She felt relaxed. How Todd could make everything all better.

Mr. Right.

"How so?" the voice asked.

"I'm sorry." Anastasia snapped back into reality. "Who is this?" "I need to report a tip about this serial killer case you people are investigating."

You people. A term only racists used, no matter what they were talking about. Great, Anastasia thought. All the case needed now was some over-zealous, Investigation Discovery-watching nut who had seen one too many episodes of *Dark Minds.*

"You should really call into the hotline, sir. I don't know why you asked for me."

"I've seen you on TV. I know you need to solve this case for your own reasons. I'm good at reading people. It's in your eyes."

Anastasia put a hand on her forehead as though she were checking herself for a fever. This guy had thirty more seconds before she hung up. "Well, okay then. Humor me here, sir. Shoot."

"I know these phones are monitored. I cannot talk about it on this line."

Anastasia did not reply. That throbbing wine headache was back.

"You there, Detective Rossi?"

Nice touch.

"Officer … I'm *Officer* Rossi. Forensic side."

"Oh. Okay, then." He sounded aggravated. "Maybe I should give this lead to someone who knows what to do with it. Obviously, you are not an investigator. You're a scientist."

"Hold on. Hold on." She thought about it. "Tell me something here that will spark my curiosity, sir. Get me interested in this call. Like, for starters, your name."

"How 'bout I say, oh, I don't know—*m-m*. Would *that* give you pause to consider what I have to be important information, *Officer* Rossi?"

Her body stiffened. She walked over to the door window into the room and looked from side to side as if he was calling from inside the building. How could this person know about *mm*? It had to be one of Lisa Marie's punk-ass friends playing a phone prank. Barton Colby was the only person outside the squad room who knew the letters *mm* were connected to the case—and it was made very clear to him that he was not to talk to anyone.

"Well, you've got my interest, sir."

"Great. Now, please let's meet somewhere so I can get you this info and you can catch this lunatic."

"Where?" Anastasia had slept maybe two hours in the past thirty. She was in no mood to meet anyone, anywhere. But she also knew that this might be the break the team needed. Chances were this guy knew nothing. He had a source inside the precinct. Or was one of Lisa's older-sounding friends, getting back at Jake and Dickie for busting Barton Colby's chops.

Either way, Anastasia decided, she needed to hear him out. "*Instinct, honey, is sometimes all we have. You always listen to it.*" Anastasia hadn't done much beat work over the years. She was strictly a lab tech and crime scene collector of forensic evidence. She had spent a year talking insecure criminals without the balls to kill out of holding hostages. But it wasn't until she joined D-15 that Anastasia Rossi was invited out into the field to investigate. Did she really want to diss this clown without hearing him out? How would Jake handle this?

Think, Rossi!

"Meet me over in East Boston, by the back of Logan, there's a Bess Eaten Donuts off the one-forty-five, Bennington Street. You know where it is?"

Keep it public. Guy could be a wacko.

"You still there?" he said.

"Yeah, yeah. Near Constitution Beach, you mean?"

"Yup."

"I'll find it."

"Be there at six." He hung up.

Anastasia wanted to go back upstairs and discuss the tip with Dickie. She called him on his cell and desk lines. No answer. She figured he was busy interrogating a burglary suspect two blues had just brought in.

So Anastasia Rossi decided to go home and rest. She'd call Dickie later. She had plenty of time before her meeting with the tipster.

52

Bess Eaten Donuts was closer to Neptune Circle than Constitution Beach. After asking a few locals, Anastasia had no problem finding the rundown coffee shop she lived ten minutes away from.

When she got home after taking the call, Anastasia made a mental note to call Dickie and let him know what was going on. That was the safe thing to do. Lying down on the couch and turning on *Days of Our Lives*, however, she fell asleep and woke up to the sound of Alex Trebek and that annoying *Jeopardy* music.

Doom. Doom. Doom. Doom. Pause. *Doom-doom-doom.*

It was six o'clock on the dot.

Racing out the door, Anastasia dialed Dickie's cell. Left him a hasty message: "Running late to meet a source at the Constitution Beach Bess Eaten in Chelsea who claims to know *mm*. Call you soon."

When she pulled into the Bess Eaten lot at 6:25 P.M., only two cars were parked up front, an Olds Cutlass and a Honda Civic. Anastasia guessed both were owned by the two patrons sitting on round stools inside the donut shop, talking to the clerk in the filthy apron standing behind the counter with a coffee pot in her hand.

None of them looked as she pulled in, drove toward the back, and parked near the train tracks bordering the north side of Logan Airport. The opposite side of the tracks was blocked off by barbed wire on top of a chain-link fence about twelve feet high.

Our Homeland Security dollars at work, Anastasia thought as she pulled in and realized how easy it was to get on to the tarmac from here.

She sat in her car and waited for her mystery man. Jumbo 757s and A-30 international flights landed behind her, rattling the rear window of her Crown Vic. Every so often, the noise subsided, but then quickly returned. Evenings were busy at Logan. Flights coming in from all over the world.

"MM," she said aloud, lost in thought. When she looked up, she watched as an old USPS Jeep with red, white, and blue pinstripes pulled into the parking lot, motored by the coffee shop's front window, then parked next to her vehicle.

Mailman.

How simple.

The guy waved as he unlatched and slid the side door of the Jeep open. He was a normal-size man. Scraggly hair underneath a worn out, greasy Red Sox hat. He had a beard that looked to be born more out of laziness than style. His crooked teeth were somewhat stained from either chewing tobacco or poor hygiene. He had little dimples, like braille, dotted about his red nose. Despite not taking care of himself hygienically, he looked to be a guy you passed a thousand times in your life on the street and never noticed.

Anastasia closed the car door behind her, approaching him with a look of surprise on her face. He seemed familiar.

"Yes, before you ask," he held up two hands, waving them up in the air as if to say, *you caught me,* "it *was* me who sold Lisa Taylor those rare flowers. We sparked up a friendship at the library one afternoon while I was delivering the mail and realized we had mutual interests. But I'm no killer. I just happened to bump into her table and noticed what she was researching. eBay—a virtual tag sale. Gotta love technology, Officer."

"You sold Lisa those flowers? Why do you look so familiar to me, sir?"

He laughed. "Well, because we kinda ran into each other in front of your apartment. I wanted to tell you then, that's why I was there. But I chickened out."

"Wait a minute … so you're *mm*? You sold the Queen flowers to Lisa Marie Taylor?" She needed to hear herself say it out loud. Then reached for her cell phone.

"I wouldn't do that … I'll leave, you'll never see me again."

Anastasia tossed the phone on the front seat of her Crown Vic as things started to register.

He sat on the driver's seat of his Jeep with his legs outside the vehicle, feet planted on the tar. A 747 shook the ground as it came in for a landing, its engines roaring like a thousand Niagaras. They watched it land, pausing, waiting on the noise to pass.

The mailman looked into the donut shop. No one inside could see the two of them. The road itself, leading into the parking lot, was blinded by thick, tall evergreens. On each side of the parking lot where they met, the walls of concrete buildings closed them in. They were in the back of the lot, away from any windows or the road. Kids partied back here late at night. On the ground around them were used condoms, flattened beer cans, empty Styrofoam fast-food cartons. Cigarette butts.

Anastasia wasn't sure about this guy. It was clear to her that she needed to get him down to D-15 for a formal interview. He likely held the key to Lisa's final few hours. Maybe the case.

"Will you come into the station to talk to us?"

"Absolutely. That's why I'm here, Officer. Lisa was a friend. I cannot believe what happened. I didn't want to just call in, you know. Or show up at the precinct. I don't like cops pointing a finger in my face. Older man, younger gal.

People talk. I have a family." He stood, walked closer to her.

Anastasia felt he looked a bit creepy and undesirable to be calling Lisa a friend. The entire scenario sounded strange. Something wasn't right. Anastasia felt her hip to see if she remembered to holster her Glock.

It was there.

For good measure, she unhooked the leather strap holding the gun in place.

The mailman talked and walked in a circle, staring at the ground. He had to keep pausing as more jumbo jets landed and taxied down the runway. He said something about how spiritually freeing the investigation had been for him. He had followed "every step" in the newspapers. "I've read every word. Seen every interview on TV. That Cooper cop, he's something. Boy. And don't get me started on Mr. Hennessey."

"Shaughnessy," she corrected with a cough of laughter. Dickie was going to love that one. "That's *Detective* Shaughnessy and *Detective* Cooper." She said it loud, as if the mailman was half deaf.

"Oops, sorry. I know how you all feel about rank and such."

Another jet. Another roar and rattle interrupting the conversation.

"You were saying," Anastasia said as the noise dissipated, "something about God and how you were called to help us out?"

Anastasia put her hands in her front pockets as though she meant to. Then moved her left hand toward her hip, casually. This conversation was getting a bit bizarre. The man was acting squirrelly and manic. She was uncomfortable with where he was taking things.

"Gut instinct is never wrong."

"Yeah, yeah. But I never said 'God.' To clear the record on that. God and me, man, we … well, you don't want to hear about that. I was referring to, like, Mary O'Keefe's body hanging there like Jesus Christ, for example. Who would do such a blasphemous thing?"

Anastasia detected a slight smirk on his face.

The facts surrounding how Mary was found had never been made public.

Anastasia rested her palm on the textured grip of her Glock. The cold steel was comforting.

"I mean, when you come down to it …" He paused again to allow another jet to land and taxi. "We are all part of Jesus's being. Little tiny cells in his resurrected body, trying to figure out our place in this world. Are you following me, Officer Rossi?" He was talking fast. Blinking his eyes a lot. Getting hung up on certain words.

Anastasia took a step away from him. A few feet separated them. She unlocked the safety on her Glock.

A jet touched down to loud squeals of burning rubber, the engines flaring up. It sounded like a hundred Mack trucks coming to a forced stop.

"The riddle is always more interesting than the solution, dontcha think, Officer?" He walked toward Anastasia.

She went to draw her Glock—but as she did, he lunged at her, going straight for the weapon.

There was a loud pop.

Then a piercing scream. The gunshot and shriek both squelched from the night air by another landing jet plane.

53

FRIDAY, SEPTEMBER 12 - 6:27 P.M.

Jake sat on the couch, feet up on the coffee table, reading through Micah's trial transcripts. A BoDeans CD played in the background on low.

Dawn was in the kitchen. Brendan played in the living room on the floor.

Dickie arrived to fill Jake in on the latest.

"Bren, little dude, can you go downstairs and put on one of those Batman DVDs, so I can talk to Uncle Red here alone for a while. Would you mind, little buddy?"

Brendan grabbed a folded-up towel from the laundry basket sitting atop the stone foundation of the fireplace. Flung it around his back like a cape, tied it with a clothespin. With his fists at his sides, arms crooked. "Sure thing, Robin." Then the boy ran away, arms stretched out in front, fake flying noises buzzing from his mouth.

"Sit down, Dickie." Jake tapped the chaise lounge in front of him. "These transcripts are something else. Graphic as hell. Not sure what I'll find here, though."

"Got a message from Rossi. Good kid. How 'bout that bag of blood?" Both waited for the other to make a comment, but neither did. It was too weird for a joke. "She said something about a breakthrough with *mm* at Bess Eaten Donuts." Dickie sounded proud. "I told her to study those notes of Lisa's. She's probably come up with some off-the-wall rookie lead we'll have a good laugh at."

Jake shrugged off the news, uninterested. He had thought about *mm* while driving back home. He wanted to call Dickie and tell him, but needed more time to consider the implications.

"Lieutenant's busting my chops. Glad you're back, Kid."

"Been gone only a day and half, Dick."

"I know. I know. I've been bearing the brunt here."

"He means well, Dickie. Matikas is just doing his job."

"Paranoid as hell, that guy. Thinks someone broke into his office."

Jake ignored the comment. He looked down at the page in front of him. Changed the subject. "MM, Dickie. I cracked the code, but it does us no good."

"It's not a name?"

Dawn arrived with some coffee. She looked great as ever. Her sweatpants—the pink ones with the white pinstripe down the sides of the legs, body tight, 1895 written across the butt cheeks—showed how well she took care of herself.

"It's simple, Dickie. *Mail Man*. Not sure how it fits, but *mm* equals mailman. He was up at the prison visiting Micah. Kind of makes sense now with the red, white, and blue paint chip you two have been working on."

Dawn turned to walk away—then stopped. "What's that about a mailman?"

Jake looked up.

Dawn put her hands over her face. Started shaking, crying.

Jake stood. "What is it, Dawn? What's wrong?"

54

The bullet hit Anastasia in the right thigh—an unimaginable pain, a golf ball shot out of a cannon a foot from her leg—with a heavy thud, followed by an excruciating burn.

Even though it hurt like hell, Anastasia managed to run toward the back of her vehicle, jump, then roll down the slight hill, onto the train tracks. The donut shop was too far. The mailman could easily tackle her in the parking lot without anyone seeing. She was on the opposite side of her car door. Her only chance was to make it to the tracks. Hide in the brush somewhere, maybe flag down a customer when the opportunity presented itself.

The mailman was close behind, grabbing at her, diving for her hair.

The gun stayed on the ground near Anastasia's car door.

"Blood is thicker than water," the man dressed like a mailman said, laughing. "You get it, Ana? You get it? I kill myself sometimes."

He jumped off the hill and onto Anastasia. Got on top of her down on the grass to the side of the tracks. They struggled for position and control. The mailman was no bigger than Anastasia. No heavier. But the searing gunshot wound and so little sleep over the past two days was working against her strength.

Anastasia gouged her assailant in the face with her fingernails. It didn't stop him. "You bitch! I'm going to cut you like I cut the others—and do it while you're alive."

"I am an officer of the law," Anastasia struggled to say, "and you are being told to put your hands up and lay down on your stomach …" Sounded as if she was reading from a card.

He laughed. A cop till the end.

Anastasia yelled, "Help!"

No one was around. It was dusk, the sun just about out of view. Anastasia felt a chill only because blood was draining out of her leg.

A jet came barreling into Logan, whistling and roaring its engines.

"Shut your mouth." He had the control back. On top of her, the mailman pinned Anastasia's arms in back of her head as she squirmed around trying to get loose. He spat in her face, a chunky slab of phlegm. "You just shut your cop mouth *right* now."

Anastasia fought him kicking and tensing up, trying to get free.

Then went limp.

He was out of breath. And let up on the pressure. "You know what it is, I like holding life and death in my hands." He wiped his mouth with the back of his wrist, using one knee to hold her down.

Anastasia spat back up in his face. "Let me go." The pain in her leg pulsed, robbing her of the ability to concentrate.

"You're wasting your breath, Officer Rossi. I am going to kill you."

She threw all her weight into her waist and, in a humping motion, lifted him off her body enough to knee him in the groin. It was enough to make him buckle, double over. She pushed him off. Then hobbled up the slight hill back toward her Crown Vic. There was nowhere to hide. She had to make it to the car. Get to her cell. Find her gun.

He leapt at her, just missing her right heel as she breached the summit of the incline.

Grabbing hold of the back bumper of his Jeep, Anastasia pulled herself up and onto her feet.

The gun was in sight.

She dragged her wounded leg. It was tight, but she made it to the Glock in time.

As she reached down, the man dressed as a mailman came from over the top of her car and kicked the gun underneath his Jeep. Then stopped. Caught his breath.

"Well now, bet you didn't expect that."

Anastasia lost her balance. Fell flat on her face.

He knelt on her back, grabbed her arms, put them behind her, snapped the handcuffs into place. In an insane burst of force, he picked her up and hoisted her into his Jeep. Then slid the door closed.

Anastasia kicked at the glass. It wouldn't budge.

He looked in all directions to make sure no one had seen them. Then opened the back door and leaned in. With the butt of her own gun, the mailman smashed the cop on the back of her head. The blow sprayed droplets of blood all over his face. He had knocked CSI Rossi unconscious. Looking at her, he watched a slow, fluid trail of blood run down her temple, follow the channel of her jawbone, then pool on the creviced indentation on her neck. Watching this gave him a throbbing erection.

Feeling triumphant, he flipped her over. How attractive. How young, too. She actually had the eyes of his mother. That whore. She sold her soul for those drugs. Brought those men into the house and did dirty things to them in front of him, sometimes making him, just a boy then, a part of it. She needed to pay. Now that he thought about it, Anastasia's hair was all wrong. Nothing like his mother's flowing blonde mane. He'd have to buy CSI Rossi a wig to keep his string going. Yes, he'd even stitch the thing to Anastasia's head—that is, after he sewed her mouth shut and cut her from her asshole to her vagina.

Bitch. You should have listened. Now you suffer like I did.

He brushed the hair away from Anastasia's face. Smiled at her. Tiny pebbles from the parking lot were embedded in Anastasia's forehead and cheeks, dried grass in her hair, a large cut on her lower lip.

Maybe you're not so great, after all, OFFICER!

55

SATURDAY, SEPTEMBER 13 - 4:48 A.M.

The garage light was on, the automatic door closed. Jake was putting the suitcases in the trunk. Brendan and Dawn sat inside the car, watching the fuzzy glow of sunlight burn through the foggy morning haze outside those four-square garage-door windowpanes.

Jake had called Father John and explained that Brendan and Dawn needed a safe house to hide in. At least until he could figure out what was going on. He could put them in a room with a standing guard, but that was no way to live. He could order a team of blues to watch the driveway and station a few more inside the house. But that wasn't going to cut it, either. He didn't want his wife and son imprisoned. Just safe. Father John knew people. Monks at monasteries. Nuns at convents. There was definitely somewhere Jake's family could be securely hidden.

"It'll be okay," Dawn said to Brendan.

"Why are we up so early?"

"Shh …" Dawn said, a finger up to puckered lips. "It's going to be okay, Bren."

"I want to spend the day at Cary's, Mommy. Why can't I, Daddy?"

"For right now, Bren, just trust daddy and mommy."

Brendan dropped his head in a huff on his favorite red and blue Spiderman pillow. He wore shorts. Flip-flops. His hair was wild. Bed head.

Dawn got out of the car and walked to the back. Jake was in motion, a suitcase in his hand, when he stopped.

"I messed up, didn't I?" Dawn said. She looked down at the concrete floor.

"No. Not telling me about the mailman would have been messing up, Dawn. It'll be okay. I'll figure it all out. As soon as I can, I'll come see you. You'll be safe where you're going."

After Father John arrived, Dawn and Brendan drove north with the priest inside the Impala with tinted windows Jake had a blue deliver to the house. After they left, Jake headed to D-15 to meet up with Dickie and figure out their next move.

In the back of his mind, that problem with Mo Blackhall nagged. Jake needed to confront Mo and have it out. All of this waiting and avoidance stalled his ability to move forward and focus on this case. His family's safety was at stake now. He needed to find the killer, or predict his next move before he killed again.

When it rains …

Inside the squad room, Jake handed off the remainder of Micah's trial transcripts to a middle-aged woman with a pale complexion they called Ing. Ingrid Swenson worked part-time at D-15. She came in on certain days and took messages, set up interviews, and answered phones when no one was around.

Dickie and Jake sat together in Jake's office, thinking, not saying much of anything, when Ing stuck her head in. "Got a minute, boys?"

Jake made a gesture for her to take a seat.

"I read through the last few hundred pages. Did you see what the state's final witness had to say?"

"No."

"Well, he talks about how this Mr. Micah carved the initials of one victim into the boy's calves. Scarred the boy pretty grotesquely."

There was some banter outside Jake's door. He got up. "Excuse me for a minute, Ing." Walked over.

It was Mo. The guy was bouncing off the walls down at the end of the hallway. Two blues watched him, laughing, pointing.

Jake took off out the door. Told the blues to get Mo the hell out of the office. "Stop making fun of the guy and get his ass home. Now."

Looked like talking to Mo today was out.

Back behind his desk. "Go on," Jake told Ing. "Sorry 'bout that."

"Well, apparently, this kid with those scars on his legs wouldn't testify. He ran away from the orphanage."

"Name?"

"Waiting on it from the DA. These kids were all underage. Juveniles. During the trial they were known as Victim A, Victim B. So on."

Dickie stood. He had an idea. He walked over and looked outside. Jake had one of the best views of the city. The sun was bright today. There were perhaps thousands of people scurrying around from place to place down on the streets. Ants marching. Dickie watched. Then turned. "You get that name checked out yet from the prison visitor's log?"

"Fake. Christopher Devlin. Cute, huh. We checked it out, anyway. No such person working for the post office in Massachusetts, Vermont, or New Hampshire. Don't ask me how he did it. He showed ID. They got him on video. But he never faced the cameras long enough for us to grab an image. Going in there, he was taunting us."

"So this Micah," Dickie walked with one hand in his pants pocket, two fingers fidgeting with his lips, looking down at the carpet, "he holds the key. He knows the boy's name."

"That might be true, Dickie. But you can't make a con talk when he's got nothing to lose and nothing left to trade."

Blood from a stone.

More noise outside the office door. Mo was being a problem. Yelling his drunken threats—"Hands off me. I can walk myself."

Dickie looked at the door, back at Jake.

"Not now. I am *not* dealing with that guy now."

Mo busted into the room. "You bastard … how *dare* you." He stared at Jake. To Dickie, "And *you*. You think you can get rid of *me*? You sonofabitch!"

The blues grabbed him. "Sorry, Cooper. We'll get him home."

Mo screamed, "You're done, Jake. All finished. Kaput." He slapped his hands together as if swatting a fly.

Jake took a breath. "Get him out of here." He closed his eyes. Paused.

One of the blues took Mo by the arm and pulled at him. "Check that file, Jake. Mancini Construction." Mo laughed, went with the escort. "Your ass is going to burn, too. Burn hard."

Dickie and Ing looked at Jake, waiting for him to respond. Jake ignored the comments. Then continued with his analysis as Mo was led out of the office. "Part of the psychology behind these predators when they get caught is knowing that there are victims out there suffering because of what they've done—and *they* hold the key to closure. Micah is sitting in that wheelchair, laughing, enjoying the fact that he knows and we don't. Locked-up serials do the same thing—think Gacy and Dahmer. They give up only a certain number of bodies and kept a few for themselves. They get off on the fact that there are families out there suffering, not able to bury their babies, but *they* know where those bodies are."

"Sick."

Ing spoke up. "Well, I'll keep reading. But it seems like one of you should go up to the orphanage and search through the old records."

"Closed about ten years ago," Jake said.

"No records for it anywhere?" Dickie added.

"There are. We're working on tracking them down."

"You Google the place?" Ing asked.

"You techies and your computer craziness. iPhones and profiles … ridiculous."

Ing laughed.

Jake frowned. Stood. Walked over to the window. Palmed the ledge. Stared out into the dead space of Boston's skyline, watched a radio station traffic helicopter hover over the Mass Pike.

56

SATURDAY, SEPTEMBER 13 - 5:45 A.M.

Anastasia Rossi thrashed around in the back of the Jeep as if someone had tasered her awake. When the mailman got her down to the marina, inside the parking lot by the docks, Anastasia intensified her struggles. That bullet in her thigh didn't seem to bother the CSI much as she fought to kick the windows out and somehow get the back door unlatched and open.

"Where in the heck do you think you're going, anyway?" The man dressed like a mailman said, watching his victim through the Jeep's rearview mirror as he backed into an assigned marina parking space. "There's nobody around. The sun's not even up over the harbor yet."

Boats were lined up along the docks, bouncing and swaying to the beat of the dark water. *The Grand Pause* was ready, waiting. He had gassed her up the previous day. Set her GPS position on the radar and could drive out of the marina blindfolded. He set up the hoist so he could hook Anastasia's legs to the end, lift her up in the air as if she was the catch of the day. Having her upside down, it would be easier to scalp and gut her. Blood rushed to the head, he knew. That first poke with the knife was going to be like crushing a bloated tick.

Killing a cop enhanced the drama. No doubt. He was feeding that greed factor he knew Jake would put his finger on sooner or later. Trauma was hardwired into his psyche.

Nothing he could do about it now. Controlling his victims gave him power over the Teacher. He needed that.

"You're a lot less congenial than you come across on television, Officer Rossi."

She refused to speak.

"Not going to give me the satisfaction of engaging in a dialogue, I see!"

There was a few beats of silence between them.

He couldn't take it. "You have this enormous chip on your shoulder. It's so obvious." He put the Jeep in park. Walked to the back. After putting on a pair of black leather gloves, wiggling each finger in its place OJ-like, scanning the marina for witnesses, he opened the door. "You think Boston owes you something because you're from New York. It's that puffy-chest attitude, like you're better than everyone else. Well, you know what, Officer—you're just like the rest of us."

Anastasia was on her back. Arms handcuffed behind her. Her feet down at the gate-style door into the back of the Jeep.

He opened it and stepped into the Jeep. Unzipped a large black duffel bag he stole from a Revere postal station. "When I thought about it, you were the perfect example for what I have planned. You represent everything the Teacher was. Everything that he took from me. And everything I can recover by killing you. Think of it this way—I am freeing you. Your death will serve a purpose."

When the mailman wasn't looking, Anastasia lifted her feet, spread her legs apart, then grabbed him by the neck in a wrestling move in between her calves. She had strong legs. Short and muscular. The bullet wound burned, but she fought through that pain. Twisting madly, he grabbed her ankles and tried to escape the tight grasp. In the tussle, she slammed his head against the window, knocking him out of the vehicle and onto the tar. He had clipped his eyebrow and fattened his lower lip on the way down.

There was a moment of hope.

This did nothing more than infuriate the killer. "Don't touch me!"

He pushed her legs upward. Thumped her feet back down on the metal floor of the Jeep. Anastasia's heels throbbed with pain—metal against bone.

"'For in all your precepts, I go forward, every false way I hate.'"

What is he talking about?

The mailman felt a warm sensation on his lip. It pulsated with his heartbeat. He looked down at the blood on his finger. Closed his eyes. It was better than cutting himself. More gratifying and sensory. His heart had never pumped this frantic when he slit his forearms or thighs.

"It's over, Miss Rossi. Don't fight it. You're going to make me do things I don't want to." He showed her the blood on his finger. "Did you know that red, for many civilizations, is the color of joy?" He licked his finger, then spat on the ground.

In the front seat, he reached into the glove box, took out a serrated hunting knife, long, bulky, and shiny. Then he grabbed the bottle of chloroform he had used on Mary O'Keefe. The roll of gauze was underneath the driver's seat.

He went around to the back door. In one violent strike, he lodged the knife into Anastasia's right thigh, just above the knee.

She screamed, but nothing came out.

He sprang forward. Placed the soaked gauze over her mouth and nose. Anastasia struggled at first. Then, as if sitting in a dentist's chair, taking in that first hit of laughing gas, her face muscles fell, relaxed. She saw stars in front of her face; little white specks dancing in the dark like fireflies.

57

SATURDAY, SEPTEMBER 13 - 10:18 A.M.

Lieutenant Ray Matikas stood in his office. He held a Louisville Slugger baseball bat out in front of himself, practiced his softball swing in slow motion. He was thinking of a way to explain how that folder went missing. The captain was going to be asking.

Ing buzzed in on the intercom.

"Yeah, Ing, what is it?"

"I have a Todd Something here on line two." Matikas walked over to his desk. The line was blinking. "Says he used to date Officer Rossi. Was supposed to talk to her last night, but can't find her. Wants to talk to you."

"Ex-boyfriend, you say?"

"Yep."

"Tell him to hold on."

Matikas hit the speaker phone button, pushed line two. "Can I help you?"

"Hi, Mr. Mathis ... I'm ... a New York firefighter." Firemen were like cops. They defined themselves by their jobs. "I used to date Ana."

"I got all that, Todd. Move on with what you need. Name's Matikas. I'm a busy guy here."

"Right. I'm worried about her. Can you call her on the radio?"

"Hold on." Matikas got Dickie on another line. "Where is Rossi, Shaughnessy? I got her paranoid boyfriend on one."

"Don't know."

"She's in today, right?"

"Don't know."

Matikas pressed the intercom. "Ing, Rossi sign in this morning? Was she at roll?"

"I checked. No."

"Thanks." The lieutenant went back to Todd. "I'll have someone call you." Matikas rolled his eyes. "Seems Miss Rossi is AWOL."

Before Todd could say thanks, Matikas hung up on him.

"Ing?"

"Yep?"

"Tell Shaughnessy to find Rossi."

Matikas stepped away from his desk and continued swinging his bat.

58

SATURDAY, SEPTEMBER 13 - 2:45 P.M.

The librarian was positive. "Look, I've never seen the girl." She pointed at the photo of Lisa Marie that Jake held in his hand.

"You're one hundred percent certain? She was here the day she disappeared."

"Do I look like I forget things, Detective?"

Actually, she didn't. Walden's Library had been part of the Cambridge landscape for the past one hundred years. Lucy May Allen had been the head librarian for twenty-five. If there was one thing Lucy could depend on in her waning years, it was a memory like a computer chip. Part of being a librarian was recalling where things were located. Your day revolved around searching.

Jake and Dickie sent several blues to shake down the local mailmen servicing the area around the library. None of them knew anything. The library's regular mailman was on a leave of absence during the period in which Lisa went missing. His replacement, said the regional supervisor, was a well-respected eighteen-year man, Charles Howard. The guy had not had a blemish to his career. According to a quick check by the department, his life was faultless, legally. Despite that, several blues headed out to Charles Howard's house in Beverly to ask him a few questions. Jake said he and Dickie would be there as soon as they finished at the library.

Jake talked to the librarian. He ran through the normal set of when, where, how, and why questions. Dickie spied a state trooper walking into the library. The tall, heavyset cop held his hat in hands. He looked glum. Something grave on his mind.

"Oh shit. This is *not* going to be good." Dickie watched the trooper walk toward them.

"Detective." The trooper nodded to Dickie.

"Trooper?"

"I need to speak with you in private."

Dickie's stomach dropped.

Jake thought: *Maddox ... Iraq. Fucking terrorist bastards finally got Dickie's boy.*

"What is it, man? Just let 'er rip."

"Outside, Detective. Not in here."

"Go, Dickie. I'll finish up."

The library smelled as they all do. A dry, arid base of flat air as though it had just been vacuumed. The staleness burned your nose. Dickie and the trooper passed by a bulletin board littered with so many announcements, they all blurred together in a quilted pattern of various fluorescent-colored papers. In there somewhere was a flier for some Berkeley flower girl with an acoustic guitar who made all of her friends promise they'd make "the gig."

They walked out the door.

Jake stared at them from the inside window. The librarian stood next to him.

"What is it? Why wouldn't you want Jake out here, too?"

Jake looked on from inside. He half-expected Dickie to fall to the ground in agony and scream, *My son. My son.* It was the only reason why the trooper would have pulled Dickie outside. Jake was the lead. If it was something about the case, Jake was the go-to man. Or maybe the Mo Blackhall ball had finally dropped. *That's it.* Jake's walking papers were on the way in the form of an indictment. The trooper was there to cuff him and lead him away.

"I pulled you out of there, Dick, because we've known each other now twenty years. Am I right? Twenty-five, perhaps. Anyway, I didn't want to say anything in front of the librarian."

"I guess, trooper. What's going on here?"

"It's, well, Dick … it's Rossi. I think you guys better come now. Like right now."

"What about Rossi? Spit it out, man."

"She's dead, Detective."

Jake walked up on them as Dickie got the news.

"Detective Cooper. It's Rossi, sir. I'm so sorry."

59

As a cop, you walk into a morgue where the body of a colleague lies in wait for the scalpel, and you feel a towering sense of revenge well up inside. You want to kill somebody. Mainly yourself. For not being there. Jake had experienced this one time before.

Casey.

Helplessness twisted his insides. His chest tightened. The moment someone you know is dead, you run through all those things you wished you'd said and did.

Heading over to view the crime scene of Anastasia's death, Jake considered what Father John had brought up last time they spoke. No matter what his father had done, no matter how he felt about the past, Jake Cooper was going to have to forgive the man. Make things good before Alzheimer's took him. Not that Mr. Cooper would have a sense of it. But loose ends were not something Jake wanted in his life. He needed closure in order to move forward. To hold on to it was no better than injecting poison.

Jake and Dickie got out of the car. It was clear the mailman had sent a message with Anastasia Rossi's murder. *Holy shit*, was all Jake could manage to think while shaking his head. Besides the obvious torture she had endured, her body had been nailed to the front door of the Old South Meeting House on Washington Street. The morning cleaning guy came upon Anastasia as he went for his keys to open the museum. Luckily, his shift started at five. No one else had seen the cop tacked there like some freak show.

Jake and Dickie had stopped at the scene before going to the morgue. With growing anger, they stood on the step, staring at the blood-stained door where their colleague's naked body had hung for hours. Jake told a CSI on scene he wanted a full report texted to him as soon as they were finished.

"Beyond the obvious, he's well into his element now, Dickie."

Tears welled up behind Dickie's eyes. That sinus pressure pushed. He did not want to speak.

Checking his iPhone, tapping in this new location, a chime went off. The profile had been updated.

Jake double-clicked the App.

Locales consistent with Boston's Freedom Trail

Jake gathered the blues on scene. "I want every other touristy destination along the Freedom Trail staked out until we give the all-clear sign."

Was worth a shot.

The drive to the morgue passed without words. Jake could see a steely determination fill his partner's face. He liked it. Dickie was on a mission now.

Dr. Kelsey wore plastic goggles. Blue rubber gloves. A yellow-stained apron. She came in from another room to greet them. Jake did not want to know what she was doing before they arrived. But from the looks of her, it undoubtedly involved a power tool and lots of gauze.

"Detectives." Kelsey took off the gloves. Then snapped on the more traditional latex. "We meet again. This has not been an easy week."

They did not respond.

Matikas showed up. For once, he had nothing more to say than, "Sorry. Losing a partner is the worst for a team. I know what she meant to you, Dick." He patted him on the back. "We celebrate her life by catching this sicko."

Matikas motioned an *over here* with his eyes to Jake.

"Be right back, Dickie. Hold tight." Jake squeezed his partner's shoulder.

Matikas walked with Jake over to the corner of the room where it was private.

Dickie and Kelsey examined Anastasia's body. Her feet were lopped off just above the ankles. Seeing Anastasia with a blonde wig sewn crudely to her scalp, not to mention her mouth sutured shut, was beyond obscene and surreal.

Corpse bride.

She was naked. Orderlies had washed her down. The string used to stitch her mouth shut was deep-sea fishing line, thirty-pound test. It would take, Kelsey said, "Oh, maybe a week to trace back to its place of origin. But we'll find it." Dickie said nothing as Kelsey bent down for a closer look. "I checked inside her mouth, Dick." An orderly came by with a clipboard. Asked Kelsey to sign off on a few bodies just brought in from Chinatown. Junkies. "He cut her tongue out."

Dickie looked at the doctor, stone-faced.

"There was DNA—skin—underneath her right fingernails, but without a donor, a profile is worthless. It will help later, though, when you guys arrest him. Oh, and the wound in her thigh is from her own weapon. We dug out a .40-caliber projectile. Ballistics say it's consistent with a Glock—though we never found her weapon."

Jake returned. Matikas left without saying bye.

Dickie looked up at the wall. Scratched the side of his face. A large round clock read forty-five minutes past six.

"I'm thinking authority figure, Dick. She represented influence over our guy. This could fit into a sketch of one of Micah's victims, but who knows. There's no doubt he's getting back at the authority figure who abused him. It's so damn typical and sickening."

Kelsey lifted Anastasia's right arm. There it was. Crystal-clear, as if typed—the letter *a*.

"M, I, C, A … at least the bastard can spell, huh, Dick?"

Dickie stayed silent.

"Means there's one more victim out there left." Jake crossed his arms in front of his chest. The intercom speaker barked something about a meeting for all pathologists. Kelsey glanced at her watch. "The *h*. Come on, Dick. We can't let him win."

"We need to go to Maine." Dickie spoke his words razor sharp, matter-of-fact. His voice a raspy, deliberate whisper.

"Pack a bag."

Kelsey stood by Anastasia's naked shoulder. She held a bunch of the wig hair in between her two peace-sign fingers as if she was a hairdresser preparing to cut it. "I'll run this down immediately. We should be able to get a good hit on where the wig hair came from. Wig hair is generally from only a few different sources. Easily traceable. Bet the sonofabitch didn't realize that!"

Jake patted Dickie on his back. "Come on. Let's blow this horror show. We're no good to Rossi here."

"One of us is next."

"We'll send Caroline to your brother's house in Michigan. Get her on a plane right away. I'll call it in when we get to the car. We'll have a team of blues surround your house until she leaves. Dawn and Brendan are safe."

"Where are they?"

Jake looked up. "Safe, Dick."

"It's not about justice anymore, Jake."

They both stared at their colleague's body. Revenge was a motivator.

"We'll find him, Dickie. It was never about justice, anyway. You know that."

"I need to make a stop before we head out." It was the first time Dickie had injected emotion into his voice. He sounded as though he had just snapped out of a trance. "I'll meet you back at the squad room."

"Can I help?"

"No. It's nothing. Just some unfinished business."

60

SATURDAY, SEPTEMBER 13 - 7:25 P.M.

Mo Blackhall stood to the left of his mahogany desk, staring into the countryside lining the back of his property. Few things were more important to Mo these days than the dozen acres of wilderness he had owned for the past thirty years. The land was all Mo had left. The bank had served papers on the house weeks ago. The foreclosure almost complete. Mo wasn't fighting it. He needed to be out by the end of the month.

That episode back at D-15 with Jake proved to Mo he had lost control—that is, what he could remember. This entire cat-and-mouse with Jake was getting old, same as running from brass. Mo walked over to the table bar and poured himself a glass of scotch. Then went back to staring out the sliding glass doors. The chestnut-colored booze cast a glare on the wall from the overhead light hitting the glass just right. Mo choked that first sip down. It burned. But then, a moment passed, and there was that warm feeling.

The tingle.

The glow. Ah … yes. That calming of his shaky hands.

His second sip was interrupted by a knock at the door.

Mo Blackhall stopped mid-sip. He knew who it was. He was expecting him.

He unlatched the dead bolt, popped the doorknob, and walked away, allowing gravity to open the door. Found himself back at the slider, his back to the visitor.

"I almost blew it," Sunshine said.

"I heard. Don't sit."

"You don't know what it's like."

"I do."

"You don't."

"It's over. I'm taking you with me when they come."

"Just give me some more time." Sunshine paced in back of Mo. "I think I can get to him. How in the hell did he know you were up north?"

"Where is he now?" Mo had not turned around.

"Packing for a trip to Maine, I assume."

"Good. But forget him."

"What do you mean?"

Mo was captivated by the maples and oaks in his backyard. They were as tall and straight as telephone poles. Perfect, like kids, really. Mo had been so out of it all these years, this was the first time he had realized how big the trees had gotten. The leaves were hanging on, ready to let go and fall to the ground. He could see him and his ex-wife out there as twenty-year-olds, throwing grass at each other, running around, laughing, kissing, talking about how many kids they were going to raise in this house.

"I should cut those two, the ones in the far north corner." Mo took a pull from his drink. He pointed to the trees with his hand still on the glass. "So the others can grown to their full potential. What do you think, Sunshine?"

"I think you need to stay sober next time you meet our guy."

Mo thought about that. "You're probably right. But is all this actually worth a shit? If that Ted Williams Tunnel lawsuit doesn't disappear, we're both going to prison. They've sent a message with the foreclosure of this house. We'll eventually both end up at the bottom of the Charles, Sunshine."

Cement shoes.

"The Tunnel investigation will take years, Mo. Hey, are you going to offer me a drink? By the time they figure out what happened, we'll be in Mexico. Then they'll go after Jake. They want his ass bad. The plan, remember? Don't lose sight of it."

"You know, evil is subjective. Good is absolute. Whether you skim off the top and people die because of it, or cut the legs off women, makes no difference. Both have the same result. We murdered that family in the tunnel—that boy and his mother."

"Come on, Mo—"

"Get out of my house, Sunshine."

"Mo, don't give in now. We're almost there. Homestretch."

Mo Blackhall took a slow sip of scotch. "You were supposed to be here yesterday, Friday. I waited for you. Fridays are not such good days, I understand. Is that why you didn't come? Did you feel that, too? Friday is the darkest day in humanity."

The Passion.

"What are you talking about, Mo? Oh, wait … that's right. You decided on a liquid breakfast and lunch and stumbled around the squad room."

"Sunday's coming." Mo turned, stared at his drink as if he was checking to see if he needed another. Twirled the glass in his right hand, watching the ice clank against the sides. "The resurrection."

The Rising.

Sunshine didn't understand the metaphors. "Come on, Mo. Don't think too much into this. I can handle it."

"Look at you." Mo finally turned. "What's with the long face?"

"Work."

"Well, since you brought it up. How many *more* will have to die, Sunshine?"

"We cannot plan on contingencies, Mo. The Carmichaels were unfortunate. That tunnel accident is not our fault."

"Get out of my house."

61

Before they left for Maine, Jake and Dickie met inside the squad room. It was quiet with no one around. Dickie was late. Said that errand he had to run took longer than expected.

Jake didn't press him.

Most of the lights were off inside the office, the rhythm of the day gone. Jake and Dickie stood by the water cooler near Jake's office. A gurgle rose from the bottom of the big upside-down bottle and a bubble burst on the top. They both looked. Here was one of those random sounds you don't hear with the noise of work and life happening around you during the day. But in the silence of the night, it took on a peculiar impression.

"I need to do a few things in my office before we leave. I'll be two minutes, tops." Jake turned to walk away. Stopped. "You all right, Dick? You look, I don't know, worried." Dickie's face had changed since the morgue. "Everything okay?"

"I'm good."

An unspoken shadow of guilt loomed over these two men, one that males rarely talk about or acknowledge. Like when a guy rattles on about his golf game at a wake, outside on the steps, smoking a cigarette. Staring at death, right there in the face, and you go on about double bogeys. It's a diversion. A subterfuge. A way to hide emotional baggage. Jake was good at holding stuff in.

Dickie wanted to clean out Anastasia's desk. Put everything in boxes. Send it away so he never had to look at it again.

He shook his head walking toward their side-by-side desks. How life could kick you in the ass without warning, rip your damn heart out. As soon as you get close to someone, *poof*, gone.

Inside one of Anastasia's drawers, Dickie found a compartment under lock and key. It was strange for her to have a secret storage place inside her desk. Why not at home? Was the woman a closet alcoholic? Dickie imagined popping the lock and finding a bottle of cheap vodka, the odorless drug of choice for the working-class alky.

Damn. How could I not see it?

Getting the little padlock to pop was as easy as jamming a screwdriver into it.

Dickie lifted the top off the box.

Notebook?

He remembered. Anastasia liked to write in a black notebook after conversations. Or sometimes while Jake and the lieutenant were in the corner discussing things she couldn't hear. And whenever she came back from a meeting.

Was the woman an Internal Affairs mole? Dickie's heart raced. He didn't want to believe it.

He opened the book and read.

Jake came around the corner, briefcase in hand. "Let's go. Take care of whatever that is later."

Dickie stuffed the notebook in his overnight bag. Walked over to the counter and left the morning desk sergeant a note, telling him to finish packing the rest of Anastasia's desk and get it out of the squad room before Monday.

They filed out the door and got into Jake's Crown Vic without speaking. Jake drove out to I-93 and over the Mystic River Bridge. He glanced at Dickie and patted the briefcase. "Little present for us left on my desk."

"What?"

The Our Lady of Peace Orphanage in Bainbridge was a three-hour hike from Boston, even with Jake in the HOV lane, cruise control set on ninety miles an hour. It would be dark by the time they arrived. Everything was going to be closed.

"My man came through, Dick."

Anastasia's notebook preyed on Dickie's mind. It was killing him to find out what she had written. He didn't want to read it in front of Jake. He needed to protect Anastasia for now. At least until he found out what she had been up to. Jake had too much to deal with as it were. Dickie figured he'd walk into their hotel room in Maine, run into the bathroom, crack open the notebook.

"Hey, you hear me?" Jake asked, looking at Dickie, then the road. Back and forth. "A list of the kids sent up to Bainbridge from St. Paul's."

"Good ole Father John. I knew he'd come around."

"With Dawn and Bren involved, I think the stakes changed his mind. Read the note."

Dickie popped the tiny locks on the top of the briefcase and read:

Jake,

Dawn & Brendan are safe with the sisters. I'll continue to check on them. Take this. But you didn't get it from me. Catch that evil man and end this madness. I'll pray for the Rossi family and Detective Rossi's eternal salvation.

Yours, in Christ,

Fr. John

"Anything jump out at you in that paperwork?"
"I see a lot of names … Micah had a lot of kids to choose from. It won't mean much until we get up north."

Jake paused as he slowed down to pass an RV traveling at the speed limit. "Dickie?"

"Yeah, Jake?"

"What's so special about the notebook you took from Rossi's desk?"

Dickie thought fast. "Nothing. Just Rossi's mind on paper. What she was thinking."

Jake gave Dickie a curious look. He didn't want to push the subject. Not now.

"You follow up with the Simmons University professor?"

"Yeah. He doesn't know a damn thing more than what he's said already. Lisa was purchasing flowers on the Internet along with other trinkets she sold. She had one of those cyber stores. Where everything came from, well, that's another question. If that punk Colby had not wiped out her computer, we'd probably have a few leads."

Jake planned to wait for Dickie to fall asleep. Then he was going to find the notebook and see if Anastasia documented anything about Mo and the assignment he had sent her on. No sense in getting Dickie involved unless he had to.

62

Jake pulled into a rest stop somewhere in the wilds of Maine on I-95. Up and down the interstate, nothing but pine trees for miles on end. Those tall, dark army-green ones that make your hands sticky. Dickie went inside, in search of something to eat. Jake waited in the parking lot. He watched a physically fit man with a sharp-dressed woman park their minivan in a handicap space. They had one of those blue and white tags with a stick-figure wheelchair symbol hanging from the rearview mirror.

Lazy bastards.

Father John called.

Dawn … Brendan …

"What is it?"

The reception was poor. Not a tower for miles. Jake looked at the screen.

One bar.

"I cannot hear you too well, Jake. But I hope you can hear me. It's Patrick O'Keefe." *The deacon?* "One of the sisters tending to him called. There's been a visitor over to see him."

"What kind of visitor, Father?" Jake hated when father was so indirect.

"A priest …" the reception was in and out, "… or, rather … like a priest," Jake thought he heard Father John say. He pulled the phone down, looked at the screen again.

Half a bar. *Shit.* He shook the phone as if it would help.

Come on.

"Say again, Father …"

"… this … priest was over there talking to Patrick."

Was that so strange? Had he heard Father John right?

"… he was asking Patrick odd questions … sort of … well, he was getting loud and used a threatening tone."

"Doesn't sound like such a nice priest, Father."

"That's just it, Jake, we … a priest at all. The sisters, they panicked, Jake … and I'm sorry, but they …"

"Again, Father? Come again? I cannot hear you."

Dickie got into the car. He was eating a doughnut. Motioning with his head, he whispered, "Who's that? What's going on?"

Jake looked concerned.

"I said"—the signal was clear now, Jake could hear the priest as if he was sitting next to him—"that I have no idea how the sisters knew where Brendan and Dawn were, but they told this priest."

Jake's heart thumped. Adrenaline filled his veins. His carotid arteries throbbed. He wanted to scream at Father. "What'd you just say?"

"I think it was this smart-aleck young priest that does all the bishop's dirty work. Apparently, this bishop is quite upset with me for helping you out. It's not in our nature here to be involved in a serial-killer case, Jake. I'm not Father Dowling."

Jake didn't know what to say.

Think this through.

"You get over to the bishop's office and talk to that priest, Father."

"Sister Rosa, she's the one who told him. She said something else that I thought was rather unusual, Jake …"

The reception broke up.

Those bars again. Jake couldn't hear a damn thing.

"What did she say, Father?"

The signal went dead.

63

SUNDAY, SEPTEMBER 14 - 7:01 A.M.

During its heyday, the Our Lady of Peace Orphanage wasn't a dark and gloomy facility conjuring images of emotionless people with decaying souls walking around like kids from a Frank McCourt book. Nor did the sisters, dressed in the traditional black and white penguin habits, slap rulers against their palms and threaten the kids with disciplinary action.

A red-brick building, Our Lady had seventy-five beds. It was equipped with a full gymnasium. Kitchen. Cafeteria. Two dozen classrooms. An old banner said Our Lady was focused on *God's Word and Goodness*. The nuns running the place were rarely seen without smiles. The priests who visited left the boys and girls yearning for their return. The teachers—save for maybe Micah—throughout the fifty years of Our Lady's existence were gentle, kind, informative. Always willing to show patience where the children were concerned.

"The homes they are from are troubled, not the kids themselves," Mother Ophelia liked to tell outsiders. "None of this is their fault."

Jake and Dickie walked onto the grounds and into the waist-high grass on that early Sunday morning. It was ten years since Our Lady had been shut down because of budget cuts and lawsuits. Strange, Jake considered, how buildings, once they stopped pulsating with life, decayed and rotted, much like the human body.

"You talk to Father John this morning, Jake?"

"Yeah, he's checking into that priest. We're moving Bren and Dawn just to be sure."

"I won't ask where."

Jake wasn't offering.

Most of the windows in the building had been shattered by vandals long ago. Jake kicked open the main door and walked in underneath a fallen timber. "Come on, Dickie."

"Remind me why we're going into this cobwebbed place John Carpenter would find attractive for a movie set?'

"Because it's fun, Dick. Move your fat ass."

Standing inside the lobby, peering into the empty rooms, Jake looked puzzled. It was as though an announcement had been made that the world was soon coming to an end and everyone abandoned the building at once. Things had been left in their place. Notebooks sat on counters next to coffee mugs and phones. The furniture was torn and covered with dust, dirt, rubble. There was an early Windows personal computer on the counter near a sign that read PASTOR'S OFFICE.

Walking down the hallway, glass crunching underneath their heels, Jake and Dickie found a door marked RECORDS.

"After you," Jake said with a magician's wave of his hand.

The room was filled with filing cabinets. They looked pillaged. Papers scattered across the floor. Unreadable. Smudged and damaged from all the water leaking into the room.

Dickie opened one of the drawers with a rusty squeal.

"Nothing."

"Open them all."

"Come on, Kid, we won't find anything here."

"We still have another hour before anything in town opens." Jake glanced at his watch. Then unfoiled a piece of nicotine gum from its plastic seat, stared at it, and tossed it on the floor before popping it. He sat down on a metal crate and, instead, took out a cigarette from a pack in his pocket, fired one up, and looked around. "Quite a place, huh?"

Dickie looked in one of the file drawers. "I see you're doing well with quitting, huh, boss?"

"Yup."

"There's nothing here, Jake."

Jake was staring at the floor. "You wanna tell me where, or, actually, why you hid Rossi's notebook from me last night?"

"Couldn't find it, huh?" Dickie smiled. Pulled open more drawers.

"Nope."

"Because I know it's killing you to know what she wrote about you."

"And?"

"And, well, a lot of things."

"About?"

"Jake, I know what you asked Rossi to do. She and I were tight. She asked, and I told her to do whatever you said. I could care less. This thing with Mo, you cannot save the guy. He's drowning. Just watch your ass. Talk is that you're going with him." Jake shook his head as Dickie spoke. Squinted his eyes. "You need to calm down. You shouldn't allow yourself to get carried away by all of it." Dickie leaned over an open drawer. "I know this case is eating you up. I realize you need to prove yourself." Dickie walked over to where Jake sat. Glanced down at him like a father to his son. "That shit with the little girl—that wasn't your fault. You'll come through it. You'll be fine."

"Appreciate the advice, Dick." Jake looked up at him and blew out a ribbon of exhaled smoke to a sound of satisfaction.

Dickie went back to digging through the files.

"I saw you last night," Dickie said. "Outside on the balcony of the hotel. Bet you didn't sleep two hours." Jake stood as Dickie continued with his guidance. "Your brother, your father, that little girl, you harp on that shit and you'll be back in the loony bin, man. Trust me. I've seen tougher cops go down. That, or you'll turn to something."

"Southie, Dick. Not a good place. I thought it hardened me growing up. Mo always told me that a kid who made it through life in Southie could survive anything. Mo was so different then." Jake walked toward Dickie. "I think I need to give all this chasing bad guys up, Dick. I'm not cut out for it anymore."

"Part of the problem is, Mo brings back all that stuff about your dad. My advice, hey, just let Mo go."

Jake dropped his head. He didn't know what to say.

"You need to keep your job, Jake. You know, there's always somebody who's going to tell you you're unworthy. Forget about making everyone happy. I understand you want everyone to like you. But you need to find that here," he pointed to his own heart, "before you expect it from anyone else."

"Shit, Dick … you TiVo-ing Oprah now?" They laughed. Jake paused. Rubbed his temples. "Just tell me what Rossi wrote."

"Rossi didn't write about any of that Mo bullshit. Pretty loyal girl. Smart, too. She wanted to impress you—and, I should note, she looked up to you."

"No kidding?"

"Yeah, she was keeping notes of meetings and cases. Like studying. She wanted to impress us both. Thought maybe she could solve this case particularly. Now, can we get out of this shithole? My feet are wet and cold."

Jake turned. "You hear that?" Sounded like breaking glass.

Dickie looked toward the door, eyes wide. "What the hell?"

"Shh." Jake whispered. "Hold on. Don't move." They palmed their Glocks. Jake inched toward the door. He whispered: "You stay here."

"You won't get an argument out of me."

"Watch my back."

Jake walked out into the hallway. Light shone in gold beams from his right, the sun just rising over the mountain in back of the orphanage. The glare had a majestic, alluring pull to it, inviting Jake to walk that way. He looked left and went for it.

Then the noise—breaking glass and blowing wind—again. Jake's stomach tightened. He turned. Dickie had his head out the doorway, covering the opposite end of the hall with his pointed Glock.

Jake continued into a hallway on his right, out of Dickie's view. There was a room, orphan beds lined up along the walls. A gust of wind came at him in through the corridor and made a whipping sound, rattling all the loose fixtures, shaking the broken glass in the windows and the beer bottles along the floor. It sounded as if a group of people were whispering all at once.

There it was again. Someone was outside the window.

Jake called out for Dickie. "Come on. Over here." With the barrel of his weapon, Jake waved Dickie over to the window.

They stood on both sides of the opening.

"On three."

As one, they popped up and stuck their guns out the window, each in opposite directions.

A tall man with white hair ran into the woods. Looked to be older. He had a shotgun in his hand. Jake thought he might have recognized the way the man moved.

Dickie leveled his Glock. "By the time we get outside, we'll never find him."

Jake used his hand, pushed the weapon down and away. "Let him be. Probably some local-yokel nosing around."

Dickie walked around the deserted room, a long and narrow space full of rusted iron bed frames without mattresses. Some of the beds had trunks—like those full of gold coins pirates pillage in kid stories—at the foot. There was debris scattered all over the floor. Fallen beams. Ceiling tiles broken into bits and pieces. Rat feces. Decomposing animal corpses. Torn up linens.

A gust of wind kicked up and whooshed through the room, as if the building took a deep breath.

The noise was ominous. It was there, but then again, it wasn't. Jake's mind filled in the blanks. "You know what that is?" He looked around the room.

Dickie shrugged. "Do I want to?"

"Echoes of the undead—the memories this building has, Dick. They're speaking to us. We've come to the right place, my friend."

64

SUNDAY, SEPTEMBER 14 - 8:04 A.M.

He slept in his priestly vestments. He had put the white collar, vest, black pants, shoes, and jacket on the night before and went out to the local Taco Bell to see how people reacted. By night's end he had blessed three old ladies with crooked backs who carried rosaries in their pocketbooks, heard one hasty confession in the restroom, and promised a young couple they were doomed to hell if they continued along the path of their marriage.

The black and whites fit him well. He considered the idea that if he had followed his first calling, he would probably be out in the world working in some parish, doing incomprehensible things to the community's children.

The man who called himself Charles Howard had blood on his soul.

He got up off the couch. Put some coffee on. No breakfast. Today was a day to let adrenaline and caffeine fuel his body. Food would only slow him down.

He straightened the vestigial tab—the white cube hiding the Adam's apple—displayed through the square cutout in his black shirt. Then looked at himself in the mirror. After fixing each button of his shirt, he patted down a few stray hairs with a wet thumb. He didn't need to shave. The two-day growth gave him a contemporary look.

"Father Rainn Meyers." He said it out loud and it sounded good. Even had a ring to it. Meyers was his namesake. He'd changed Randy, his given name, to Rainn, only because he liked the way it looked on paper. Rain was how he felt, anyway. Gloomy, wet. Irritating. Who liked rain?

"*You were chosen,*" he heard the Teacher say, "*because I knew you could take it, Randy—and you would continue what I taught you.*"

Fawning over himself in the mirror, he considered the idea that not every abused kid grows up to be an abuser. It took an unusual breed. He knew he was one of them.

Special.

Chosen.

He straightened his jacket by pulling down both front flaps at the same time. Brushed a piece of lint off his shoulder. He could hear the coffee machine in the kitchen making that familiar, pleasant steam-popping noise as it percolated. It was almost done. Smelled good, too. Fresh, like the morning should.

He pointed and talked to himself. "Time is short. I must get on the road. Busy day ahead."

He turned. Stopped. Went back to the mirror. "Father!"

Sitting at his kitchen table, Rainn Meyers checked his watch. The convent was a forty-five-minute drive. On the way, he needed to make an additional trip off the beaten path. Just in case.

Micah.

This time the image of the Teacher's face brought with it a smile.

65

SUNDAY, SEPTEMBER 14 - 8:12 A.M.

Dickie pressed the VOICE MAIL button on his cell phone. Put the speaker to his ear. Listened. He and Jake were parked outside, facing the Bainbridge Sheriff's Department, waiting for the sheriff to arrive. It was a small building. Looked like maybe an old, converted schoolhouse or library.

"You have two messages …" the mysterious cell phone lady's voice said.

Beep: *"Honey, I made it here okay. I'm fine. Don't worry 'bout me. Love you."*

Caroline. Such a bastion of purity. Always doing the right thing.

Beep: *"Shaughnessy, Matikas …"* Dickie hit pause. Tapped Jake on the shoulder. Pushed SPEAKER: *"We found something on the Taylor kid's computer… and zeroed in on a postal station out of Revere … that paint chip backed it all up. Tell Cooper—asshole must have shut off his phone— word is that his boy Mo is being indicted any moment now on extortion, bribery, and corruption charges, the papers will be filed soon … I'm hearing there are several others under the indictment, but no word on names."*

Jake stirred in his seat. He didn't like the sound of that. He looked out the window, focused on the hedges. *Ted Williams Tunnel.* Jake saw himself as a young cop running over to a construction trailer at Mo's request to pick up a package and bring it to the station house.

Don't ask, don't tell.

Mo had involved him.

Sonofabitch.

"Yo, there's the sheriff now," Dickie said, slapping Jake on the arm. And they watched a monster of a man, six-four, three hundred pounds at least, blue jeans, Stetson. He exited a black Chevy Tahoe and marched up the steps toward the sheriff's department front door.

"Thought they did away with the cowboy hats after those two troopers got sucker-hit with bats because they couldn't see beyond the rim of the hat?"

"Why am I thinking … Chuck Norris and Billy Jack?" Dickie offered.

"Let's not fuck with this guy, Dickie. He's all business—that's obvious."

"Sheriff?" Dickie yelled, opening the car door. "Sheriff?" Dickie flipped through his little notebook as they walked toward the stone steps. "Sheriff Townsend? Can we get a minute, sir?" Dickie sounded like a reporter. He had called ahead the previous day for an appointment. But the deputy laughed at him. Something about "appointments being for you city folk."

The big man turned. Looked at the two of them. Spat a dime-sized tab of chewing tobacco on the steps and, without answering, continued into the building.

Jake and Dickie picked up their pace.

The sheriff stood on the opposite side of a wooden saloon-like gate into the small office area. There were three desks cordoned off by a partition. "Cal, show these boys here to the conference room, would you?" The sheriff opened the door to his office and slammed it shut behind him.

Deputy Cal Sheraton said, "Follow me, boys."

They walked behind the vivacious deputy to the rear of the building.

"The sheriff here, well, he took the liberty of collecting all the records he could find for Our Lady after your lieutenant called last night and told us you was coming."

"Why would you people laugh at me when I asked for an appointment?"

Cal smiled at Dickie. "The sheriff here doesn't meet with people, Detective. He's got the business of watching over a county to contend with. Just the way he does things is all. Don't take offense."

Dickie and Jake looked at each other. Strange country people.

Inside the conference room were ten boxes of files, a few additional folders of medical records, and a large crate of remainders from the orphanage—diplomas, medals, certificates.

"Sheriff says you might want to go out and talk to Buster Turbach. Buster's the only employee from that old place there who is still alive and living in town. Buster's old. But sharp as a new sickle."

"Can we thank the sheriff?" Jake said. "Can you ask him to come out here?"

"Nope, busy. Doesn't want to be disturbed." Cal used his fingers to make quote marks, as if *disturbed* was a new word for him. "You need anything, however, you just call on ole Cal here, and I'll take care of it for y'all."

Jake wondered if they were in Maine or Kansas.

"We were out at the old Orphanage. Some old guy with white beard, overalls, a shotgun, scared us half to death. Any idea who he is, what he wanted?" Dickie asked.

"Nope."

"Where's Buster live?"

Cal took a piece of paper from his front pocket, stuffed it inside Jake's suit coat pocket as Jake followed his hand. Cal tapped the pocket. "You'll find his address and directions on there. Buster don't have no phone. Now, anything else?"

"Deputy. Anything else you can tell us would be helpful. We're looking for a kid who might have caused some trouble up here in town after getting out of the orphanage. Anything like that." Jake wasn't sure what he was fishing for.

Cal tapped a finger on his lips. "Not sure, Detective. None of that rings a bell."

"Anything you think of, let my partner here know. He'll be around most of the morning going through these boxes."

Dickie rolled his eyes.

"Well, the Meyers kid. Sumbitch done put a pickaxe to good ol' Charlie."

"What's that?" Jake jerked up his head quickly. "Any reports on that would be helpful."

"Nope, can't help you there just yet. That case is still open. You'll have to get your DA to call our guy and get word to the sheriff that you good old boys from the city need to dig into the file. Otherwise, sheriff here, he won't let you see it."

"Goes by the book, does he? Well, okay, Cal. Thanks." Jake decided not to push it. He turned to Dickie. "You go through these files. I'll pay a visit to Buster and get what I can. Call the DA and get her ass working on that Meyers file."

"Ask Buster 'bout ole Charlie and that Meyers kid. He can tell y'all what that sumbitch evil kid done did. I think he escaped from the orphanage, went on a rampage. Something like that." Cal whistled as though he had dodged a close call. "I was a boy then. But heard things."

Dickie sat down. Put his head in his hands.

"Get going on that reading. I'll bring you back a coffee."

66

SUNDAY, SEPTEMBER 14 - 9:00 A.M.

Jake had explained to Dawn in a text message that she needed to take Brendan, Mother Lucinda, and maybe a sister or two, and drive to LOCATION NUMBER TWO. What Father John had told him about that rogue priest asking questions was too close for comfort. It was time to move.

Early that morning they left St. Catherine's Convent in the Lynn Woods Reservation, coats over their heads, hustled into the cruiser. In that unmarked vehicle, they were driven south on I-95, past Wakefield, Reading, and Lexington, onto Route 2, then down into the Walden Woods section of Concord. Father John owned a cabin near Walden Pond. It was given to him some thirty years ago by a man whose son Father had saved from a heroin overdose. The cabin was surrounded by over two hundred acres of preserved forest. If you didn't know where it was, good luck.

Father John sent two state troopers Jake had called in up to the cabin. One walked the grounds to make sure a stray mailman wasn't lurking in the bushes somewhere. The other guarded the end of the driveway. Both carried M-16s and pistols.

Dawn sat with Mother Lucinda on the back deck of the cabin. It was a gorgeous day. Birds chirped loudly, as it was spring. The wind blew in soft, gentle, warm drifts. A bright canopy of morning sun shone on their backs. Brendan played with a model plane. Colored. Picked wildflowers and gave them to Dawn and Mother.

Dawn felt safe here. The nuns were comforting.

"You're very kind to come here with us, Mother. I appreciate your hospitality."

Mother Lucinda smiled. Bowed her head, eyes closed.

"I don't think the troopers are necessary way out here, Mother. But you must understand my husband. Before anything else, he is a police officer."

"I do understand, Mrs. Cooper." They both looked toward the driveway entrance. One trooper held his M-16 off to the side and paced the entrance to the driveway. His partner, roaming around the grounds, called on a walkie-talkie every once in a while to ask if everything was clear.

"I'm sure we'll be able to leave in a day or two. Go back to our homes."

Mother blinked her eyelids.

"Is Father John coming today?"

"I do not know."

9:25 A.M.

Father John planned to meet up with Dawn. He told Jake he would watch after his family and decided the only way to fulfill that promise was to stand by their side. He packed an overnight bag and his hunting rifle, a .22 caliber gun his father had given him the day he turned eighteen. It was difficult getting rid of the gun. Nostalgia pulled it back every time the priest went to toss it. Placing it in the car, Father wondered why he was even bringing it. Was he going to actually shoot a man if the opportunity presented itself? Did the rifle even work?

He tossed his bag in the backseat. Placed the gun under the driver's seat. Pulled up, looked left and right, then took off out of the rectory driveway.

From St. Paul's, the cabin was an hour's drive. A nice, quiet, relaxing ride into the heart of Massachusetts' beautiful woodlands. The ride gave the priest time to consider all that had happened recently. He did not question what role God played in any of it. Yet knew there would come a time when Jake would pester him about this. Jake needed answers to the big questions. He would knock on the rectory door one day, ask Father John to resolve how a compassionate God could allow such a morally corrupted soul into the world. He would demand to know how a caring God could create a human being who scalped women and cut their legs off. *"And I don't want to hear about free will, Father."*

Two weeks ago, when Jake first heard Mo was possibly involved in a scandal going back all those years, during the Big Dig era, Jake showed up unexpectedly at the church. He was broken and bitter. He questioned his future, not to mention his faith. He and Father John sat outside on the front steps. Jake said he didn't want to go inside. He was thinking of leaving the BPD and the Church. "Everything! Screw it. Maybe all of this," he raged, meaning the Church, "is just a scam. Some 'thing' dreamed up by ancient men hungry for power and wealth." They could hear kids yelling and having fun at the playground nearby. Cars whizzed by, beeped. Waved to the priest. "Nothing makes sense to me anymore, Father."

"Jake, you need to let it all go. Just show up and not think about the big picture. That's faith, son. If Mo broke laws, he will need to take responsibility. Same as you."

"Come on, Father. We either believe or we don't. Faith is measured by belief. It's a gift—you've said it yourself. I lost that gift on the day that little girl stopped breathing underneath two feet of dirt. Maybe I never had it."

Father John understood how Jake could fuse the two— and both, his faith and Mo included, had let him down.

"You're here, Jake. You believe enough to sit with me and talk about it."

"Where else would I go?"

"That's fine. I understand that—"

Jake cut him off. "I need to not come here for a while. I hope you understand."

Father John put his arm around Jake's shoulder. "If you don't believe, Jake, then what I'm wearing, this tunic, the amice, alb, cincture and my normal everyday collar and blacks, it's nothing more than a silly costume. This church is nothing more than a set. I must look like a fool to you."

Jake walked away. The first time they spoke after that day was when Father John showed up at Jake's house, unannounced.

As Father John came out of the memory, he took a sharp left off Route 2 and onto the entrance for Route 126. He was ready for the final descent into the Walden Pond State Preservation.

The priest wasn't paying attention as he drove. Because if he had been, he would have certainly noticed an SUV, black with tinted windows, that had gotten on his tail as he left the church, trailing about a half-mile behind him.

67

Buster Turbach would have looked less like a redneck had he purchased himself a good set of dentures. Playing with his gums, as if grinding grass like a cow, didn't help. His lower jaw poked outward, the front end of a surfboard sawing back and forth.

Buster stood in a pumpkin patch, most of which had rotted into the ground because of a recent drought. He smacked at the roots of an old elm with an axe, stopping every so often to take off his hat and, with a hankie he kept in his back pocket, wiping his brow.

The dirt driveway left a trail of dust behind Jake's Crown Vic. He drove the half-mile strip into a gravel lot in front of Buster's white clapboard farmhouse.

Buster walked toward Jake's car as though he was expecting him.

"Mr. Cooper, I presume." The farmer stuck out his hand.

"Detective Cooper, actually."

Buster laughed. "Right. Okay. Let's clear this up now. That big city crap won't work with me out here, son. I have the info you want. Be glad to give it to you. Just don't play any silly, city-slickin' games with me. I'm a straight shooter."

"Fair enough." Jake sounded defeated. "I'm in no position to bargain."

"Come on in then." Buster took off his gloves and—like two chalkboard erasers—slapped the dust from them.

The storm door whined as Buster opened it ahead of Jake.

"Nice place you got here."

"Wipe those feet, Cooper, would you?" Buster let the handle go and the spring swung the door back and slapped against the frame.

In the kitchen, magazines were stacked as if they were being distributed from Buster's house. Dishes were piled in the stained sink. The cat litter box hadn't been changed in, Jake guessed, weeks.

"Sit." Buster had to clear off a chair. "What is it, exactly, that I can do for you, Detective?"

"Tell me about Stuart Micah. You worked up at Our Lady during his day?"

Buster sat back in his rocker. Took a deep breath. "Good ole Mr. Micah." He explained how much the kids at Bainbridge liked Micah, trusted, and looked up to him. "He was just that kind of teacher. He knew what to say. They ate it up. He selected a group of kids as the years passed. Kids that, you know, were drawn to him more than the others."

Jake tapped out notes on his iPhone as Buster spoke. Snapped Buster's photo without the old man suspecting anything. Emailed it into the database as they spoke. Looked up every so often while he waited for a response. "How many kids we talking 'bout, Buster?"

"Oh, I don't know ... five or six."

"When did the problems begin?"

"Started with one kid, Alston Sinclair, or so he called himself. His real name was Corey Hatch. The kid talked about how he was from Rockefeller blood and his family would come to rescue him one day. He was delusional, but nice. Well, Micah saw that vulnerability in the boy. Exploited the hell out of it. The boy came forward but had a hard time explaining himself. No one believed him."

"Did you?"

Buster picked up his pipe. Packed it. "Naw. I thought he was full of shit, to be honest. We all did."

"What changed your mind?"

Buster smiled. Jake could see his pink gums, white tongue. A faint chime sound went off. Jake had his response from K-PAC.

"What was that there noise?"

"Just the phone." Jake flashed the screen at him. "Somebody called me."

"Well, two more kids came forward. Then that one kid, the Meyers boy, escaped. Disappeared. I started to go back and think about things. I started to look for—and you should appreciate this—clues."

"Meyers. Cal mentioned him. What about this Meyers boy?" Jake allowed Buster to talk while he read the text report.

SUBJECT FROM BAINBRIDGE, ME,

WORKED FOR M.A.S. MAINTENANCE

FROM 1963 TO 2001. DOB: 7/6/1923.

SS# 002-45-8991. NO FELONIES.

"Rainn Meyers, who went by Randy at the time, was a smart kid. Lots of potential. Much smarter than the others. Mr. Micah took a true liking to this one. The kid was fascinated with animals."

Jake didn't realize Buster was so observant. "Let me change the subject for a moment. What'd you say the name of the company you worked for was?"

"I never done said that. But I worked for Masterson, Atlas, and Stevenson Maintenance—at least that's what it said on my check." He laughed a phlegmy gurgle.

"Great. Continue. What happened next?"

Buster sparked his Bic. Brought it down on top of the packed tobacco. Took a deep pull from his pipe. Smelled like vanilla. A heavy, thick cloud of blue-tinted smoke hung there between the two of them. Buster reminded Jake of a character from *Hee-Haw*, a variety show he used to watch with Casey when they were kids. "Well, this Meyers boy, he was ultra-religious when he showed up. I think, and you'll have to go back and check the file, but I think, well, he done come from St. Paul's, down in your neck of the woods."

"What'd you say?"

Buster got up and took two cans of Narragansett beer out of the fridge. Jake thought it was kind of early, but what the heck, he didn't want to insult the guy.

"Yeah … St. Paul's Church in South Boston, I believe. That be it. Why, does that mean something to you, Detective?"

"Ah, yes, actually, it does." Jake took a pull from his beer. The taste reminded him of being a kid, drinking hot hose water that had been sitting in the summer sun all day.

"There came a time when Micah became unnerved when he heard or saw that the Meyers boy and one of the sisters was talking. Micah would stop class in the middle if he saw Meyers talking to anyone in an authority position. Run over. 'What are you two talking about?' The Meyers boy, he would turn and run, lock himself in the bathroom. Or take off into the woods."

"How old was the kid then, Buster?"

"Oh, Meyers must have been maybe sixteen by then. No one wanted to believe him. He started telling these crazy stories of being taken down into some basement at night by Mr. Micah. Finally, a priest came in to talk to the child. Thought he might have been possessed." Buster rolled his eyes. "Sat him down, got his entire story. It was awful. No one wanted to hear it. This is, what, I don't know, early eighties? Things was different. People didn't talk about that stuff like they does today.

"So the kid, you know, he spins this wild yarn. Then he lifts up a pant leg one day and there they are, these fuzzy scars. Never forget 'em. The kid's own initials carved on the meaty portion of his calves. Must have been burned in there or something. It was frightening to look at. Had the texture of nightcrawlers."

Jake was overwhelmed by this detail.

Buster continued. "No one believed him still. We thought he did it to himself."

"No kidding. Did you?"

"Yep. Some time later, everyone's asleep, the boy packs a bag and takes off."

"Gone?"

"Like a raccoon shooed away from a garbage can with a rock."

Okay …

"Any idea where he went?"

"Well, this is where that file comes into play—the one Cal—what a bastard he is, friggin' wannabe sheriff—wouldn't let you see. Howard Charles Markmann. Old Howard lived by himself about three miles south of the orphanage. They found him three days later when the neighborhood mailman reported an odd odor coming from the kitchen."

Jake stood. "Continue … please, I need to make a call."

"Take a moment and make your call."

Jake dialed Matikas. He was gone. "Ing, tell Ray to check out the name Rainn Meyers with the post office. See if you can nail down a postal carrier by that name. Meyers is our guy. I want him taken into custody immediately."

Jake paced as he apologized to Buster and asked him to continue.

"Howard Charles Markmann, a good man, God-fearing. You know what I mean."

"I do, Buster."

"Well, that Charlie worked hard all his life. Retired. Wife passed on. Lived alone. Someone took a pickaxe to him. Sheriff found a rabbit's foot there on scene."

"And?"

"I saw the Meyers boy with the same little relic. You know the kids how they had those lucky rabbits feets, all purple colored and stuff. The Meyers boy liked to tie his to a belt loop."

"That's some story, Buster."

"I ain't got to the best part yet. Later, clearing out Meyers's room, cleaning, checking inside walls and underneath floorboards, I find this box." Buster got up, walked over to the closet. He returned with a cigar box, old and tattered. "This one here." He handed it to Jake. "Don't tell Cal I done kept it."

"Smells."

"The Meyers boy. He kept his little treasures in there."

"'Treasures,' Buster?" Jake had a *here we go* look on his face.

"Animal parts. Squirrel legs. Rabbit legs. Cat legs. You name it. After killing the animals, he must have kept them as some sort of souvenir. He dyed them all a whitish blonde by pouring bleach on the fur. Things began to make sense after that. I used to find dead animals all over the property—many of them missing limbs."

"Question, Buster. Does Markmann have any family still livin' up there by the old orphanage?"

Buster pondered the question. "You know what, as a matter a fact, he does. Brother. Name's Louis. We called him Loopy Louie."

"White hair? Feels pretty protective of the old building?"

"Uh-huh. He bought the old place after his brother was killed. No one never knew why."

68

SUNDAY, SEPTEMBER 14 - 12:39 P.M.

Jake was on his way to pick Dickie up when Dr. Kelsey text messaged. He pulled over and called the pathologist.

"You ready? I got something."

"Figured."

"A match to that indent we molded from Lisa Marie's back."

Jake had nearly forgotten about it. "Go ahead."

"It's from a 1999 Shimano deep-sea fishing reel. The base, where all the gears are housed. The molds match perfectly."

"You're good, Doc." Jake was impressed. "Excellent work."

"We're working on the dealers in the area. He could have gotten it online, but I doubt it. Those items, people like to try them out before they make a purchase."

"Let me know when you do. And thanks for the call, Kelsey, not to mention staying on this. It's Sunday."

"Least I could do, Cooper."

Before pulling back out into traffic, Jake keyed the information into his profiling program. Then sent an email to the K-PAC computer with the new details.

12:45 P.M.

Dickie wondered if Cal had turned the heat on in the room

to bust his chops. He had sauna-like sweat pouring off his brow. His red hair, now a dark maroon, was saturated. Digging through the files was actually not that bad of a job. Beyond the fact that the dust made him a little congested, Dickie tossed aside files easily after determining that the years did not correspond with their case.

Then he picked up a tattered manila folder, its corners crushed and torn. Looked at the name on the little tab.

And that handwritten, faded marker pen changed everything.

The file contained Micah's medical and educational records. Combing through, Dickie ran into a document with several diagrams stapled to it. The drawings appeared to be a room inside the orphanage where one of Micah's students had been sent for detention. Apparently, a boy, *Randy Meyers, 16, a transfer from St. Paul's Parish in Southie*, acted out in class one day. He grabbed a fellow student by the throat and choked him to the ground. The incident caused peripheral bruising around the kid's neck, sending him to the infirmary. That same day the Meyers boy pulled a knife on another student. He was placed in a special time-out room overnight.

Stuart Micah came forward and said he wanted to go in and speak with the boy. The sisters had a meeting. Micah knew Meyers best. So they agreed.

Micah spent two hours talking to the kid.

When he left the room, the boy carved Micah's name with his index fingernail all over the walls. Took him all night to do it. By morning the tip of his finger was bloodied and worn down to the middle of the nail.

"Holy shit," Dickie said, slapping the page.

69

SUNDAY, SEPTEMBER 14 – 1:00 P.M.

The man dressed as a priest did not own a gun. There was no emotion, no sense of power, behind the trigger of a weapon like that. On the other hand, there was not one chance in a million that Detective Cooper had sent his wife and child into hiding without some sort of armed guard. There had to be cops protecting Dawn and Brendan. The only way to get to them, the man who called himself Rainn Meyers knew, was to drive into where they were hiding, past the cops, then back out the same way.

"Use your head, not your muscle." It was the one idiom that made sense Meyers had taken away from Father John O'Brien, his childhood parish priest.

Steve's Market was near Baker Farm Drive, a mile from an unnamed dirt road that led to Father John's cabin. It was the only general store for miles. Steve's had been a staple since—so the sign out front proclaimed—1926. Steve sold Walden knickknacks. Fuel. Soda. Live bait for fishing. Maps and SAVE WALDEN WOODS refrigerator magnets.

Father John pulled into Steve's parking lot to refuel. Meyers stayed far enough behind the priest so as not to be seen. He sat with binoculars, watching and waiting. A winning chess player, Meyers knew, had to be patient.

After pumping fuel, the white-haired clergyman walked into the store to pay. Looking on, Meyers hoped the priest would get caught up in a conversation with the clerk, which would open up that little window of opportunity he needed.

After blessing the store per Steve's hasty plea, Father John got back into his car and pulled out of the driveway.

As he turned onto the unnamed dirt road and disappeared into the woods, Meyers popped up from behind Father and put a straight razor against the priest's freckled neck. With such a small frame, Meyers had managed to wiggle his way into the backseat floorboards, covering himself with the Father's suitcase and trench coat. Returning from the store, Father John never thought to look in the back.

"Keep driving." Meyers sounded angry with his serial killer stage voice. "Do not touch anything but the steering wheel, or you will meet Jesus Christ today. I promise you that, Father."

Father John looked in his mirror. He couldn't get a clear view of the face.

"It's okay, Father. You wouldn't remember me, anyway."

That voice. Father John recalled its distinctive affect. "Take me," Father John said, driving through the woods. "Kill me. Leave the woman and child alone. They've done nothing to you."

"The perfect martyr." Meyers laughed. "Jesus would be proud of you." Father John's insides turned over every time the man used the Lord's name in vain. Randy Meyers pressed the razor more firmly. "Keep driving, Padre."

The road was riddled with ruts and large stones. Father John had to carefully watch where he was going. As they passed over the larger potholes, the shocks on his 1997 Ford Taurus not what they once were, Meyers bounced up into the mirror's small rectangular window and Father John got a good look at him.

"You're a priest now, I see."

"Funny, Father. And you're a comedian." He nicked the priest's skin to let him know the blade was not in his hand for show.

"This can end now, son. Right now. No more killing."

"End? There is no *end*, Father. There is only a lull. Does persecution ever *end*? You should know all about that." He had a tough time keeping the knife steady. Every bump sent his hand out a few inches, away from Father's neck, then springing back, nicking a flabby section of skin hanging over the priest's collar. The white cube of Father John's choker was flecked with blood spots.

"I do know, son. Whatever happened to you, it can be overcome."

"It's too late for that now. Much too late. I need to finish what I started."

"You do not have to."

Meyers pushed himself up closer to the back of the driver's seat. A rosary Father John had hanging from his rearview mirror crashed against the windshield as he hit the road ruts. Meyers got right in Father's ear and whispered, "If I see cops, I slit your neck like a water balloon. We clear on that, Father?"

"Yes, son."

"Stop with the 'son' business. Won't work with me."

Father John finally got a good look at him. "Randy Meyers."

"You *do* remember." Meyers laughed mockingly. "Well, they call me the Optimist now. Just keep in mind, if you're thinking of martyring yourself, today would not be the time to do that. I will kill you and drive the car there myself." He pressed the blade against Father John's neck again. "Are we clear on that?"

"Yes, Randy."

Father John's loaded rifle bumped the back of his left foot. He had no idea how he was going to get to it without Meyers seeing him.

70

SUNDAY, SEPTEMBER 14 – 2:15 P.M.

Matikas had tried calling Jake and Dickie all weekend. Neither cop had answered. They were either blowing him off, or were out of a serviceable area. Matikas guessed the former. He even called the Bainbridge Sheriff's Department, but Deputy Cal explained that Jake had picked Dickie up already. "Oh, musta been, what, an hour ago. They done took off outa here like there was a corn feed sale somewheres."

The lieutenant pulled the phone away from his ear. Looked at it. *This guy serious?*

Screw Dickie and Jake, the lieutenant told himself. This was his collar. He was only calling them out of courtesy, anyway. Matikas had the post office run that name, Rainn Meyers. The clown in human resources wasn't happy about getting up on a Sunday morning, but Matikas convinced him that he'd have a Boston blue up his ass every morning on his way to work if he didn't help. Thus, within a half-hour, Matikas found himself at the Postal Operations Center office on Brookline Avenue, holding the addresses of two Rainn Meyerses employed by the post office over the past twenty years. It was such a rare name. One guy was twenty-five. Died in a car accident six months before the first murder.

Scratch.

The other guy was single. He lived in Winthrop by himself. Just turned forty. He'd had some trouble on the job saying perverted things to a few women on his route. His boss took him off the road two years ago. He'd been on medical leave—suing the government for discrimination—for the past year.

No one had heard from him.

"That paint chip," Matikas asked the cop riding to Meyers's house with him, "we get a match?"

"No, but there's an indication," the cop said, reading from a report, "that this Meyers dude liked to dress up in his mailman's uniform on his off days and approach females. Says here many of them were college kids."

Matikas pumped his fist. "This is our guy. You ready for your first big bust, kiddo?"

"He even bought himself a used mail truck, the report says."

Matikas felt a sense of urgency. Even anxiety. He'd show up Cooper and Shaughnessy, those arrogant pricks. He'd gain the captain's trust back. He could see a photo on his wall of him and the captain, side by side, city service awards in hand.

Two troopers made it to the scene merely an hour after Matikas ordered them to watch the house. Both reported seeing "curtains move" in one of the bedrooms.

Meyers was home.

Five cruisers followed Matikas. Depending on the layout of the house, the lieutenant explained over the two-way, he wanted to surround the place. "Drive on the lawn. Tear it up. I don't give a shit." He told the team to take action in three swift moves—pull up, approach the door with weapons in hand, kick it in. "Let's grab this sonofabitch and get him on the floor, facedown. No questions."

"Riley?" Matikas said to the cop riding with him.

"Lieutenant?"

"After the collar, you call your source at the *Globe* and leak the arrest. Use the name 'Optimist' in your description.

Make sure you give him our names. Tell him we have no idea where Cooper or Shaughnessy are. Got it?”

“Consider it done, Lieutenant.”

71

SUNDAY, SEPTEMBER 14 – 2:25 P.M.

Jake and Dickie were on I-93, driving past Medford, near the suburbs of North Boston. Dickie checked his voicemail—or calls he didn't want to answer as they came in. When he heard Matikas's voice announce they were converging on Rainn Meyers's house, Dickie looked at the digital time display on the dashboard.

"Move it, Jake. Matikas got a lead on Rainn Meyers. They're at his house."

Jake was furious.

Dickie hit the button for the blue light and siren.

Jake floored the gas pedal.

"Ray … what a bastard."

72

SUNDAY, SEPTEMBER 14 – 2:32 P.M.

One cop set his right shoulder against the doorjamb leading into Rainn Meyers's small, single-family Cape-style home at the end of Summer Street in Winthrop, the back of the home facing the Belle Island Reservation. Matikas and his crew stood on the stoop, weapons in hand, badges hanging from their necks, blue BPD windbreakers fluttering in the wind coming in off Broad Sound. It was cloudy out. Looked like rain. A blue wearing a bulletproof vest, helmet, and face shield, brandished a double-barrel shotgun and faced the door.

As ordered, the other blues surrounded the house.

Matikas motioned with a head nod that it was time to go in.

"Police!" screamed the officer dressed like Robocop as he kicked the door in, and they all flushed into the living room, one after the other.

Rainn Meyers was not there.

Matikas ran toward a bedroom down the short hallway.

The door was closed. "Shh ..." The lieutenant heard a television.

One, two, three ... he whispered, counting off with his free hand, motioning for Robocop to kick this door in, too.

The bedroom door came right off the hinges.

Rainn Meyers was in bed, just waking up from the ruckus going on inside his house. Around him were the remnants from a recent delivery pizza and powdered doughnut binge.

An old western on American Movie Classics flickered on the television. John Wayne, Richard Widmark.

There was a poster of Bruce Lee, that infamous *Enter the Dragon* pose, tacked to the wall above Meyers's bed. A Shih Tzu ran around in circles, barking, wagging its rat-like tail. There was dirty laundry all over the floor. Had the smell of a locker room on game day.

Meyers weighed, Matikas guessed by looking at him, about four or maybe five hundred pounds. He reminded the lieutenant of one of those guys you see on the Discovery Channel who cannot get out of bed and needs the fire department to help.

"Damn," Matikas said. He holstered his pistol. Put his hands on his waist. Walked over to the window, spread the curtains to let some light in. "Get on the radio. All clear here."

Just waking up, Rainn Meyers said, "I thought you were my housekeeper."

73

SUNDAY, SEPTEMBER 14 – 2:43 P.M.

Jake and Dickie were almost at Meyers's house. Dispatch called and explained the false alarm. They looked at each other, then busted out laughing.

Jake got off the exit and headed back toward the squad room.

Getting out of the car in the parking lot, Dickie said he needed to go home and pack up a few personal items Caroline forgot to take with her. Then FedEx them to Michigan.

"Let's hook up later today."

"Right."

Jake texted Dawn.

HOW ARE ALL OF YOU DOING?

Dawn answered as though she had been waiting.

FINE … FATHER JOHN IS SUPPOSED TO BE
HERE SOMETIME THIS AFTERNOON—I'M
TOLD WE'RE MOVING AGAIN!!!!????.

Jake typed out his answer, sent it, put the phone away.

LET'S LEAVE THAT THERE. DON'T SAY
ANOTHER WORD ABOUT IT. FEW MORE
DAYS. HANG ON. BE STRONG. I'LL SEE
YOU TODAY OR TOMORROW MORNING.

The next order of business was Mo. Jake needed to talk with Mo while he had a chance. Jake hadn't eaten lunch. So he grabbed a sandwich at the deli on the ground floor of the Patriot Building, ate it while on his way over to Mo's. It was time to end all this bullshit with his mentor. Once and for all. If the feds were coming for him, Jake needed to know what to expect. How deep he was involved. He couldn't live—or work—while constantly looking over his shoulder. Part of him wanted to drive straight to HQ and lay it all out for the captain. Tell brass what he knew and what he thought he had done per the Big Dig. Let the chips fall. As he drove and ate, Jake considered how it would go. "Kickbacks, Captain," he heard himself saying. "I knew but I said nothing. After I put this sonofabitch serial in prison, fire and indict me. But let me finish this."

That plan, Jake knew, might foil the investigation. He couldn't afford to put Dawn and Brendan in danger. On top of that, there was loyalty involved. The Southie code.

You don't rat. No matter what.

Mo was a perfectionist when it came to cleanliness. On patrol, if he found so much as a foil gum wrapper on the floorboard of his cruiser, the guy went spastic. He hated disorganization. That's why, when Mo opened the door to let his former student in, Jake knew right away things were as bad as they could get for Mo Blackhall—he was at the end of a long rope. The inside of Mo's house was disgusting. Empty cartons of food scattered among beer bottles and cans and strewn newspapers. All sorts of different documents spread about the floor in Mo's office as though he was searching for something he couldn't find.

"What is this, Mo?" Jake had to step over things walking in. The kitchen stunk of rotten food.

Mo tried to tidy up as Jake made his way into the house. But there was no use. It was obvious the guy had given up.

They walked toward the slider. Dog hair was piled up in the corners like tumbleweed. "You'd think the pooch goes out in the middle of the night for secret chemo treatments," Mo said, trying to lighten the mood, "with all the hair he sheds. Look at this shit."

Mo hadn't shaved in four, five days. He had the beginnings of a gray, white, and black beard. His eyes sagged. His face had that puffy, red, alcoholic bloat to it. Jake thought of a woodsman, terribly downtrodden. But most of all, tired. Yeah. That was it. A man tired of running.

Mo slid the door open, inviting Jake to walk outside with him. "No one can hear us out here. Sounds paranoid, I know. But look at me, Jake. Do I look like I shouldn't be?"

"Mo, what the hell is going on?" Jake was as confused as he was angry. "Why'd you take off on me like that? Matikas said something about an indictment. What am I missing here? Come on, man, talk to me."

Mo shrugged. "Embarrassed, I guess. It's hard to face you sober." Changing the subject, "You should have used me on the Optimist case, Jake." There was pleading in his voice. "I needed that *one* thing. One last feather to go out on."

"That's bullshit. I've seen you get drunk as a hobo and brag about sleeping with the fattest, ugliest skank you could find. You have no shame, Mo. Your pride is gone. This isn't about solving a murder."

Mo knew why Jake was there. "I was running an errand upstate. Trying one final move to get out of this. Let's leave it at that."

"Out of what? What do you mean, 'errand'?"

"Jake, come on. The less you know …"

Jake didn't want to hear it. He wanted Mo to say he was having a rough time and things would be okay. A few weeks, a month, Mo would be back in the game. Jake shook his head. Put his hands in his pockets. Mo walked toward the wooden chair swing near the edge of his property. Jake followed.

"What's going on? *Talk* to me, Mo. Maybe I can help. How is the Teddy Williams Tunnel lawsuit connected here?" Jake had a good idea, but wanted Mo to confirm his suspicions—and also tell it to the wire Jake was wearing.

"I don't know how this happened, Jake. I never expected people would die."

There was movement in the woods behind them. Leaves cracking. A squirrel chasing nuts.

"Were you paying someone off up north?"

Mo thought about it. "Freakin' bartender. I gave him a c-note to keep his trap shut." He waved his trembling hands around. The skin on Mo's palms was yellow, Jake noticed. His eyes, too, held a jaundiced hue. "You don't want to know, Jake. It won't do you any good now."

Mo pulled a half-pint of Black Velvet from his back pocket. Before he could take a swig, Jake grabbed the bottle and threw it into the woods. "Tell me what's going on here!"

Mo looked with longing at the shrubbery where the bottle had landed. "It's over, Jake. There was so much money floating around during that Big Dig. You have to understand how hard it was for me."

"What have you done?" Jake was startled by this revelation. He assumed it was a few thousand dollars here and there. *Coffee and donuts,* the old-timers called it. Local merchants liked to give cops free stuff. It was a community thing. But he could tell by the look on Mo's face it was much more involved. "You're stronger than that, Mo. Come on. What are you saying? How deep have you gotten me involved." Jake paced. Put a hand on his forehead. "Tell me."

"The Big Dig, Jake. Everyone was making money."

Jake put his head down. He couldn't believe this. His cell phone buzzed. "Yo? Kinda busy here, Dick."

"We got our break, Kid. Meet me at your house in an hour."

"What is it?"

"The name … the name … but I need to show you."

Jake hung up. "Mo, I need to get going. We're close to getting our guy. Let's talk tomorrow or Tuesday."

Mo did not speak.

"Hold on, Mo. We'll fight this. Together. Just a while longer."

Jake went to walk away.

Mo called after him. "Mayor Devino, Jake, we go way back. I owed him."

That stopped Jake in his tracks. He turned.

Mo raised his voice. "I always taught you to pay your debts. Remember, there are only three sources of morality—object, intention, circumstance. I failed all three, Jake."

"You did *what*?" Jake looked down at the ground as his temples throbbed. "Two people died in that Ted Williams accident, Mo. What the hell are you talking about?"

Mo stared at nothing, tearing up. "I know …"

"Last time I checked, we were supposed to save lives." Jake walked over and poked a stiff finger into Mo's chest. "Two," he held up the peace sign, spoke slowly. "Two. People. Died. Mo. You got me involved in *that*?" Jake stared into Mo's sad eyes.

Mo didn't speak.

Jake started for the house. He had a hand on the sliding glass door handle. "I'll call a few people, Mo. Find out some things. Just give me a few days. We'll turn ourselves in. Figure this out."

"Why didn't you just follow Casey into the service, Jake? I've always wondered. I gotta know."

Jake considered this. He didn't want to talk about it. Not now. Then said: "No guts, Mo. I was scared of dying over there. No fucking guts. That's me."

Jake walked in, closed the door behind him.

Mo stared into the woods, not knowing Jake was gone. He said, "Our plan was to groom you. Bring you into the fold with us. But when I began to see how good of a cop you were, how much tougher than I could ever be, how far you had come from that neighborhood, I couldn't do it."

Jake was out in front. Inside his car. The blue light above him on the roof spinning and flashing. The siren wailing.

On his way home.

74

A manila folder in his hand, Dickie paced in Jake's driveway.

Jake pulled in, chirping the tires to a stop.

The house was empty, the shades pulled. It had that no-life look to it, same as when families go on vacation. A tell-tale sign to home invaders was the porch light on during the middle of the day.

"What's up?" Jake slammed his door shut, tore off his sunglasses.

"I could have explained it over the phone, but I had better show you this. I took one of the files from the sheriff's station house like you told me to."

"Naughty boy."

"Listen, you were right. I found something. There was a report in here about that boy, Rainn Meyers, who supposedly killed the neighbor after escaping."

"I know all this already." Jake was impatient. "Come on here—"

"Just shut up and listen for once. I did a LexisNexis on the name. Look at this newspaper clipping." Dickie shoved an article published by the *Augusta Gazette* in Jake's face. It was a short piece about the break-in and murder of Howard Charles Markmann.

Jake took the article. Walked toward his garage. The next-door neighbor started his lawn mower, pushed it into gear, began cutting his grass. The noise reminded Jake how out of the suburban loop he was.

"Read it," Dickie said.

HOME INVASION ENDS IN MURDER

Suspect Sought by Sheriff

BAINBRIDGE—Howard Charles Markmann, 57, a retired Port Henry school teacher and lifelong resident of Bainbridge, was murdered by an intruder last night. The intruder broke in, killed Mr. Markmann with a pick-axe. Nothing appeared to be stolen.

Asked if residents in the tiny town should be concerned, Sheriff Buford Townsend responded, "Not at all. Isolated incident. The only thing missing was Markmann's wallet and a few papers from his desk. We have a suspect."

"Sonofa*bitch*. How'd we miss that!"

"Exactly."

"You run that name and see what turns up. I'm driving straight to Walden."

"I'll call Father John and let him know."

Jake wondered why Dickie would say that. Then, "No," he shook his head quickly, "don't alarm them. I'll text Dawn. They're supposed to be moving to a seminary near Hampton, anyway."

The new locale was in Bangor. A retreat center.

Jake sped off.

Dickie stood, stunned, watching Jake drive away. Sure that Jake was out of sight, Dickie took out his personal notebook, licked the end of his pencil, wrote something down.

Near Hampton seminary…

75

SUNDAY, SEPTEMBER 14 – 3:24 P.M.

Father John forced a smile as he pulled up to the trooper standing guard along the gravel driveway leading to his cabin. The priest was no actor. Nor was he thrilled about lying. Today would be a test of will.

Rainn Meyers looked at his prisoner. He brandished enough of the razor hidden under his left thigh to remind Father John who was in charge. The priest did not doubt that Meyers would lift that blade, slice his throat, then slash the cop in the face before either of them knew what happened.

"Father Charles Howard, you got it?"

The priest said he did.

"Officer," Father said, rolling his window down.

The trooper leaned in. He looked at Father John's passenger. Then raised the barrel of his M-16 into the opening of the window. Nodded. All business. "Who's that, Father?" He pointed to Meyers with the barrel of the gun.

"That, my good son, is Father Charles Howard, from Reading. He's here to speak to the child and Dawn. Counsel them about what's going on. Detective Cooper approved the visit. Encouraged it, even. Please call the detective and ask."

Rainn Meyers did not like the addition of that last part. He ground his teeth. Blinked his eyes. Rolled his tongue across his bottom lip. Took a deep breath.

"I haven't heard anything about this," M-16 said. "What's up with your neck? Nick yourself shaving?"

"Indeed. Darn dull razors."

"Hold on a minute." M-16 stepped away from the driver's side door. Lifted his walkie-talkie, said something they couldn't hear.

Father John sat still, looking straight ahead. Bounced a finger on the steering wheel. The air coming into the car was noticeably colder out here in the woods, a cool dampness to it. Father John could smell the sweet, pungent aroma of the pines all around them.

"Shut off the car," M-16 ordered, leaning down, pointing his weapon at them.

Meyers stayed calm. "Keep cool," he whispered to Father. "You are going to do this."

The cop was on his radio again. Clicking and talking cop-speak to his counterpart, who was walking out the front door of the cabin.

Dawn, Mother Lucinda, Brendan, and one of the sisters stood in the doorway, looking on, wondering what was going on.

Both cops stood on each side of Father John's car. "Get out," M-16 said sternly, as he had been trained to. The second trooper had a shotgun pointed at Meyers's head.

"Everything okay, son?" Father John asked M-16.

"Just fine, Father. Get out." He used the barrel of his weapon to point.

He stepped out, and walked away from the vehicle. "Listen, Officer. Father Charles is, well, he's not in the best shape. Problem with his legs." The priest put a hand up to shield the side of his mouth, whispered. "He's in the early stages of multiple sclerosis. Doesn't want anyone to know. He's soiled himself. Needs to change his Depends."

"Meaning?"

"Well, he really shouldn't be getting out of the vehicle until we can get him into the house. Maybe you can carry him. Detective Cooper is not going to like this. But if you insist."

M-16 looked over the roof of the car at his partner. Motioned with his eyes for a huddle. They talked in back of the car.

"Fine," M-16 said, approaching Father. "Get back in. We're going to allow you to pass. If you need us, there's a radio inside, on the kitchen table. You press the big button on the right side, then you speak."

Father John drove away.

M-16 and the other cop, standing at the end of the cobblestone driveway, watched Father John and his companion drive toward the cabin.

76

It took Rainn Meyers exactly three minutes. He and Father John hustled into the cabin. Meyers grabbed the boy at razor point. Made a slight cut along his neck—nothing too deep or dangerous—to prove how serious he was. The boy cried. Meyers then held the razor to the boy's neck and led Dawn and Father out of that pile of logs as effortlessly as he had walked in.

Father John drove. Dawn was forced to sit in the back seat where Meyers had Brendan choked underneath his arm.

"Tell the kid to stop the bawling or I scalp him in front of you."

Dawn pleaded with her son. "Brendan, please, honey … listen to the man."

Meyers felt great about himself. Just like that, he had what he wanted—the ultimate prize. *Dawn*. He could care less about the kid. Or the priest.

Dawn was his *h*—the final sacrifice.

"Don't hurt him." Dawn fell apart quickly as Father drove. She put her hands over her mouth. Tears streamed down her face. Her heart melted like wax. One moment she was talking to a nun about faith, the next she was staring at the man who was going to kill her son.

"I will if I have to."

Father John hoped Dawn could keep the killer distracted enough so he could grab his rifle underneath the seat.

As they exited the gated area of the cabin driveway, Meyers gave a smile to the trooper, along with a sober warning via the walkie-talkie he took from the cabin. "Drop your weapons. If you follow us, you will listen as Detective Cooper's *only* child is being gutted like a fish—his wife maimed in the face for life."

The two troopers could only watch them—and their careers—drive away.

Onto the main road, Meyers made his order clear to Father John. "You pull up to that convenience store and shut the vehicle off."

Father John took a right into the parking lot.

"Now, we need to do this quickly as possible. Mrs. Cooper, you stay in this car with me."

Father John opened his door. The overhead light turned on. That irritating *ding-ding-ding* chimed to let him know he had left the keys in the ignition.

"Father, don't you go running off on us now."

The priest stopped.

"Okay, Mrs. Cooper. You come over here." The killer let go of Brendan. Then grabbed Dawn and put the razor to her throat. "You, kid, you get into the front seat with the priest." *Ding. Ding …* "Father, close your damn door. Now!"

Meyers pulled Dawn out by her hair, then got her in a headlock. He leaned inside the car through the open passenger-side window, looked at Father John. "Drive away. Go west, toward Route 2. Do *not* look back. Give that radio to Mrs. Cooper."

Father John looked at Dawn. "Go," she struggled to get out. "I'll manage."

"No."

"Go, Father."

"I will kill that child, Father. You don't want his blood on your hands."

Father John put the car in gear. Drove away slowly. Brendan cried.

When Father John was out of sight, Rainn Meyers forced Dawn into the back of his SUV. He handcuffed her to a metal bar holding the spare tire in place. Then stuck a piece of silver duct tape over her mouth.

He looked in both directions. Steve had a phone to his ear, watching from the storefront window. Those two police officers from the cabin came barreling out of the dirt road, breaking speed records as they whisked past the parking lot and Rainn Meyers, not noticing a thing.

With the wild squeal of rubber sliding on tar, Meyers took off with his prize eastbound, in the opposite direction.

77

SUNDAY, SEPTEMBER 14 – 6:31 P.M.

After escaping from Bainbridge as a child, Rainn Meyers killed Howard Charles Markmann and stole the man's identity. Dickie processed the addresses for every Howard Charles Markmann and any other combination of those three names who had ever worked for the post office.

The trace did not take long.

He came up with Charles Howard, Beverly, Massachusetts. Howard fit the description to a T. Not to mention there were no other combinations of the three names working for the post office anywhere in New England.

Dickie, along with a team of blues and two cars of state troopers headed to Beverly as soon as he acquired the address. Not for one moment did they think Charles Howard, whose real name was Rainn Meyers, would be home. Dickie knew, however, it was as good a place as any to start looking.

6:44 P.M.

"Gone," the trooper said over the radio.

"What?" Jake was puzzled by this word. *Gone.* He was on his way up to the cabin to be with his family.

"Sorry, Cooper … he had the priest by the neck … said he'd gut your kid."

Jake turned the radio off. He could not listen. He turned his vehicle around and headed back to D-15.

The anxiety of knowing Dawn was going to be killed numbed Jake. The images pounded on his fragile sensibilities. Father John had the boy, that was the only silver lining. They were on their way to meet Jake at the squad room.

Walking in, Jake ran into Matikas. "How the hell did he get into that cabin, lieutenant? Two troopers just let the guy drive in, I suppose?"

"He was dressed as a priest, Jake. Come on. We'll find the bastard."

"Before or after he kills my wife?" Jake walked away.

"Let's not go there, Jake," Matikas said, following behind. Everyone in the office stopped what they were doing and looked on. "We're not sure that's what he wants. I spoke to that FBI profiler. This is something that is, well, it's the 'end game' for the guy. He's going to use Dawn as a pawn to get something else."

"What *else* could he want? Dawn is *h*!"

M-I-C-A-H.

Father John walked in with Brendan. The boy darted into his father's arms. They hugged for a long time.

"I want him here. I want my son guarded under lock and key with cops all over the place."

"We're in a police station, Detective Cooper," a blue said.

Jake stared at the young cop. "Brendan doesn't leave here."

"Where's Mommy, Daddy?"

78

SUNDAY, SEPTEMBER 14 – 6:48 P.M.

Dickie put his weight and anger behind the kick and the door broke in two, a piece of it hanging off the hinges. He and the boys from the state police, along with a team of D-15 blues, were inside Meyers's small, two-bedroom ranch. They dug through things they knew a search warrant would cover. Dickie told one of the blues to call Jake and tell him it was going to be a while before he came up with anything. "There's shit everywhere. Boxes upon boxes of stuff. A damn darkroom, for cripesakes."

At the station house, preparing to go find his wife, Jake didn't care what was going on inside Meyers's house. He wondered instead how he was going to find Dawn. He had to collect his composure. Falling apart, Jake knew he was no good. He needed to key the new information into his iPhone, call Kelsey to see if she had made any progress with the fishing reel. The focus had to be on what he could control, which Jake knew from experience was always easier said than done.

Father John stayed quietly by Jake's side.

Dickie called. "Put me on speaker. Get the lieutenant."

"Just say it," Jake yelled. "Come on here. What do you have?"

"A brochure. It's from the Museum of Science. There's an exhibit going on through next week. Rare flowers. This guy had a brochure out on the table. Marked tomorrow's date on a calendar he left next to the brochure and, of all things, a copy of *The Strange Case of Dr. Jekyll and Mr. Hyde*." There was a pause. Sounded like Dickie picked the book up, flipped it over for some reason, stared at the back cover, put it back down. "He's sending a message. All this shit was left here for us to find."

Jake did not answer.

Dickie knew why.

"We're going to continue searching this place through the night, Jake. If we find something else, I'll call."

79

MONDAY, SEPTEMBER 15 – 6:00 A.M.

"Wake up! Come on." The Optimist slapped Dawn on the face. "We have work to do."

Dawn was groggy. Her body was sore from being tied up all night. She was thinking how she was going to convince Meyers that she suffered from seasickness. When he wasn't looking, she stuck a finger down her throat and vomited.

The sky was opening up over the horizon.

Rainn Meyers made Dawn sip from a bottle of water. "I need you alert and alive this morning. The rest of…"—he stopped. "Well, Mrs. Cooper. How you fare the rest of the day is going to be entirely up to you."

The sun was an orange ball of fire, a daisy yellow as it reflected off the water. The swells were running about four feet. Not too bad, considering a ferocious tropical storm off the southern coast of Maine had sent many of the Grand Bank fishermen from Gloucester south and into Boston Harbor to wait it out.

Dawn was disheveled. She had a gash on her forehead from when the Optimist had pulled her out of the back of the SUV. The wound throbbed. It felt swollen and infected.

"I'm not going to say it again, Mrs. Cooper. Move your ass. Now!" The Optimist was right in her face. Nose to nose. Dawn could feel his hot breath hitting her mouth.

Dawn managed to raise herself up alongside the bench seat on the bow. She used the stiff white cushion as leverage to stand. Her legs wobbled. Her hands were handcuffed in front.

Still, she was alive and had made it through the night. If his plan was to simply kill her, she would be fish bait by now.

Denny, she found herself thinking. She could see Denny Garcia in this man. Maybe that relationship with Denny could help. *Optimist ... he is going to give me choices.*

"I had a plan to leave your corpse inside King's Chapel." He paced in front of her. "You know, that wonderful landmark downtown. I was going to prop it up on the altar. But then, oh, I don't know. Something told me I was taking things a bit too far. Blaspheming such a sacred place, in front of God's face like that. It would secure a place in hell for me—and to be honest, Mrs. Cooper, if there's the slightest chance"—he held two fingers almost closed together in front of her eyes to make his point—"for me to be redeemed, I thought something like that would blow my chances." Then he laughed.

Meyers jostled Dawn clumsily and aggressively by her shoulders. Set her down on the cushioned bench seat. Then walked back and forth in front of her, tapping the blade of a ten-inch knife on his palm.

Thinking.

Dawn was tired. In a lot of pain. But her strength was there. She could call it up when needed. She decided, however, to act as if she was drifting in and out of consciousness. She opened her eyes. She closed her eyes. Allowed her body to sway with the motion of the waves.

"I have something for you. You wait here." The Optimist rubbed the knife down the bridge of her nose. "And don't you go running off on me now."

The killer emerged moments later from the small cabin below deck with a package. It was bow-tied. Wrapped with a shiny blue paper that matched the sky. He set it gingerly on Dawn's thighs. Cradled her chin in his palm, lifted her face up to look at him squarely.

"Open it."

She wished she could puke on it.

"Go ahead, please. Open it. It's for you."

Dawn didn't move.

"Here, nudge over. Let me slip in there and help you out."

Get him to talk about the past ...

He tore open the package. Lifted the top of the box off, as if it were cheap chocolates you give out on Christmas.

"Have a look inside. Come on."

Dawn moved a bit, but refused to look down.

"Oh, well, if you must." He grabbed the back of her head by her hair and forced her face down into the box. His voice changed into a deep, croaky tone. "I said *look*."

Dawn could only feel the brittle softness of tissue paper against her face.

"Little memento for you, Dawn Cooper," he said, bending down, whispering in her ear. "Savor this moment—because it just may be your last."

80

Sunshine stopped by the house after not hearing from Mo all day on Sunday. Last Mo had said, Jake Cooper was on his way over to talk. That was a day ago. Sunshine called Mo several times but got no answer.

He knocked several times, curious to hear what Jake wanted.

Drunken sonofabitch is probably passed out.

"Mo," he shouted, "you in there?"

He walked around to the backyard, hoping to look in through the sliders. The shades were drawn, blocking his view.

Mo's pooch, Magnum, barked relentlessly.

The mutt's yelping followed Sunshine as he stepped around the outside of the house, trying to get a look in through a window.

"You in there?" Sunshine yelled, his hands cupped around his eyes, looking into Mo's bedroom.

More barking.

He walked back around to the front of the house. Before turning the last corner, brushing up against an azalea plant and row of prickly evergreen bushes, by the gutter he noticed a way in. There was a small rectangular cellar window that opened from the bottom with a crank. It was cracked enough for Sunshine to get his thick sausage fingers underneath and pull.

It was a tight fit, but Sunshine forced his gut through the small opening, falling in and onto the concrete floor of the basement, groaning and brushing dust off himself as he struggled to get up.

"You here?" He only yelled to make it look good. He stared up the basement steps. "Hey, Mo?"

Out of breath, Sunshine made it to the top. Opened the door.

The living room was dark. The air-conditioner was set so high Sunshine thought he could see his breath. The air was crisp, heavy, like the inside of a restaurant walk-in cooler. Still, cold or not, the smell was pungent and sobering. He pulled a hankie out of his back pocket, placed it over his nose and mouth. "What the hell?"

Turning the corner into Mo's office, Sunshine discovered the embattled cop on the floor, blood and brain matter on the wall behind him, the carpet a halo of tissue, skull, and bone underneath his blown-apart head.

With a crinkled look of disgrace and disgust, Sunshine stepped over Mo's body, walked toward his desk.

Reaching inside the top, middle drawer, he felt his way around to see if that file was still taped underneath the drawer.

Thank heavens.

Sunshine walked to the door, used the same hankie to cover the knob, took one last look at Mo's bloated and decomposing corpse, then out he went, file in hand, ready to meet the rest of his day.

81

MONDAY, SEPTEMBER 15 – 10:00 A.M.

Brendan slept on a cot in the conference room down the hall from Jake's office. Jake sat in a chair next to his son, feet up on the table, his suit coat—now a blanket—strewn over him.

First thing in the morning, Dr. Kelsey called. She said the fishing reel that made the indent on Lisa's back was sold by only a handful of retailers in the Boston region. Jake got up and spent hours going through records provided by K-PAC, looking to see if any one of the five dozen retailers made sense to the geographical locations of the case. Jake's iPhone did not have a sensible comparison to make a judgment and returned a report that was of little use. When the chime came in with the bad news, Jake stood behind his desk, the iPhone cocked back in his arm like a baseball, but then stopped, thinking better of throwing it against the wall in frustration.

He sat. Palms on his forehead, elbows on his desk. *What have I done?* He'd begged Matikas for a murder case. A second chance to prove himself and redeem that little girl. Now Dawn was a victim. Probably cut into pieces. *For what?*

After falling back into his swivel chair, Jake had an idea. The diesel fuel lead, coupled with his theory of a boat, and now this fishing reel, meant they needed to be looking for a marina. Only problem was, there were ten marinas named on K-PAC's list of "potentials" Jake had received via text after keying in the latest information.

"Damn it."

He looked down at the phone and thrashed the ENTER key repeatedly. Kept pushing it down. "Come on!"

A blue knocked and walked into his office with Krispy Kreme doughnuts and coffee.

"Thanks, man." Jake put the phone away.

Brendan came into the office as the blue walked out. "Is Mommy okay, Daddy?" The kid rubbed sleep from his blue eyes. He had his favorite source of comfort these days, a red Let's Rock Elmo!, with him. "I want to see Mommy."

Jake got down, eye-level with his boy. "She's in trouble, buddy. Daddy is going to do everything he can to find her. I promise, okay?"

Brendan collapsed into his father's arms. Then backed away and stuck out his pinky. "Promise, promise?" he said, referring to a gesture they had made up. Jake had been working so much overtime that even Brendan noticed, calling him on it one day. Jake apologized as Dawn stood behind him with raised eyebrows and an I-told-you-so gaze. Brendan made his dad pinky swear he would try to make more time for them. And so Jake linked pinkies with his son. "Promise, promise, buddy," rubbing the top of his head, messing his hair up.

They ate doughnuts together without talking. Jake took Brendan down the hall where Father John was just getting up. "Don't take your eyes off him, Father."

"Jake, I need to do more. This is all my fault."

"No, don't go there, Father. You could not have done anything." Jake and Father John had spent three hours the previous night going through every detail of what happened. He blamed himself for not putting his family under house arrest in some state police barracks up north, where they could be watched until it was over. That was stupid and selfish. Jake said he allowed his ego to override his instinct.

Jake went to the locker room to take a shower. Shave. Change into some fresh clothes: jeans and black T-shirt and dark blue BPD-issued windbreaker. He always kept an extra set of clothes at the office. Putting on his pants inside his office, the tears came. Not a crying fit. But more of that feeling before you sneeze. Sinus pressure. The well-up. He saw himself burying Dawn—that is, what was left of her. He envisioned himself standing graveside, his arm around Brendan. Scores of people, heads bowed, lined up along her mahogany coffin on each side. The image was so clear. He couldn't help it. His experience told him Rainn Meyers had taken Dawn for one reason.

I have to find her ...

As he pulled his shirt over his head there was a knock on the door.

"You got a minute?" Matikas poked his head in, never sounding so courteous.

"Dawn?"

"Jake, can I come in?"

Matikas entered. He had a somber look about him, shoulders drooped, eyes darting around. Jake stood in front of the mirror slipping on his windbreaker. "Just spit it out. They found her, right? I've prepared myself, Lieutenant."

"You had better sit down, Jake."

The comment startled him. Jake whirled around. "What is it?"

Matikas looked down at the carpet. Took a breath. Sighed.

"Come on, Lieutenant. Time is not what I have right now."

"It's Mo, Jake ... he's gone."

Jake froze. "What?"

"Dead. I heard the call this morning on my way in. I radioed over to the Lexington PD to confirm."

"What do you mean, dead? I just saw him."

"Shotgun blast to the head. Killed himself. Anonymous tipster called it in."

Jake closed his eyes. He should have known. Mo sounded desperate, as if he was going to, well, take the easy way out. He had that don't-worry-everything-will-be-all-right tone to everything he said. Jake knew it, too. In his gut. As he sat in his car getting ready to head home to meet Dickie that day, he felt it. But he had more important things to do.

He worked at a kink that had popped up in his neck, kneading it gently, before telling Matikas, "Call his ex-wife and tell her to take care of this."

"Of course," Matikas responded.

82

MONDAY, SEPTEMBER 15 – 10:07 A.M.

The Optimist asked Dawn why she didn't like the gift. He had gone to so much trouble to pack and wrap the thing.

Dawn took it out of the package and held it up—a wig?

"No." He laughed, then stood. "That whore your husband worked with—it's her hair. I scalped her like an Indian."

Dawn struggled to hide her disgust. She was being held prisoner aboard a boat in the middle of the ocean by a madman. He was, at any time, going to kill her. She needed to get her strength up so she could employ her psychological knowledge and skill to beat him. Her only chance was to talk him out of whatever he had planned.

Go right at the trauma, Dawn knew. That was the key. Get him chatting about why he ended up this way. It was a crapshoot. He would respond hot or cold. Did Dawn want to take that chance?

What else do I have left?

Out in the middle of Cape Cod Bay, the Optimist anchored. He sat for a while, legs up on the bar in front of the steering column. He had his arms behind his head, relishing the plan he had dreamed up for Dawn and Jake.

Dawn said something.

He turned. "Did you want to talk now, honey?"

Dawn had her head bowed. She nodded.

"Go right ahead." He stood.

"You, I … I." It was no use. She was out of breath. Her lips moved, but nothing came out. She tried again. "This child I counsel, he's a lot like … you."

The Optimist didn't respond immediately. He picked at one of his cuticles with the tip of his knife. Had a serious gaze about him. With a curdled face, he walked over, grabbed Dawn by the hair, put his knife to her throat. She could feel the razor-sharp edge digging into her skin.

"That psychobabble, it will not work with me, you stupid shrink. Don't you *dare* try that shit with me." He shoved her hard against the side wall of the boat.

"When … when … did … it happen?" Dawn was not going to give up easily.

Point out vulnerabilities.

He pushed the knife against her skin, drawing a straight line of blood. "I said to stop that right now." He became transfixed by the sight of the blood. Shook his head.

Keep him talking …

The Optimist then walked to the other side of the boat. Stopped. Lowered a small, Navy SEAL-like rubber rescue raft with a ninety-horsepower engine down into the water. Tied it off. He had taken anything of value off the boat the previous night and loaded it into the SUV before they departed the marina. He had no idea why he did this, but couldn't seem to stomach seeing all of those body parts he had collected and froze end up at the bottom of the Atlantic Ocean. Didn't seem right.

Dawn started to say something as she watched him lower the boat, but he stifled her—"You make another peep, I will decapitate you."

She didn't move.

After making sure the raft was secure, he walked over to Dawn. Grabbed her wrists. Dragged her toward the stern as she pulled in the opposite direction, trying to fight with him. Not giving in.

"Get up on your feet or you go for a swim."

Dawn let out a desperate scream the Optimist didn't think she had left in her.

He stopped. "Was that you?"

"*Yes*," she said with as much hate as she could muster.

He was pleased—a player. "Now this is what I appreciate. Spunk."

He let her go and walked over to the cabinet where he kept his knives.

"I knew you had some fight left in you." He licked the blade of his serrated knife, nicking his tongue, drawing blood. "Believe me, I would love nothing more than to gut you and watch your colon fall out on this deck like a Slinky. But I am a killer who offers his victims options." He spit a mouthful of blood in Dawn's face. "At least that's what the papers say."

Dawn swallowed. "My husband is going to skin you alive."

"Ooo …" He said it in a mocking fashion, wiggling his fingers out in front of her. "Scared of the Dawnster's threats."

He squinted one eye. Then grabbed Dawn by the back of the head once more, put the knife to her throat. He made a short, quick slit. A slow trickle of warm blood ran down her neck onto her chest. A droplet fell on the deck in front of her.

"Lick that up." He pushed her mouth into it. "I cannot stand a mess."

The Optimist put the knife down. Pulled out a pair of titanium handcuffs he had purchased online (two sets). Dragged Dawn toward the steering column.

"Time to get on with this."

There were two one-inch-thick metal bars protruding from the sleeping cabin below deck, bolted to the main control room. The Optimist took one of Dawn's ankles, slapped one side of the cuffs around it and the other side around one of the bars.

He did the same with her other leg.

Dawn stared down at her imprisoned feet. "Oh my God, what are you doing?" She grabbed hold of his hair and pulled. He backed off, smiling. Took a breath. Went back to work.

As he finished handcuffing Dawn shook the steering column as hard as she could, trying to get loose.

Nothing moved.

The Optimist held the serrated knife up in front of Dawn and slowly moved it toward her cuffed ankles.

"There's a soft spot in the bone, down here close to your Achilles heel." He turned his leg and pointed to his. "It's softer there near the joint. Have you ever deboned a chicken, Dawn? You'll know what I mean."

Dawn had a bruise under her left eye that was starting to pulse and swell up.

"If I were you, Mrs. Cooper, I'd snap the bone with your hands once you get through the skin. Ever see that movie *127 Hours*, where the mountain climber gets trapped under a boulder and … well, whatever. Same thing. Like near the thigh and the leg. It's not really that hard to do. You're a psychologist, right? You can talk yourself into anything, I'm sure."

Dawn was immobilized by the fear of his proposition. The blazing sun alone would kill her. As a child, she suffered repeated nightmares of drowning and being buried alive. Looking at him, listening to this, she wondered now if she would choose one of those methods over dehydrating on this deck, or bleeding to death.

"Oh, yeah. Almost forgot the most important part. I wouldn't be a good killer if I didn't make things a bit more interesting for you."

Confused, Dawn watched him walk toward the back of the boat.

There was a plug in the far corner. He bent down, unloosened the nut holding it in place. As soon as it came loose, seawater spit out of the tiny opening as though Sprite soda overflowed from a shaken-up two-liter bottle.

Meyers had uncorked the boat's drain plug.

"You probably have about, oh, maybe an hour. Perhaps two. Give or take. You need to make up your mind, Mrs. Cooper, but give yourself, I don't know, at least ten minutes to get through each leg. That knife you're using is rather dull. Miss Rossi's bones were hard as ceramic."

Dawn looked at her legs. She had the knife in her good hand. The Optimist walked over to his cabinet, took out a chef's knife, placed it in the crook of his back, then jumped over the side of the boat.

Dawn heard the splash.

Then an engine fire up.

Looking out toward the west, Dawn Cooper watched the tiny image of her kidnapper inside that rescue raft disappear over the horizon.

She looked down at her legs. Then at the knife in her hand.

The first cut was going to be the hardest. After that it was about survival.

She put the knife up to her right ankle and slowly glided the jagged, scalloped blade across. She could taste a steely electric shock on the tip of her tongue as she broke through the skin and blood trickled down the sides of her foot slowly, mixing in with a bit of the seawater swirling around the deck, running into the side channels.

83

Jake was getting ready to head out to Rainn Meyers's house. If nothing else, he could help the search team and maybe get an idea of where Meyers was holding Dawn. But the clock, he knew, had just about timed out on Dawn.

As Jake collected his keys and radio, Dickie called to say forget about it. "I know where the showdown is going to occur."

"What do you mean, 'showdown'?" Jake stood in his office. Stared out the window. Below was the busy Monday lunchtime rush. All those people shopping. Visiting friends. Running errands. Grabbing a quick sausage-and-pepper sandwich on a hard roll. Jake wanted to be one of them. A normal guy. Doing regular things.

"Yeah." Dickie was energized. "Showdown. OK Corral-like. He set it all up."

"Dickie, what did you find?" No emotion.

"An invitation. You need to get over to the Museum of Science immediately, Jake. 'Member that brochure I was telling you about? The flower exhibit?"

He waited, but Jake didn't answer.

"Well," Dickie continued, "the museum has a conservatory on the second floor—it's part of that exhibit. Full of rare flowers. Trust me, Kid, this is where you'll find him. That is where he gets his inspiration. It plays into what we've uncovered here. Get over to that museum now. I'll call Ray, get it shut down, and have a team of blues meet you there."

84

MONDAY, SEPTEMBER 15 – 12:10 P.M.

The Plant Conservatory was inside Boston's Museum of Science on Route 28, just off Storrow Drive. The Museum displayed one of its most prized possessions on a grant from the John Kerry Foundation. It was a Titan Arum, or *Amorphophallus titanium.* The rarest flower in the world. But more famously, it went by another name.

The Corpse Flower.

Oddly shaped, much in line with a cactus, this massive botanical freak of nature grew up to ten feet tall. It looked like some sort of a stem-cell experiment gone terribly wrong. At times it emitted an aroma considered to be the nastiest smell on the planet. Hence its nickname.

"This plant is one of the wonders of the botanical world," one of the museum's botanists told reporters the previous Friday morning, unveiling the flower for the first time.

The exhibit drew thousands of visitors over the first three-day period of the 3rd Annual Museum of Science's Rare Flower Exhibition. Definitely the star of the show.

Jake raced down Storrow Drive. The Longfellow Bridge and Massachusetts General Hospital was a blur on his right. Cars pulled off to the side of the road in front of him as sped toward the museum.

Matikas called and demanded that the Museum be closed.

"But only the day," the museum conservator said. "I'll give you that."

"A cop's wife's life is at stake here, you bowtie-wearing prick," Matikas replied angrily. "You'll do what we tell you to."

It was 12:16 p.m. Jake took a hard left onto Route 28. The museum was in his sights.

Matikas radioed to say the museum had just ushered patrons and employees out of the building. There wasn't time for a complete sweep. "But the conservator is certain the place is completely empty."

Jake kicked the knob off the radio. It went dead.

Dawn.

Cooper had based his value on being a cop and his professional standing in the community on what his father thought of him. It was as if being a cop, completing the transformation from Southie bad boy to golden-child lawman, somehow justified his existence. He thought of *Rocky*, his and Casey's favorite movie. Adrienne, Rocky's girlfriend, asked why it was so important to win. Why Rocky needed to be the champ. "Then I'll know I'm not a bum," Rocky said.

It was clear to Jake now as he headed for the parking lot closest to the conservatory that his identity and self-worth—the conditions for his life—were with this killer. No one else—and nothing—mattered. Likewise, he needed Dawn in the same way he needed to kill the man who had violated that space. He was a slave to original evil. He knew that. But there was salvation there, too. He could see that clearly now.

As he got out of his car, Jake knew deep down that Dawn was dead. He was on a mission of payback at this point. Nothing more.

85

MONDAY, SEPTEMBER 15 – 12:19 P.M.

Other exhibits in the museum included an entire wall of Queen of the Night flowers. This was where the Optimist had spent a lot of his spare time the past few weeks. The greenhouse had become a place where Rainn Meyers could fulfill the final wish he had for himself.

Dickie was right. The Optimist had set it up to end here. He knew Jake and his team of cops would storm into the museum's greenhouse conservatory at any moment. They would wave guns and threaten. Tell him he was cornered. There was nothing he could do.

What a damn joke.

Meyers hid in a closet when the museum announced it needed to close "for routine maintenance." He knew it was about him.

"'*Our hearts are restless until they rest in Thee.*'" He wondered if it was the Teacher or Father John who had given him that Bible passage. He couldn't recall.

He walked about the greenhouse, feeling the petals of the Queens brush smoothly against his open palm, almost as if he was giving the leaves high-fives. It was here where he came up with the idea to place that lone seedling underneath Lisa Marie's body. And also to leave the brochure with today's date, leading Jake and his cronies here. They would think it was all some sort of master plan. Some crazy serial-killer thing. But it was nothing more than a ruse. A well-thought-out plan to kill one last victim.

Police were so easy. So predictable. Too damn gullible.

As he walked around, the Optimist pictured what was about to happen. Jake was going to point his gun. *Where is my wife?*

The Optimist saw himself laughing in the cop's face.

Waiting for Jake, the killer pressed his nose up against the glass. He stood in the conservatory alone. He wondered which path Dawn had chosen. It was over by now. She'd made her choice. As he watched cops barrel into the parking lot three stories below, he pictured Dawn on the bottom of the Atlantic. Bloated and blue. Her hair swaying in slow motion, like algae, with the surf. Eyes wide open. Fish swimming around her.

Who wanted to live a life on stilts—stubs of flesh and bone—anyway?

She was better off dead.

"There they are now." His hot breath bounced off the glass back at him. "What a pack of fools."

Jake had pulled in, banked his Crown Vic to the right, skidding to a stop, television cop-style.

And, *What a surprise.* Here we have Father John. He would tell Jake, "I got her into this. I need to be here to help get her out."

The Optimist shook his head, laughing.

86

MONDAY, SEPTEMBER 15 – 12:23 P.M.

Every piece of furniture had its place, not to mention those little coasters underneath each leg. There were two paintings on the walls. A reproduction of Edvard Munch's "The Scream" and a nameless beach landscape setting he had probably bought in Cape Cod. The Queen of the Night flowers were lined up on the mantle above a fireplace filled with three birch logs, perfectly pitched on a metal grate. Inside the Optimist's spotless house, Dickie pried open the padlocked door to the basement. No sooner did he reach the last stair, did it become clear that he had hit pay dirt.

In an old photo album with a sticky white cardboard backing, a clear sheet of plastic covering the photos, Dickie found a scrapbook dedicated to Jake, Dawn, and Brendan. There were common photos of Dawn and Brendan going about their lives. In the park. At TGI Fridays, eating and laughing and being half a family. Miniature golfing. Then Jake at the Boston Public Garden crime scene. Dawn coaching soccer. Brendan getting off the school bus.

Beyond that were boxes of black-and-white photographs of women's legs. Hundreds of pairs. Skinny. Fat. Long. Short. Every leg type imaginable.

Dickie flipped through the photos. "What a sick sonofabitch …"

"Detective?" The call was from upstairs in the kitchen. "Come here."

Dickie put the photos down, ran up the stairs.

"Have a look at this."

Inside the freezer were several Ziploc bags of frozen blood. Dates were written on the front with a Sharpie.

"Damn." Dickie reared away from the macabre display. "He was keeping track of each victim."

"You think he drank it, too, Detective?"

Dickie wasn't about to gratify that rookie question with an answer.

Behind the bags was a small amount blood inside an empty 35mm film cartridge. *The sweat of equity* written on the front of it. It was the Optimist's.

Back in the basement, Dickie located a large Tupperware-like see-through tub. It was full of electronic gadgets, navigation charts, maps of Boston Harbor and Cape Cod Bay. "Jake was right."

Putting that aside, Dickie pulled out a GPS system for a car. It was a portable unit that plugged into the cigarette lighter.

A state trooper stood over Dickie's shoulder, looking on. Dickie sensed the cop—literally breathing on his back—had something to say. So he turned.

"It's your stage, Trooper."

"Oh, thanks, Detective. I just was thinking. You can probably find out his normal, everyday comings and goings by looking at the history in that thing. A GPS works like a computer, leaving an imprint of every move the driver makes. Saw it on Discovery once … that *How It's Made* show."

"Take it outside and have one of the techs hook it up so I can get into it. Call me when you're ready."

87

MONDAY, SEPTEMBER 15 – 1:23 P.M

The Plant Conservatory was three flights above the parking lot. Strategically positioned over the museum's lab. A set of executive offices sandwiched in between. This section of the museum was part of a new construction project. The roof and walls of the conservatory were glass. Inside the greenhouse were two doors—one leading to the east side of the museum, another down into the back parking lot. In the small foyer by the east-side door was a stairwell of about ten steps heading up, dumping you out onto the roof.

"Well, well, well." The Optimist gripped the handle of his knife with force. "You came."

Jake had not entered the greenhouse. He stood outside the open glass entrance, opposite the east-end doorway. Several troopers and BPD personnel stood around. "Wait here," Jake whispered, explaining how he wanted things handled. "Do not come in without my signal."

During the commotion of arriving at the same time, Father John rushed past everyone and made it inside the museum before anyone could stop him. He was working his way up the back stairs. "Let him be," Jake told two blues who went after the priest. "This will be over before he makes it."

The Optimist moseyed through a row of flowers displayed on large boards like plants for sale at Home Depot. He bent down and pulled a stem and its petals up to his nose every so often. He seemed calm. He knew Jake was not about do anything foolish until he knew for certain the status of his wife.

"Ah …" The Optimist took a slow breath in through his nose, eyes closed. "The rare but fruitful-smelling Alchemist Rose." He leaned over the flower.

A moment of silence pulsed.

"Tell me, Detective, what would you put over her coffin? Roses or carnations? I have you pegged as a carnation guy." He used the knife to point at Jake. "Am I right?"

Jake had one foot in the greenhouse. He exchanged a glance with the sharpshooter sent in by the FBI, a guy who did not miss. "Get a bead on him, but stay back. When you have a clear shot, take it. But do not kill him. Hit him in the shoulder."

Head nod.

Jake walked underneath a hanging, vine-y plant of some type and into the room, not taking his eyes off the target. He had swiped out his Glock back at the office for a .357 Magnum he rarely shot. Now it was pointed out in front of him, cop-like.

"Where is she?" Jake said. He pointed the weapon at the Optimist's head, one eye squinted.

"You cannot come up with anything better than that?"

Jake walked toward the killer.

"Hey, hey. Don't you come too close. You're making me awfully nervous."

A row of flowers four feet wide separated the two of them. It was a line of wild orchids. Jake did not take his eyes off Rainn Meyers.

"Put that gun down, Detective, or you'll never find her. Which reminds me. Can Dawn swim?" He laughed. Took his Red Sox cap off, threw it at Jake.

Jake lowered his weapon. "It's over, Meyers. You're done."

"You haven't changed much, Jake. Just taller. Broader shoulders, maybe. But that baby face of yours, it's still the same."

Jake didn't know what Meyers was talking about.

"Oh, you don't remember me? How come? All that 'instinct'"—he tapped the back of the blade against his palm—"you cops are supposed to have. And Detective Cooper does not recall a fellow parish member and altar server? I've been told I was invisible as a child, but shame on you, Jake. You're not a good Catholic."

Jake thought it would help if he could place Meyers into some context of his life. Maybe talk about old times. But the face was unfamiliar.

The Optimist changed the subject. "That Alyssa Bettencourt, she should have never rejected me. She started this. You know that, don't you. All I did was approach her in Quincy Market and show her some photos I was nice enough to take. I couldn't help it, Jake. Or do you prefer Sundance? Anyway, Alyssa resembled my mother so much—that is, of course, until I cut her into pieces and fed her to the sharks."

Nothing. Jake studied the room. He looked for the best corner to back the Optimist into. He wanted to keep him talking.

"From there, you know, saving Alyssa's legs for the Taylor family, I just went with the flow. Did what felt right."

Jake kept his eye on the Optimist. The sharpshooter had him dead-on, even though the killer kept moving.

"And you thought I was stupid, Detective, didn't you? I'll have you know, I was an honor student. 'Golden child.' That's what Mr. Micah called me. Imagine that."

Jake grew tired of this psycho's trip down memory lane. "Just try to think about how this will eventually end, Meyers." Jake had a composed affect. Perfect cadence. All business. Zero emotion. "You are not going to leave here on your feet. No matter what."

The Optimist looked down at his knife. He ran the tip of his forefinger along the sharp edge, making a fine paper cut. He waited for blood to emerge. When it did, in a controlled rage, he screamed. "What makes you think I want to live, Detective?" He paused. Lowered his voice to a calm note. "What is it that makes you think you can dictate when I live and I die, anyway? *I'm* the one who makes those decisions."

"First chance I get, I'm blowing your fucking head off."

"Promises, promises. *Tsk, tsk* on you. Now put that gun down, like I said."

"My wife is dead, Meyers. I know that."

"You think you're so smart," the Optimist yelled, spittle spraying from his mouth.

"I don't."

"You see, Detective, we're not so different, you and I. Our teachers have let us down—haven't they? Maybe you ought to take my lead. Let redemption guide you. My teacher, he's still alive—dying a miserable death in prison. Yours, well, we all know yours was a dirty cop who couldn't live up to his responsibilities. He took the easy way out. Didn't I just hear that on the radio this morning?"

Mo.

The Optimist walked up to the glass door on the east end of the greenhouse. He stood in front of a large case of flowers, reached for the door handle.

"You walk out that door, Meyers, I'll shoot you in the back." Jake held his weapon chest-high, pointed at the madman. The door led to the rooftop. To the left side, a stairwell led down the stairs into the back parking lot.

"You ever read C.S. Lewis, Detective?" The Optimist let out a guttural laugh. Waited. "No, right. What am I saying? I didn't think so."

Jake kept his Magnum poised at eye level. His heart thumped. He wasn't prepared to fire. He looked over at the sharpshooter, who couldn't keep the Optimist in his sight long enough to get a good crack at him.

"Great Christian writer, that Lewis. The Catholics love him. Anyway, Lewis said we all have this 'ordinary idea' of a 'natural self with various desires and interests.' He suggests that we all 'know something called morality and decent behavior' have a grasp—Lewis called it a 'claim,' I think—on the self. We are hardwired, Detective, to understand the demands of morality and society. Imagine. We know better. It's instinct."

"Stop moving toward that door, Meyers."

The Optimist heard something. Footsteps. He stopped in front of the door.

Jake heard it, too. He pointed his weapon at the door, then back at the Optimist.

"As I was saying—"

The door flew open and almost hit the Optimist in the shoulder.

Father John stepped out. The priest was out of breath. Huffing and puffing. Beads of sweat ran down his crinkled brow.

Jake refocused his sights on the Optimist. "Father, don't move."

The Optimist lifted the knife over his head, slasher-film-like—and then lunged at the priest.

88

MONDAY, SEPTEMBER 15 – 1:39 P.M.

Dickie stood outside the Optimist's house. He leaned over the hood of his Crown Vic. Trooper Styles by his side. They searched through the GPS's history. The idea was to find a pattern. Anything that might lead them to Dawn.

"Detective?" A blue walked out the front door. He had a book in his hand.

"Yeah?" Dickie sounded distracted. "Kinda busy here, Officer."

The cop held up a three-inch-thick version of the King James Bible. "Check this out."

Several pages were flagged with Post-Its. They all contained a reference to drowning. Dickie read Matthew 18:6 to himself: "*But if anyone causes one of these little ones who believe in me to sin, it would be better for him to have a large millstone hung around his neck and to be drowned in the depths of the sea.*"

"Hey, Detective," another blue yelled from the porch. "We found a laminate machine—must be how he got into that prison to talk to prisoner Micah."

"Thanks." Dickie never looked up. He wasn't paying attention. In his mind, he kept repeating that phrase: *Drowned in the depths of the sea.*

"Detective Shaughnessy?" Trooper Styles was still panning through the GPS files. "I think I know where he keeps his boat. Look." He pointed to a list of about two dozen trips to the same North Shore marina over the past two weeks.

Dickie stared at the readout. "Same location. He kept going back there." Then, Dickie took his radio in his hand and keyed, "Jake, you there?"

No answer.

Dickie put the radio against his forehead in frustration.

Drowned in the depths of the sea.

"Call the Coast Guard and Harbor Patrol, Trooper. Come on. Let's move."

89

MONDAY, SEPTEMBER 15 – 1:41 P.M.

The Optimist grabbed Father John by the neck. Whirled him around, using the priest as a shield. He had gone to stab Father John, but thought better of it, stopping mid-strike. He had another idea. Something more practical to his endgame. He whispered in the priest's ear. "Don't do anything stupid, Padre." Then looked at Jake. "Drop that weapon, or I expose the priest's larynx and juggle with his Adam's apple."

Jake obliged. He knelt down, placed his gun on the ground. Stood with his hands raised above his head.

Holding the knife blade to Father John's neck, the Optimist walked him toward the door. "Open it." Father did as he was told.

"I'm wondering, are you going to answer that call, Detective? Seems your partner has some information for you. We'll wait."

"Call me on my cell, Dickie." Jake threw his radio at the Optimist, just missing his head.

Jake took out his iPhone, put it between his shoulder and ear. He bent down and picked up his gun. Held it out in front of himself.

The Optimist and the priest stopped in front of a large Judean date palm plant by the door. He leaned down and rubbed his face against the leaves.

Jake dropped the phone from his shoulder on purpose, refocused his attention back on the moment.

"Do you know the story of the Masada, Detective?" The Optimist gripped the priest's neck tighter. Closed his eyes. Took in a deep breath through his nose. Pinned the knife to Father John's neck, drawing blood. The priest struggled for air.

"You need to put the knife down, let the priest go. Then tell us where my wife is." Jake had learned a few things throughout the years. Stay on point. Stick to the basics. Don't get into any good-and-evil conversations with a perp holding a hostage. It fuels their rage. Most of all, let them do the talking.

"Let me tell you about the Masada. They say the Jews committed suicide on the mountaintop sanctuary of Masada. But that's not true. Six men killed all the women and children on Masada—with machetes! Can you imagine that? Women and children."

Father John looked to be changing color. "I'm choking," he said in a raspy voice. "Please, Randy. Let's talk about this."

"Women. Incredible, isn't it?" The Optimist squeezed a tighter grip on the priest's neck, jamming the knife even further into his flabby skin. "One of the men then killed the five others afterward, and he—that *one* man left behind—committed suicide. Masada was not a mass suicide or a massacre by the Romans. It was mass murder, and *one* suicide. You should know your biblical history, Detective."

It was hot inside the greenhouse. Jake kept having to rub beads of sweat from his brow. His T-shirt was soaked from his neck down along his spine.

Like the cop he was, Jake ordered, "Get on the ground, put your hands behind your back."

"… I cannot breathe," Father John struggled to say.

"I told you, Father, *not* to speak."

The Optimist backed the priest toward the door.

Jake followed each step, making sure not to crowd the psycho.

With his foot, the Optimist jerked open the door. Then dragged Father John into the small foyer.

Jake rushed to the door, stopped it just before closing.

The Optimist dragged Father John with him up the stairs. At the top was a one-way door leading out onto the rooftop.

Jake lost sight of them. He did not walk in. The rest of the team moved closer, swarming around Jake. A blue got on the radio. "He's heading up to the roof. Get a bird over here now."

"No helicopter." Jake sounded firm. "I want the building surrounded. We do not push him."

"It is already, Detective."

"Good. Seal off this entryway and any other entrance or exit from the roof. I'm going up there—alone. I don't want anyone following too close. All he has is a knife."

"All that we know of, you mean."

"Right. Whatever. Toss me your radio."

Jake pulled his foot away from the door, allowed it to close. He put the radio in his back pocket. Took off his windbreaker, dropped it on the ground.

Up on the top stairs landing, Father John gave it one more try. "Please, Randy. Give yourself up. Listen to me. I can help you."

The Optimist closed his eyes. He bounced the back edge of his knife off the bridge of his nose. He was thinking as he took deep, quick breaths, psyching himself up.

Father John said, "You don't need to give in to evil, Randy."

The Optimist opened his eyes. Raised his head. Stared eye-level at Father John, looking through him.

He pictured his mother. Her long blonde hair flowing over one side of the bed. Her head jerking up and back as one of those men pumped his way deeper inside. He could hear her moaning. *I like that … harder*. He was in the closet inside her room. *Harder, baby*. She didn't know he was there.

The little boy closed his eyes.

Harder. Yes. Yes ...

Every once in a while he'd open his eyes, look through the slats in the door. *Yes ... oh, yes.* His mother's head bounced as if she were on a horse.

There was a hiccup in his mind. Silence. He snapped out of it. Smiled. Lifted the knife over his shoulder—in what seemed to be slow motion—and stabbed the priest in the chest with one overhead motion, burying the blade somewhere near his heart. He looked into the priest's eyes, pulling the knife out of him slowly. Then licked the cold steel while watching the life drain out of Father John's face.

The priest gasped. Grabbed at his chest.

It didn't take much, but the Optimist gave the priest a nudge. And Father John tumbled down the stairs, finally landing and rolling into the door.

90

MONDAY, SEPTEMBER 15 – 1:59 P.M.

Jake heard a thump. Turned. It came from inside the foyer. He opened the door with caution. Saw Father John struggling to breathe. Hyperventilating, his legs bucked as though he had gone into an epileptic shock.

Jake grabbed the priest by the arm and pulled him into the greenhouse. "Get him some help!" Stepping into the foyer slowly, Jake took a cautionary gaze up the stairs. He did not want to get stabbed in the face if the Optimist was waiting in the shadows of the dark. Kneeling by the railing, using the corner brick as cover, Jake pointed his .357 toward the roof entrance and took a step.

A beam of light brightened the stairway—then it went dark again as Jake heard the door above close.

After hurrying up the stairs and kicking the door open, on top of the roof, Jake looked in all directions.

The Optimist was nowhere to be found.

Walking on the rooftop with guarded composure, Jake thought of what Dickie had said on the phone moments ago. *"We're on our way to the Back Bay Marina. We think she might be on his boat."*

Jake knew Dawn was dead. And now he needed to kill her killer. Revenge was all he had left.

Standing on the roof, the Charles River at his back, the wind blew fiercely. Jake could hear the stifled hum of traffic running north and south off in the distance on I-93. He spun around, three-hundred-and-sixty degrees, the city's blurry skyline twirling in his vision. A part of the building jetted out over the Charles.

Where are you?

Jake ran toward the south edge. He looked down at the roof of a second building below, the Planetarium. It was connected to the conservatory. Just a short jump—about five feet—down and on top of the next rooftop. It was the only way the Optimist could have gone. Every other area of the roof led to a dead end.

Jake leapt.

Landing on both feet, he heard something. Movement. Stones grinding against shoes.

He turned.

The Optimist popped out from behind a large heating and air-conditioning mechanism. It was taller than him. In between Jake and Optimist was a glass skylight as big as a garage door. They had to be careful, or risk falling through.

The sun burned hot through the wind. Jake could smell the tar from the roof heating up, melting. In all that was going on, he couldn't get the thought of working construction that one summer before joining the BPD out of his mind, patching potholes all over the city. It was that hot asphalt odor. So distinctive. Memorable.

The Optimist held his knife as if he were a carnival performer, ready to toss it at Jake like a dart. They stood about ten feet away from each other on opposite sides of the skylight. Jake had a clear shot. He could end it right now.

"You're finished. Lay down. Put your hands behind your head."

"Curious. Your partner, Detective. Did he have good news for you?"

"We have her, Meyers. Back Bay Marina. She's alive."

The Optimist turned red-faced. He screamed. "Don't you lie to me! Do you think for one minute I would *allow* her to live?"

Jake felt a pang in his gut. He swallowed. No response.

"Control, Detective. I controlled her destiny—and now you control mine. Funny how it all worked out, huh?"

The Optimist walked closer to the skylight. Tapped his knife on the glass.

"I should just kill you, Meyers. What do we have between us? Nothing. You're just a piece of shit. A psycho this city could stand to get rid of."

Lined up along the roof of the building Jake had jumped down from were a group of five officers, each dressed in riot gear, armed with rifles, kneeling, their weapons pointed at the Optimist. Jake spotted them out of the corner of his eye.

The Optimist looked. "I bet you gave orders not to follow, didn't you?"

Jake made a break for the Optimist, running right at him, screaming as loud as he could to cause a distraction. He had to go around the skylight. As he approached, the Optimist jumped on the skylight, breaking shards of glass in a circular pattern, like splashing water. It was loud and unsettling. A few stray slivers, sharp and pointy as icicles, hit Jake as he got down on his knees and covered himself with his hands.

If he survived the fall, the Optimist was now inside the Planetarium.

Jake got up. Brushed himself off. Looked in the through the hole. It was dark. He could see a ticket counter, a mess of glass, spurs of wood from the broken window frame all over the floor. He stood above the area of the Planetarium where patrons waited in line to get in. Twelve feet down.

Probably not enough to kill the sonofabitch.

"Surround the inside of the planetarium." Jake tossed the radio after giving the order. The team of riot police came up behind him. "I'm gonna finish this now for good."

91

MONDAY, SEPTEMBER 15 – 2:09 P.M.

The Optimist hid under the ticket counter. After jumping through the glass, he hit the ground and rolled. As he did, pieces of glass embedded into different areas of his body. He was huddled in the corner. Cold and shaking, he looked at the cuts all over his hands and legs, several small pieces of glass sticking out of his ankles and elbows. His right side burned. Looking at it, he noticed an elongated, triangular-shaped shard of glass protruding out of his skin near his appendix. Blood flowed from it steadily. It was an odd feeling. There was no significant, throbbing pain from the lesions, but more of a numbing sensation, reminding him that he was supposed to feel pain.

Huddled there in the corner underneath the ticket counter like a wounded animal, that sense of helplessness he had endured after the Teacher chained his leg to the furnace in the basement and abused him came back. He saw Micah grab him by the back of the head—the memory almost an out-of-body experience—and inch his face toward the furnace door as a fire raged inside. He could hear him. *"You tell anyone and I'll douse you with gasoline and burn you alive."*

Small shards of glass fell from above as Jake walked around the opening on the roof. He must be contemplating how to jump down, the Optimist considered. The bits of glass fell in front of Rainn Meyers and bounced off the red carpet.

Blood ran down his forearms and the side of his hip. His socks and underwear were saturated.

The Optimist felt the game had played out exactly how he had planned. That "incongruous compound of good and evil" was there in everything he and Jake did. He said those six words over and over in his mind. *Incongruous compound of good and evil.* A quote from the book—*The Strange Case of Dr. Jekyll and Mr. Hyde*—that kept him company all those nights when he believed the world was against him. When he realized his sins had sent him to Bainbridge. Nothing else. Robert Louis Stevenson's tale had become Randy Meyers's reality.

Every thought I ever had centered on self.

There were two of him. He knew that now.

Jake landed directly in front of the counter, his calves facing the Optimist. The trip down from the roof was loud and surely painful.

The killer who could not resist the temptation stared.

As Jake hit the ground, the Optimist stabbed the detective just above his knee, in the meaty ham-shank section of his thigh. As Jake reacted, grabbing his leg and falling on his back, it gave the killer enough time to crawl out from underneath the counter and limp his way into the Planetarium.

92

MONDAY, SEPTEMBER 15 – 2:15 P.M.

Clutching his thigh with both hands, Jake Cooper thrashed on the floor.

Out of the corner of his eye, he saw the Optimist head into the Planetarium. Taking a lesson he had learned running on the streets of Southie, the cop reacted without thinking. He tore off his shirt and ripped a long strip from it. Then yanked the knife out in one quick extraction, screaming in pain and tossing the knife on the carpet, before tying the strip of cloth around his thigh in a makeshift tourniquet.

It burned—lemon juice squeezed on an open wound.

Jake stood as upright as he could. Caught his breath. Checked his gun to make sure his .357 was loaded and ready. Then hobbled into the Planetarium, the barrel of his weapon leading the way.

It was dark inside the immense, sphere-shaped room. It smelled of cleaning fluids—bleach and Pine-Sol, the same synthetic, fake-fresh odor the precinct took on after the night crew finished its work. The dome-like screen covering the ceiling gave off a bit of light because it was so, well, white. The red-and-black exit signs brightened up the aisles. Yet it was hard to see anything beyond a ten-foot radius of where you stood.

Jake heard a seat rattle. Then a tired laugh. "She begged for her life, Detective." The Optimist's voice echoed loudly throughout the empty room.

Jake's leg stiffened. Cramped. The makeshift noose kept the bleeding to a minimum. But it hurt like hell.

"What's happening here, Meyers?" Jake looked down the rows and aisles of seats. Bending down as far as he could, he didn't see anything.

"I hear the trumpets of angels, Detective." The Optimist had a hard time speaking. "Oh, how beautiful they sound. They're singing my name."

"This is over, Meyers."

"As you know by now, Jake, I am not a rapist. But I need to tell you that I did have sex with your wife. It was not fun."

Jake squeezed his eyes closed as a mountain of rage welled up.

"You know, I was going to bury Brendan and leave a map for you to find him—with a window of opportunity, that sort of thing."

Jake flashed on an image of the little girl. Her mouth full of dirt. Her fingernails broken and oily from trying to dig her way out of the hole. Her favorite stuffed animal—a Webkinz seal—still in her arms. The pathologist had confirmed Jake was minutes away from saving her.

"I'm going to kill you, Meyers," Jake whispered. He knew the killer could hear him.

"Doing that to Brendan, I thought, shit, maybe it would be *too* much. Send you over the edge. Then our game would be over. No more fun."

Jake heard a soft squeak from the rubber sole of a shoe, a gym floor during a basketball game. It came from over by the stage in the middle of the room. The Planetarium's projector, a praying mantis-looking apparatus, stood tall as a man, its dome-shaped ball, the singing end of a microphone, pointed toward the ceiling.

Jake dropped to the ground. His butt nearly touched the floor. He had his back against the side of the stage. His thigh throbbed. He fought through the burn, which had turned into a pure toothache-like pain magnified by a thousand. He felt a trickle of warm blood run down his leg. He now knew where the Optimist was hiding. He was close enough to see his shadow, faint as it was, casting an outline beyond the planetarium's projector. He could hear his labored bleeding.

He's hurt.

The Optimist hid on the opposite edge of the platform, just beyond where the projector was bolted to the stage. He had no idea where Jake was, or that Jake knew his location. He kept looking in different directions. It was no use. His vision was blurred. He had bled so much from being cut by the glass, the puncture wound to his appendix hemorrhaging so profusely, he was dizzy. Falling in and out. Running a fever. Sweating. Rocking back and forth.

He sat on his butt. Back against a waist-high wooden wall. Held his side.

Jake was quiet. He moved with the grace of a burglar, making little noise, inching his way along the edge of the stage. Closing in on the Optimist, he could hear him wheezing, taking long, labored breaths, hospital machine-like.

Darth Vader.

About five feet from his target, Jake stopped. He walked eight paces out in front of the Optimist, who could not see him.

But the killer heard him. He looked straight ahead.

"That you, Jakester?" he somehow managed to say in a raspy, hoarse tone.

Jake set a good bead on his target. The light from an overhead exit sign projected just enough to give him a clear vantage point.

The Optimist spoke as loud as he could through the pain. "Jake, did you know that sin and evil are … are … ow … manifestations of self-centeredness and pride … shit, ow … that lead to oppression against others?" He bit his lip. Tried not to groan. It was over.

Jake did not say a word.

"'A qualm has come over me,' Detective." He laughed. "That's R.L. Stevenson." It was his favorite line from the Dr. Jekyll and Mr. Hyde story.

Jake lined up the sight on his .357 with the Optimist's forehead—that tiny space between his eyebrows.

"You see the monsters Southie produces … I am evidence. But then, so are you, Detective. We are not so different."

Jake looked over his shoulder toward the entrances. He heard something. Back-up was preparing to enter the room. He could hear them stirring. He and the Optimist had ten more seconds alone. The Optimist was ready to pass out.

Jake whispered over the barrel of his weapon, one eye closed, his Magnum still locked on the Optimist's forehead. "I'm going to do you a favor."

"Like a wounded horse." The Optimist reached up, hit the switch over his left shoulder. The projector popped on, blasting a night sky above them onto the ceiling screen. It was as though he was back out on the ocean at midnight, staring up at the open heavens.

Jake closed his eyes. Dropped his head. Not taking the gun off his mark.

He couldn't do this. He wasn't a killer. The Optimist was no threat any longer.

"You're the same as me, Detective …"

The two sets of double doors leading into the planetarium popped open. Matikas called out Jake's name. Teams of blues dressed in face-shields and body armor, semi-automatic rifles, trekked down the aisles in lines.

"Over here," the Optimist said, raising a hand as high as he could, speaking with everything he had left. "I want to give myself up."

As he smiled at Jake, no doubt mocking him this one last time, he whispered, "I win!"

The detective said, "Eat shit and die, asshole." Then took the shot and hit the psycho square in the forehead, dropping him to the floor, spewing the back of his head into a million little pieces.

THREE WEEKS LATER

93

SUNDAY, OCTOBER 6 – 4:16 P.M.

Jake was behind the wheel of an old Chevy S-10 pickup. For October, it was pretty warm out. Enough to make you sweat.

Jake and his passenger rattled down a dirt road, the flimsy wheel wells of the truck leaving a dust cloud along the shores of Lake Winnipesaukee. Country music—some irritating song about a barbecue stain on a white T-shirt— was on the only station the AM radio was able to tune in. Brendan, sitting shotgun, smiled as Jake brushed the kid on top of his head. "You know what they say, buddy. Bad day of fishing is better than any day in school."

"Right, Daddy."

Shutting off the radio, Jake pulled into the dirt driveway leading to the cottage. The vacation was almost over.

Father and son got out and slammed the truck doors at the same time, as if they had rehearsed the move. Jake opened the whining screen door to the cottage and Brendan walked in before him underneath Jake's arm.

Dawn sat at the table reading the Sunday paper, looking over her shoulder, half-smiling. She had a quilt her mother had sent draped over her back. She did not get up. "Catch anything?"

Jake and Brendan took off their jackets. "Nope."

"Missed a whopper." Brendan spread his arms out to show his mother how big the fish "probably" was.

"Tellin' fish tales already, huh, kiddo?"

Jake kissed Dawn on the cheek. She clutched his hand on her shoulder and squeezed. Brendan got himself a Coke.

The letter Mo sent posthumously arrived a day after he blew his brains out. It sat on the table in front of Jake. He had brought it with him, along with his final report. He read the letter several times, but wanted to quote from it in his report. They were scheduled to head back to Boston in two days. Jake needed to be done with this case. It was time to move on.

Mo was no wordsmith, but his points were clear and concise. Jake did the legwork to check out the claims Mo had made in the letter. All of it turned out to be more or less fact.

It was kickbacks, as Jake had originally thought. Mo took money from Mancini Construction, who was responsible for the collapse in the Ted Williams Tunnel that killed two members of the Carmichael family. The problem—besides enormous greed—was the concrete, which was not up to spec. The company had saved hundreds of thousands of dollars using the cheap stuff. Mo made sure all the permits and paperwork were in order by paying off several inspectors. He picked up the bottle again because he knew the feds were in the process of indicting him. HQ had never considered going after Jake, as IA had it under good information that Jake didn't know what he was doing when he picked up and delivered packages for Mo. You solve the state's most high-profile serial-killer case and you are entitled to a little leeway and under-the-rug sweeping. Jake wasn't sure he was continuing in his role as a cop anyway.

Shaking his head for the umpteenth time, Jake couldn't believe who had helped Mo. The last person Jake would have ever suspected of being on the take was Lieutenant Ray Matikas. Apparently, Matikas knew people who helped fix some of the paperwork. It was Matikas who found Mo dead and walked out of his house with a file the feds later found in Matikas's car.

Sunshine.

Dawn got up from the dining room table. Walked to the couch, leaned over Jake's back. "Whatcha reading?"

"Old news." Jake said, smiling. "Go take a nap. You need your rest."

94

Dickie stood at the podium inside the BPD union hall on Congress Street. "Please hold your applause." He had to repeat the statement several times. "Please."

Standing over Dickie's shoulders, looking sheepish in suits two sizes too small, were Adam Bales and Russel Cannon. Both men were humbled by the loud cheers, slaps on the back, and anonymous atta-boys from the crowd. The *Globe* and *Herald* magazine had written about the two men. They were interviewed on the CBS Nightly News and WBZ-TV's *Crime Night Live*. Heck, even Matt Lauer invited them on the *Today Show*, but they refused.

Neither man cared for all the attention. They were fishermen, first and foremost. That would never change. Their fathers and grandfathers fished. They would teach their children to do the same. It was intertwined in their DNA.

"Dawn Cooper is alive and well today," Dickie said into the microphone, looking behind him, "because of the heroism displayed by these two gentlemen." Applause broke out as the men looked at each other. "I want to read something Detective Cooper emailed me this morning. He couldn't be here. He's up north with his wife and son. I quote, 'To Mr. Bales and Mr. Cannon, my wife and I want to express our gratitude for what you did that morning. The only reason you came upon that sinking boat, my wife close to drowning, was because you were out on the ocean doing what you love. You could have driven by, called the Coast Guard and waited it out. You didn't. You risked your lives to save my wife, same as you do every day out on the Grand Banks for the sake of feeding your families. Thank you.'"

The storm off the Maine coastline that morning had sent scores of fishermen further south, toward Boston and the Cape. Bales and Cannon decided, "by a mere stroke of divine providence," Cannon told ABC News, to head into Boston Harbor, dock for the day, then head back out after the storm broke. They came upon *The Grand Pause*, called it in, then decided, after seeing Dawn struggling to keep her head above water, to make the rescue attempt themselves. There was blood all around Dawn, swirling in salty swells, attracting all sorts of predators. Blue fish, they knew, were more of a threat in Cape Cod Bay than sharks. They needed to act quickly.

Dawn had started cutting through her legs, couldn't go through with it, and decided to give in to death.

Cannon used the net hoist on their fishing rig to keep *The Grand Pause* afloat while Bales went in with a torch and cut through the handcuffs.

"If I can follow up," Dickie said, feedback from the microphone squealing throughout the hall. "As I hand these two men our most coveted honor, by leaving you all with something Jake once told me." After a few inaudible shouts, the audience quieted. "Jake asked me one day if I knew what concupiscence was. I looked at him as though he was speaking Chinese or something." Some in the crowd laughed. "'It's the magnetic pull of evil,' he explained. 'It's that devil on your shoulder—the desire to sin that is in every one of us.' I made some stupid joke that day and … oh, well, you don't need to hear it, too. My point is. These two men standing here prove that there is also the pull of goodness in many of us. They heard that call and answered. Thank you for hearing me out."

Standing ovation.

95

MONDAY, OCTOBER 16 – 12:16 P.M.

Jake parked his Chevelle in the only space available near the Cumberland Farms convenience store outside Logan Airport in Chelsea. It felt good to be back in the saddle, the smell of the city wafting up around him. For a city boy, nothing compared to good old-fashioned taxi exhaust choking your sinuses after a few weeks in the country.

He walked up a grassy knoll incline strewn with garbage off to the side of the road. When he reached the summit, he turned and took in what was the best view of Orient Heights, East Boston, the highest point in the city. Jake liked it here. Save for the roar of the jets taking off from Logan, the atmosphere comforted him. He loved looking out at the well-settled, hardworking community of blue-collar Bostonians and the backdrop of downtown's saw-toothed skyline.

Home.

Fifty yards ahead, Jake stood on the concrete patio inside the Madonna Queen Shrine. Off in the distance, he spied the man he had come to see.

"Thought I might find you here. Always was your favorite place in the city to say a rosary."

Father John turned. Walked slow. Jake could tell it was not by choice or from old age. The man was in pain. This, after several weeks of healing.

"Nice to see you, Jake." The tranquility in the priest's voice was familiar.

On the street down below, a car honked. A man yelled something in Spanish to his wife, who leaned out of one of the three-decker windows. The squeal of a city bus's brakes squelched them both out.

"Thought we might have lost you there, Father." Jake hadn't seen Father John since he was airlifted with a punctured lung from the Museum of Science that afternoon. The Boston diocese sent Father John to one of its hospitals in Canada specializing in heart and lung surgery. The knife entered his chest cavity, just missing his aorta. Rupturing a main vessel, however, the priest had endured two heart attacks in the weeks following the incident and needed an operation to get him back on his feet.

"Never, Jake." They hugged. The priest stepped back for a minute and stared at the cop. "Let me just look at you."

Seagulls from a nearby landfill squawked their whiney cries overhead.

"Glad you're on the mend, Father. Nice to see you up and around. Sorry I didn't make a visit."

"No need to apologize. You had your hands full with Dawn, Jake. How is she?"

"She'll be okay. The wounds went deep. Strong girl. Never thought she had it in her to even consider the idea. She's antsy to get back to work."

Father John squeezed his rosary, looked up into the sky. "Thank God above."

"Father, without your instinct—"

"No, no, no."

They walked, taking in the shrine, its piety, the unspoken sacredness between them while standing in such a divine place.

"The papers get it right, Jake? I never heard how."

Jake dropped his head. Stared at the Virgin Mary before him. "Yeah." Then, looking down at the concrete, fiddling with his sunglasses, he had no idea why, but Jake Sundance

Cooper lied to his priest. "He came at me and I shot him. That's about it." He had written the same thing in his report.

"You taking some more time off, or …?"

This was the burning question. Jake wasn't sure himself. "Being a cop, Father, it's like you're in the mob. Once you're in, you're in. There's very little faith left in justice. Besides, I am thinking about taking my investigative skills and putting them together with my writing skills and taking on a new career."

"We have Dennis LeHane and Robert Parker already, Jake."

"Yeah, I wasn't *quite* thinking along those lines." Jake smiled.

"Well," Father John said, unsure if Jake was joking, grabbing him by the shoulder and squeezing, "regardless what you do, I need to remind you that faith is a funny thing, isn't it? We all have faith in *something*." They looked up at the immense statue of the Madonna Queen. "The belief of Don Orione here, the great man who erected this fine structure, was that beside every work of charity lies a work of faith."

Jake nodded.

"Abide with me, Jake," Father John concluded. "There is hope for the hopeless.

Author's Note

This is a work of fiction. That means I changed some things to suit my own narrative needs. There is no D-15 or CSU-6 in the Boston Police Department, for example. Like a lot of things in this book, I made it up.

I want to thank John Paine and Jim Thomsen, two editors who truly made me look a helluva lot smarter than I am.